THE BOOKS OF ALEXANDREA

THE BOOKS OF ALEXANDREA

Book 1: The Book Club

Louisa & Elise,

2022

Take Magic Back!

Enjoy!

JH Nadler

JH NADLER

ISBN 978-1-7370098-1-8
Library of Congress Control Number (LCCN) 2021917075

This is a work of fiction. The characters and events portrayed in this book are fictitious.
Any similarity to actual events or persons, living or dead, is coincidental and not intended by the author.

Cover design | Jason Nadler
Cover photo | Sergey Nivens, licensed from Shutterstock
Cover photo of the Author | Irvin Simon Photographers
Illuminated Letters | William Morris, public domain

Printed in United States of America

Published by WorkingCat, Inc
Wading River, NY 11792

Visit **jhnadler.com**

For Laura

My Beatrice. My Bonnie. My Zelda.
No amount of thanks will ever be enough
for your support, conviction, or enthusiasm.
This book exists because of you.

Table of Contents

Chapter One

eath was coming for Alexandrea Hawthorne. A sense of impending doom embraced her like the arms of a drowned man, cold, wet, and unwanted. It narrowed her vision, caused her head to ache and ears to ring. Words crept up the stairs to her bedroom armed with knives, slicing at her brain with every syllable.

The terrible feeling had arrived with the uninvited guests. As if by entering her home, they had transformed it into a mausoleum. She held her breath, straining to listen to the conversation. Hearing their words—barbed accusations cutting her mother—Alexandrea knew they had come for her.

"Are you even listening to me?"

Alexandrea jumped at the question. Charissa, eyes locked on her phone, poked at the device. "Isn't that so adorable?" She flashed the screen at Alexandrea, a video. Kittens tracking flour across a countertop.

Alexandrea looked without seeing.

"Here's another; it's even more adorable."

She returned her attention to the doorway. *Can't Charissa feel what's happening?* Dread billowed up the stairs like smoke from a fire, choking her. *No, she only cares about her stupid phone.*

Who were these men threatening her mother? They spoke with a strained familiarity, like they were at the end of a lifelong feud, awaiting its violent conclusion. Alexandrea faced what seemed like an inescapable outcome, the end of a long and meticulous plan.

*   *   *   *

Though the morning had offered no portents of what the day would bring, in retrospect, Alexandrea wondered if her parents had known. Her father's agitation and her mother's unusual mood should have given her pause.

Waking, she had dressed and gone downstairs to make breakfast for herself and her father. Her mother Holly was an ER nurse at the hospital, and her overnight shifts frequently spilled into the mornings. On such occasions, it was left to Alexandrea to feed her father. She found Peter wandering near the front door. He would walk past, pause, pivot to look outside, then turn and walk past again. She set a hand on his emaciated shoulder, her touch calming him, and with gentle pressure, she guided him to the kitchen.

Alexandrea could remember no time when Peter had held a job. As far as she was concerned, he never had—or done anything else, for that matter. Most days he'd wander from room to room, occasionally regarding her or her mother, but usually not. She typically found him in front of the television. Some days, she turned it on for him. Peter had all the impact on his surroundings of a lamp with a broken bulb.

Sitting her father down, she flipped on the coffee machine and set about making scrambled eggs. When the food was ready, she fed him, a forkful at a time, as he stared expressionless at whatever lay in his line of sight. Her mother often told her to eat her own breakfast first; Peter wouldn't complain if his food got cold, and he never did. But Alexandrea, like Holly herself, rarely heeded this advice.

Alexandrea tapped the fork on his plate, impatient for him to swallow. Holly sometimes told Peter stories as she fed him, about her day or touting their daughter's latest achievements. Sometimes she'd wax poetic over his chestnut eyes, which sparkled with every dream and wish he couldn't express. He never nodded or smiled, though. He chewed mechanically, opening his mouth after each swallow. Alexandrea never spoke to him like this. She only told him what she wanted him to do. He was as likely to acknowledge her as was the fork in her hand.

He'd been like this all her life.

On rare occasions when Holly was melancholy, she'd reminisce about her and Peter's love affair, the romance that had culminated in Alexandrea's birth. She told her daughter everything. Everything except how he ended up like this. When asked, she would only change the subject. *What should I defrost for dinner? Looks like rain, don't you think?* She never refused the question, but it was clear she wouldn't discuss it. The truth, it seemed, was too painful. This could not have been the life her mother had intended, after all. Alexandrea suspected Holly had not been happy since before she was born. What was Peter like back then? The answer, she sometimes thought, might quell her resentments. But whatever it was, she also feared it. What about her birth could have made him like *this*?

Peter finished eating, or rather, Alexandrea fed him the last bite off his plate. If she continued, she knew he'd keep going. To look at him, he barely ate at all, but this did not seem to concern Holly, and he never expressed hunger. He was a living thing without care, a zombie minus the consumption fetish.

She wiped his mouth.

When the kitchen was in order, Alexandrea deposited Peter into his chair—so he'd be out of the way while she vacuumed—and turned on the television. A grave voice lamented the plight of polar bears amidst melting sea ice. She paused from time to time to watch, curious if the tragedy affected her father. What, if anything, ticked behind that vacant expression?

At one o'clock, Holly's car pulled up the gravel driveway, which ended well short of the house. Holly drove past it onto the lawn as she always did, right up to the front steps. *7756672 County Road B—drive right up to the house.* Alexandrea had heard her mother give these instructions so many times, she once believed it was their full address. She could always tell if someone had been invited by her mother by where they parked.

Not that they had many guests. Her Aunt Abby—not a real aunt, but a close family friend—hadn't come in almost a year. And Peter's actual sister—his twin, Heather—hadn't been around with Billy and Rosemary—*her* twin children—in months.

Once a week, Holly would do their shopping on her way home from work. One day, she had returned with a girl Alexandrea's age. "I think you'll be perfect friends," she had said. Alexandrea was bereft when Charissa's mother picked her up a few hours later without even leaving the car. She had so enjoyed the girl's company, it never dawned on her that Holly hadn't found her in the produce aisle.

Holly came in like a dervish. "Why wasn't the door locked?" She hollered at Alexandrea, who was only feet away.

"You were coming up the steps."

Her mother's concern melted into a smile, strained with exhaustion. "Thank you." This had been her third consecutive overnight at the hospital.

"Dad's fed. Downstairs is vacuumed. I'll make you some eggs." Holly often chided Alexandrea for up talking, so Alexandrea hoped she had taken this as a question.

"Eggs... um, that sounds nice. I'm starving." Her mother seemed distracted.

Alexandrea whipped up another plate in no time, and as her mother ate, leaned on a chair watching her. "Um, it's Saturday," she said expectantly.

"Eggs are perfect. Thanks." Holly set down her fork and touched her daughter's arm. She didn't speak.

"Mom, it's *Saturday*," she repeated, giving the word extra significance.

Holly stared at her. It was like she was taking her in, drinking up every detail.

"Charissa's coming over in, like, two hours."

Holly knocked the fork with her elbow; it spun across the table. "Please tell me you're kidding." When Alexandrea shook her head, she added, "Today? Why today—no. No, not today. She can't."

"You said, Mom. I asked you two weeks ago; you said."

Holly reached across the table for her fork. "You'll have to cancel. Postpone—just, no."

"Whatever. You do this all the time." Alexandrea shoved off the chair and turned to leave.

"Alexandrea, stay," her mother ordered, and the girl froze. "I do *what* all the time?"

Her mother was right; going back on her word was *not* something she always did. "Mom, you said though," she whined, hating the sulk in her voice. "I invited Charissa *two weeks* ago. I asked again *last week*."

Holly softened. "And I said *yes*, huh?"

Alexandrea nodded.

Holly's lips moved as though mouthing numerals in a calculation. "Nothing different," she mumbled to herself. Then to Alexandrea, "If I said it, I said it. If that was the plan for today, Charissa can come over." She paused, looking away contemplatively. "It's been a long couple of days." Then she blinked. "I know it's beautiful out, but I want you two inside. You can play in your bedroom."

Alexandrea's was a life defined by rules. Rarely had she questioned them. At fourteen, she had yet to kiss a boy or go on a date; she had never owned a phone, computer, or television; she had never even traveled to town or gone to a real school. The scope of her world consisted of her home—this house—and the spaces around it. Visits from her friend were all she wanted. But unlike Alexandrea, who loved exploring the woods by the road, mucking about in the garden, or stirring up the chickens and chasing them about their enclosure, Charissa preferred indoor activities. For her, poking at her phone was more exciting than getting mud on her shoes, and Alexandrea's lack of a game console or a computer was horrifying.

"Bedroom," Alexandrea repeated. "Got it. I think I can twist Charissa's arm."

Holly smiled. "Charissa's a sweet kid. She's good company for you; I'm glad you got to know her. I just wish she could take her eyes off her phone to notice the world around her." Holly touched Alexandrea's arm again, rubbing it as she might pet a puppy. Her eyes met Alexandrea's, but they appeared to look inward as if searching for a solution that wasn't there. Her expression was distant.

It wasn't so much Charissa's company Alexandrea enjoyed, as her stories. Charissa went to the public school and had lots of friends—even boys. She even went on *dates*, or so she said. Charissa said Alexandrea was her one friend that didn't know any of the others, so she could tell her everything, all the schoolyard gossip. She was like an explorer newly returned from some savage continent, recounting stories of wars and truces, of great loves and glorious tragedies. Her words were windows into another world.

Holly hadn't yet settled in for her customary afternoon nap when Charissa arrived. Alexandrea thought better of asking why; her mother was acting strangely, at once frazzled and affectionate. When Holly was frazzled, she typically gave her daughter space—and

Alexandrea usually steered clear of her as well—but she could not seem to keep from checking in every few minutes. Alexandrea almost would have called it invasive. Not that she minded, really—so long as it stopped when Charissa arrived.

A car pulled up to the house. Charissa bounded up to the porch, and Alexandrea opened the whining storm door before she could knock. She led Charissa upstairs. Each step had its own signature creak, and Charissa repeated a few steps, creaking out a not-unmusical tune. She giggled and looked to Alexandrea for an approving laugh. Alexandrea had learned where to step to avoid the creaks, but Charissa's antics gave them an unexpected charm.

They cloistered into Alexandrea's bedroom. Her white satin comforter was cool to the touch as they sat with their backs to the wall. Charissa took out her phone and began showing Alexandrea what her other friends were up to—an endless procession of photographs and video. Alexandrea wasn't sure if she felt jealous or bored looking at them, or some combination of the two. Nothing felt natural. The backgrounds and locations seemed to exist exclusively for their selfies. These were what intrigued Alexandrea, places she had never been, things she had never seen in real life. The screen was only a few inches, and it was smeared with fingerprints, but Alexandrea couldn't look away.

Charissa nodded to the doorway, running a finger through her short brown hair. Peter stood lurking outside the room. Alexandrea thought only *she* knew how to avoid each creak. He stared into the bedroom. He inhaled deeply, held a moment, then let his breath out in what almost sounded like a sigh, something he did from time to time. Then he turned and disappeared as silently as he'd arrived.

Charissa giggled. "Your dad is so creepy." She immediately seemed to regret her words. "I mean, you know, the way he was standing there. He's just quiet and, you know." Her body stilled, and she slackened her jaw in imitation of Peter. "My father said there's a drug made from blowfish that makes people into zombies."

"He can't help it," Alexandrea said, defensively. "He's... not all there. It's not his fault.

"Was he always like this?" Charissa whispered. "I mean, he is your father." She laughed nervously. "What made him this way?"

"Who's this?" Alexandrea pointed at the image on Charissa's phone, hoping to change the subject. "Why is her hair like that?"

But Charissa wouldn't be turned. "He's brain-damaged, isn't he? That's horrible. When I told my parents about your dad, they said I shouldn't be afraid and that your mother was amazing for caring for him. Is it okay to talk about? I always wondered but was afraid to ask."

Sighing, Alexandrea gave in. "It's fine," she said. "Mom sometimes talks about how he used to be. I guess I know him like that because of her." Her eyes drifted back to the empty hallway. "I do wish he was normal. He could talk to me or sit with me and actually be there. Mom talks to him all the time, but he never even grunts." She faltered. "I've seen her leaning against him like she's trying to get him to hug her or something. She does it when she thinks they're alone. I think she misses him a lot."

Charissa tisked. "So sad. Do you think he, you know, understands? Is he sad inside too, do you think? My dad says that would be horrible. It would be, right?"

Tears welled in Alexandrea's eyes.

Alexandrea slid off the bed. "Be right back," she said, stepping into the hall. She found Peter in her parents' bedroom. She slid her arms around his bony frame and hugged him. He made no move to reciprocate. "Love you, Dad," she whispered. She opened her arms, and it was like the embrace had never happened; her father looked no different than before. She rubbed her wet eyes and was about to return to her bedroom when Peter's shoulder bumped hers sharply. She scowled. *So much for being affectionate.* He bumped her again as he wandered back into the hall.

Alexandrea found herself regretting having Charissa over. The girl's words echoed in her head, and soon she just wanted to be with her parents; she wanted to hug them both. *Mom must be sad. She never shows it.* Holly always spoke to Peter as though he were cognizant. Her recollections perhaps may have dabbled in melancholia, but they carried in them a joyful tone. *What if Mom's trying to sound happy for his sake? Or mine? What if Dad's sad inside because I never talk to him or hug him? Does he feel I've ignored him all these years?*

As Alexandrea pondered these painful questions, her ears suddenly popped. Her stomach tightened. "Did you feel that?" She pulled on her earlobe to reduce the pressure.

"Feel what?" Charissa lowered her phone.

"My ears are ringing," Alexandrea replied. "They just popped. Everything feels weird. Like my stomach and chest are being squeezed."

"Maybe you're getting your period. Cramps are a bitch."

Alexandrea winced. "I don't feel right." Her head swam. Her stomach pushed up into her chest, and she could barely breathe.

She heard her mother downstairs. Talking to her father. Alexandrea was glad that, for a moment, Peter was getting some attention. Except it sounded as though she was having a conversation. Question, answer, statement, reply. Alexandrea heard changes in her mother's tone but couldn't make out the words; her ears rang disruptively. Except Holly didn't normally answer on Peter's behalf. She never *reacted* to him; how could she?

What's happening? Alexandrea strained to listen. She could tell her mother was saying something important.

Tap-tap-tap. Charissa re-engaged her phone, poking the screen and messaging other friends. *Rude,* Alexandrea thought, but she was glad for Charissa's distraction. She felt a queer achiness, like she was running a fever, but she knew she wasn't. This was something else entirely.

A car turned off the road, crunching along the gravel driveway. Had Holly already called Charissa's parents to get her? Alexandrea knew her mother wasn't thrilled about Charissa's visit, but that wouldn't have been like her. *Who else could it be?*

Alexandrea's speculation ended when the car stopped. Her stomach quivered. Charissa didn't understand the significance when the car parked—still on the gravel.

Alexandrea knew exactly what it meant.

Chapter Two

our doors opened. Four pairs of shoes crunched on the gravel.

"She's definitely here?" a man asked.

"She's here," a second man replied. The hall window's thin glass muffling their words.

The third voice spoke. "You're sure this time?"

"I am," the second voice snapped.

"What's the plan, then?" asked a fourth voice.

Alexandrea heard a laugh. The second man, maybe? "We knock, and she lets us in. In and out. Quick."

Sounds of Holly scurrying about filtered up from below. Stomach acid gurgled in Alexandrea's throat, like she was on the verge of throwing up. Something struck the storm door so hard she almost thought she could feel it, and a rush of energy raced silently up the stairs. Alexandrea held her breath. She looked at Charissa, wondering if her friend sensed it too, but the girl only made a face. "What?"

Alexandrea peeked out towards the door, expecting to see someone lurking. Her chest thudded. No one was there. Turbulent air rose in the hall, like heat off the sunbaked pavement.

She jumped at a second knock. The aluminum door vibrated with an angry, electric buzz. Downstairs, her father shuffled to the door. Blood pounded in Alexandrea's ears, but she thought she heard her mother say, "It's time, Peter."

The front door groaned open. The storm door squealed its dissent. Four sets of footfalls entered their home.

Holly addressed the newcomers. She didn't sound shocked at their arrival; in fact, her voice carried a sarcastic bite. *Does she know them?*

Charissa startled her, tapping her shoulder. "Are you listening to me?"

Something bad was happening; Alexandrea felt the weight of it, crushing like an anvil.

The voices downstairs grew heated. Still, she could only catch snippets. Her ringing, squealing ears muted much of the conversation.

"I know she's here..." said one man. "...stole her from me." "She was never... yours," her mother snapped. "...wasn't your choice."

"Peter knew what he was sacrificing," Holly argued. "He did that willingly, not for you." Alexandrea edged back into her room and climbed onto her bed. *What are they talking about? Stole me?* Her satin comforter felt deathly cold against her palms. She cringed at the menace in the men's voices; it was like watching a pack of dogs encircle her mother. The emotion in Holly's words rose with each reply. She knew they would take her daughter.

A single flight of stairs separated Alexandrea from the newcomers. She couldn't escape without walking past them. She was trapped. She didn't understand why she feared these men so, as though she was awaiting an inevitable death to climb the stairs. Alexandrea tried to recall what her last words to Holly had been. At least Charissa had inadvertently compelled her to embrace her father. That would suffice for goodbye.

A clutching tightness twisted her insides from throat to groin. She felt like she was caught in a snare.

Charissa was oblivious. Could she not sense Alexandrea's distress? The way her heart fluttered or body trembled? Did she not see the cold sweat covering Alexandrea's skin? No, the girl noticed her distraction, but nothing more. Again, she threw out her accusation. "Are you even listening to me?"

Alexandrea jumped. She realized she was experiencing two worlds, the living and the dead. Upstairs, they were still in the former; as downstairs transitioned to the latter. The voice in her brain telling her she was being ridiculous was muzzled by terror.

Charissa held out her phone. "Isn't that so adorable?" Momentarily distracted by kittens, Alexandrea lost her bead on what was happening downstairs. She offered a half-hearted acknowledgement. Charissa still hadn't looked up. "Here's another; it's even more adorable."

Wave after wave of dread washed over her, drowning her, catching her in swirling eddies and an undertow to the bottom of a deep, frightful sea. She wished she understood where it came from.

Who were these men who came unannounced and unwelcomed, and brought death into her home? No one who was invited parked in the driveway, and no one who wasn't came in. Was that why she was in such a panic? Was that what was wrong? Was this an overreaction? A misunderstanding? Was she inventing the danger, or did she feel rightfully imperiled? Every rational impulse told her she was overreacting, but the feeling rose from her gut, infecting her throughout. Her skull felt as if it were about to explode.

For reasons she couldn't quite fathom, Alexandrea recalled their last few visitors, Charissa's parents, Aunt Heather, Aunt Abby, all of whom had pulled their cars right up to the house. She recollected how excited she always was seeing Abby jump out of her truck and run up the front steps. And Abby returned her enthusiasm. Heather would spend her visit with Holly and—until he wandered away—Peter, but Abby had always spent most of her time with Alexandrea. Playing, talking, buying clothes and toys and gifts. *Why am I thinking about Aunt Abby? Why now?*

Charissa held out her phone and huffed. Alexandrea signaled *one minute* with her hand when the report of a gunshot startled them.

Silence rang, upstairs and down.

Charissa mouthed, "Was that a gun?"

Alexandrea's head throbbed too much to acknowledge the question. Charissa blanched and let out a scream that ended in choking sobs.

Erratic thudding—a violent struggle—issued up the stairs.

Alexandrea dug her fingernails into her scalp. She couldn't release the explosive pressure in her skull.

"She's right up those stairs. I'm claiming what was never yours to keep," growled one of the voices.

"She has a name," her mother spat back. "She's a child, my child." Alexandrea had never heard her mother so disgusted. A thread of desperation ran through her voice; as she continued, it only seemed to grow. "Why her? There's got to be some other way. Some other child. Just let her alone."

"You knew. Or why hide her? Jeremiah doesn't know…"

Alexandrea's ears howled, drowning out everything.

"Why her? Shouldn't *she* get a say? Shouldn't she hear what you plan for her?"

"Holly, we all… You had to know I'd find her."

"I knew you'd try."

"All these years, you've lived dreading today would come, didn't you?" Alexandrea gripped her fingers tight. Her palms were slick with perspiration. "How sad, always looking over your shoulder, waiting..." She strained to hear above the squealing pain exploding in her skull. "You're both such idealistic fools. Did you... betray me? You made... and broke..." Her head rang like a bell. "Where did it get you? Look at Peter. There's nothing left. He... he made that sacrifice for me, for the greater good. Not for you or even her."

"You can't know him and... protected her... to my little girl."

Charissa clutched her knees, eyes wet with tears, chest heaving with uncontrollable sobs. For the first time, she seemed aware of what was going on around her. Her first instinct, of course, was to turn to her phone. She dialed the police.

"Enough stalling," another male voice spoke. "Why are we talking to her if the girl is here?"

"If you think..." Holly's voice fought to be heard in Alexandrea's thrumming ears. "...just hand her over..." Her mother interrupted herself. "Peter? How? Matthew... What are you doing to him? What have you done?"

"Yes, hi, hello? There's a—okay. I'm, ah, my name is Charissa Tylerson. There's a man shooting downstairs with a gun." The words came out mashed together like a single word.

"Don't make this more difficult," another voice drawled. "Don't cause someone to get hurt."

Alexandrea heard her mother sob before clearing her throat, "You will *not* take my daughter. Not today. Not ever. I won't let you have her."

"Holly, please." The voice protested. "You're giving him no choice."

Charissa continued into her phone. "The address?" Her lips moved as she took a moment to remember. "Seventy-seven, fifty-six, sixty-seven, two." She checked with Alexandrea, who nodded. "That's County Road B; drive right up to the house... Cross street? I mean, I gave you the address, can't you just plug it in?"

Bodies crashed into bodies below, into walls and furniture. Holly cried out, "Alex, don't let them take you!" Her yell ended with another sharp gunshot.

Charissa started and nearly dropped her phone. "Hide?" She echoed an instruction from the phone. "I'm in my friend's bedroom. Where the heck am I supposed to hide?"

Alexandrea trembled. Her legs wobbled. She could barely see through the swarming chaos in her brain. *Did I just hear my parents die?* She thought she was going to throw up. Her stomach quivered, and her heart plummeted into her abdomen. *No. They're fine. They have to be fine. They can't be dead... because of me. Mom didn't want Charissa here. Is this why? Did she know?*

Alexandrea stared into the hall as Charissa attempted to crawl under the bed. Could she help Charissa hide? *If Charissa survives, she could tell the police.* But she didn't move, didn't speak. She didn't know what to do.

A single set of footfalls approached up the creaking stairs.

"You better be in your bedroom."

The steps drew closer.

Plywood splintered as the bedroom door burst open, colliding with her dresser. Charissa screamed from half under the bed, kicking her exposed legs. Alexandrea scarcely heard or noticed. Her attention was snatched by the figure in the hall.

Her father stood in the doorway; a sneer painted across his face. He gripped a pistol in his hand, the sight sent needles of pain into Alexandrea's eyes. She blinked as if staring at the sun. Then she gasped, and her eyes widened as the gun grew larger and even more menacing.

"I've waited a very, very long time," her father said. Alexandrea had never heard his voice. She wondered if his first words—words of anger and malice—would be the last she ever heard.

A second set of footfalls—lighter than the first—took the stairs.

"Do something," Charissa chanted below, "Do something; do something…"

Peter cast a distracted glance down the hall, tracking the gun with his gaze.

"Get out, Alex!" It was her mother.

Holly's small frame pushed past Peter into the room. She met Alexandrea's eyes and screamed, "Go!" before she spun back defensively. The gun roared. The air swirled with heat.

Alexandrea shrieked, frozen in place as her father murdered her mother. The gun repeated its violent howl. She wanted nothing more than to obey her mother and leave—not just leave but disappear. But Peter stood between her and escape. And how could she think of leaving Holly? The weapon spat fire, hot cackling laughter, like it took no greater joy than destroying whatever lay in front of it.

A scream shredded Alexandrea's throat, pulling her emotions, draining them out of her. Her body clenched around the sound, and she closed her eyes, expelling every atom from her lungs.

Her ears popped, cutting short the blood-curdling noise. Her mind couldn't unravel the confusion: the firing gun, Charissa screaming under the bed, her mother, those strange voices, her father—her own *father*?—and something else, bigger than them all; it was as though the room grew too small—or the air too big—and it threw her aside.

A shock wave bearing an awful stench buffeted her, coating her in thick, sticky dust.

What's happening? Mom? What was that? Mom, are you okay? Mom, what happened? Her mouth moved, but the sound was a buzz. She opened her eyes to silence—*I've gone deaf*—and her room savaged by an explosion. Bodies lay tossed about the room, disturbing mote-filled air as they stirred. The door was no more than a wedge of splinters hanging from the top hinge. Her dresser, now faceless, spilled clothing like a gaping abdominal wound. Her mother, thrown beside her at the foot of the bed, shifted, still breathing, Alexandrea was relieved to see, though bloody burns covered her body. Her father had been at the epicenter of the explosion. His shoes marked where he had stood like footprints in his dust.

Another man lay in the hall, crumpled and broken, his face a mask of pain, decorated with lacerations. The drywall had shattered where he'd hit it.

Dust roiled around Alexandrea in turbulent patterns, as though a wave of intense heat entered the room.

Her skull wailed.

Her mother fought to stand.

Footfalls crashed up the stairs. Cursing voices cut through the painful ring in Alexandrea's ears.

Holly choked out a whimper. "Why are you still here?" She found her feet and clutched Alexandrea's shoulders with both hands. "You have to go. Now." Holly pointed to the wall by the bed, her face softening. A flare in Alexandrea's head momentarily drowned out her words. When it subsided, she said, "It's okay, Alex. You know it turns out okay. Now, call the mist and go."

Alexandrea glanced back at Charissa, as though the other would clarify what her mother said, but the girl's unconscious body lay in the corner.

"Leave her," her mother pressed, stroking Alexandrea's face, but never looking at her. "Bring the mist, Alex. There's nothing more for you here."

What mist? She didn't understand what her mother was saying.

Alexandrea gasped, hissing the *s* in *mist* as a disk of brilliant light spilled from Holly's chest. She touched her mother, laying a shaking hand to her breastbone, right over the glow.

Two men appeared in the hallway with a third lurking behind. One peered into the bedroom, and another knelt beside their fallen associate. They looked like television detectives in their slacks and dress shirts. "Matthew's neck is broken, George," the kneeling one said. Then after a brief pause, "Did you hear me?"

"Yeah, Gary, I heard. Is he dead?" Her head shrieked.

Gary touched Matthew's chest, "He's alive, for now." He glanced at her father's empty shoes. "Peter's obliterated. George, it wasn't supposed to happen like this. No one gets hurt, remember?" He stared at Holly as he spoke. "She wasn't supposed to be this strong yet."

George shook his head. "I don't know. She did this?"

The sensation of needles stabbing her brain was excruciating.

The third man slipped past them. "It was her," he grinned.

"Be careful, William," George warned.

William nodded. "I am."

"Alex, please," her mother pressed, "focus." Alexandrea's ears rang and squealed. "Take Matthew's... now GO!"

Alexandrea wanted to scream. Her skull might as well have been turning inside out. The men were right there. How was her mother so calm? "What are you talking about?" Her words were a whisper. She stood motionless, no more than an object between her mother's palms. Sticky, red flowers bloomed across her mother's shirt. One below her shoulder, one on her abdomen. The disk on her chest smoldered bright.

"Alexandrea." Gary rose from the stricken Matthew and entered the room. His voice was firm and angry, and perhaps a little frightened. "That's not your mother. Don't listen to her." He reached for Holly—*into* her—his hand grasping the glow in her chest. His fist shone red. "Not anymore."

Alexandrea stared in horror. Her father was dead. Her mother dying. The realization washed over her like a wave of icy nails. "Mommy," she whined.

Gary tugged on the light. A fine, glowing filament connected his fist to her mother's chest. It sparked but gave no slack. He yanked harder, throwing his weight into it, but the line slipped through his fingers, causing him to tumble back.

"Why'd you do that?" William asked. He turned to Alexandrea, and whispered in a soothing tone, "I know you're scared, but things will be okay."

George shouted, "William, what are you doing? Grab her!"

"I won't touch her," William hissed back.

Holly smiled.

"Go," her mother pushed her towards the wall. Her words were disjointed, barely audible beneath the intermittent buzzing in Alexandrea's ears. Holly didn't seem to be speaking to her at all. Perhaps blood loss had muddled her mind.

"Mom? What?" Nothing made sense. Alexandrea's head felt like it was being cleaved in two.

"Don't touch that wall," Gary commanded. Then to her mother, "Tell your daughter, or I'll do unspeakable things."

"Mom?"

"Go," Her mom ordered. "Now." Alexandrea didn't know how to comply. Holly grabbed and pulled her. Alexandrea collided with the wall. *Did she try to go through the wall?* Waves of heat washed past Holly, distorting undulations, like the mirage on a hot summer blacktop. They reached the wall. Plumes of smoke erupted from the sheetrock. *Did my mom do that?*

William whispered to Holly. His words made no sense. "The loop is closed. Get her out of here."

George crowded them. Alexandrea's mother released her, her eyes closed, her face washed over with defeat. "You can't have her," she sobbed.

Gary grabbed Alexandrea by the forearm. She tried to pull free, but his grip was like a vise. "Come on, girl."

William tried to free her, "Don't do that, Gary. You saw what she did to Matthew."

Gary released her, pulling back as though he'd been clutching a corpse.

A thick, roiling fog bubbled up to Alexandrea's right. None of the men seemed to notice it. Holly stood away from it, her legs trembling. She gazed into Alexandrea's eyes. Her lips were blue. She had never looked so pale. Holly blinked once then collapsed.

"Mom!" Alexandrea knelt beside her mother, tears streaming down her face. "Mommy?" and then, "Holly? Say something, Holly." Her hands shook too much to feel for a pulse. Because she knew her mother no longer had one.

Alexandrea wasn't sure when the child appeared.

A sweet, almost angelic face stared at her mother with large, dark eyes.

"Where'd you come from?"

The small child, perhaps three or four years of age, didn't answer.

Long, chestnut curls swept around cherubic, brown features. Wrapped in fabrics of riotous colors and patterns, the barefoot child could have been a boy or a girl; Alexandrea couldn't tell. Its open expression was sorrowful yet consolatory. This child understood extraordinary loss.

The child leaned closer as if to offer Holly a secret.

Holly rose. Alexandrea screamed. Her mother still lay on the floor, yet she was sitting too, half in—and half out—of her own dead body, as though she were peeling herself from a sleeping bag.

"What's happening?" Alexandrea asked, first to the child, then her mother, then anyone and no one in particular. "What's happening?"

William shouted, "We need to get out of here."

"Calm down. Charon's come for the mother," George reassured the others, but his tone belied the words.

"I'm not leaving without the girl," Gary shot back. "Matthew needs her." He motioned to the crumpled form in the hallway. "More now than ever."

The child ignored Alexandrea. It knelt beside her mother, stroking her cheek with a delicate touch. Holly made no move to acknowledge it, not even when it offered the other hand as if expecting something. Did she even see it? "Not yet," she said, answering Alexandrea's doubts. "I've got to see my daughter safe."

The child favored Alexandrea with a dispassionate look, then turning back to her mother, it held its hand out once more. A demand, this time.

Alexandrea's mother held her in her gaze. "I can't stay, but I won't leave until you're safe. Go. Please, Alexandrea." She nodded towards the wall of mist. "Walk into it."

Alexandrea stared at her mother. She stared at the mist.

"Please, Alexandrea, please."

William and George were at the door, spots of light emanating from each of their chests now too.

"Where are you going?" Gary reached for Holly's glow.

Both William and George began to shout, "Don't do that."

Rage contorted the child's face as Gary wrapped his fingers around Holly's light. Alexandrea cowered against her bed, watching the child's skin split and tare away in ribbons; its bright clothes wilted before her eyes, falling into piles of scrap. Muscles shriveled and disintegrated, but its pointed skeleton grew *larger*. Before Gary could lift a defensive hand, the living nightmare—now gigantic—sliced a bony claw into his chest, extracting *his* glow. Flesh parted at the creature's terrible touch, ribs separating around its knuckles. With a sharp snap, the shining tether between Gary and his light burst into a shower of falling sparks.

Gary crumpled to the floor. Alexandrea gasped. There were two Garys, now, one dead on the floor with his chest ripped open, the other standing before her.

The other men cringed and recoiled. Alexandrea wanted to run from the towering, skeletal thing; she wanted to hide, wanted to protect her mother.

George backed through the doorway. William remained just inside the room.

The gruesome creature regarded its bony hand and the glow it had pulled from Gary's chest. Then it returned its attention to her mother. It held out its hand once more. Gary's glow was gone.

The standing Gary passed between them. He shot Alexandrea a wistful look before disappearing into the mist.

"Follow him," Holly hissed.

"What about..." she started. She couldn't leave her mother. Or her friend. But no one in the room paid her any mind. *Is Charissa safe?*

George cursed and disappeared into the hall.

William addressed Alexandrea. "It's okay. No one will hurt you." He edged out of the room then turned back. "He won't stop, you know. Matthew needs you too much. He thinks he's the only one who can stop Jeremiah. He doesn't understand." Back in the hall, he knelt beside Matthew's injured form.

As Holly took Alexandrea by the shoulders, Alexandrea realized she had never felt the full weight of her mother's gaze. She felt herself pressed back into the wall of mist. She expected the mist to be chilly or wet as it embraced her, drawing her away from the room, but it felt like nothing. She watched the creature through the foggy veil. Cold, empty eyes met hers. She cringed, but no glow emanated from her chest.

"Don't be afraid," her mother whispered. "You're safe from the Reaper; it has no interest in you. Your father and I saw to that. Find Aunt Heather. She'll know what to do."

Alexandrea stepped backwards, deeper, further from her bedroom. Nearly lost in the fog, she watched her mother grasp at the glow within herself. She gazed on her daughter one final time. "I'm ready," she said, and she handed her glow to the skeleton. Bones relaxed; flesh knitted back together, and it was the child that took her mother's hand. Holly followed it into the mist.

Alexandrea staggered. *What just happened? Is my mother really, truly dead? My father? Both, gone? I never said goodbye.*

Who were those men? What did they want with me? Will Charissa be okay?

She took a deep breath and another step forward. Further from her bedroom.

Further into the darkening mist.

Chapter Three

For eight nights, Alex had awoken from the same nightmare. She greeted each morning, bolting from her pillow, sticky with sweat and with a fresh, desperate cry on her lips. This morning was no different.

"It was a dream," she repeated the familiar mantra, "just a dream." She breathed deeply to calm her pounding heart. It was always the same, always terrifying.

Cool air washed across her legs as she lifted away the sheets. Her bedroom, a third-floor attic, was a study in discordant angles. With no walls in any traditional sense, its converging rooflines rose from the floor to peak in the center of the room above her bed. Headroom diminished the further she moved from center. To reach the space behind her dressers or trunks—the room had no closets—Alex had to stoop. A cupola rose from the ceiling, with a window aimed in each cardinal direction. These opened, allowing the room to breathe. Navy curtains surrounded attic-pull stairs, which were always down, granting access to the rest of the house.

The whole floor belonged to Alex. Stifling in the summer, freezing in the winter, but it was hers.

It was Saturday. Her cousins, Rosemary and Billy, had planned a whole day exploring the trails and fields just beyond their dead-end street, where fallow farmland abutted the untouched state park. The Adirondack Mountains of Central New York State weren't the majestic granite behemoths of the West—or so she had read. But worn by time into steep, undulating hills and ridges, the local range begged for exploration. Sometimes she'd discover fossils of seashells and coral, anachronistic on old mountain trails. She had accumulated a small but treasured collection of these, displaying them on her dresser.

Wandering the woods was one of Alex's favorite ways to spend the day, and she hoped escaping her normal, familiar surroundings might help her forget her nightmares, if only for a few hours.

The scene was never far from Alex's mind. She sometimes found herself replaying it in her head without even realizing. The strange, dangerous men. That giant skeletal *thing*. Her mother's protracted death. It seemed so real; it was *her* childhood bedroom in the dream, her father just as she remembered him. But of course, none of it had happened. Peter and Holly died four years ago. Alex had come to Heather's to spend the day with Billy and Rose. She remembered feeling ill—almost as though she knew—her head hurting so bad it threatened to split open. Then Heather broke the news.

Her parents had died in a car accident.

She didn't remember much from that time, likely from the trauma of her loss. She couldn't recall a funeral—or any sort of service—only moving into Heather's attic.

Now, she saw her parents in her sleep. Four years of vague impressions and missing memories had given way to crisp, clear visions of their faces. And each night she lost them again, making her ache for them all over. She hadn't realized how little she had come to think of them recently.

Alex couldn't guess what this fantastical and disturbing dream meant. It was like a mosaic of lies cobbled together by her brain. There was one truth about her parents' deaths she could be certain of; it formed on her lips as a question she used to ask every day: "Why wasn't I in the car?"

Alex shook the dream from her head as a dog sheds water. A glance at the clock showed she had overslept. She pulled on her clothes, which lay crumpled by her bed, and tied her long auburn hair into a ponytail before easing her way down the ladder to the second floor.

Aunt Heather's room was empty, so were her cousins'. Alex washed her face in the bathroom. Her eyes in the mirror reflected the nightmare's lingering images. Like a stain on her waking moments, every morning, it grew more permanent. If only the face she saw— her reality—could reconcile the real memories with the false. She eyed herself in the mirror. A comic splash of freckles peppered her pale cheeks. Inspecting her skin for new pimples or blackheads, she rubbed the crust from her eyes.

Alex galloped down the stairs to the kitchen. Rosemary was setting the table for breakfast as her mom tended the stove. Billy poured milk and juice into glasses. Beside him, on the counter, the coffeemaker burbled contentedly.

"You've rejoined the land of the living," Heather said without looking up from a skillet of spitting sausages.

"Sorry," Alex said before launching into her customary response. "I hoped if I slept late enough, I'd get breakfast in bed." She exaggerated her disappointment. "I guess I didn't sleep late enough to find out. This time."

"Yeah," Rosemary clattered a fork atop a plate. "I'm sure one of us would bring you breakfast. The Hawthorne breakfast special, a bucket of ice water."

"That's not nice," Billy said to his twin, "but it *is* funny." He smiled at Alex as if to reassure her.

"Funny's what matters," Rose laughed. "But I wouldn't *really* do that, would I, Billy?"

"You might," Billy laughed. Rose scowled.

At eighteen, Alex was two years older than her cousins.

"What's left to do?" Alex looked around the kitchen; Heather was nearly done cooking; the table was set. She poured coffee into a mug and placed it beside the stove for her aunt.

"Oh, *now* you're here to help," Rose mocked, hands on her hips. She returned Alex's glare with a smile.

"Something the matter?"

"Something the matter?" Rose mimicked. Then, in the same voice, she added, "I sleep late and don't thank anyone for doing all my chores."

"What are you talking about?"

"Rose set the table," Billy interjected.

"I see that," Alex replied. "Sorry, I forgot her medal."

"I see that..." Her cousin started to repeat Alex's last statement but couldn't help breaking into laughter.

Alex looked at the others. "Am I missing something?"

Heather put down the coffee mug and began plating breakfast. "You guys are going hiking today?"

"Yeah," Alex said. "You said it was okay."

"You've been oversleeping a lot," Heather said. "Everything okay?"

"I'm just not sleeping well," Alex replied.

"Rose took care of the chickens and the rest of your chores this morning too."

"Thank you, Rose," she said in earnest, "I didn't know."

Rose bowed. "One day I'll call on you to make it up to me, and you can't say no, no matter how horrible or dangerous the ask."

"Really?"

"That's how favors work."

"Then I take my *thank you* back. *I* never asked for a favor, Rose. Don't forget that part."

Rose put her hands on her hips again. "You want me to undo everything? I will. I'll put everything back how I found it. Don't test me. I'll put those eggs right back in the chickens." Then she burst out laughing.

"You can do that?" Billy asked, and Alex started laughing too.

Still giggling, Rose offered them an impression of a surprised and unhappy chicken before Heather answered. "No, Billy, your sister cannot—and *would not*—put eggs back into the chickens. She made a joke."

Billy frowned. "I know; I was going to too. I was about to say *that proves which came first.* I'm not dumb."

Heather nodded. "No, you're not." Carrying their plates to the table, she regarded her niece. "Why aren't you sleeping well?"

Alex didn't want to talk about the nightmare. If Heather had questions, she didn't know if she could answer them. She just wanted to forget it and hope it didn't come back again tonight. "I'm okay. Just restless, I guess."

"Why do you think that is?" Heather poured coffee for everyone, refilling her own mug. "Something I should know?"

Alex tightened under the weight of her aunt's scrutiny. "What do you mean?" She joined the others at the table.

Rose swapped her toast for her brother's, only for Billy to lick it before handing it back. Heather shrugged, following the twins' antics with neither amusement nor concern. She returned her attention to Alex. "You seem distracted and cranky; that's not like you. I mean, if there's something you want to talk about…"

"I haven't been sleeping well, Aunt Heather, that's all," Alex heard frustration in her voice. She tried to speak evenly, though her thoughts returned to the vivid nightmare. "Maybe it's all the daylight, you know, circadian rhythms. Plus, the attic's warming up."

"Don't wait until it's too uncomfortable. You know where the fan is; you don't need me to set it up. Or you can always sleep downstairs on the couch."

Rose laughed. "Or you can share my room. He won't mind, will you, Billy?"

Billy made a face. "Shut up."

"If you're sure that's all." Heather ignored her children. "You'd tell me if something's bothering you?"

"Of course." Alex turned to Rose. "Thanks for taking care of my things this morning. It means a lot to me." Rose stuck out her tongue and clucked. "Those poor chickens," Alex said. "But I mean it, thanks."

Rose grinned. "Nothin' but love for you, sis."

The words warmed Alex's chest. She felt for Rosemary what she imagined she might for a twin of her own. She sometimes worried about her cousin coming to resent her; although Heather treated her like a daughter, and Billy and Rose, like a big sister, she knew she wasn't. Just as Rose was getting old enough to move into the attic herself, here had come Alex, forcing her to keep bunking with her brother through the remainder of her teenage years. Wishing they really were sisters, Alex sometimes counted their similarities; they both had blue eyes, freckles, and a wicked sense of humor, but in some ways, they couldn't have been more different. Alex's hair was redder while Rose's leaned more brown; Alex was much taller at five foot ten, leaner, and more athletic, while Rose, only two inches over five feet, was curvaceous and very pretty. Of course, not all sisters looked alike. Alex sometimes wished she looked more like her cousin.

"Alex," Billy called to her, "we're hiking today? Right? Saturday, for hiking?"

"That's the plan." She grinned at his barrage.

"That's good," he said. Scrunching his face, he added, "Today is a good day. It's the day we went. It's the right day."

The girls stifled a bout of laugher—largely due to a preemptive glare from Heather. Alex felt bad though; she didn't want Billy to think they laughed *at* him. It was just strange. Lately, he'd begun talking about things they were doing—or going to do—as if they'd already happened. Heather insisted it was just a phase he was going through.

"Don't laugh at your brother," Heather scolded.

"We weren't laughing at him," Rose shot back. "Sheesh, Mom, we're next to him."

Heather met Alex's eyes, shaking her head; Alex liked to think her aunt saw her as—if not quite an equal—a peer, someone who could share in her exasperation.

"He said something funny, Aunt Heather. We weren't laughing at him." She turned to Billy, who grinned at her. "It is the right day, isn't it, Billy?"

Sixteen and lanky as a scarecrow, Billy carried an angelic face and mop of wavey chestnut locks atop a body that was nothing but knees and elbows. He stood taller than Rose and, though not quite Alex's height, was in just about every way that could be measured, the opposite of his twin. Whereas it had been a shock when Rose did Alex's chores, Billy was always eager to help. Where Rose was graceful, Billy was awkward and clumsy. But that only added to his charm. He was sweet to everyone and especially kind to Alex. And she adored him.

Alex saw that her aunt worried about the boy, like she knew something bad would one day happen, like he was born under a sorrowful star. Heather insisted he required their constant attention. "He's too trusting." She warned. "Billy is special. He'll always choose kindness, even when it brings him suffering. One day you'll understand." She talked like he was so young, but something about him always struck Alex as very old.

"Anything happening besides hiking today, kiddoes?" Heather dipped her toast into the sausage fat and runny yolk left on her plate.

"We're hiking. What else is there to do?" Rosemary's frustration at living an hour's drive from any typical teenage haunts sometimes came out in passive-aggressive shots at her mother. Getting anywhere worth going required a car, and Heather's car, like an untended garden, was overgrown by weeds.

"And what exactly are you getting at?" Heather asked.

"Nothing."

"Then why'd you say it?"

"Never mind, okay?"

Heather sighed. "We live here for a reason, Rose. Remember that. I was born in this house. Our family lived here for generations. You were born here; so was I. You don't just walk away because you want to live closer to shopping."

"I know," Rose said into her plate. It wasn't the first time she'd heard this speech.

"I know it's far from everything. I know you want to get out and have friends and go to stores, but there's more to life than shopping and being silly."

"*I know*, Mom," Rose's tone implored her mother to stop.

"One day you'll see this is the absolute best place to grow up. You'll thank me and apologize for giving me a hard time. When you learn to make do with what you have, to enjoy the small things, the free things that nature gives you, you'll be very happy."

"I know," Rose groaned.

"I like getting lost in the woods," Alex tried to change the subject.

"Lost? How do you plan to get lost?"

"It's a figure of speech, mom. Sheesh." Heather's lecture had completely exhausted her daughter's patience.

Alex didn't always understand her cousin. She missed her own parents every day. She'd forgotten so much, the car they drove, where they'd been going, or even the date of the accident. *Perhaps it's a sign that I'm healing?* She wished Rosemary knew how lucky she was to have her mother.

The twins still saw their father. Mostly for holidays, and the occasional weekend, but Alex didn't remember him. According to Heather, she hadn't seen Eric since before he and Heather had divorced. From the return address on his annual birthday cards, he lived close by.

Alex found that it took a good measure of alcohol before Heather would discuss him and the pain he'd caused. They divorced after Rose and Billy's births, and he'd remarried to start a new family. "He left me," Heather would whimper, "but I made him do it. He didn't understand sacrifice, so he found a woman who wouldn't ask it of him."

Billy chewed his sausage thoughtfully, a troubled look on his face. "How can you get lost in the woods?" He walked his fingertips along the tabletop. "We walk on the path." His marching fingers reversed. "Same every time. We can't get lost. Someone could think they're lost, but they never are."

Heather coughed, "Where'd you learn that?"

He declined to answer, his face flushing red. His eyes shone remarkably blue.

"He's being weird, Mom. He's being an ass."

Billy cracked up. "She said *ass*, Mom, not me." He giggled too much to say more.

"You just said it," Rose pointed at him.

"You made me," tears of laughter fell from his eyes.

Heather's expression said she'd resigned herself to the chaos.

Chapter Four

lex stood with Heather over a rack of drying dishes. Several inches taller, she looked down at her aunt. The gulf between *status* and *stature* was awkward.

"Sometimes I wish you wouldn't stand so close," her aunt said with a wince.

Alex made a face. "What?"

Heather wiped the counter. "It hurts my neck looking up so much."

Alex stepped away.

"Better," Heather said, some tension lifting from her face. "I like looking at you. I see bits of your father, and it reminds me of when we were all kids." She groaned, "I remember, when I was your age, my parents were so old. I hope I don't seem that old to you."

Alex shook her head. She'd never describe Heather as old. If she weren't so busy being their mom, Alex thought, she would have made a great older sister.

"In my head, I feel no different than you feel. One day you'll know what I mean. You think being an adult means something special, like something magical is bestowed on you, but so far all it means to me is more responsibilities and less stamina."

It was hard to reconcile her aunt's words to what she saw every day. Heather was a ball of positive energy. She never sat still. Cooking, cleaning, running a classroom, shopping, tending the garden, laundry, managing the lives of her two kids—three, counting Alex. Yet she was always present, always available. As far as Alex could tell, Heather's only personal time was her monthly Book Club meeting; it was the only strictly personal time she demanded. Alex sometimes wondered if she had other friends. Exhaustion haunted her some days as shadows peeking around the corners of her eyes, or clinging to the last syllable of a word. But her enthusiasm never seemed to flag.

Echoes of Heather's youth lay scattered in the old photos around the house: the new mom or the expectant mother; Heather as a bride; graduate, student, teen; Heather and Peter as kids. In more than a few, Aunt Abby posed beside her. *Would we have been friends?* Her aunt had long brown hair back then. She was pretty.

Heather turned from Alex to the table, where she had placed the weekend newspaper. Dolly, the family cat, perched atop it, limbs tucked under her. "Oh, you're not allowed on the table, but you think my paper's fair game?" A minute-long battle of wills ensued, ending as Dolly jumped up for a third time, just to prove she could, then scattered papers to the floor as she immediately jumped down.

Alex watched Dolly prance upstairs, intent, probably, on curling up at the foot of her bed.

"Aunt Heather, can I ask you something?"

"Of course, Alex," Heather replied, meeting her with consequential eyes. "You can ask me anything, you know that. Is there something you want to tell me?"

"I was hoping I could have—that you would let me, that is— get a summer job. I'd like to make some money this year."

"What do you need money for?" Her aunt sounded disappointed.

Alex was quiet.

"Oh. That."

That. It wasn't the first time Alex had tried to have this conversation. It never seemed to go far.

"Oh, that," Heather repeated in a different tone. "Now's not the time. You should stay in home classes a while longer. I've been researching special programs to help qualify you for scholarships."

Alex bit her lip. *More of the same, though she's never mentioned any 'programs' before.* "Is this about the money or about me leaving home?"

Heather leaned against the counter and rubbed her forehead. "It's about doing what's best for you, what your parents wanted. It's not time yet."

"What did my parents want?"

"They wanted you to be happy, safe, and strong. Like all parents want for their kids."

"Won't going to college help me have those things? Or are you saying I'm not smart enough yet?"

"Of course, I'm not saying that. You're plenty bright. That's not it at all. We have to talk about this eventually, sweetie, but now's not the time. Billy and Rose are changing, and I don't want a black cloud following you around on your hike. This isn't *no*, Alex; it's just *not now*. It's too late to enroll for September, anyway."

Alex sighed. There was no arguing. She felt like Heather didn't want her to go but would never give the real reason. She offered a reluctant, "Okay. Whatever. Fine."

Alex slapped some peanut butter sandwiches together for their hike, slicing Heather's homemade bread extra thick, practically daring Heather to criticize her. She wrapped the sandwiches in cloth napkins then filled a canteen with water and placed it all in her rucksack.

Perhaps feeling their silence had gone on long enough, Heather asked, "Was that *Okay* to placate me? You're not agitated about this?" Alex shook her head. "Good. I don't want there to be hard feelings between us. You can come to me whenever anything is bothering you." Alex nodded. "Anything. No matter how small. You know that, right?"

"Yeah."

"Good. Enjoy your hike." After a pause, she pulled Alex in for a hug. "Keep my babies safe," she whispered.

Chapter Five

They passed the chicken coop and the gardens where Heather grew her vegetables and herbs in neat little rows. The road was usually deserted, and they thought nothing of walking three abreast.

The further they wandered, the freer they felt. Rose's walk became more animated; Billy poked around looking for curios and interesting objects. They walked in silence past increasingly sparse houses, the mid-June sun, intense but not yet hot. A dry breeze carried scents of soil and fresh-cut grass, and Rose's rucksack bounced on Alex's back. These times were special to Alex. Without Heather nearby, she felt Rose looked up to her; she no longer worried that the girl resented her. In truth, she wasn't sure where she got the idea; it wasn't like Rose had ever said anything.

The pavement ended at the street's close where broken chunks of macadam and bluestone gave way to a dirt road, which soon faded to overgrown tire ruts before disappearing into the growth.

They followed a meandering path through the taller grasses to the edge of the fallow farm. Every few hundred feet faded yellow and black signs hung tacked to a tree, warning that this was state land and forbidding hunting without a permit. Ahead lay the Old Witch's Shack, a tumbled stone foundation in the woods, which local lore accorded countless fanciful stories from witches to serial killers.

They reached their path, where the grass never grew too high, and the air was always cool. Trees lined the natural trail, reaching high overhead, intertwining their branches, stirring and tickling each other in the breeze. Years of fallen leaves and broken limbs littered the ground, which dropped away on either side. Saplings and vines grew wherever light reached the wooded floor.

"I heard you and Mom talking about college again," Rose broke the silence. Her heavy breathing punctuated her words as they drudged the first of many long inclines. "What did she say?"

Alex took a preparatory breath. "The usual." Everyone knew what that meant. As Alex had approached eighteen, she had grown excited at the prospect of college, but it had been nearly a year since she first brought it up, and Heather wouldn't have it.

"Why do you wanna go?" Billy whimpered.

"Because," Alex thought for a moment, "that's what comes next. There's only so much Heather can teach us. We've been home-schooled all our lives." Billy didn't seem convinced. "I want to visit the places we've read about. I want to see what I've been missing."

"So not because of us?" He sounded anxious.

Alex rested her arm on her cousin's shoulder. "No, bud; *us* is the best thing I have."

"You two want to be alone?" Rose smirked.

Billy blushed. Alex slid her arm from his shoulder and grabbed Rose, making exaggerated kissing sounds. "There's enough love for you too," she laughed.

They reached the clearing by the Old Witch's Shack, and Billy ran ahead. The canopy opened wide, showing a blue sky with not a cloud in sight. Sparse grass tangled with vines and crawling weeds around the stone foundation. Built on a gentle slope, it came up to their waists up front, dropping to knee height on the other end.

Billy climbed on all fours up a collapsed pile of stones as Rose and Alex hoisted themselves up the side to meet him. They'd once tried to map the foundation, but it was all but impossible to tell where walls might have been. A rough black crater in one corner marked the remains of a fire pit. No walls, no roof, no chimney remained.

"It's funny," Rose began, "the top was once the bottom. All that's left is the floor."

"Do you think it's creepy?" Billy asked.

"No," Rose answered.

"Why?" Alex asked.

Billy shrugged. "Someone lived here. Now they're gone. They slept and ate here. Walked right here."

Rose giggled, but Alex understood. Billy had captured her own feelings about the place, like she could reach through time and touch the people who'd called this home. Looking across the clearing, she tried to imagine it through a window or open doorway. "Was this their land?" She wondered aloud.

"It's a state park," Billy replied. "They couldn't own it."

"It wasn't always. Before it was a park, someone owned it," Rose replied.

Billy looked down. "It's a small house if they were rich."

"Why do you think they were rich?" Alex asked.

Billy shrugged. "If they owned all that land, they'd have to be."

Alex looked into the woods. The hilly ground was riddled with stones and boulders. "Wouldn't have done them much good. They couldn't farm here. It's just far away from everything."

"I bet this was a bedroom once."

Alex looked at Rose. "What makes you say that?"

"There's the kitchen; there's the living room." She pointed as she spoke. "So these had to be bedrooms, here and here, and I bet that was either a bathroom or a closet."

Alex shook her head. "Probably neither. I bet they had an outhouse. Maybe it was all kitchen."

Billy looked up. "They slept in the kitchen?"

"If they called it that," Alex guessed.

"Speaking of," Rose interjected, "I could use a little energy. Maybe we all split a sandwich. You made sandwiches, right?"

Alex nodded, and they sat down in a line with their feet dangling over the foundation. Alex broke the first sandwich into thirds and handed out two of them. She saw now how ridiculously thick she cut the bread, as did Rose, evident by her quizzical look. Billy made noises as he tried to open his mouth wide enough to take a bite.

They stared into the woods. Billy giggled and pointed out acrobatic squirrels chasing one another. They passed the canteen between them, its water warm and tasting of plastic, but it helped get the thick bread and peanut butter down.

"What do you think it's like?" Rosemary said no one in particular.

"What what's like?" Alex asked.

"Out there." Rose nodded towards the woods. "It's an hour to the store, and Mom never lets us go with her. We've never been anywhere except the few places Dad takes us. He took us to the city once—not the real city; that's, like, six or eight hours away. New York." She offered the name with a flourish. "I'll probably never go, not unless someone's life depends on it." She paused a moment, still intent on the woods. "Is everywhere like this? Just hundreds of kids sitting in their own woods, wondering what the world is like? Or do kids in the city wonder what it's like for us? We read about all these places in Geography and History. Do people really live in gigantic cities? Can they even imagine a place as Podunk as this?"

"Po-dunk," Billy repeated. "It's not po-dunk; it's rural."

Rose continued as if she didn't hear, "Sometimes I pretend those places are made up. I pretend there's no one but us, and I'm not missing out on anything."

Alex sighed. "I barely remember my parents' house." She recalled it more from her nightmares than any true recollection. "If Heather didn't let us come into the woods unsupervised, I think I'd wonder if she was keeping us prisoner."

Rose gasped, "Right? I think that all the time!" She turned her body to Alex. "It's like those stories where people think they're alone but they're secretly in some crazy experiment, being studied."

Billy looked up. "Who's studying us?"

"Ever think we're in the middle of nowhere for a reason?" Rose's voice dripped with melodrama. "Hidden on purpose?"

"Hidden from what?" Billy wasn't getting Rose's joke.

Rose gave him an incredulous look. "Do I have to spell it out for you?"

"Spell *what* out?"

Out of nowhere, Alex's head started to throb. In only a few seconds, it felt like it was exploding. She winced and rubbed her temples.

"You okay?" Rose looked concerned.

It was excruciating. Her ears rang as if she had steam whistles blowing inside them. Then just as suddenly, it stopped. "One of my migraines," Alex said. The pain had vanished, but it still hurt in her memory. "I haven't had one in a while…" This wasn't entirely true. She got them in her nightmare. She remembered getting them as a child, usually when Heather or Aunt Abby was over. "I don't know, I think it happens when I get excited."

"But you're okay? You don't need to go home?"

Before Alex could answer, Billy piped in. "We can't go home. Not from here. We still haven't gone to…" his voice fell to a whisper, "Sacrifice Stone."

They both looked at him queerly.

"I'm fine," Alex said, even as Rose chided Billy. "You know Mom hates when you call it that."

"You mean Picnic Rock?" Alex asked. "Since when do you call it that?"

Billy made his guilty face. "I started when I saw it."

Rose rolled her eyes. "You're so weird."

"You know Mom hates when you call *me* that," Billy mimicked his sister's words.

"And if you tell, so will *I*, and she'll never let you come out with us again."

"Keep it up, Rose," Alex warned, hoping to diffuse things, "and Heather won't let any of us out again."

"Not like it matters." Rose tossed a chip from the foundation into the woods. "It's just an old house. None of the stories about it ever happened. It was probably so boring whoever lived here just moved away and forgot about it."

"We happened here," Billy said.

Alex patted the boy's shoulder. "What if it's not this place, what if it's Heather?"

Rose squinted, "What do you mean?"

"She never lets us do anything. Never takes us to the store. You at least go places with your dad. I never go anywhere. What can we do without asking Heather's permission, like, fifty weeks in advance? Even if I met a boy, and he passed the Heather test, what would that be like? Heather, can I go on a date? Heather can I kiss him? I mean, if we decide to, *you know*, will your mom be right there wagging her finger at me?" She raised her voice and tried to imitate her aunt, "You didn't get permission for intercourse."

Rose and Billy laughed.

"It's just crazy," Alex sighed. "Sometimes she seems so cool, like she wants to be my friend, wants me to confide in her. I just don't get her."

"Amen," Rose added. "You think she's bad now, you should have seen her after Dad left. She's loosened up since you came along."

Alex fell quiet. She was not often made to feel like she wasn't a part of the family.

Rose seemed to sense she hurt Alex's feelings. "I, um, get what you're saying, though. I mean, what's she afraid of?"

"Sometimes, it's like Aunt Heather still thinks I'm a kid, then in the next breath, she'll talk an hour to me about being a single mother, or about how she fell in love with your dad. She's sharing. She'll talk about sex and using protection like she's preparing me in case there's a guy hidden in my bedroom, and the next moment, she shuts the conversation down like I'm a little girl who has no idea what sex is. Sometimes I just want to," she pursed her lips, unable to express what was on her mind, "just… *you know*."

Rose grunted her agreement. Her enthusiasm proved too much for Billy. "Enough," he said, jumping down from the wall and walking away, muttering to himself. "You think it's easy for me, boobs wherever I look?" He paced back towards them. "Mom treats me like a baby. She'll say I'm so young then I'm growing up too fast. Which is it? She talks to me like I don't know things. Believe me, I do. I know."

Rose edged closer to Alex. "It was fun sharing a room when we were kids, but now…" She shook her head. "It's tough enough finding privacy to get dressed in the morning, or change for bed, but when he thinks I'm asleep, he starts." She motioned with her hand. "You'd think he was paid by the mile."

"I hear you," Billy shouted back. "You do it too."

"Nope," Rose said, looking at Alex before giggling. "At least as often as he does. And I'm just not bouncing all around my bed."

"That's what I'm talking about," Alex sighed. "A little privacy; is that too much to ask?"

"Hey," Rose chided, "you get to sleep in the attic all by yourself. You can do whatever you want. You could sleep in the nude and no one would know."

"How do you know I don't?"

Rose grinned. "Because I never heard you ask Mom's permission."

Alex laughed; Billy cupped his hands over his ears.

"I bet if someone was crazy enough to climb to the roof," Rose went on, "you could sneak him in and out without Mom ever knowing." She looked back to make sure Billy wasn't listening. "First you'd have to meet someone, though."

"I kissed Mark White once," Alex confessed. "But it wasn't a real kiss."

"You kissed Mark White?"

Billy's fingers, still over his ears, parted slightly.

"It was like, last year, before he went to college. I wanted to know what it was like to kiss a boy, and sometimes I'd see him around. It was funny; when I asked, he wanted to prepare. He must have chewed half a pack of gum."

"What was it like?"

"I don't know, less of a kiss and more like warm, wet mint." Billy retched.

Rose's giggle broke the silence. "I can't believe you kissed Mark White."

"What of it?"

"He's completely unworthy. He's totally kissing above his level."

Alex shrugged. "He seems okay. Heather doesn't like his family, but he always waves at me when he passes. I didn't think anything of it, you know? It's not like there were a lot of options."

Rose made a face. "I guess. He was definitely kissing *up*, though."

Billy made another retching sound.

"What about you, Rose?" Alex winked. "You ever kiss a boy? Was he minty fresh?"

A grin broke Rose's stern expression. "I kiss boys all the time. I'm what you call a professional."

"Oh? Name one."

Rose snorted. "His name's Billy."

"No," Alex mouthed, unsure if her cousin was joking.

"We kiss all the time, don't we, Billy?"

Billy's eyes widened. He shook his head violently.

"Sure we do, Billy. Tell Alex."

"We do *not* kiss." Billy was adamant.

"When we go to sleep at night, I kiss you goodnight, don't I?"

"Here," Billy corrected her, pointing to his cheek. "No mint gum."

The girls laughed so hard they slid from the stone foundation before they ended up falling off.

Rose looked up. The sun was cresting the tops of the trees on the southeast side of the clearing. "Do we want to walk all the way to Picnic Rock?"

"Sacrifice Stone," Billy corrected, chanted his version of the name. "Sacrifice Stone, Sacrifice Stone! That's the place we have to go today!"

"Picnic Rock it is," Alex said, returning the first sandwich's cloth and the half-empty canteen into the rucksack. They said goodbye to the Old Witch's Shack and departed on the trail that would take them back into the woods.

Chapter Six

hey wound their way deeper through the towering hills, around protruding boulders the size of cars and houses. It was a long, steep walk, about an hour at a comfortable pace. They would have another hour at Picnic Rock, before starting back. Sun dappled the earth through the trees; leaves fluttered and waved in a breeze that carried fragrances of late spring wildflowers and the ionized air from a distant thunderstorm.

The final incline painted their bodies with perspiration. Cresting the mountain, they came to an overlook. The land rose like the spine of a gigantic creature then fell away into a steep slope littered with spilled stones and scree. A giant, flat stone sat cantilevered over on the edge, perfectly level in the center of the crest. Picnic Rock. Though almost precariously balanced on the cliff, it had never budged. Though not for want of trying.

They took a minute to catch their breath and stare in awe at the gigantic stone. It appeared suddenly as they emerged from the woods, blocking the sky; beyond it lay the valley with sweeping views of forever. A jumble of boulders and large rocks served as stairs to the flat top. The stone was the size of a small house, plenty large for a picnic. Tufts of grass pinched through a soft-edged crack running its length, as if all the time sitting on the mountain's spine was slowly cleaving the stone in two. Perhaps one day it was destined to become two separate formations, but for now, it didn't appear bifurcated.

Alex walked to the far edge with her cousins and looked out into the valley. Trees and grasses, distant shades of greens and browns, all bled together. Shadows of clouds skidded over the land, chased perhaps by the dark clouds lurking beyond the next distant ridge.

Bathing in the sunlight, breathing the electrified air, feeling closer to the sky here than anywhere else they knew, the threesome stood on the cusp of land and sky, their feet on one and heads in the other.

Billy feigned a jump and laughed at Rose's panic. They dangled their feet over the edge. The drop to the ground was ten or fifteen feet. The cliff was dangerously steep and littered with rubble. Names and dates tattooed the west-facing side of the rock, many in spots unreachable from top or bottom. More recent names were scrawled in paint or marker, covering the green and brown lichen. Others were scratched into the surface, but the oldest and largest were carved into the stone itself. It must have very important for *Jonathan William Frost, 1826* to leave his mark on the world when he hammered out the oldest and largest name in perfect, precise letters.

Alex sat to the left, with Rose between her and Billy. Rose picked at the lichen; Billy craned his neck, pointing out a V-shaped flock of birds. Rooting through the bag, Alex first handed a headband to Rose, whose windblown hair was sticking to her sweat-dampened face, then she distributed their thick sandwich halves and passed around the canteen. "It feels good to be here," she said, "away from everything."

Rose rolled her eyes. "You didn't need to come here. We *live* away from every-thing!"

"You know what I mean. Look." She pointed at the dozen tendrils of smoke rising from the valley. "Each one of those is someone getting away. We all came to the same place and we're still alone."

"It's sad when you say it that way," Billy remarked.

"Maybe we can convince Mom to let us camp here overnight," Rose suggested. "We could light a big fire right here. We could set up a tent right there." She pointed back to the edge of the woods.

"I don't think we're allowed to have a bonfire." Alex thought for a moment. "I don't know how I'd feel spending the night. Would we feel safe after dark?"

"It's only, like, an hour to walk home."

Alex checked the time. "We left the house two hours ago."

"And stopped at the Witch's Shack. If we walked straight here, it wouldn't take an hour, I bet."

"It might be fun," Billy agreed. "I bet you can see all the stars in the sky that ever were."

"It's no different from the sky at home," Rose said.

"But there you can only see all the stars that are," Billy defended, "not all that ever were. This rock has seen them all."

Rose offered an exaggerated, "Oh," and turned to Alex, giggling. "We should see if she'll let us. If she says no, who cares? The next time we want something we can remind her she didn't let us do this."

Alex could discuss most disagreements with her aunt, whereas Rose and Heather butted horns and shouted. Maybe that was why Rose relied on such manipulative strategies, and Alex didn't.

Alex pulled out a bottle of sunscreen. "Your cheeks are getting red." Rose smeared some on her face, before turning to Billy. "Give me your face," she said, smearing it on him. "Rub it in yourself."

Alex applied a little herself, watching Billy rub his face like he was trying to take off the skin. She sighed. "It's so beautiful here. It's like you can see forever."

"Almost," Billy remarked. "Some things I can't see from here, no matter how hard I try."

"I sometimes dream about this place," Rose said absently. "I'm in a dream, and there's a trail right over there," she pointed to where there was no path. "I follow it to a house. Outside it's small, but inside it's immense. Some rooms aren't finished but most are. There's furniture and curtains, and books, and everything. It feels like I'm home, even though I'm dreaming. Sometimes I expect to see you, Alex, but you're never there. Billy usually is. He never says anything to me. He just sort of stands watch. He's so serious. I think he's protecting me." She patted his shoulder. "You're a good dream-brother that way."

He smiled back. "I like the fireplace. The one in the kitchen. You can see through to the living room."

Rose looked back to Billy. "You dream about it too?"

"Only when you do."

By her expression, Rose was a little unnerved. "Alex, why don't you visit my house in your dreams?" she asked, making light of it, Alex thought, to hide her discomfort.

"I guess I've never been properly invited. Honestly, I feel a little left out."

"Do you ever have a dream like that? You know, where you're somewhere you've been, but it's different?"

The storm clouds started clearing the distant mountain. Alex heard the rumble of thunder, as quiet as her own heart. The wind picked up from the west as if brought to life by Alex's awareness. It wasn't more than a breeze, but it arrived laden with the smell of moisture and static electricity.

At last, Alex replied, "I have a dream where I go somewhere, but it's not pleasant."

"Where do you go?"

"I'd rather not talk about it."

Rose repositioned one leg up on the rock and turned more to Alex. "Alexandrea, tell me. Where do you go? I told you mine, and Billy messed it up." She turned to Billy and half-jokingly remarked, "You need to find some friends of your own when you dream." Billy shook his head.

Alex took a reflective moment. "I'm in my bedroom," she started. "I mean where I used to live with my mom and dad—when these men come."

"What men?"

"I don't know exactly, but if you want to hear about it, stop interrupting me."

Rose motioned that she would speak no more.

"My parents are just like I remember. Probably the same age they were when the accident..." She didn't complete the sentence. "Dad was, I don't know, strange. In the dream, I mean. He was always like a zombie; you remember?"

Rose nodded. Billy whimpered, "He made me sad."

"In the dream, it was like he knew something was happening. Then these men come, and a bunch of stuff happens. Then my dad has a gun, and is screaming at me."

"He wasn't a zombie?" Rose was confused.

"He was, but he wasn't. I think my mom exploded him to dust." Even now, she could see his form collapsing into cinders.

Rose opened her mouth to ask another question but distilling her confusion to a single line of thought proved too much.

"Then the wall turns to mist, and all this other crazy stuff happens."

"Crazier than your mom exploding your dad?"

Alex motioned to her chest. "These silver things start appearing on everyone. They look like glowing disks. There's this little cute kid, but then it's this horrible monster. It's like this giant skeleton." Staring off, Alex's eyes may have been seeing the landscape, but her mind was projecting the mist onto it. She could see the thick smoke, roiling like an uneasy sea.

Rose's voice cracked as she said, "Go on."

"The skeleton goes like this to my mom." Alex showed Rose, holding her hand out. "It sounds so ridiculous when I say it out loud, but it's the same, night after night. It seems so real. Anyway, my mom gives the monster her disk. It turns back into the kid. I'm scared, but she tells me to go, so I walk into the mist. Then I wake up."

"What? That's in-sane. Are your dreams all this messed up?"

"Lately, that's the only one I have."

"What?"

"Every night for the past week. Exactly the same."

"You don't give your silver coin to Charon." Billy's hands formed a circle in front of his chest.

Rose looked up. "Billy, what did you just say?"

"Charon. The child—the monster. It looks scary, but it's not unless you try to trick it. You can't cross over unless you pay with your coin."

"Coin? I don't have a coin," Alex answered warily.

"You don't?" Billy sounded surprised. "Because you're dreaming."

The girls stared at Billy.

"You give Charon your coin, just like in stories, to pass when you die. You throw a coin in the fountain for luck. Silver dollars are the luckiest, but most people throw pennies. They never get any luck, though. But you're not buying luck; you're tossing coins to confuse Charon. I think that's where the tradition comes from. Toss a fake coin so Charon goes looking for it and won't come for the real one. They're not the same kind of coin." He looked at them. "I keep you safe. I walk with you to your dream house. My coin is tarnished. Mom didn't keep it safe for me. She ruined it. She meant to but didn't mean to." He looked at Alex, "I protect you. I can't do everything I should to keep you safe, but I will when I have to."

Rose's eyes grew wider with each word. "Billy, what are you talking about?"

"My job. I keep you both safe."

"Who told you this?"

Billy started to cry. "Don't tell Mom. I have to keep you safe."

"Mom knows you're with me in my dream house?"

Billy cried out, shaking his head, his body wracked with choking, retching sobs. "She says not to, but I have to. I have to."

Alex crawled to her cousin to try and soothe him.

Rose wrapped an arm around them both. "I think we should start walking back. I don't feel good out here anymore."

Alex nodded. "As soon as Billy's able."

Rose pulled a few napkins from the bag. She wiped her brother's face and held them under his nose. "Blow."

It took Billy a few minutes to find his composure. Rose asked if he was ready to head back. "Another minute," was his answer. "Please don't tell Mom."

"Okay," she promised her brother. "This is our secret." She took Alex's hands; Alex could feel her trembling. Then she whispered too low for Billy to hear. "When we get home, I think we need to tell Mom about our dreams, yours and mine. Maybe even about what Billy said."

Alex shuddered. "You just told him you wouldn't. You can't betray his trust."

Rose nodded. "You're right. You'll help me figure this out?"

"What's he doing?"

The question seemed to surprise Rose, and if she said anything, Alex didn't hear. Stretching past the younger girl, tumbling over her, she reached for Billy, clutching at air as he leapt into open space.

Alex fell on top of Rose. The girls crawled frantically over each other, twining themselves into a tangle of arms and legs. Then they froze together, wincing in shock and horror at the sickening thud from the rocks below.

Chapter Seven

ose scurried to her feet, wiping dirt from her trembling hands. Staring over the edge of the great stone, her unbelieving eyes fixed on the crumpled and bloody body of her twin brother.

Alex's hands trembled. She felt like throwing up. "What happened? He jumped? Why would he do that?" She spoke aloud to herself. "What do I do? What do I do?" She repeated the question, trying to clear her head, assemble any kind of plan.

"Oh god, oh god, oh god, oh god..." Rose chanted beside her.

Rose stood with her feet at the very edge. *Is she thinking of jumping too?* Alex could almost hear the thoughts in her cousin's head. She could hear Heather's accusations demanding why they had not prevented the unpreventable. No amount of wishing would undo this, or heal Billy's broken body, or turn back time to before he jumped. *Was he so afraid we'd tell Heather that he tried to kill himself?*

"We have to get to him." Alex studied the terrain. Minutes ago, the way out past Picnic Rock seemed too dangerous, but now, nothing else mattered.

"What do we do?" Rose screamed, repeating her cousin's question. The words echoed back from the valley walls.

We were always sisters, Alex thought despite herself. Then, face stained with tears, she regarded Rose. *I'm the adult here.* "We have to get to him. He needs our help."

Rose gulped. "How?" She looked down then back at Alex. "Help? How? He's dead?"

Alex wasn't sure if Rose was asking or up talking. "He's breathing. We have to help him."

"How? What can we do? We're so far from home. What can we do? Look at him. Look at my brother." Rose turned away, tears flooding her face. "Billy, why'd you jump? Why'd you have to do that? I wasn't going to tell. I wasn't. Why'd you jump?"

"Come on, Rose," Alex said, trying to stay calm. Her hands trembled. She swallowed to keep from throwing up.

"But," Rose sniffled, "he's, he's—look at him. What can we do?"

Billy lay over a small, curved boulder. His head rested on patchy grass; his legs were splayed, and one arm was twisted beneath him. Wherever Alex looked, there was blood, his face, his hands, a patch on his thigh, all dark and red.

Alex took a deep breath. When she didn't throw up as she exhaled, she called to Rose, "Come with me." Rose froze at the edge. "Rose," Alex whispered, "Billy is hurt badly. Only we can help him. You understand? You and me, Rose. No one else is coming."

Rose stared, tears wetting her face, snot running from her nose. "What are we…"

Alex waited a beat, but Rose added nothing else. Alex didn't know how to do this alone. She grabbed Rose by the shoulders and steered her to the stepping stones. "Come on," she urged. "We're all he has."

They rounded to the far side and stepped over the rocky crest. The world dropped away before them. Behind, Picnic Rock towered. The drop was steep, but from here, Billy seemed closer. Alex started towards him.

Rocks clattered overhead as Rose skidded, nearly falling. "It's too steep," she complained.

Alex took the slope backwards, on all fours. "Come on, Rose," she called up. "Walk like this."

Rose clutched a sapling. "I can't."

"Turn around and walk like me." Alex looked ridiculous, her ass high in the air as she walked on her hands and feet, but didn't care.

Rose shouted to her, "I'm afraid."

"It's okay," Alex said. "You won't fall. I'm here. If you slip, you'll slip into me. We have to get to Billy."

Rose whimpered. "I'm scared, Alex. What's he gonna be like?" She gulped air. "What if he's all gross? It's our fault. We brought him here. Every time I see him all messed up," she sobbed, "I'll know it's because of what we did."

Alex had held similar thoughts. If Billy died, how would she ever face Heather? What if he was disfigured? Her aunt would curse her and kick her out of the house. And Alex wouldn't blame her. "Rose," she tried to maintain her composure as hysteria crept closer and closer, "if we don't help him, none of it will matter. He'll die."

Rose wiped her face, her gaze volleying between Alex and her brother. She nodded, less in agreement than to convince herself.

They scrambled from boulder to boulder, grabbing saplings and tufts of grass, vines—whatever would not rip from the ground— gradually working their way to Billy.

Alex's concentration was intense. Five minutes may well have been an hour. Billy was just out of reach when Rose lost her grip. She screamed and toppled into Alex. Half the tuft in Alex's grip tore loose, and with Rose practically climbing her, they collapsed to the ground. They slid a few feet, pebbles and rocks grinding against their skin.

"It's hopeless," Rose sobbed, head down in the dust.

Billy was within reach. He faced them, eyes open. He tried to smile.

"He's right here, Rose," Alex whispered. She helped her cousin up. The ground around Billy was stable, a small horizontal island jutting up from the slope.

"I slipped," Rose quivered. "I thought I was gonna die." She looked at the oozing scrapes on their arms and hands. "I'm sorry, Alex."

"We're okay. We can do this." Her words seemed to calm Rose. She wished they could do the same for her.

Alex knelt beside Billy and stroked his forehead. Blood matted his hair. "Hey Billy," she cooed, "that was really dumb." He grabbed her and pulled her close. She put her hands gently against his sides. "Give me some napkins," she said, handing Rose the rucksack. "Wet them with the canteen." She forgot to say please. "Please," she added. She cringed; the word sounded like she was asking the impossible.

Alex gingerly wiped away Billy's blood, surveying him for injuries as she went. A gash lay above his right eye, and scrapes covered his body; here and there, she found patches of raw, abraded skin that looked like grated cheese.

With a suppressed whimper, Rose joined her cousin. Widening a tear in the left thigh of Billy's jeans, she revealed the pristine white tip of bone breaching his skin. They both stared at it. It looked fake.

Rose collapsed onto her brother. Billy grunted, but he did his best to hug her back. Kneeling beside them, Alex added to the embrace.

"Okay," Alex said at last, "let's stop the bleeding."

They looked at his leg. The gash was coagulating and gross, but there was no bone sticking out. It must have been a trick of the sun.

Billy groaned, "Why does everything hurt so bad?" His eyes rolled back before popping open as though he was slipping in and out of consciousness.

"I'm trying to think," Alex said. "I know what we're supposed to do, but not exactly." She stood, long auburn hair sticking to her damp face, sweat staining the armpits of her t-shirt. She counted on her fingers, "He's breathing. He's not bleeding too bad." She pointed to his forehead and his thigh, the two worst visible injuries. "He's got this and that, but I don't know what else."

"Billy," Rose called.

He whimpered. "Don't shout. I'm here."

Rose lowered her voice. She wiped her forehead, smearing dirt on her face. "Can you wiggle your fingers and toes?"

His fingers didn't move. Alex started to despair. It felt like a dream, but she knew it was very real.

"Why do I have to?"

Alex growled; he hadn't even tried.

"Because," Alex and Rose said together; Alex let Rose finish, "we need to see if you can."

"You guys." His fingers wriggled, and his feet, encased in boots, made small circles. He groaned again. "See?" he told them.

They weren't going anywhere, not yet. Alex lowered her voice to keep Billy from hearing. "We're, like, two hours from home. You're not supposed to move an injured person, but…" she trailed off, pointing to him.

Rose asked, "When we don't come home, Mom'll find us, right?"

Alex shook her head. "In two or three hours, if we're lucky, she'll start worrying. When we still don't come home, maybe then she'll come looking."

"That's too long," Billy moaned. "I have to pee. I'm fine. I can walk back."

Neither paid him any mind.

"Rose, by the time Heather gets here, it'll be after midnight. It's gonna get cold. We'll be here till morning."

"I have to go sooner," Billy insisted.

Rose was getting upset. Tears welled in her eyes. "You could run back and tell Mom. You could run the whole way. You'd be there in no time."

Billy started moving, "Guys, I'm fine." Putting weight on his leg, he screamed and dropped back. "It's okay, I'm good," he whimpered.

Alex held her response to Rose. Her cousin was sixteen. Crouched there, sweaty, filthy, a very pretty girl stained with dirt and tears, she looked so young. Alex understood why Heather was so protective; Rose was a child. *I'm always asking to be treated like an adult,* she thought, *and here I am, life and death in my hands, and I just want someone to tell me what to do.* But that wasn't what adults did. "More responsibility and less stamina," she muttered aloud. Then to Rose, "We can't rely on Heather."

"Guys," Billy was still trying to convince them he was okay.

I hope I'm doing the right thing. I hope I don't hurt him worse. "We have to get him to the top and we—"

Rose interrupted, "To the top? Are you out of your mind? We almost died getting here!"

"Stop shouting," Billy mumbled. "You're hurting my head." Alex half expected him to be grinning. He wasn't.

The girls leaned in and held him. Alex wanted to say they loved him, tell him he'd be okay, but the weight of responsibility made it difficult to breathe. Billy's life was in her hands. She felt utterly helpless, yet *she* was the one they were looking to. Billy looked fragile and broken; she needed him to understand that her resolve to help him was absolute. "You're going to be okay," she whispered. She sat back and their eyes met. "You will be okay, Billy. Do you understand? Rose and I will make sure. You have to trust us. We need your help, and it's going to hurt. Do you understand?"

Billy nodded. "I think the hug helped," he said.

Rose put her hands up. "Seriously? Boobs make you feel better? You're a freak."

He nodded. "Don't tell Mom what I did, okay?"

Rose looked at Alex. "I don't know how we're gonna pull that off, Billy. She'll wonder why you're all broken."

"I had to do it," he said, "so I could do it. It wasn't right now. I protect you and keep you safe."

Alex whispered to Rose, "Maybe he hit his head. He's not making sense."

"See," Billy said, "she understands."

Alex examined him, trying to remember everything from the Health and First Aid class. "He's not really bleeding anymore." She pointed to the gash on his forehead and the congealed blood around the flap of skin. "That could be good... or shock. His color is fine, so maybe not. I don't know."

"Could he be bleeding, um, inside?"

Alex nodded then shrugged. "Nothing we can do if he is." She pointed to his leg. "We have to make sure that doesn't get worse."

Billy groaned. He pointed up to Picnic Rock. "I'm okay, I think."

"This is okay by you?" Rose asked.

He tried to sit up. "The hug helped. Maybe another?"

Rose shouted at him, "You're so gross. I'm your sister." Still, she knelt at his side and wrapped her arms around him. "Oh, Billy," she whispered. "Why'd you do this? Alex says you're gonna be okay. She has a plan. She'll get us out of this mess. You hear me?"

While Rose spoke to Billy, Alex surveyed. They were nearly twenty feet from the crest. It was steep, but not impossible. *Was there an easier way up? How do we get him to the top?* She tried to take stock of their options. He might think he was capable, but his injuries said otherwise. *Maybe he's in so much pain he's not feeling it anymore.*

She had an idea. "Stay here," she told the twins.

"Where are you going?" Rose sounded alarmed.

Billy pointed up. "She has a plan," he repeated his sister's words.

Alex scrambled up the cliff-face and disappeared over the edge. It was easier going up. After a few minutes, Rose called out in concern. "Are you okay, Alex? Don't you dare leave us!"

"I'm almost ready," she shouted back.

As she came down the edge, Alex heard thunder from the forgotten storm that now obscured the far side of the valley. But her main concern was daylight, their one finite resource. They still had hours, but she figured this day wouldn't end until well after dark.

Alex returned with several thick, long branches and placed them beside Billy. Tearing apart the rucksack, she used the fabric and strings to tie three together, enough to cradle in and drag him up the slope.

"That's not going to work," Rose protested.

"It will," Alex said as she removed her shirt. "take off your shirt. We need to splint his leg in case it's broken."

"I'm fine," Billy argued, sucking air through his teeth as Alex tied her shirt around a branch and his leg.

They drank the last of the water and abandoned the canteen and the sunscreen. It pained Alex to drop their belongings, and to litter, but they couldn't carry everything back. They ate the crushed sandwich and filled their pockets with candies, leaving everything else behind.

"We need to work together," she told Rose. "We can do this; inches at a time."

Rose nodded. "Tell me what to do."

"Billy, this won't be easy for any of us." Alex fitted the frame under and around him and showed him what to hold to support himself. "But we can do this."

"I know." His eyes opened only while he spoke.

We will do this.

Alex grabbed the top of the frame and took a few cautious steps up the cliff. "Push," she told Rose.

Rose complied strenuously.

"Not so much," Alex tried not to shout as she almost fell backwards. "Inches."

They took turns pushing and pulling, scrambling up a foot or two at a time. Twice they had to stop when a rucksack string snapped and needed repairing, but Alex's design held. Billy grunted and gritted his teeth each time they lurched him up. He'd pant when he was still and kept telling them, "It's okay; I'm okay."

Alex reached the top first. "Almost there, Rose," she said. Rose remained focused; her face soaked with sweat. Alex expected her to push too hard, to try to reach the top in one effort, but she moved the frame an inch or two until, finally, they were both on the same side of the rise.

Rose cried. They leaned Billy and the frame against Picnic Rock, and Alex embraced her. The sudden relief that they were at the top overwhelmed Alex too, and she sobbed into her cousin's embrace.

Standing there, holding Rose, their bodies trembling and sweaty, Alex felt her strength returning, as though Rose was feeding it into her. Reaching the top may have been the hardest part, but they still had far to go.

Chapter Eight

eady?" Alex asked.

Rose wiped her face, smearing dirt everywhere.

"You're making it worse," Alex told her.

Rose grunted. "Worse? Look in a mirror."

Alex examined her hands. Thick grime hid her scraped palms. Black filth outlined her fingernails. She had touched her face countless times, pushing hair out of her eyes and wiping sweat away. She imagined what she looked like and laughed.

"I'm ready," Rose said after a minute.

"You're both so dirty," Billy said. "When did you take off your shirts?"

Alex patted his head. "You missed the show, buddy."

Billy grumbled, "It's okay. It wasn't really a show."

Alex resumed her place at the head of Billy's frame and began dragging.

Rose watched for a moment. Without the angle of the cliff, reaching the base of the frame proved awkward. "How do I push?"

Alex paused. "We'll take turns, okay?"

Rose didn't respond.

"You coming?"

Rose snapped out of her daze. "It's too far. We'll never make it."

Alex hesitated. "Do you hear yourself? We already did the impossible bit. This," she motioned with her hand, "is the easy part."

Rose followed as Alex pulled the frame, two or three steps at a time.

Around them, the path, the trees, the undergrowth that they marveled at on the way here grew ominous. Leaves blocked the light. Branches hooked the frame. Pebbles and roots snagged the legs. It was as though nature wanted them to fail.

Alex looked around. "This doesn't even look familiar."

"Maybe one of us should walk ahead?" Rose suggested. "Maybe walking normal will make it feel right."

"That's a good idea."

Rose took the frame. "We should switch before you're too tired."

Alex walked ahead. Rose was right, she realized, finding familiarity with her regular pace. Behind her, Rose panted and grunted each time she took two steps and pulled the frame. Each time, Billy moaned.

More than halfway to the Witch's Shack, day transitioned to night like a pull-chain light going out. They hadn't noticed the setting sun until the cold night air crept across their sweaty, half-naked bodies. The girls stood, shivering.

"This sucks." Rose's voice quivered from the cold.

"Heather's gotta realize by now," Alex breathed. "Hopefully, she starts looking soon. I don't know how much either of us has left." Someone coughed a short distance off the path, startling her. She stared into the deceitful dusky light; it could be anything or nothing.

"Who's there?"

A rustle of leaves answered her question.

"I think we should go," Rose whispered, adjusting her bra straps. "My skin's grinding off. There's sand everywhere," she pulled the waist of her jeans to show her red, abraded skin.

Alex understood how Rose felt, but kept listening. "The Witch's Shack can't be much further. Let's get there, then figure what comes next." Alex worried they would have to stop there for the night.

"This isn't a good place," Billy mumbled. "The woods try to be scary." He stared at nothing. Alex pulled his stretcher with renewed enthusiasm, hurrying forward as if something was chasing her. A rustle. The clearing of a throat. Breathing. Snapping twigs. Noises off the path could be branches in the wind, animals, a psycho-killer. As long as it remained noise. Alex focused forward. She told herself she was imagining things.

Every few minutes, the girls switched. They worked hard. The night air chilled their skin, yet their faces dripped perspiration. Their eyes burned and hands blistered.

Alex handed off to Rose. Almost immediately, Rose stopped and whimpered, "My arms are falling off." She took the frame back, despite her own screaming muscles. "We've got this, Rose," Alex said, possibly lying. "We're close."

"That's what you said before." Alex couldn't make Rose's face out in the dappled moonlight but knew she was crying.

Alex ignored the sounds she still heard around them. Her body wanted to drop the frame and run, but she would never abandon her cousins. Rose either hadn't noticed, or she was relying on Alex even to decide when something felt threatening. Alex's heart drummed from more than just exertion.

Not wanting to stand still, Alex pulled the frame. "I know, Rose." She pulled. "It's impossible." Pull. "It's so far." Pull. "Billy's hurt." Pull. "We're so tired." Pull. "What do you want to do?" Pull. "To stop?" Pull. "Is that what you want?" Pull. "To give up?" Alex had once read that some predators will wait until their prey is exhausted. Even if it was her imagination, she couldn't stop, couldn't let the wind think it had her good and tired.

Eventually, Rose sobbed, "I just can't. Not anymore. I'm going to collapse."

Billy comforted, "I'm sorry, Rose. I tried to walk."

"We can't stop."

"I know, Alex. I don't want to. I'm just," Rose took a breath, "I'm done, but I'll keep trying. As long as you keep trying, I'll keep trying."

All three snapped towards nearby rustling.

"It's a deer," Alex reasoned as she pulled. "We're scaring animals trying to sleep."

Another, closer. Breathing. A moving glint passing through moon-lit shadows.

Billy pointed, "He's there. I saw him."

Rose panicked, "Someone's following us, Alex. Do something."

Drawing breath was difficult. Alex worried that agreeing would make it true. "Ignore it. Keep going." They were slowing, tiring. It wouldn't be long before she couldn't move anymore. Before they became exhausted prey.

Rose walked beside Alex. "Maybe someone's only trying to scare us?"

Alex wanted to believe that. "Why? They see Billy's hurt. Why wouldn't they help?"

"We're half-naked in the woods." Rose's tone was intended more as narration than dialogue. "Two girls, alone, exhausted. It sounds like a horror movie."

She had a point.

Snapping twig. Crunching footsteps sent a chill of panic down Alex's spine. Coming closer.

"We were safe on the cliff," Rose snapped. "You should have run to get Mom."

"It's okay if I'm alone in the woods?" Alex heard the accusation in her tone but couldn't stop. "It's okay if Alex gets raped and murdered as long as Rose is safe? You're tired and scared. I am too."

Rose glared with the ferocity of a rabid animal. When Alex stood upright, half-leaning on the frame, Rose rushed her, screaming, "I hate you, Alex."

Alex could have restrained her if she had her arms free. She shouted, "You'll hurt your brother, Rose. I'm going to drop him. It'll be your fault."

Billy cried, "Please don't drop me."

Rose fell still, heaving sobs.

"I'm sorry, Rose. I didn't mean to shout. I'm scared. I—"

"Me too," Rose interrupted. She held Alex, fighting to stop her tears. "I don't hate you."

Alex's nose ran from her own tears and the cold. She tried to sniffle but snorted in Rose's hair. Rose cackled. "You're disgusting."

This was more than a rustle. Like someone charging right at them.

Despite the terror written across her face, Rose snatched the frame from Alex's hands and pulled with the ferocity of a wolf caught in a trap.

Billy grunted at being lurched.

Then the charge stopped. Alex could see nothing. "Who's there?" she called. Whoever it was, they were hidden from her eyes.

"Shhh," Rose hissed.

They continued, pressed on by fear, hands blistered and raw, shivering in the cold. *What are they waiting for? We're too tired to put up a fight.* The sounds, the rustling, the footsteps, followed them. Chased by their imaginations and perhaps something more sinister, they found the strength to push forward. Nothing had harmed them yet, but there was no telling what might happen if they stopped.

"We're close," Alex said, taking the frame.

Rose shouted towards the sounds, "I see you. You're not scaring us, asshole."

He—Alex assumed it was a *he* because what woman would be so cruel—didn't seem to care. He followed them, sometimes a dozen feet from the path, sometimes so close they thought they could make out his shape, thin with a severe hunch. In the deceptively dappled shadows, he looked nearly decapitated, as though his head rested against his shoulders rather than sat above them. He seemed to be carrying something as his hands didn't appear to swing. A flat box or a book. His eyes flashed moonlight as he met their gaze. He followed them, walking parallel to the path through thickets and underbrush.

"That's poison ivy, you're walking through," Alex called. "You'll be miserable for weeks. Why not just come help us?"

Rose hissed, "What the fuck are you doing?"

"We could use another set of hands." Alex continued, "Please. If you're trying to scare us, congratulations. Job well done." She was tired of being frightened. "Either help us or go away."

The man remained still, unmoving. Alex began to doubt her eyes. Was that even a person? She stared until she saw a tree trunk vaguely resembling a man by a trick of vines and moonlight.

"Where'd he go?" Rose scanned the forest. She'd lost him too.

Alex pulled harder. She couldn't tell if her palms were sweating or her blisters weeping. Adrenalin drove her heart into a fever beat, causing her hands to tremble but giving her strength.

Just as she convinced herself that shadows and wind had conspired with her imagination to scare the crap out of her, the man caught up again.

Rose started speaking, but Alex interrupted. "Look!"

Silhouettes of branches and leaves opened ahead to the glistening sky. The moon shied behind a bough, its waxing orb near full. Even in darkness, this place was familiar. Although the stone foundation did nothing to assuage their fears, Alex felt a wash of relief at the sight. They were nearly there. They dragged the frame now, without pausing. They wanted to touch the foundation. To call out, "base," as if somehow that would protect them.

They gave the last of the strength for that final pull. It was just a rotting foundation, and she was sick with thoughts of what might happen when they reached it, but she wanted to believe their stalker, who had ignored many opportunities to harm them, would just continue on. What if the stone foundation was his destination too, though? Alex dreaded meeting him in that tumbled ruin.

Sometimes he wasn't there. Sometimes he was. Sometimes it seemed the moonlight made patterns of leaves and branches that looked like a person. Sometimes exhaustion made them see things too.

They entered the clearing like they were crossing the boundary into a protected realm—like a graveyard or hallowed ground. Fifty feet, forty, thirty to go. A voice muttered something; Alex's head and ears ached too much to discern. The moon shone a spotlight onto the foundation. Their pace quickened. Their arms and backs ached at the strain. Tears streamed down their sweaty, filthy faces. Their bodies trembled, begging them to stop, but they denied these exhausted demands.

Just feet away.

The rustling circled the clearing. Was the bent man going around them? Going away? Or trying to cut them off? They reached the stone foundation, and it became clear he wasn't alone. Two additional sets of footfalls rushed towards them. Bouncing beams from flashlights appeared, blinding the girls. This was it. They recoiled, preparing to be attacked. Rose clutched Alex. "Oh no," she whimpered before she screamed in terror.

"You better have a good reason for being out here."

Rose collapsed at the sound, sobbing in relief. "Mommy," she screamed. "Help us!"

The flashlights lowered from their eyes.

Heather called back to them. "I'm coming, babies."

Heather rounded the foundation, her flashlight dancing; the rustling to the side became frenzied. Heather shone her flashlight in that direction. The other flashlight, further back, did the same. The rustling ceased. All they had illuminated was a swirl of blowing leaves.

"Someone's there, Mommy, he's been following us for hours!" Rose cried as she shouted, her body shivering. Alex was shivering too, but she didn't think the cold alone was responsible.

"Abby," Heather shouted, pointing to the woods with her flashlight, "check that out."

Alex's heart lightened. "Aunt Abby's here?"

Heather nodded. As she joined them, panting, she asked, "You're filthy; where are your clothes?"

Her flashlight scrutinized the girls. It found Billy, his arms twisted in the frame, blood smeared and dried on his face. She dropped to his side.

Alex held the frame and wrapped an arm around Rose, the chill unbearable.

Billy smiled and weakly waved, "Hi Mom. Good to see you."

"What the hell happened to you three?"

Abby stomped through the woods, her flashlight bobbing.

There was so much to explain. Alex didn't know how to start; her words cut off as Rose answered. "We walked out to the Picnic Rock, we sat and talked."

Heather interrupted her daughter as she examined her son. "Don't tell me a story. What happened?"

In Rose's preparatory breath, Billy winced. "I fell off the rock. It's not their fault."

Heather's eyes studied him. "Why would you say that?"

Billy made a face. "If I didn't, you'd ask why they weren't watching me."

Heather couldn't argue. "What were you thinking?" Heather pleaded, examining the cut over his right eye.

"He's gone. They okay, Heather?" Alex closed her eyes. Abby's voice was not motherly or particularly feminine, yet hearing it always made her feel better. She couldn't explain why, it just did. Maybe it reminded her of home, of being a child.

"*Him?*" Alex asked. "Who is he?"

"N-Nobody," Heather stuttered. "Whoever was following you." Then she shouted. "I need your help, Abby!"

Abby ran towards them. She was a densely built, stocky woman wearing jeans and a sleeveless muscle shirt, the only thing Alex had ever seen her in. She must have had a closetful of sleeveless shirts. She looked heavy, but her body moved solidly.

Abby inspected Alex, her face pained, tears glistening in her eyes. She hesitated to touch her. "Are you hurt? Are you okay? Turn around, let me check your back." Alex felt overwhelmed.

"I'm okay, Aunt Abby, now that you're both here." She turned to Rose and Heather. "I was so scared. Billy's hurt." Alex couldn't explain it, the fear, the terror finally melting away. As it dissipated, she realized how frightened she had been. The tears came. "I'm sorry, I don't know...." Alex saw Abby focusing on her when it was Billy that needed help. "I'll be okay," she said, wiping her face.

Abby trained her flashlight on Billy. When she saw his leg, she muttered, "We've got to get him to the hospital, right?" She ran her fingers through her short, dark hair. She looked to Heather for guidance. Then at Alex, "Only him, right?"

"The girls are exhausted, Abby." Heather studied them both. Something in her cadence suggested she was choosing her words with purpose. "They dragged him all the way from Picnic Rock."

"Picnic Rock? Why, that's," Abby shined her flashlight into the darkened woods, "at least a couple miles."

"It was far," Rose said. "We've been dragging him all day."

"Enough talking," Heather said. "Abby, can you carry him to the truck?"

Abby grabbed the frame. It seemed effortless for her. When Billy groaned, she leaned it against the stones and patted the boy's head. "Stay here," she said to the group. "I'll get the truck."

Heather looked around, "You're not supposed to drive near the building."

"Fuck them," Abby spat, her dark eyes flashing. "Billy's hurt, and that contraption is falling to shit. Let them slap my wrist for taking my truck too close to the building."

Rather than arguing, Heather knelt and stroked Billy's face. "My baby." She winced when he grimaced, her touch getting too close to a bulbous swelling on his forehead. She kissed his cheek and stood to face the girls, wrapping them both into a half-hug. "You guys are freezing. Abby will be here in a sec."

Rose and Alex shivered against one another. The door to Abby's truck squawked open before the loud engine choked and sputtered to life. Headlights, light-bars, fog-lights; there seemed to be all manner of lights mounted to the truck, and Abby turned them all on. The truck lumbered out of the brush with Abby navigating the thick tires around the larger stones until she pulled up beside them. Jumping out, she hefted Billy up by his shoulders—the frame collapsing around him—and slid him into the back seat. She moved like he weighed nothing. He groaned at being moved but never cried out. Heather came around to help pull him in. She made room for Rose and pointed Alex to the front seat. Alex clambered up, tightened the seatbelt around her and cranked up the heat. The blowing hot air felt magical against her cold, bare skin.

Abby climbed in. "Everyone belted in or holding on?"

"Just get us there," Heather replied wearily.

Abby looked at Alex. "You good?"

Alex nodded. Out of the woods, in a warm truck, the hot air blowing against her. She was good. For a moment she thought she saw the man again, just outside the lights. *Is he smiling?* He disappeared. *Was he even there?*

"I'm good, Aunt Abby."

Abby stared at her, long enough she had to say something. "Pretty bra."

Alex looked down at herself. She was filthy, her bra soiled and sweat-stained. She looked at Abby, who shrugged and put the truck into gear and turned around.

Until they cleared the woods, the ride was excruciating. Each bounce and bump knocked an expletive out of one of them, except for Billy, who slept undisturbed.

Twin ruts in the headlights guided their way. In far less time than it would have taken to drive back to the dead end, they pulled onto a paved road. "I didn't know there was another way. How'd you know?"

Abby shrugged. "It's a thing."

Abby didn't say another word. The wheels squealed as she turned down their street and flew past their house. The hospital was over an hour away. Alex had never been there before. *It figures; I'm finally going someplace, and it's somewhere I never wanted to go.*

Abby was definitely speeding, almost daring the police to pull her over. Alex had seen police escorts on television shows and wondered if they got one, would they get there any faster?

Chapter Nine

eather made three calls from her cell. Each time she reported back to Abby. "No answer. Where is she?"

Now that Alex was warm and safe, the full gravity of what had happened was hitting her. She felt sick. Her head throbbed and ears rang. It came and went. It had been happening since the woods, she realized; her body had masked the pain while she needed to be brave and strong. She didn't tell anyone; this was Billy's emergency. These headaches always passed on their own.

Heather and Rose held Billy in the backseat, trying to soothe him. He was awake more than asleep, his pain coming in waves. When it was at its worst, Heather would chant a litany of soothing words to calm him, stroking his face until he quieted.

At last, Abby pulled her truck into the hospital parking lot. She drove towards the "Ambulance Only" bay. Tires screeching, the truck skidded to an abrupt stop between two ambulances.

"Hey," Abby shouted as she leapt out, "I need help!"

A woman and man standing beside one ambulance walked over. Before either could ask, Abby answered. "I've got a teenage boy who's banged up. It's been hours."

The man looked at his counterpart. They both wore windbreakers with the words, "Ashburn Volunteer Ambulance" over a caduceus with a six-pointed EMS star. "You got this?" he asked his partner. The woman climbed into the backseat. She questioned Billy about his injuries, her tone measured and soothing. The man ran into the hospital.

Alex went to stand beside Abby. She felt the overwhelming need to be next to someone she trusted. That sensation of wanting to touch "base" again.

"He'll be okay?"

Alex didn't know what the expression on Abby's face meant. "Let's let them do their thing," was her reply.

The man returned, clutching a battered yellow backboard, with two others in tow. One wore lavender nurse's scrubs, the other was in a blue uniform with, "EMS First Responder" printed on his breast pocket and across his back.

It took longer than seemed necessary. At one point the woman said, "Nice job on the splint, ladies." The trio slid Billy from the backseat onto the backboard, placing him on a yellow and black mechanical stretcher, which a fourth person had wheeled out. Though they had only yards to go, they secured him to the stretcher before bringing him inside.

Heather and Rose walked beside the stretcher down the long hallway with Abby and Alex trailing close. The next nurse they saw raised a commanding voice into a room whose occupants Alex couldn't see, "One trauma and two exposures, possibly an assault. Get a kit."

A team of three nurses, two women and a man, each in different colored scrubs, hurried from the room. A woman in yellow scrubs appeared with blankets to wrap around Alex and Rose. She smiled at Alex as though they were acquainted, though Alex had no recollection of her. Her face was narrow; she wore no makeup, and her dark hair was pulled back into a bun. Her large, brown eyes sat close together, and her face was marked with what looked like empty piercings: eyebrow, nose, lip.

The nurse mouthed something to Heather. *They know each other?*

Before Heather could reply, the commanding nurse pointed in her direction. "Are you Mom?"

Alex had read that hospitals smelled of antiseptic, but the smell was not what she thought of as clean. She tightened the stiff, white blanket around her arms.

Heather explained what happened as best she could. Unsupervised hike. Billy fell off a large rock. The girls used their shirts to make a stretcher and splints. Carried him for miles. When they were late, she went looking for them. Here they are.

The commanding nurse turned to the others. "Take the boy to Room Five. The girls can share seven."

"The girls don't need examinations," Heather contended.

Yellow Scrubs put her hands on her hips. "Heather says they're fine. I'll give them a once-over to make sure. She's a friend, and I trust her."

The commanding nurse nodded. "Be certain; it's your call. And I want a signed RMA for each of them."

A male nurse in green scrubs with tennis rackets spoke gently to Billy as he wheeled him down the hall. "Hey buddy, can you tell me your name?"

"Yes," Billy replied.

"What is it? What's your name?"

"Billy. Billy Hawthorne." The nurse wrote it down.

"Do you know where you are, Billy?"

"Yes."

"Where's that?"

"Hospital," was Billy's reply. "I've been here lots of times."

Alex assumed it was his head injury talking; she couldn't think of a single time he'd been here.

"Can you tell me what happened?"

"Yes."

They turned and disappeared through a set of doors.

Yellow Scrubs left Commanding Nurse to speak to Heather. She beckoned Alex and Rose and then looked each of them over. "You two okay? No cuts, scratches, infections?"

The girls both nodded.

"Nothing else happened, right? No one else was there? Just the three of you?"

Alex and Rose looked at one another. "Just us," Alex answered.

The nurse looked at Alex, "So no one *did this* to you?"

Alex understood; her previous statement wasn't a lie. "No." Certainly, two young women without shirts would arouse suspicion, but there was a valid reason for their appearance. "We needed to make splints," she explained. "It was our shirts or," she hesitated, hoping the joke would land, "our pants." Yellow Scrubs chuckled. Alex added, "Is Billy going to be okay?"

Yellow Scrubs patted Alex's arm. "I can't say, but between the two of us, my money is on him getting home after the weekend." She looked at her tablet. "Since we're not treating you, we say you *Refuse Medical Attention*," she pointed at the title of the digital form. "Clean yourselves up while I fill these out." She opened a heated glass-fronted cabinet, pulled two more white blankets, and handed one to each girl. They were coarse and itchy like the others but very warm. Alex wrapped the second blanket around her shoulders while Rose held hers, a warm bundle against her chest.

Rose looked like she was fine so Alex tucked into the bathroom. She was aghast when she saw her reflection. "Why didn't someone tell me how I looked?" Her reflection didn't answer.

Why isn't Rose this filthy? Alex was a disgusting, grimy mess. Blood and dirt smeared her face, except where tears had deposited rings of caked grime around her eyes. Between her state of undress and the filth, she understood why the nurse suspected she had been assaulted. Alex made a mess of the bathroom, splashing water onto her arms and torso. The dirt caked before letting go, and she had to wipe and dry herself with dozens of not-particularly absorbent paper towels, which were spilling from the trashcan before she was done. Clean enough, Alex wrapped herself with the blanket and tried to tie it about her shoulders to make it look less… blankety. Nothing worked.

Stepping out, she hissed at Rose, "Rosemary, why aren't you filthy?"

Rose answered sheepishly, "There was a container of wipes in the backseat."

Alex recalled Rose emerging from the truck mostly clean. It hadn't registered until now. "So you don't share? I looked like you dug me out of a grave."

"I tried," came Rose's reply. "I tried to pass them forward, but you were holding your head and didn't answer. I should have tried again."

Yellow Scrubs placed her tablet in its charging cradle and led Alex and Rose to a waiting room. The room wasn't full. People clustered in evenly distributed, solitary groups, clans separated by tables and empty chairs.

They approached Heather who was looking at her phone. "Billy's doing okay," Yellow Scrubs informed her, giving her a polite hug. "He's sedated. They'll check out his head and leg and look for anything else. I shouldn't say, but," she flashed an awkward smile, "you know. He looks worse than he is. Family's allowed in the ER so you can see him."

Abby, who had just returned from parking her truck, touched Heather's shoulder. "I'll wait here."

"Thanks," Heather said. She turned to Yellow Scrubs, "Nancy, could you find out if Marta is working?"

Yellow Scrubs—Nancy—said, "She's already with Billy."

As they followed Nancy from the waiting room, Alex looked back. "Aren't you family, *Aunt* Abby?"

"You know I'm not really your Aunt," Abby replied as though revealing a shocking secret. "I'm not related. But you are. Go."

Nancy left them in an empty room. It was a quiet five minutes before they wheeled Billy back in.

Billy lay in bed, a white sheet up to his throat with only his head and left arm visible. His head was bandaged. A square of clear tape covered the IV needle in the crook of his left arm, and a thin tube running from his nostrils to up behind his ears hissed quietly. His breathing was shallow. His eyes peeked open. Heather let out a sigh. She caressed her son's cheek and whispered, "The last time I saw you in a hospital, you were visiting me." She looked around as though no one was supposed to hear that. "Poor Billy," she whispered. "I wish I could make you all better." She sobbed. "Is this what you meant? Is it beginning?"

Alex tried to stand out of the way, but there wasn't room. The fact that doctors and nurses weren't racing about worried her. They always did on television.

Rose and Heather took opposing sides of the bed, holding Billy's hands.

"Alex," Heather whispered, "come here." She traded places with her niece. "Hold his hand. Stroke his arm. He knows we're here, and it'll make him better."

Alex did as instructed. She ached seeing Billy like this.

A while later, the doctor came in with an air of authority, her shoes clicking as she walked. She was tiny, a compact woman, her frame hidden beneath her stiff white coat. It was impossible not to recognize she was in control. Alex felt her power and tried to see what about her made everyone else give her the room. She walked up to Heather. Her dark brown hair was tied up in a tight bun on top of her round face.

"Miss Hawthorne," she said, her tone even and deep, her accent crisp, "I'm Doctor Patel. We took your son for a CT scan to help determine the best course of action. It'll be read within the hour.

I don't want to make promises, but it's my opinion that he'll come out of this just fine. So far, everything looks right. You're welcome to stay, but I'd feel better if you went home for some sleep. I'll keep you updated, but right now he needs you to be strong." She motioned to the two bags of intravenous fluids hanging from a pole on the bed. "We're keeping him comfortable."

Heather looked up. "I'll be here when he wakes up. I have a friend who can take the girls home."

Doctor Patel nodded.

Heather looked to the girls. "Let's go find Abby."

Doctor Patel called after her, "Miss Hawthorne? Marta is waiting to see you."

As they walked out of Room Five, a darker-skinned woman met them, immediately embracing Heather. "I'm so sorry," she breathed. "He'll be fine, but it's got to be so hard on you right now."

As they let go of one another, Heather wiped her eyes. "Marta, you've met my daughter, Rosemary."

"I haven't seen you in forever. You've grown up." Marta leveled her hand to Rose's bust to show Rose's height when they last met. Then she embraced the girl. "I heard what you girls did. You're heroes."

"And this is my niece, Alexandrea."

Marta didn't embrace Alex. Her tan eyes swept Alex up and down as if trying to learn something about her. Her lips puckered like she exaggerated a kiss. She was a very slender woman, tall and thin enough that Alex wondered if Marta could fit into one leg of her pants. Alex was creeped out by just how thin and tall she was. *How do organs fit in her body? At least Doctor Patel is proportioned.*

"*The* Alexandrea?"

Heather laughed nervously. "Yes, my niece. She's lived with us since her parents were taken," she glanced at Alex, apologizing for adding, "in a car accident."

Marta looked perplexed. "I thought you said—"

Alex's ears rang, her head once again felt ready to explode. Then just as suddenly, it was over. Concern washed over Heather's face. Marta seemed confused, looking between them before understanding dawned. "Alexandrea," she repeated, as though discovering the name after trying to remember it for years. Then she surprised Alex with a big hug. She was strong. She pinned Alex's arms to her sides under the blanket. "I've heard so much about you," she said with a warmth that Alex questioned. "It's so good to finally, really meet you." After an embarrassed pause, she added, "Although I wish under better circumstances."

"How do you know one another?" Rose chimed in.

"Book Club," they answered in unison.

Marta added, "I met your mother here when you were just a sea-monkey in her belly."

"Abby's here," Heather told Marta.

"Of course she is," Marta replied, displeased.

"Be nice to her. I couldn't have done this without her help."

"That's what she's there for," Marta sighed. "To help."

Heather was silent for a second. "Girls, go to the waiting room and," she paused, searching for a better word but finding none, "wait with Abby."

Rose and Alex thought the same thing; they both said, "You'll tell us as soon as you hear about Billy?"

Marta answered, "One of us will. Your mother has a small army of friends here. We've got you guys covered."

"Thanks," Alex said. Rose repeated.

"You hungry?" Marta asked before they could leave.

"Starving," Rose answered first.

Marta turned away and resumed speaking with Heather.

Rose looked at Alex as they left the room, "Was she taking a survey?"

They turned down the hall to the waiting room. Rose asked, "What was that all about?"

"Huh?"

"I don't remember Marta at all." She mimicked the woman's voice, "When I last saw you, you were boobs tall."

"That was good, Rose," Alex complimented. "You sound just like her."

"Thanks," Rose replied proudly. "Mom's hosted a couple Book Clubs, but that was before you. She just met us, and she's crapping on Abby and talking about you like you're all my mom ever talks about. Is she a bitch or something?"

"Marta is a bitch," Abby said, holding the waiting room door open for them. "She can't help it; it's baked in." The girls fell to laughter.

"She's not a bad person," Abby explained. "She thinks she's important. It's a Book Club thing. I'm not really a member and she likes to point that out."

Alex asked, "Why aren't you *really a member?*"

"I'm not so much for reading their kind of books. I go for the drinks. And Heather will cancel if I don't come."

"Ugh," Rose said. "She's weird." She mimicked Marta again, holding her arms at odd angles. "*The* Alexandrea?"

Alex laughed, pulling the blanket up, noticing people staring at them.

"You're really good at that," Abby said. "She's not a bad person," Abby repeated. "You get used to her. It's a..." she paused, "Book Club thing."

Nancy approached them, carrying two trays. "Marta sent this to you."

"Thanks," the girls replied in unison. Abby took the trays, and they sat down.

"Now I feel a little guilty," Alex said.

"I don't," Rose replied. "So what if she's nice to us once? Doesn't mean she's suddenly not a bitch."

Tomato soup with rice, sliced turkey on whole wheat, unsweetened iced tea, and rice pudding. The girls barely chewed, realizing with the first bite how famished they were. Rose held up her sandwich and joked, "I've never seen bread so thin. That's how I know Alex didn't make the sandwich." She pretended to fit an impossibly large sandwich in her mouth. Alex laughed. Rose rubbed her arm. They ate the thin sandwiches.

About an hour later, Heather joined them. She sat beside Abby. Rose was out cold, leaning against Alex, who had her eyes closed, too haunted to sleep. Her mind kept replaying Billy jumping off the rock, interspersed with images of that man—bent neck and glowing eyes—staring out of the mottled shadows in the woods, smiling.

"Thank you," she said to Abby. "I know how the other women can be. They don't get it. I mean, I don't get it, but whatever. Today would've been different if you weren't around. Thank you."

Abby shook her head with a faint smile. "It's why I do it, Heather. We've been over this. They don't want to accept me because I'm not like them? Fine. They don't understand. They don't have a choice. Then again, neither do I."

"I don't want you to think I take you for granted."

Abby shrugged. "I *want* to be here."

"I'm grateful you are."

"Me too. You have no idea." Abby sighed, "It's been hard staying away."

Alex opened her eyes. "How's Billy? Any word?"

"I'm still waiting on Patel."

"What's taking so long? Tests were hours ago."

Heather shrugged. "We're not the only ones here, Alex. Maybe it's better they're not all over him. Marta said it means they don't think he's in danger. Some people are much worse off."

Alex closed her eyes again.

"Alex?"

Alex opened her eyes.

"Can we talk? Not here."

Abby reached around Alex to shore up Rose's head. Alex slipped away and Abby slid into her place. She and Heather walked to an empty hallway. The rooms were dark, their occupants asleep. It felt private.

"Hear me out; I'm not looking for someone to blame," Heather began. "Nothing can change what happened. I need to know everything that happened today."

Alex took a deep breath. "Billy didn't fall."

She expected Heather to react. Matter-of-factly, she replied, "Of course he didn't fall."

"You knew?"

"I'm not stupid, Alex. I know my son. What happened?"

Alex tried to parse out what led to Billy's leap. "He sort of, you know, he was sitting, and then he just got up and leapt."

"You know how before I told you and Rose *not* to tell me a story?"

"Yeah."

"I'm asking for the whole story. Something happened before he tried to kill himself," Heather said patiently. She looked around as though verifying they were at the hospital. "Years and years ago, just down this hallway, a good friend of mine told me something very important would happen here. I need you to be honest with me. I need every detail."

Alex wasn't sure what Heather was talking about. "We got out to Picnic Rock," Alex began.

"From the house? You went straight there?"

"Well, no. We left the house and walked down the street and through the field to the woods."

Heather made a face. "I don't need you to recall every footstep, Alex."

"That's why I started at Picnic Rock. I mean, we walked to the Old Witch's Shack first and hung out there for a while. I asked where they wanted to go next. Billy got excited and begged to go to Picnic Rock. He was chanting, *Sacrifice Stone, Sacrifice Stone.*"

Heather grimaced. "I hate it when he calls it that."

"It's what he said. You told me to tell you what happened."

"You're right," Heather nodded. "Go on."

Alex waited a beat. "We were sitting, and after a while, we ate and started talking. Oh, when we got there, Billy pretended to jump to scare Rose. He wasn't serious," she added, noting Heather's expression. "At least he didn't seem it that time."

Heather was nodding. "And then?"

"Rose started telling me about this house she visits when she's dreaming."

"She's been having that dream all her life."

Alex stared at her. Her aunt was acting like nothing was out of the ordinary. "Billy talked about it too. Rose said she saw him there, and he made it sound like he was. You know, like he was in her dream or something."

Heather closed her eyes and took a steady breath. "He knows I don't like that he goes there."

Alex was shocked. She felt lightheaded. "He said you've said that. Aunt Heather, what is this about? He goes into Rose's dreams? Is that a thing people can do? I'm kind of freaking out."

"What else?" Heather pressed.

"Tell me what's going on first."

Heather pursed her lips. "I need you to tell me."

Alex made a face. She tried waiting for her aunt to say something but then Heather put her hands on her hips and she knew she had lost. "Rose was sort of wigged out so she made a joke and asked me about my dreams. I told her, and then Billy started acting really strange."

"How so? I mean, how was he acting strange?" Alex felt the weight of her aunt's concentration.

"He started talking about coins and fountains and how you let his get tarnished."

Heather gasped, her eyes filling with tears. "He said that about me? Then he already knows. *It is starting.*"

Alex stood silent.

"He must hate me. He must think I'm a monster." Heather shook her head and looked at the ceiling. She was fighting back tears.

Alex whispered, "What are you talking about? Billy loves you." She saw as Heather's gaze returned, tears streaming down the woman's face.

Alex didn't speak. She'd finished telling her story.

Heather had a false start trying to regain the conversation. "Billy said these things after you talked about your dream?" she finally managed to ask.

Alex nodded.

"Why didn't you lead with that? Tell me everything you told them. About your dream."

Alex recounted her nightmare, including every detail she could recall. Her parents, the home invasion, the gunshot, her mother exploding her father, the child, the mist.

"That was last night?"

"Yeah."

"Last night was the first time?"

"What?"

Heather's eyes had widened to saucers; she looked crazed. "Alex, how long have you been having this dream? Was last night the first?"

"No. I've been dreaming it for over a week. Eight," she said, "I think eight nights."

Heather started to speak. Several times. At last, she said to herself, "Okay, I can deal with this. He told me, I do this." She took another breath and returned her fists to her hips. "I know what comes next." She looked up at the ceiling again, hyperventilating. "He told me. I agreed. Fuck, I tried to do this to Rose. What was I thinking?"

She started walking away before grabbing Alex by the wrist, dragging her.

"Heather? What's happening? What are you talking about?" Heather didn't answer, she pulled Alex at a near run.

"Did I do something wrong, Heather?" Alex started trembling; tears welled in her eyes. "Why aren't you talking to me? Say something!"

"Abby," Heather shouted as they cleared the doorway to the waiting room. The people still sitting here—some new, some from hours before—glared indignantly. "I need you to take Alex. Go to your house."

Abby looked up, startled. "My place?"

Heather nodded. "I need you to take her now. I need to talk to Marta and Nancy and see how quickly we can get a..." she struggled to get her mouth around the words, "Book Club meeting together."

"Is it time?"

Heather nodded again. "Please keep her safe. I'll put Rose in Billy's room." she reached out and caressed Rose's sleeping face. "It's no coincidence we're here tonight." She motioned to Alex. "She's been having the dream. *The dream.* For over a week."

Abby bolted upright. "Okay Alexandrea," she announced with a sense of haste, "we're getting out of here."

Rose groaned. "I'm so tired. Can't I sleep here?"

Abby looked at Heather, who motioned like she was shooing them.

Alex turned to her aunt. "You're freaking me out, Aunt Heather. Please tell me what's going on."

Heather looked at the door. "You wouldn't understand no matter how I tried to tell you. You will, but you have to trust me right now. Abby will make sure you're safe. Nothing will happen to you while she's around."

Before Alex could argue, Heather grabbed a still-sleeping Rose and ran out of the waiting room.

Alex watched her go, leaving her to endure stares from the waiting room crowd. Her heart pounded. In her mind, she kept seeing that man in the woods, his sparkling eyes and grin.

"What are you waiting for?" Abby called from past the automatic doors. "Come on."

Alex wrapped herself in the blanket. Outside was cold, the sky reddening as dawn approached. She followed Abby to the truck. For a while, they drove in silence, but by the time Abby had pulled onto the main road, Alex couldn't take it anymore.

"Abby, please tell me what's going on."

Chapter Ten

bby watched the road, her headlights doing little to improve the predawn light. She said nothing for the first few miles. Alex sat, curled in the front seat, her mind racing. *Is this about the man in the woods? It has to be. Why wouldn't Heather just say that?* With no sense of what was happening or why, she felt abandoned.

The sky burned from darkened red to a brighter pink. The trees blurred by the side of the road. Alex waited for Abby to say something. Abby returned her wordless queries with an opaque expression. She looked like she didn't know how to start.

"Heather's concerned for your safety," Abby said at last. "She wants you someplace safe."

Alex kept thinking back to the woods. She hadn't slept since Saturday morning, nearly twenty hours ago. She kept seeing Billy in mid-leap, the valley sprawling beneath him as though the entire planet were receding from his body. She saw, and felt in her mind, the slips and falls she and Rose had suffered, her tenuous grip on some dubious weeds. She didn't think about it then, while the roots snapped out of the dry soil, but now she understood how lucky they had been. They cheated death. All three of them. And the man in the shadows might he have been a trick of foliage and light and exhaustion. Nothing about him made sense, his appearance, his crooked neck, the way he followed them, as though his whole purpose was only to frighten them. As though scaring them might accomplish something. *Who would do that? Who would leave us without helping?*

"Abby," Alex began, "why does Heather think we're in danger?"

"What gave you that idea?" Abby said unconvincingly. Then she sighed. "Not we," she whispered. "I'm not—I mean, I am, but only by association."

"Association to what?"

Abby took her eyes off the road for three full seconds. "To you, Alex."

Alex had no reply. *I'm putting others in danger? What did I do?* She tried to understand what had Heather so concerned. She thought back to the hospital, the words that passed between them. *Was there a reason Heather said we didn't need examinations?* Alex hadn't question it at the time. She kept coming back to her dream. That was the moment Heather changed. *What about it bothered her so much?*

Alex listened to the tires drubbing on the road's expansion joints. She kept thinking, analyzing, replaying. Nothing made sense. She waited for Abby to offer some critical clue that would join all these disparate thoughts into a cohesive plot. Abby—Aunt Abby—the family friend who for years couldn't wait to see her, to play with her, to be with her, was silent. Maybe Aunt Abby was gone. Maybe that was why she visited infrequently. "Why aren't you telling me anything, Abby?" Alex asked. "What makes Heather think I'm in danger?"

Abby took a preparatory breath. She motioned like she was about to explain but offered only a heavy sigh.

"She used those words, right, that I'm *in danger*? She didn't explain, yet you practically chased me out of the hospital. That sounds like you know."

"I know."

"A little help here," she cried, exasperated. "Please Abby, what's going on?"

Abby eased off the accelerator. The truck slowed from below eighty to below seventy. "Alex," she said, "I'm begging you to trust me. I can't tell you. I want to, believe me, I do." Her voice rode a wave of pleading emotion. "But I can't. If I could, you have to believe I would." Alex glared. She took a deep breath. "It has to do," she said, pausing between every word as though pulling them one at a time from a bag, "with your parents."

This flummoxed Alex. *My parents?* "Abby, they've been dead four years."

"Believe me, I know. After you, no one misses your dad more than me."

This stung; Alex couldn't say she missed him. He and Abby were friends before Alex was born, before he was the only way Alex ever knew him. "Did they, what? Kill someone in the car accident?

And that family wants revenge?" After she said it, she realized it sounded ridiculous.

"I can't, Alex. I can't say more. This is so hard. I wish you could understand. It's tearing me apart. Really, it is. I want to tell you; I need to tell you; more than you know."

"Cut the shit." Alex's frustration was coming out. "Don't say you want to. What's stopping you? Tell me why you can't."

"My job is to protect you. That's why."

"You're making no sense. Do you hear yourself? Are you keeping me safe by not telling me? How will I know I'm in danger? What if, I don't know, kittens are after me? If I don't know, what'll stop me from petting one?" *Could I have used a worse analogy?* "Stop telling me I have to trust you. How can I if you won't tell me?"

Abby inhaled. Alex heard her anger in the trembling vibration. When Abby spoke, she realized it wasn't from anger at all. "Alex, your parents did something. They, um, they, weren't in a car accident."

The air evacuated the cab, and Alex sat suffocating. When she found breath to speak, she said, "What?"

Cautiously, Abby began to reply, "Four years ago, your parents—"

Alex's ears shrieked. Her head throbbed like every blood vessel within it had swelled to bursting. She clutched at her temples, fingers digging into her scalp, eyes squeezing out tears as she pressed them shut. She wanted to growl in pain, but even trying to breathe threatened to make her vomit.

And then it was over. The pain lifted as abruptly as it came. The sudden absence felt orgasmic. Alex cried out, gulping air, her body doused in sweat. It was as though a thousand knives had been pulled from her brain. "Dammit. That was the worst friggin' headache I've ever had." The concern on Abby's face made her even more worried. "What," she asked. "Is that what I'm in danger from? Is that going to keep happening? You're worried about headaches? Why are you looking at me like that?"

"You've had these headaches before."

"So?"

"Do you remember when?"

Alex shrugged. "On and off, most my life. You know that." She recalled times in her youth when Abby would hold her as she suffered through the excruciating waves of pain.

"Were you ever alone when you had them?"

"I don't know. Maybe not. No. I don't think so."

"When did they stop?"

Alex had that answer. "About three years ago." Not long after she started living with Heather and the twins.

"Why do you think that was?"

"I don't know; I assumed hormones. I grew out of them?"

"What else happened around that same time?"

Alex shook her head. "What's with the questions? Yes, my parents died, and then my headaches stopped. But not right away. Those first few months at Heather's were the worst. I thought I had a brain tumor."

"It's not a tumor."

"I know that." Alex slapped her thighs in frustration.

"Please don't be angry with me, Alex. Please. Not with me." She closed her eyes for a moment. "Let's get you someplace safe. We'll get you some clothes, get you settled, let you sleep. It's been a long day for everyone, and we're all exhausted. Being tired means we make stupid mistakes."

Alex squinted out the window, mouthing a voiceless complaint.

I thought I knew Abby. This was the woman who had spoiled her, who couldn't wait to spend time with her. That was Alex's childhood, though. She rarely saw Abby anymore. Maybe she had never known her. She swept her eyes over the woman behind the wheel. Abby was in Heather's Book Club? Abby wasn't someone who attended a book club. Book clubs were like high tea, erudite and elitist. Not Abby's scene.

Alex disappointed herself for the thought; she was judging someone who had never been anything but kind to her.

Chapter Eleven

he drive into the dawn was silent until Abby cursed the glare of myriad pits in her windshield glinting in the harsh morning light. She half squinted, half yawned as she slid on sunglasses. "Heather wants me to take you to my place. I say we stop at your house first." She glanced at Alex. "You need clothes, and while I'd lend you mine," she pinched the shoulder of her sleeveless muscle-shirt, "most of them look like this."

Alex shrugged. "You're in charge."

"Trust me, Alex. I am not the one in charge."

Alex laughed. *We're both following Heather's instructions, like it or not.*

Abby pulled off the main road. "Grab enough for three days," she said, rolling through the still morning neighborhood. "T-shirts, jeans, oh, and panties. Don't forget underwear. Socks if you wear them. Maybe a light jacket. Only what you need for day-to-day."

Alex giggled at the way Abby said panties like it was a fancy expression for underwear or having the word in her mouth discomforted her. "I need to feed Dolly."

Abby mouthed the words, "Feed Dolly," as though adding it to her mental list. "No, she needs to come with us. Just be quick about it. No dawdling."

Alex crossed her arms. "Do I strike you as a dawdler?" The tension dropped from Abby's tone, and Alex couldn't maintain hers without it.

Abby grinned. "You've grown up since you were the kid I knew, but Heather's told me plenty. You're prone to dawdling."

"Just because I have trouble waking up at the crack of dawn doesn't mean I dawdle."

They pulled into Heather's driveway. Alex let the blanket slide from her shoulders. She snuffled. "Mind if I take a quick shower? I'm disgusting."

"I said no dawdling. There's no such thing as a quick shower at your age. Do it at my place."

Alex shrugged. She felt mature in recognizing this wasn't a fight worth having. She left her blanket in the truck and walked to the back of the house; Heather left the back door unlocked. The morning air chilled her bare skin. *Did I steal that blanket?* She used to like this bra, but she couldn't wait to put on something clean, something not caked with grit and sand that abraded her skin. She didn't care if she never wore this again.

Entering, she flipped on the kitchen light and took the creaking staircase to the basement. The open risers and bare-wood treads reminded her of a prehistoric skeleton. A painted two-by-four served as a railing. She always bound up and down these stairs in case they collapsed, an irrational fear, but given all the noise, she took no chances.

One small window on each wall let in some dirt-filtered dawn light. Spiders strung webs throughout the open joists, like tattered curtains covering the open ceiling. The bare concrete walls and floor smelled wet and acrid. She grabbed the cat carrier from atop of the drier and made her way upstairs, heading first to the bathroom.

The screen door creaked below.

Jeez, Abby, Alex thought, grabbing toiletries, it's only been, like, a minute.

She washed her face and wet a towel to wipe as much of her torso as she could. If she couldn't shower, at least she'd get some dirt off. She slipped it under her bra and her jeans, hoping to get the abrasive grit out. When she dropped the filthy cloth, she could almost hear Heather complain about the dirt stripes on it. *Use soap. There's no reason for a towel to get this dirty.* Alex dumped the towel in the hamper. *Heather might complain, but at least I didn't leave it out.*

Alex climbed the steep attic ladder to her bedroom. The cupola let in bright morning sunshine, but she turned the light on out of habit.

Dolly perched precariously balanced on her headboard, staring blankly into the space between Alex's dresser and desk. She made an unfamiliar sound, a guttural yowling growl. Alex followed Dolly's gaze to a wood-framed photograph of her and her parents. She was eight and awkward, like a puppy that needed to grow into its ears, paws, and tail.

Alex scooped Dolly up. The cat resisted, hissing and yowling, delivering a pinwheel of needle-like claws. Alex coaxed her into the carrier and locked it. Dolly made threatening noises, which Alex was certain were cat-based profanities.

"Everything okay up there?"

"Just getting the cat," Alex shouted down. "She didn't want to go peacefully."

"Hurry up."

"Be down in five."

Alex placed the carrier on her bed. A shudder ran through her shoulders. She checked the room. Dolly sometimes stared into empty space. It had never bothered her before. She had also been half-naked for hours; that didn't help. She opened drawers and pulled out clothes. The faster she gathered her stuff the sooner she'd be at Abby's and be clean. She threw everything on her bed and looked for a bag. She took out a long-sleeve T-shirt and, grinning at her ingenuity, tied the arms and filled it. Lastly, she picked out clothes to wear now. She placed them on her bed and started to change. She left her filthy clothes in a pile at the foot of the bed. She'd take them to the hamper on her way out. Heather would definitely have something to say about them moldering in the bathroom. As she moved, she noticed an unpleasant odor coming off her body. She preferred showering before putting on clean clothes; at least she'd be in clothes. She looked at her naked body in the mirror, rubbing off the last of the sand and examining the raw, red stripes where her bra straps acted like sandpaper. As she pulled on some underwear, the framed picture of her parents fell flat on the dresser.

She stared at it, but nothing looked to be amiss.

Alex sat on the bed to pull on jeans, then clasped her bra and pull on a T-shirt, still eyeing the toppled picture, when Abby called up, "Let's get a move on!"

Her ears began to ring, and her head suddenly threatened to explode. Dolly hissed. From downstairs, Abby cursed. Furniture clattered and banged, and it sounded as if the kitchen table was upended. Then her head went calm.

What was that? Her heart raced. "Abby? You okay?" *Stupid question. Maybe she fell?* Alex spun around as hands grabbed her arm.

"Don't scream."

She jumped, her heart exploding in her chest. She tried to pull away; the young man's grip was strong. She screamed.

Downstairs, Abby shouted, "Get out, Alex!" More furniture crashed across the floor. Something shattered.

The man stood between her dresser and desk. *How long has he been here? Was he watching me undress?* There was something familiar about him. Something told her he was dangerous.

Alex screamed and kicked. The man collapsed, clutching his groin. She ran to the opposite side of her bed. Downstairs, many somethings shattered.

"Stop, I'm not here to hurt you." He spoke in winded gasps. He had short, dark hair and large, wide-set brown eyes. He looked a few years older; maybe in his early twenties. He was dressed like he'd just come from the office.

Alex's heart did not so much beat as vibrate as the man inched forward. She inched back, looking for a moment to run.

She cringed at the sounds from downstairs, a thousand something's shattering against one another. Abby grunted. A deep voice started to shout before another crash caused them both to curse. Alex's head flared up again, but only for a moment. It started again then stopped, and then again, over and over. "Abby!" she screamed between bursts.

The young man held up his hands. "Easy. Easy there. Come with me and this will be over."

Alex squared up to him. "I'll take my clothes and the cat and go downstairs," Alex told him calmly as she picked up her shirt-sack. "If you try to stop me, I promise it'll be the last mistake you make." She couldn't believe she threatened him. She hoped he didn't see her trembling hands. She had no plan how to follow through.

"I'm not here to hurt you," he repeated, leaning against the dresser. "If you just come with me, I can explain everything."

"Explain what?"

He took a breath. "We need you to—" the squealing in her ears cut off his words, nearly crippling her.

Alex dug her fingernails into her scalp. She screamed through waves of excruciating pain. His hands rose defensively, his head turning away as though a locomotive was barreling toward him. Then it stopped.

"Please don't. Calm down, please. It's okay." He emphasized his *pleases*. He kept begging her not to do something she wasn't doing. He crept closer to the attic stairs like he wanted to leave, as though if he crept slowly enough, she might not notice until he vanished. All Alex was doing was rubbing her temples.

His reaction to her pain shocked her. She hurt, but he was threatened by it. "We're okay?" He asked, lowering his hands and opened his squinting eyes. "Good. Thank you. Thank you for not, you know."

They both jumped at a loud snapping sound from downstairs. It didn't sound like something breaking, but like a sharp pop.

"For not what?" Alex's heart raced. She couldn't catch her breath.

He looked nervous. He started speaking but his words drowned as Alex's head raged. She clawed and screamed, nearly collapsing in pain.

He clamped his mouth shut and turned from her as though expecting something horrible. The pain receded, and Alex seized the opportunity. She rushed forward and knocked into him with the full weight of her body.

He didn't seem to lose his balance; he just transitioned into the open space above the staircase. His head clunked into the opposite side of the attic opening as he dropped straight to the floor below. Alex grabbed her shirt-sack, the cat carrier, and raced down the ladder. She leapt over him, stopping halfway down the living room stairs.

The main floor was ransacked. Broken plates, knick-knacks and glassware spilled from upended furniture. Broken drawers lay scattered about the floor.

Alex surveyed the damage. She wanted to get out of the house, as though being outside meant safety. Again, she thought of touching *base.* "Abby?"

"You shouldn't come any closer." The voice was raspy and dark. Deep enough to make Alex's insides rumble.

She took a step to the left, revealing Abby sprawled on the floor with an older man kneeling behind her. One arm was wrapped around Abby's chest, holding her upright—she looked unconscious—while the other held an opened book. His head seemed to jut forward, not up, from his shoulders.

Alex couldn't breathe. She'd seen this man before. She'd watched the injury that set his neck into such a fierce angle—her father exploding to dust throwing him across the hall and into the wall outside her bedroom. In her dreams, they called him Matthew.

"You were there," she hissed. "Last night, that was you in the woods."

"It was."

Alex took a step forward. "Leave her alone."

Matthew's expression shifted. His head was bald, except for a ring of salty hair above his ears. The lines on his forehead deepened in surprise or concern, furrowing the top of his scalp.

"Where's the boy? What did you do to my son?"

"He's upstairs." Alex took another small step. Matthew gave her all his attention.

"Dead?"

"Not dead. He fell."

"Fell? He fell?" Matthew sounded surprised.

"I pushed him."

"Pushed," he repeated, finding the word trite enough to grin.

Alex trembled, but Matthew seemed distracted. *Why does he assume I did something to his son?* "Abby and I are gonna go. You can rob this place or whatever. Just let us alone."

"Robbery? That's what you think? I'm a *burglar?*"

She nodded.

Matthew's eyes processed.

"I'm sorry about last night. I tried scaring it out of you. It was all just disappointing." He squeezed his arm around Abby, studying Alex. "You should show me something."

She was immediately nauseous. "Show you what?" She felt sick. "Don't hurt her," she begged.

"I need to see you have it," he started to speak. "You should—" Excruciating pain dropped Alex to her knees.

When the pain stopped, the man seemed to consider his options. "He warned me. Now William's gone. Jeremiah's figured things out by now." He looked at her. "You don't have it, do you?"

"Have what?" She looked at her empty hands. She did not possess whatever he was searching for.

He shook his head. "Nope, you don't. I wondered last night. I thought you were playing games with me. You can't." He looked around the room, trying to clear his head. "I was so sure, but she's no use without it."

Alex feared what he'd do to them if she couldn't produce what he wanted. "Without what? What do you think I have? Tell me and I'll give it to you."

His mouth moved, but Alex only experienced anguish. It was short-lived. She broke out into a sweat when it passed.

"She can't even hear it," he said. "If she had it, she'd have used it by now. Protected herself. Tried to hurt me." He looked at Abby. "Unless she was a decoy. They made me think it was her to protect another." He wasn't speaking to Alex; he was trying to convince himself. "They were not that conniving. It's got to be her."

"What are you talking about?" Alex used a broken chair to push herself to her feet. "Who do you think I am?"

"Peter's daughter."

Alex couldn't breathe. Two simple words left her empty and cold. She waited for him to say anything else, but he appeared to be waiting for her. "If I don't have what you need," she said, slowly, "then you can leave?"

"Yes, another time, another way. The motivation's not strong enough." He motioned to Abby. "Trade you? Yours for mine?"

Alex felt the balance of power shift, but she wasn't sure why. "You mean you fetch your son and get out of my house?"

"No. I mean I let you let me."

Alex took another step forward. Matthew disapproved. He started to speak.

Alex clawed at the air, tensing muscles distorted her body. Dolly yowled at her side. Teeth clenched, Alex tried not to crumble to the floor again. White spots blotted out her vision.

When it abated, the ringing in her ears echoing like distant thunder, she sucked air, cold sweat washing over her, soaking her clean clothes, making them cling. She shivered.

Matthew rolled Abby onto her side. She grunted; her swollen eyes fixed on Alex. He collected his book and stood. His hunch looked painful. "We'll figure it out," he told Alex, matter-of-factly. "Figure out what's blocking you." He dusted himself off. "I wondered why I couldn't find you. It's like you don't even exist until you're in front of me." Nothing he said made sense. Maybe he was crazy. Maybe he was a cult leader who'd convinced the unconscious man upstairs to follow his insanity. It sounded like, although he was leaving, this wasn't the last she'd see of him.

"Why are you doing this?"

His tone softened. He spoke to her the way Heather spoke explaining a difficult problem. "There're things I can't get through to you. Once I figure out how, there are important things you'll do for me. Working together, you and I can fix everything wrong in the world." He walked past her and climbed the stairs. Alex's gaze tracked him the whole way.

When he returned a minute later, his son's full-grown body hung weightless in his arms. At the bottom of the stairs, he faced Alex.

"I know they think you're special, Alexandrea," he told her. "What they don't understand is, without me, you're nothing."

"I've been called worse."

The old man grinned. "I'll figure out how to provoke you."

"Provoke me?" Alex felt provoked. "How'd you know my name?" *How'd he know my father's name?*

He turned, kicked the storm door off its hinges, and walked out.

Alex raced to Abby. Abby looked up, her face distorted by bruises. Her lip split and her arms covered in deep scratches. "I'm so sorry, Alex," she croaked. The swelling caused her words to slur. "I was stupid to bring you here." She fingered the remains of her necklace, a glass charm shattered and ground into the floor. "Lucky for me you were here." Alex wasn't sure if Abby was addressing her or the charm; all clues pointed to the shattered glass. Alex had done nothing worthy of Abby's praise.

Alex looked out the windows to prove to herself that the man had left and wasn't sabotaging Abby's truck or setting fire to the house. She saw no sign of him. Instead of pulling Abby to her feet, she collapsed against her and sobbed. Abby placed an arm around her. Alex hugged her, feeling once more like she was touching *base*.

"Was it him?" Alex sobbed into Abby's shoulder. "He's the danger?"

Abby rubbed her back. "Some of it," she whispered.

"Why'd he do this? Why'd he hurt you if he's after me?"

Abby shushed her. Her arms squeezed tighter, calming Alex. "Just cry it out. Hold on to me and let it out."

A few minutes later, Alex helped Abby to her feet. She grabbed her shirt-sack and the carrier and helped Abby out the door. They saw no signs of the old man or his son outside.

Once in the truck, Abby locked the doors and sat frozen in her seat. She hit the steering wheel, startling Alex. "Stupid, stupid, stupid," she repeated. "Heather told me what to do, and I fucked it up. I brought you right to him. I can't believe I was so stupid. I almost ruined everything. Everything!"

Alex watched Abby talk herself into tears. She leaned over and embraced her. "Abby, you didn't know. I'm okay. We're going to be okay." She tried to stifle her own tears as Abby held her, her body shuddering. "That was him," she whispered to herself. "From my dream. Matthew and..." she fought to recall the name, "George." It felt wrong to say it, but she had to. "George."

She fell silent, chilled to the bone. Why do I know him? Was he in my dream the way Billy was in Rose's?

She wanted to let out all the emotions, the fear and anxiety, the hatred and revulsion, but right now Abby needed her to be the strong one. She would hold Abby for as long as the woman needed.

The further in the past the incident became, the more Alex's emotions swirled, the more her mind worked over the event. She had tried not to consider it at the time, but she suffered through the best possible outcome. She had been so vulnerable. He had been in her bedroom. Even as she undressed and changed, she never saw him. She cursed him, the pervert, disgusted and grateful at the same time. Things could have been so much worse.

Abby radiated warmth. Whatever she had been through, Alex realized, Abby had borne the brunt of it. She took a physical beating to protect her. Alex's chest swelled. Abby may be the sole reason she was still alive. Those men didn't expect a woman to put up such a fight. What started as an embrace became more; Alex held her, her *base*, her safety. Here, with Abby, she felt protected, even if it was all in her head. She tried to speak, to thank Abby for being there.

"Abby, I want to..."

"Shhh," Abby whispered.

After a few minutes, Abby slid free from Alex, who shuffled back into her seat. Abby started the truck and turned them around. Only when they were back on the main road, in the early-morning streetlights, did she see how bruised Abby's face and arms were.

Abby shook her head. "Stupid. I should have listened to Heather and brought you to my house first." She hit the steering wheel. "Just gone to the store. I can't make these mistakes."

Abby knew more than she let on. Alex inquired, "How were you supposed to know they'd be there, Abby?" The question reeked of accusation. "Why were those men there? What do they want with me? Did you know? Did you know they were coming for me?" Abby was quiet. "Abby, a guy was hiding in my bedroom; I didn't see him. He watched me change. He grabbed me. He scared me half to death. I thought he would kill me, or worse."

"They came for worse."

"And you still won't tell me anything." Alex looked out the window.

A few minutes passed in silence. When Abby spoke, her voice quavered more with each word, "He came at me. I didn't matter. I don't matter to him. He was going to kill me. He knew why I'm here. He..."

Alex's ears squealed.

"...then you came downstairs."

The pain dissipated.

Abby sank back in her seat. "I'm grateful you got him to leave."

"I didn't do anything." Alex shook her head. "The guy in my bedroom, his son, George, he—I don't know how to describe it—acted like he was afraid I was going to hit him."

"Maybe he fears you for a reason."

"Abby, please. What—"

Abby let out a tremendous sigh. "Please stop asking me that, Alexandrea."

"Stop calling me Alexandrea, first of all. My name is Alex now, Aunt Abby."

"Fine, Alex. Then I'm just Abby. If I could, I'd tell you. If I could, I'd tell you everything, everything I know."

Alex felt a stab of regret. Did Abby just take away her honorary aunt status? Why is she so afraid of telling me? "What's stopping you? Heather?"

"You wouldn't understand."

Alex wanted to scream. She held it in, trying to remain rational. "Abby, my cousins are in the hospital. Some men just tried to kill us. Or just me. Just maybe, I should know why. You seem to know, or at least you give that impression. What doesn't Heather want me to know?"

"I can't tell you because you can't hear it, Alex. You. *You're* the reason I can't talk about it, not Heather. You can't hear it."

"I can take it. Whatever it is. Just tell me, please."

Abby sighed. "Fine. You asked for it. I'll tell you everything I know." She let out a long, centering breath. "I promise I will not stop until you tell me to. Is that what you want?"

"Yes."

"Fine."

Abby slowed the truck down a little. She looked at Alex. "To start, you were supposed to be born—"

Alex clutched her head as agony crashed across her skull. She wished Abby would stop, but she kept talking, and as long as her mouth moved, Alex struggled to bear the pain. She couldn't hear anything Abby said as a dozen simultaneous squealing, squeezing, stabbing migraines muted everything. As soon as the woman's mouth stopped moving it ended. The pain vanished, but before Alex could take a breath of relief, Abby spoke again. Alex tried to concentrate, to prove her point, but she could barely exist under the torment. Abby continued, stopping, starting, and stopping again. Alex had a moment to recover, to catch her breath, and then Abby would inflict some more. It was like torture, like drowning.

"Enough, enough," Alex screeched, throwing her hands in the air. "Please stop, please stop! I'm going to be sick."

Abby wagged a finger. "Don't you dare throw up in my truck."

Alex looked at Abby, her eyes tearing, her body soaking in sweat, her head felt only the prolonged echoes of pain. "What is that?"

Abby cocked her head. "Really?"

"You're talking *now*. I can hear you *now*. Is there something about *what* you're saying?" Alex couldn't help but feel deflated. "Right? That's why you can't tell me, I literally can't hear what you're saying?"

Abby replied, as though counting her words. "I'm told it's what happens when your brain is presented with two realities."

"Two?"

"Well, that's what I'm told. Your brain knows one thing to be true and is told something so completely different that it can't reconcile the information and boom."

"It's less *boom*, more *aaahhh*."

"I hope you know I'd never intentionally cause you to hurt."

"I do. I asked you to. Honestly, I don't think I've ever been in so much pain." After a thoughtful pause, she asked, "What do you mean by *two realities*?"

Abby raised her eyebrow. "Really?"

Alex saw Abby's incredulous expression. "No. No, that's okay."

"And I only told you a little. I don't know the whole story."

Alex's voice quivered with nerves. "How did this happen to me?"

Abby cocked her head.

"I know, I know," Alex replied. "I can't hear it." She looked out the window. "I'm not sure I want to."

Chapter Twelve

he sun rested in the treetops when Abby pulled her truck off the road and onto a narrow, rutted path. The truck pitched and bounced as it crept through what became a gully, the uneroded sides rising to the middle of the doors as the truck squeezed between.

"Sorry," Abby apologized. "Been meaning to get this road fixed. It's just always the lowest priority. I don't own it, but I'm sure one day I'll get stuck and starve to death in the truck."

Alex half-laughed, unsure Abby was kidding. Abby tried to lighten the mood, but Alex's head raced: The twins. Matthew and George from her dream. Heather. The pain in her head. What wasn't she comprehending? The more she tried not thinking about them, the more she did.

The path leveled out, bordering a field of three-foot-high corn stalks to the left and woods to the right. The truck crawled to avoid kicking up dust.

"This your farm?"

"I rent space. Pat, the farmer, is related to a friend. I rent out a barn."

"You live in a barn?" Alex blurted, picturing sleeping on bales of hay.

Abby laughed, deep and long, punctuated with winces. "No, I don't live in a barn."

The driveway curved downhill to a large, weathered structure with peeling red paint, gaps in its planks, and missing shingles. Visible as Abby drove around the side, was a small mobile home. Spinning objects—maybe cut-up soda bottles on strings—festooned a green canvas awning over the door. It was not what Alex expected.

Killing the engine, Abby eased herself out of the truck and limped to the door. "Whenever you need a place to stay, this is your home too."

They entered into a tiny kitchen/living room with immaculate white cabinets. The air smelled of lavender and citrus. On the couch to the right of the front door, two gray tabby cats lay curled on a white blanket.

They yawned and stretched as Abby pet them. "This one's Marty," she explained like she was talking to a baby. Alex didn't know Abby capable of such sounds. "You can tell because when he's happy his tale goes straight up." Exaggerated rises in pitch peppered her speech. Marty immediately made for the cat carrier to investigate. Dolly hissed from inside. Marty fled deeper into the trailer; his very straight tail now bent between his legs. Abby stroked the other cat. "This one is Quest."

"Marty and Quest?" Alex asked.

"I'm not good at names." Her tone became cute again. "Quest is for Question, because her tail looks like a question mark." Quest purred loudly as Abby scratched her back.

Abby led Alex through the kitchen, past the bathroom to the bedroom. "You can sleep here. I'll take the couch."

"Don't let me inconvenience you," Alex defended.

"I'm not. I typically fall asleep on the couch watching television."

"I feel like I'm kicking you out of your own bed."

Abby gently squeezed her shoulder. "It's all good, kiddo. If I didn't want to take the couch, I wouldn't."

The bedroom made up the back third of the trailer. Not what she'd expected, Alex found the room femininely decorated. A full-sized bed dominated the space, covered in a white, fluffy blanket trimmed with lace. Matching decorative pillows lay atop two plain pillows by a brass and porcelain headboard. Alex looked out the larger of two windows. Outside she saw only a barn and fields.

As though hearing her thoughts, Abby offered, "I could dress it down for you. I have a plain blanket."

Alex declined.

"Once you close the door, let Dolly out. The litter box is in the pantry, opposite the bathroom." She opened a dresser drawer, scooped out a pile of muscle shirts and stuffed them into a different dresser drawer. "Put your things in here. Get settled, take a shower, get comfortable. Food or nap first?"

Alex didn't have to choose, exhaustion won. "Nap."

"Please shower first." Abby kidded, "Don't soil my clean sheets with your stink." She smiled, looking uncomfortable until

Alex smiled at her joke. "When you wake up, I'll make us lunch, dinner—whichever time it is—and then show you around. Good?"

"Thanks, Abby."

Abby grinned. She stepped out and closed the door.

Alex opened the carrier and pet the now cowering Dolly.

"You're free, stop being a 'fraidy-cat. I know you miss Heather and Rose and Billy. I do too."

Dolly took one look around and made two frantic laps around the room before hiding under the bed, out of reach.

Resigned to letting Dolly acclimate on her own, Alex refolded her clothes and neatly put her things away. She stepped from the bedroom and closed the door behind her. The bifold door to the pantry lay open to her right, litter box on the floor. Alex found a bowl and cat food on the kitchen counter and a small note that read, "For Dolly. I'm outside to give you privacy."

After feeding Dolly, Alex went into the tiny bathroom. A small wooden vanity and sink sat beside a white toilet with a blue fuzzy lid. Once the water in the standing shower was hot, she stepped in. She wanted to scald away two days' filth and memories. The heat was intense on her raw skin, but she just wanted to be clean. The water at her feet ran brown. Even soaped and rinsed, Alex stood in the stream.

"Why didn't Abby call the police?" Alex whispered to herself. "What triggers these headaches? Why isn't anyone concerned about them?"

After drying herself and dressing, her long hair wrapped in a towel, Alex returned to the bedroom. Dolly snored on a pillow. Alex slid under the sheets. She lay facing Dolly, petting the tuxedo cat's soft fur. She worried wouldn't be able to sleep with so many thoughts spinning in her head.

And she dozed right off.

Alex opened her eyes confused. Nothing looked right. "Abby's," she reminded herself. Waking in a new location after a deep sleep meant reality failed to match expectation. It took her a minute to remember why and how she'd gotten here. The bedroom door was ajar. Rubbing her eyes, she made her way to the kitchen.

Abby lay on the couch, petting Dolly. "You were tired."

"How long was I out?"

"It's after three... about six hours." She looked at Dolly. "Someone started banging the door." She looked at Alex, "I didn't want the ruckus to wake you, so I let her out. She's notified Marty and Quest she's in charge."

"That's impolite." Alex glared at Dolly.

Abby sat up. Dolly hopped down and walked the perimeter of the room. "If they didn't want her in charge, these two wouldn't have it." Abby's two gray cats sat like gargoyles on top of the fridge, their paws curved over the edge, their heads touching the ceiling, green eyes following Dolly.

"You hungry?"

Alex clutched her stomach. "Wow, am I starving."

"I'm not much for cooking," Abby warned. "It's just me. I've got sandwich fixings, or some frozen dinners."

"What would you eat?"

"Sandwiches it is." Abby stood, walked past Alex, and pulled a loaf of rye bread from the pantry. "P-B and J or sliced turkey?"

Alex remembered the thick-cut sandwiches she'd made for the hike. *Was that only yesterday?* "Turkey's great."

"Mayo or mustard?"

"Mustard, if it's spicy."

"We're going to get along great."

A short while later Abby presented her with two heaping portions of sliced turkey between two well-mustarded slices of rye. Abby placed four glasses on the table, filled the larger two with sparkling water, then added ice and a little bourbon to the tumblers.

"I'm not old enough to drink," Alex told Abby.

"What?"

"I'm eighteen. The drinking age is twenty-one."

"I didn't get that," Abby cupped her ear with her hand. "Maybe I can't hear you when you talk about these things."

Alex grinned. "Thank you for not clutching your head to get your point across."

"That'd be funny. Insensitive, but funny." Abby laughed. "I won't tell if you won't. After the day we've had, I think we deserve a little buzz—Not like that!" Abby shouted as Alex poured the beverage into her mouth. Alex choked, her eyes watering. When the coughing passed, Abby explained, "Small sips."

She had never drunk gasoline, but Alex figured it probably tasted like bourbon. She'd stick to water.

"How did you and Heather meet?" she asked when her sandwich was more than half consumed.

Abby's mouth was full. She started talking but stopped, motioning that Alex needed to wait. She washed the sandwich down with water before taking a large sip of bourbon.

"I was friends with Peter first."

Alex fell still.

"Peter, your father," Abby clarified.

Alex tried not to sound snotty, "I know who Peter is. I didn't know, I mean, I assumed you were friends with my Mom."

"I met Holly years later. You maybe thought we were friends because the Peter you knew wasn't much of a talker. Peter, Heather, and me went to school together, from kindergarten through high school."

"What was he like?"

"Your dad?" Abby grinned. "He was a jerk."

Alex wanted to ask so many questions. In her memory, her father shuffled around the house. He was not someone you could be friends with. He was almost a thing, like an ottoman that was often in the way but also needed feeding and cleaning. Abby knew him before that. "And Heather? What were they like?"

"Completely inseparable."

"Don't make me pull every detail out of you. I can finally hear you explain something."

Abby took a bite and washed it down. "At first, I didn't really know your father and your aunt. Not for years." She paused and gestured to herself, "I was built like this, even as a kid. My mom called me big-boned. Everyone else called me fat. She was right. I'm just thick." She guffawed.

"Well, I lived near your father. He was a tall, scrawny kid who hung out with the girls. He's where you get your height. The girls liked him. It was at that age when girls and boys weren't supposed to like each other. Our backyards touched. I walked home from school by myself. He and Heather walked together, sometimes just a few steps behind me. When we got to my street, I'd half-wave, and they'd half-wave." Abby demonstrated, barely raising her hand from her waist.

"One day in sixth grade, this boy started giving me shit. Robert Cerrillic." She sighed. "I don't remember what I did to provoke him. For weeks, he made fun of me: my weight, my face, my boobs. It was bad. One day, in the middle of class, I don't even remember what he said, he got me crying so badly I peed myself, right there in the classroom."

"That's horrible." Alex reached across the table to rest her hand on Abby's.

"No one was home to bring me a change of clothes. The nurse cleaned me up and sent me back to class, stinking of pee. Things were different then. Walking home, I didn't feel like waving, so I just went on my way." Abby stared into a middle distance. Alex read sadness and disappointment in Abby's expression as she critiqued her younger self, as though experiencing the emotions all over again.

Alex tried to remember what Abby looked like as a child, the kid in Heather's old photographs. This Abby seated before her would never cry because someone called her names. Alex felt she was losing part of the story. She wanted to understand Abby better, by imagining the hurt child rather than the strong adult. Maybe, seeing that version, she might know her father a little better too.

"I started down my block. Peter ran over to me, yelling. I thought he was coming to start with me too. I turned around and exploded, crying every profanity I knew and telling him to leave me alone. I blamed him for everything. Funny that I could confront Peter, who did nothing wrong, but to Bobby, I couldn't say a word.

"I remember like it was yesterday. Peter got into my face and just stood there, staring at me. I'm sure he smelled the pee, but he didn't let on. He said, *If you want him to stop, all you have to do is tell me.*" Abby smiled.

"I couldn't ask for help; that's what babies did. I think I feared he'd make fun of me. I mean, I felt nothing but self-pity and self-blame, so I told him I was fine." She held up her hands. "I mean, imagine me, stinking, miserable. Of course I was fine." She laughed and wiped an eye. "I went home and cried. I never told my parents what happened, but I'm sure my mother knew. I mean, my clothes stunk of piss in the hamper. Why she never thought to ask, I don't know. I think I was both relieved and hurt by her silence.

"The next day at recess, Bobby calls me names like *pee-pee girl.*" Abby laughed. "I mean, really? Looking back, I think, how could *pee-pee girl* make me cry? Some words can have a lot of power. Then Bobby started pushing me. I pushed back. Maybe he thought I was a weak girl, or that I was a fat, weak girl. But I was a fat, angry girl. I knocked Bobby right on his ass. I barely tried, but I decked him. I could tell I embarrassed him in front of everyone. He got up frothing at the mouth. I knew I was in for it.

"This whole crowd gathered. Kids from our grade, younger kids, even the older kids wanted to see. They were chanting and excited for a fight. Real *Lord of The Flies* playground stuff. It terrified me. He was going to embarrass me again. This time, in front of everyone. I mean, yesterday he made me pee with words. What would happen if he hit me? Then your dad caught my eye, hands in his pockets like he was just hanging out with nothing better to do. When he saw that I saw him, I nodded to him; I wanted Bobby to stop.

"Peter walked right up to Bobby, pulled him away from me. He said something to Bobby; I don't think anyone except Bobby heard. Then the two of them started shoving, sort of like you'd expect two boys to shove." Abby mimicked them fighting, "*Oh yeah? Yeah!*"

"Then it stopped. Bobby backed off. Peter said to him, and I'll never forget this, 'Abby and me are best friends. We walk home together every day. Don't make me remind you.'" Abby's eyes teared up. "He said it with such conviction that I believed it." She repeated the words with wonder. "*Abby and me are best friends.*"

"That worked?"

"Worked?" Abby laughed. "Two months later, Bobby asked me to the sixth-grade dance. We were friends throughout high school. We only lost touch after he went away to college."

Alex's chest swelled with pride.

"Nothing changed; I was still the fat girl," Abby mumbled. "But everything changed. I walked home *with* Peter and Heather. We were best friends."

"I can't believe you knew my dad. That's so cool."

"Years later, when Peter'd been married to Holly for, I don't know, at least a year, and Heather was dating Eric, I felt like I was losing them. That was when your aunt let me in on some things. And it was like we renewed our friendship. I was in their lives again."

Alex nodded. "You, coming to the house when I was a kid, was, like, my favorite thing. I couldn't wait to see Aunt Abby."

Abby blushed. "That's nice to hear."

"But then you stopped. I thought maybe I did something wrong."

Abby shook her head. "Not you. Never you, Alex. By the time you were born, your father, you know what he was like; he did something really brave. It took everything from him."

"Brave? Mom made it sound like one day he was and the next he wasn't."

"Your mom did her best. She couldn't tell you just like I can't. Sometimes she and I talked about it, but we saw what it did to you. You suffered for it." Abby shook her head, her voice cracking. "We'd try to find things for you to do, but you wanted to be wherever I was."

"That's why I had those headaches?" Alex said, "It was you all along?"

"I couldn't be around you because when Holly and I got together, we'd reminisce, and it hurt you. That's all Holly and I had to keep us together. I saw Heather, but she was having issues with Eric. That's when she inducted me into her Book Club. She wanted to keep me in her circle."

Alex laughed. "It sounds like it'll be cool and exotic, except then you say Book Club."

"When a bunch of women need to meet and don't want their husbands snooping around, no one questions Book Club."

Alex grinned, as though she were discovering a universal truth. "You're saying it's not really a Book Club?"

"It's not, Alex. And yet, that's exactly what it is."

Alex felt giddy. She'd learned something about her family she hadn't known before. It was as though a closet had opened and she'd found all her lost toys. She wanted more. Alex wanted to press until Abby said something she couldn't hear.

"What else?" She leaned forward. "You knew them. What were they like? What really happened?"

"I don't think I can say more. I'm sorry, Alex. Everything is interconnected. It'll set off your head."

Alex tried to dispel her frustration but wanted to learn more. "Can you tell me about, you know, yourself? What you do, you know, for work or fun? Tell me a little if, I mean, if you can."

Abby chuckled. "I was planning to show you after lunch. So you've seen my mansion," she joked with an exaggerated sweep of her arm. "For work and fun, I do the same thing. I'm an artisan. I pull glass and make necklaces and charms. My workshop is in the barn. The kiln should be rocket-hot by now. I want to make something for you."

Alex was touched and curious. There were many suppositions she made about Abby from her appearance, and none were correct. Abby looked like she'd be more comfortable behind the wheel of a truck than someone with an artistic soul. Alex remembered the Aunt Abby she knew as a kid. She now saw her through a different lens. *Is this part of growing up? Does adulthood cast a different light than childhood?*

Abby opened the barn doors. Two dozen bare bulbs hung from parallel black wires which were strung back and forth over the space. Large propane and oxygen tanks stood in a row, segregated from the rest of the equipment. A long, narrow bench, its thick wooden top burnished smooth, delineated the right side of the workspace. Archaic-looking tools were grouped in miniature half-barrels at one end. A collection of leather cloths and a stack of damp newspapers separated the tool buckets from a water-filled barrel, its glassy surface spinning dozens of drowned insects in lazy circles. To the left, hung a supply rack covered in plastic totes, which were filled with baubles and glass balls. In the center of it all, stood a large concrete block, radiating waves of heat. Two doors clasped one another on the front face of the block, bisected by a glowing seam. At the seam's center a small, round portal offered a view inside.

Alex felt the rush of heat from the kiln as Abby showed her the contents of several battered plastic totes. Some contained pieces of broken glass, separated by their multitudes of colors, but most contained small, shiny black beads.

"This is your cousin," Abby boasted, rattling a tote of beads. She withdrew it as Alex reached to touch them. "Please don't touch them," Abby begged. "No one touches them in this state, not even me."

"I'll bite," Alex replied, not taking offense. "How is that my cousin?"

"Rosemary," was Abby's reply as she replaced the cover and returned the tote to its shelf. "I have Heather right here," she tapped another tote. "Heather, the person, supplies me with herbs. Things she's grown and nurtured, so they're..." she struggled for the word, "special." She grabbed another tote. "This one's rose petals. I use the kiln to convert them to ash. It has to be crazy hot and happen really fast so the essential oils don't burn away. I roll them into clear glass, form tubes, and cut them into these beads."

Alex looked at the other totes. "How can you tell them apart?" Amidst the totes, a single jar propped carefully on a shelf caught Alex's eye. A solitary bead unlike any of the others sat inside; it was so black it almost looked like a hole.

Abby smirked. "My special labeling system." She pointed to a series of nondescript hashes in the corner of each tote. Taking a small scoop from the tool bucket, she narrated as she worked. "I gather some glass in the heat, and I use these tools to work it, pull a small piece off the mother and start adding to it. For you, I'm just adding beads, no color. I add a bead or two of various herbs. I have to get the glass molten first, see, look here—this is called the glory hole. Funny?"

Alex laughed at the name, but she was sure she was missing the joke.

"Supposedly, each herb has a purpose. Health. Strength. Protection. Once blended into the glass, they stay pure forever. Then I work the beads. Usually, I don't blend them or let them touch. I pull and twist everything together to make a design inside itself."

Abby heated the glass inside the kiln by twisting a large pole she called a *punty*. When it was good and hot, she placed the punty in a rest, glowing clear glass stuck like chewing gum to the end. She collected beads from random totes. Alex wasn't sure if she took any Rosemary or Heather. Using pliers to pinch and pull and wet newspaper to smooth, she worked in the beads before sending it briefly back into the kiln. When she opened the jar and used tongs to take out the solitary black bead. Before Alex could ask what that one was, Abby had worked it right into the small glowing lump.

"It's like honey," Abby said, concentrating. "If I don't keep it moving, it'll ooze off. Maybe fall on the floor and get contaminated, or everything will mix wrong and it'll be ruined." She sprinkled some water to cool the punty then worked with her tools, pinching, pulling, and smoothing. The wet newspaper flamed wherever it touched the molten glass. When the cooling glass became less workable, she returned it to the glory hole.

After considerable work, Abby announced she was done. She scored the glass just above its attachment to the punty, then with a drop of water, the seam broke apart. Gripping the disk in a large leather mitt, Abby held it out to Alex for a closer inspection. "Don't touch. It's still hot enough to burn off your skin. It'll take hours before it's cool."

"It's beautiful," Alex mused. It was silver-dollar sized, but it wasn't like she'd expected. A tiny sphere, obsidian black and round, marked the exact center. Ovals surrounding the center at various distances created an illusion of depth far greater than existed. From the right angle, the disk-shaped pendant looked spherical. It had such depth, Alex couldn't take her eyes off it until Abby rested it in the annealer to cool.

"I'm glad you like it," Abby smiled warmly. Although her bruises were yellowing and fading, the wide, genuine smile made her wince. "It's very special. Like you."

Chapter Thirteen

lex stirred in bed, awakened by daylight streaming through the windows. The small room glowed pleasantly, dreamily. She stretched, luxuriating in the restfulness of an undisturbed night's sleep; her first in weeks. Her hand clasped the warm glass charm which Abby had given to her just before bed, strung on a silver necklace as fine as a thread. When Alex was upright, it rested flat on her décolletage. There was an obvious front and back, the back slightly textured so it wouldn't slide with every movement. Just holding the charm, the glass disk that had already brought her recurring nightmare to an end, brought her comfort.

Abby was awake, her footfalls reverberated through the structure. Still, Alex had slept better than she could recall in weeks. With all she'd experienced, she wanted to believe it was the result of the charm. With Abby she felt safe, perpetually touching *base*.

Rising from bed, Alex looked at her form in the mirror, for the first time recognizing the features that differentiated Teenage Alex from Adult Alex. The past forty-eight hours were unlike any she'd experienced. Before her, the change was unmistakable. Her bruises, her raw skin was healing well. She felt transformed.

Once dressed, she stepped from the bedroom. Dolly trod up to her and rubbed against her ankles until Alex stroked her black back.

"Morning," Abby said from the kitchen table. She sat with a cup of black coffee and several pages of yesterday's paper strewn about her. Marty and Quest each sat in the center of their own page. "I could tell the moment you woke up. Very little dawdling," she joked. "Sleep well?"

Alex stretched again, touching the ceiling. "Yeah. Best night in weeks. You? Regret giving up your bedroom?"

Abby laughed. "Naw. It's all good. I slept great. In a coma. Cats walking on me didn't wake me until the sun came through the window." She slid from behind the table. "What can I get you for breakfast?"

"What you have?" Alex paused. "Any news?"

"I'm waiting for Heather's call." Abby made a face that seemed to say, *We can only wait.* She opened a cabinet. "Make yourself at home. Coffee. Cereal. Yogurt. Pans there." She pointed to the cabinet beside the range.

Alex opened the fridge. "Eggs?"

"Go for it," Abby replied.

"Can I make for you too?"

Abby thumbed her coffee mug. "If it's not too much to ask."

"Not at all." She stared at Abby for a moment longer than was perhaps polite, causing Abby to look down at her paper. What yesterday were swollen, dark bruises on Abby's face, today, were barely yellow smudges. Not even her lip showed signs of the previous day's trauma.

Alex's deep sleep had done a good job burying her memories, but in the morning light, she found they were quickly resurfacing. She tried not to think about them, but George and Matthew still skulked through her mind. She took a deep breath to blow the growing emotion away and replace it with concern for the twins. She wanted Heather to call and put an end to at least one unknown.

While Alex scrambled four eggs and made toast, Abby thumbed through the paper before having to negotiate with either Marty or Quest for the next section. The cats were obstinate. It was as though Marty was content with Real Estate but adverse to Styles. Quest was particularly fond of the Book Review.

As Alex served breakfast, the phone rang.

If Alex wanted convincing things weren't yet normal, their reaction was all the proof she'd have needed. They both jumped to the jarring music from Abby's cell.

Abby held the phone to her ear.

"Hi, Heather. We're fine, all good by us. How's Rose and Billy? Really? I see. Better than they thought? I wonder why?" She smiled softly at Alex. "It's Heather, obviously," she whispered. "Oh, that's great. Yeah. She's right here. I don't think you should go home yet." Abby paused. "Heather, Heather, Heather," she repeated until given a chance to speak. "I brought Alex to the house, yesterday." Heather said something at which Abby winced. "I know. It was stupid. We're okay, but Matthew was there." She paused. "No, we're fine. Alex is fine. The house took the brunt of it." She listened for a while. "No, Heather, you're right but it's done. I thought I was being smart. I'll be more careful." Abby was quiet, and apparently so was Heather. "Where will you stay in the meantime?" She made a face for Alex, as though sharing a joke. "Yeah? Marta's doing that for you? That's nice of her. Oh? Eric's going to take the kids? Is that a good idea, right now—not that it's my place to say. Okay. Yup. Okay." Abby looked at Alex and continued to nod. "Gotcha," she said at last. "Book Club. Tonight? Marta's coming here? Well, I could just... If Alex is here for a while, I want to make it feel like home for her. I know. Believe me, more than anyone else, I get it. We'll see. I'll do my best. I'm glad they're okay, Heather, and that you are too. We've been sick with worry." She looked at Alex. "Both of us. I'll have her ready. Love you too, Heather. Glad everyone is safe. No, she's no problem at all. I absolutely adore your niece. Yeah, well, yup. Bye."

Abby hung up the phone and ate a bite of egg. "These are good," she told Alex with a hint of surprise.

"I could figure out most of what Heather told you. But not all. No headache, though."

Abby took a sip of coffee. "Marta's coming later to pick us up. Book Club tonight. You're the guest of honor. You're finally gonna learn what's what."

"Marta's picking us up?"

Abby made a face that didn't match her tone, "Don't let the name fool you. Book Club can get wild. And this girl will be having something strong to drink tonight."

"I'm glad you're not driving then," Alex said glumly. The idea of spending time with Marta didn't thrill her. A half-hour at the hospital was more than sufficient.

The conversation stalled, and they finished eating in silence.

"Your charm works," Alex said after breakfast. "I didn't have my nightmare last night."

Abby's eyes traced Alex's face, eye to eye to mouth and back. "I like to think the charm will do more than look pretty, but it didn't stop your dream."

"Then why didn't I have it last night? First night in weeks, except..." Alex trailed off, realizing she hadn't slept the night before and so didn't have the dream then either.

"I don't want to get your hopes up, but tonight will enlighten you."

"Tell me about it, Abby." Alex proffered the charm. "Maybe with this you can?"

"It's not that kind of charm either," Abby replied, shaking her head. "It won't stop your headaches."

"Then what kind of charm is it? I mean aside from *pretty*?" Alex regretted her tone even before Abby winced.

"Tonight, Marta will take us to the meeting. You'll meet the whole Book Club. I bet every one of them will be there, eager to meet you. We'll go someplace sacred. What happens there should help some of this make sense." She sighed, "You'll meet everyone at Eric's house first. Dinner, I think. That way you can get to know them a little."

"I honestly don't remember meeting Eric."

"You haven't seen him since you were a baby. I don't think he visited after their marriage fell apart."

"Heather tells me a little, but she's cryptic."

"It's all related, Alex."

Alex put her hands on the edge of the table. "Tell me," she begged, pointing at the charm.

Abby made a face. "You, Marta, your aunt, are all—" and the squealing kept Alex from hearing anything else.

Once Abby finished, her face drawn into a caustic smile, Alex sighed. "It was different that time."

"It's not that kind of charm."

Chapter Fourteen

he waiting filled Alexandra with slightly less dread than the not knowing. Abby could say nothing to prepare her that wouldn't cause her pain, and her head had made clear it wasn't that kind of charm.

Abby drummed her fingers on the table, cognizant of Alex's anxiety. Then she perked up. "I know. Let's pull some glass."

"Okay."

"You don't sound interested."

"No, it's okay."

"Then it's settled, we'll wait here, bleeding out our eyeballs in boredom."

"I said it was okay," Alex said, exasperated.

"It's okay that it's only okay." Abby winked. "I thought maybe it would be fun. I figured I'd teach you to do it."

"Me? You mean…" Alex motioned like she was twisting a pipe with her hands.

"Yes," Abby said, "I'll teach you. You'll make something."

Alex realized how her earlier tone might have been mistaken. "Why didn't you say so?"

Her first effort at blowing glass was a disaster. Abby swore it was a valiant attempt, but the simple glass ball was a lopsided mess.

*   *   *   *

"You ready?" Abby closed up the barn.

"I guess," Alex replied. "I'd be readier if I knew what I needed to be ready for." Abby made a face and Alex answered, "I know."

"Marta will be here in…" Abby looked at her wrist like she wore a watch, "about an hour. Gives us time to sit and reflect."

Alex looked around the barn for a clock. She saw none.

Abby grabbed two old, green folding chairs leaning beside the barndoor. "I'll set these up."

"I'll do it," Alex took the chairs from her.

Abby nodded before disappearing into the trailer, leaving Alex to find a shady spot to sit. She re-emerged a minute later with two glasses of golden liquid. "See if you like beer."

Alex knew better than to argue. They sat, and Abby took several refreshed gulps. Alex slurped, mostly foam. It was noxiously bitter. "I'm supposed to like this?"

Abby laughed. "You don't have to. I'll get you something else."

"That's okay."

"You sure?"

Alex nodded. She sipped the cloudy, effervescing beverage, convinced she'd get used to it if she persevered. She couldn't imagine ever outright enjoying it.

"I like the face you make. Every time you sip." Abby mimicked her pinched expression.

Alex stuck out her tongue.

Abby sat back. "It's nice to end a day like this. Cold beer, sitting in the shade. The barn gets hot and I don't realize how tired concentration makes me." She took a deep breath and motioned to the view with her beer. "Corn makes a great neighbor."

Alex almost agreed out of politeness. The air smelled grassy. The corn stalks swayed, their large leaves rubbing, giving the breeze a voice.

As though sensing Alex's apprehension, Abby said, "Heather will be there. And you've already met Nancy and Marta at the hospital."

"They're all in the Book Club?"

"Counting me and Heather, there's eleven."

"That's all?" Knowing she wasn't meeting a crowd helped Alex's anxiety. She tried another sip. It was disgusting. She couldn't understand how Abby enjoyed something so gross. She twisted her glass into the grass. As soon as she sat back, she felt like she could relax.

"Thanks for today," Alex said after several silent minutes.

"My pleasure," Abby raised her beer.

The sense of peace and relaxation ended with a distant billowing of dirt. A car, speeding beside the cornfields, approached the barn.

"I guess that's Marta," Abby sighed. Then she looked at Alex. "I get it. Your cousins. Matthew. The headaches. This is the key that unlocks it for you. I've got your back. Nothing will happen to you so long as I'm alive."

Dust coated the copper-brown two-door convertible. It skidded to a stop in the gravel, generating a cloud of dust that rose away on the breeze. The windshield washers came on, grinding dust before spraying fluid made mud. The door opened, and Marta emerged in a huff.

She didn't look at all like the nurse Alex met at the hospital. Tall and thin, Alex was expecting. Marta wore makeup, mostly lipstick and eyeliner. Compared to the nurse Alex met, Marta looked pretty. Her latte skin glowed. Last Alex saw her, she wore loose-fitting scrubs. Now she wore black leggings and a fitted, sleeveless tunic. She looked posh, her left wrist wrapped in a clunky bracelet. Her hand hovered over the car door before her fingertips pushed it closed. She made a disgusted sound. "How am I going to get this clean?"

Alex started to rise but seeing Abby making herself more comfortable, stayed seated.

"Good to see you, Marta," Abby said, not hiding her sarcasm. "There's a garden hose and spigot just inside the barn if that'll do."

Alex looked at Abby, surprised by her tone.

Marta made a sour face but ignored the comment. "You ready to go?"

"Can three of us fit?" Alex asked.

"It's not like Abby can drive tonight with what's supposed to happen to her."

Alex panicked. "What's supposed to happen to her?"

Abby glared. Marta shrugged apologetically. "Let's go, kiddo," Abby said and stood.

"What aren't you telling me?" Abby made a face. "Unless someone can explain to me what's happening to Abby, I'm not going," Alex said.

Marta started to speak; Alex grit her teeth and held her head, groaning.

Marta looked at Abby for the first time. "Is she kidding?"

Abby shook her head.

Marta was quiet. Alex wasn't moving. Abby started for Marta's car.

Alex said to Abby, "You're not going to say anything?"

"I don't want to hurt you."

"Then I'm not going."

Marta held up her hands. "Whatever, kid. Heather sent me to pick you up. If that means Abby and I kidnap you, so be it."

Alex bristled; Marta's condescension annoyed her. At eighteen she saw herself on the cusp of adulthood, but around people even a few years her senior, she felt like a child. They never stopped reminding her, either.

Abby put her arm around her, "Get in the car, Alex. Please don't make this harder for me than it already is." Alex tried to argue but found she couldn't. Not with Abby. She walked to the car and climbed into the backseat. It barely functioned as a seat, and Alex sat across it.

Once everyone was settled, Marta turned the car around and headed out to the road. Abby twisted to face Alex and pretended nothing had happened. "Did you have fun today?"

Alex decided not to brood. "I did. That glass ball was disgusting. I hope we can do it again."

"You'll get better."

Alex leaned forward and touched Abby's face. "You don't have any bruising left. You must be a fast healer."

The car swerved. "Really," Marta snorted, "she has no clue?"

Abby shook her head. "Nope. She has no idea what's in store for her tonight. None of you do."

Chapter Fifteen

lex stared out the small side rear window as they snaked through residential streets lined with large houses set on sprawling, landscaped lots. Every house looked alike, a collection of randomly placed cubes providing a puzzle for the roof to solve. The lawns were all dark and green, striped and glossy, decorated with gardens and shrubs so neatly trimmed they looked like they might have stopped growing out of fear of retaliation.

"Heather's ex lives here?" It was much bigger than Heather's house.

"Personally, I don't get how Heather tolerates being around him and his *new family*. She needs to leave William and Rosemary with Eric tonight." Marta shook her head. "I mean, *come on*, she's Heather. Who leaves Heather?"

Alex stopped looking. She had greater thoughts on her mind. *What's coming? Not knowing is worse than knowing ever could be.* She could feel uncertainty creeping up on her like a cold, wet hand.

"Abby?"

"Yeah?"

"What should I expect?"

Abby shared a glance with Marta. "I wish I could tell you. Truth is, Alex, I don't know what you'll experience."

"You all talk like you do."

Marta said, "Heather knows. Maybe she—"

"She doesn't," Abby interrupted. "She knows what she was told. She knows what she has to do, not what will happen to Alex."

Marta stared at Abby. "Really? I thought Heather, you know, knows."

Abby replied, "She knows enough."

They pulled up to a house with stacked stone surrounding the door. A half-dozen cars shared the brick driveway which was still large enough for Marta to pull in. Alex recognized Heather's yellow car, out of place without the overgrown grass surrounding it. That car always looked just right in front of their house. It was so incongruous here, she could only imagine how impossible it would be for *her* to fit in. They got out, and as they approached, the imposing dark-red double front doors opened.

Rose ran out in jeans, an oversized white dress shirt, and bare feet. She gave Alex a suffocating hug. "Everyone's here," she said. "I can't wait for you to meet my dad. Can you believe he lives here?"

Alex held Rose, not ready to let her go. "Are you okay?"

Rose nodded. "I'm great. Really." Rose bounced; Alex could feel her excitement.

"I was so worried. No one can tell me anything."

Rose nodded as their embrace slipped. "Mom told me. I'm so sorry, Alex. I wanted to be there for you."

A man held the door open. Alex knew him from a photograph in Rose and Billy's bedroom—the only photograph of him in their house—in which they were still kids and he was secondary in the frame, like he had wandered into the picture just as it was being taken. His face was long and thin. A large mustache which was not in the photograph, tickled his pointed nose, curling over his upper lip, and a pile of shaggy brown hair capped his head, looking as though he had combed it with his fingers. Trim, but with a stomach like an inflated basketball, he was not at all who Alex would put with Heather. His facial features were strong and linear, giving him an air of authority. Seeing him now, Alex saw little bits of Billy and Rose.

"This is my dad," Rose beamed.

"You must be the infamous Alexandrea Hawthorne." He extended his hand. "Nice to meet you. Last time I saw you, you were still in diapers. I'm Eric, Rosemary and William's dad."

Alex shook his hand. "I'm glad diapers were the impression I left. I hope to do better." She watched his eyes sweep over her. She was a little taller, and he kept eyeing her feet, trying to see if her hiking boots had a heel.

Abby said hi as she walked into the house. Eric acknowledged Marta. He stepped inside ahead of her and closed the door after her.

Heather hurried to Alex, her eyes looking swollen and tired. "It's so good to see you, baby," she said, hugging Alex just a few seconds longer than Alex was expecting. "I'm so glad you're okay. You are okay? You weren't hurt?"

"No," Alex said, glad Heather asked. "It was scary, but I was fine. Abby, on the other hand…"

Heather saw Abby. "Thank you for keeping Alexandrea safe."

Abby nodded and gave Heather thumbs-up.

Alex worried about Abby. When they were together, Abby was a powerhouse of personality, her friend and protector, but here, amidst the crowd, she appeared cowed and out of place. Not one of the other women said a word to her. She slowly faded into the background, leaving Alex alone.

Billy hobbled over to Alex, balanced on a wooden crutch, and gave her a one-armed hug. "They said my leg and my arm both looked like I broke them weeks ago." He demonstrated by wiggling his leg. "This is just to take the weight off. Weird, right? Dunno when that happened. You know what? I wanted a cast, so everyone could sign." He scribbled in the air with his free hand. "The doctor said I didn't need one. Doesn't that suck?"

"I guess. Glad you're home. I haven't stopped worrying about you. I can't imagine how scary it all was."

He leaned close to Alex, almost touching shoulders, to have her ear. "I wasn't ever scared; you know why? Because after I jumped, when I was in darkness, I knew you were there." Then he seemed to shake off the thought. "You saved my life. I won't forget that."

Alex didn't know what to say. She didn't understand why he'd jumped. She wanted to ask. *Why, Billy? Why'd you do it?* Did he even know? His raving about coins, about fountains; she was surprised she could hear it. Alex wanted to believe there was a reason. She stammered, trying to find the appropriate words. "I, um, I'm glad you're out of the hospital. I'm so relieved you're okay."

Before either of them could say another word, Heather grabbed her. "There are some people I want you to meet. I mean, they want to meet you too. You are the guest of honor." She waved her words from the air as though they swarmed around her mouth. She led Alex, from room to room, person to person.

"Alex, this is Donna, she's our elder stateswoman of the group."

Donna was grandmotherly in appearance, somewhat stout. Her gray hair was curly and a little thin. "You're tall," she remarked, eyeballing Alex as they shook hands.

"I guess," Alex replied.

"You guess? Fact's a fact, young lady. You nervous about tonight?" Heather started to interject, warning Donna that she was about to hurt Alex's head, but Donna shrugged her off. "Ah, all I wanted to say is that my knees are shaking. To think, tonight I get to be a *real bitch*." She winked at Heather, who rolled her eyes.

Donna presented the woman at her side. "This is..." Alex clutched her head as Donna spoke. "What? What happened?"

Heather shouted to the group, "Ladies, it still affects Alex, even if you don't say it to her. Keep off-topic a little longer, okay?" She turned to Alex, "You okay?"

"I'm getting used to it."

"Anyhow," Donna continued as though nothing had happened, "we taught high school together until I retired last week."

Alex caught part of the name just as her head started hurting. Was it Linda or Lydia? She was embarrassed to ask and hoped the other would introduce herself.

Linda-or-Lydia stepped closer; hand extended. She appeared closer to Alex than Heather in age. Her straight brown hair was shoulder-length, cut neatly across the bangs, just above her eyebrows. She wore a pretty white sundress with the rattiest canvas sneakers Alex could recall ever seeing. They weren't dirty but polka-dotted with holes that showed her bare feet.

"Hey, Alex," Linda-or-Lydia's large brown eyes smiled. "Good to know ya." She looked to Donna and then Heather, perhaps uncertain what she could say, and as a result, she said nothing.

Heather brought her to another collection of women standing in a tight circle across the room. All three were drinking red wine from large, stemmed glasses, but one held her glass in one hand and the bottle in the other. "This is Colette, Betty, and June."

All at once, the three women turned to her. One was almost as tall as Alex, her skin luxuriously dark, her smile and eyes bright on her stunning face. She wore her hair pulled back into what looked like a round, curly crown at the crest of her scalp. She waved with her free hand. Her long, bright blue fingernails swirled hypnotically in the air. Alex could have just stared at her face, and might have, if a shorter woman with flaming red hair sprinkled with colorful plastic barrettes that looked like bows and butterflies didn't sing, "Hey."

"Hi," Alex replied, taking one extended hand as the other shook aggressively. Her t-shirt was white with black shoulders. Over her chest, was a cartoon image of a cat, its tongue out, paws up, with middle claws extended. Underneath it read, *Good Kitty*.

The third, older than the other two, passed the wine bottle to the first, saying, "Don't go far with that, Colette," so she could shake Alex's hand. She was a slender woman, not as tall as the first. Her shiny, black hair was pulled in a ponytail. Her features were fine, her dark, Asian eyes sparkled as she smiled. "Good to meet you, Alex, I'm June," she said sincerely. "I canceled a business trip to be here. I don't do that for anyone."

"Thanks." Alex was piecing together their names. This was June, Colette was the tall, elegant woman now holding the bottle, which left the red-haired to be... Alex had forgotten her name. Already. She leaned over to Heather, "I wish everyone wore name-tags."

"See," June pointed at Heather. "I told you. No one likes them but they change the world. Wars could be avoided. I make my team wear them at meetings. No sense making people guess."

"Excuse me." Heather stepped away, leaving Alex with the trio.

"Your team?"

June smiled. "Work nonsense. There isn't enough wine." She proffered her glass to Colette. "Don't let my glass get dry. Makes it harder to clean."

An arm slid over Alex's shoulder. She thought it was Heather, but when she looked up, she didn't recognize the woman. She had several piercings: eyebrow, nose, and lip. She grinned, wiggling a stud with her tongue. Alex hoped she wasn't using it to wave hello. "Good to see you again, Alex."

"Yeah," Alex said politely. *Who are you?* She smelled of cigarettes. Nothing struck a note, though.

"Heather asked me to finish showing you around. She had to attend to someone. Who's next? Who have you met already?"

Alex gulped. "Um," was all she said.

"I know," the woman shook her head. "I hate it when you meet a whole bunch of people at once and can't remember. At least we met the other day."

When did we meet?

"Nametags," June said, tapping her chest. "Save the world."

"I think," the woman said, looking at Colette, June, and the woman whose name escaped Alex, "that you still need to meet Carrie and Rachel."

"Could be," Alex said. "Those names sound new."

"*Could be*," the woman laughed. "I like you, kid."

Alex's head screamed. She clutched her temples. It only lasted a moment.

"Hey," the woman screamed, "cut the shit. Every time one of you does that, you hurt her. What's wrong with you?"

"Thanks," Alex whispered.

"Yeah, no worries," the woman said, playing with her lip ring again. "They mean well. They're excited and forget themselves." Her voice rose to make clear she wasn't speaking just to Alex. "It's a big day for everyone."

"That's what I keep hearing."

"This is Carrie," Alex's new escort said, pointing to a petite woman in dark jeans and a black tank top whose arms were covered in tattoos. Her near-black hair was short and spiky. She didn't look much older than Alex. "And this is Rachel." Rachel was Rose's height. Her face looked round. She wore a powder blue three-quarter-sleeve shirt with fine navy horizontal stripes. Red denim shorts, rolled at the hem, dug into her thighs.

"Hey there," Carrie said, extending a tattooed arm. Alex found herself caught by the designs. There were skulls and knives, but also skillets and realistic depictions of food. Here and there, she saw scripted words wrapped in winged hearts or made to look like they were written on parchment. "Excited to meetcha. You're so tall! I keep asking Heather to bring you to the restaurant, but you know how she is. She knows I won't charge her, so she doesn't come." Carrie rubbed her arm in a way that almost looked bashful.

"Nice to meet you, Carrie. You're Rachel?" Alex asked more because it seemed strange to tell her, excited to repeat their names. She was glad the woman whose name she didn't know was providing clear introductions.

"That's what my mom tells me," Rachel smiled. Her thick eyeliner made her brown eyes look feline.

Alex giggled at her joke.

"So," Carrie said, her face red and bashful despite how tough the tattoos and cropped dark hair made her look. "Tonight. Yeah. You."

Alex was starting to recognize what she was seeing: reverence. These women were all here to see her. It was downright bizarre. "Yeah, me," she replied. "No clue."

Carrie made a face. She looked at Rachel then back to Alex. "I'm here for you," Carrie said. "I don't know what that means or what I'm supposed to do; but know that. Tell me you need me and I'm there."

"Thanks," Alex replied. "I don't know what I'm supposed to do, either."

Rachel's face looked sad. "You don't know?"

Carrie motioned to Alex and said to Rachel, "Duh, you saw what happened when you started yapping before."

"I know," Rachel said. "But you don't know anything? Like you don't know that we're—" Alex's head exploded in pain. "I'm sorry. I'm sorry. I'm sorry," Rachel repeated, hesitant to touch her. "Oh, jeez, I'm so sorry. Please be okay."

Alex held up a hand, catching her breath. "It's been happening a lot lately. Abby tells me whatever we're doing tonight should make it stop."

"You will freak," Carrie enthused, "when you finally hear what's going on. Freaking freak out."

Alex looked at Carrie, at her tattoos. She was a handsome woman, more masculine than feminine, yet it suited her.

Carrie caught her staring, "What?"

Alex didn't know what to say. "I just like the, um," she pointed to Carrie's arms, "ink."

"Oh, cool." Carrie pointed to several pale lines on her forearms. "These," she said, "are kitchen tattoos. That means I burned myself. After a few of these I decided it was okay to get one not by accident. You know, something with meaning." She leaned in, "Only, I learned there's no such thing as getting just one. I'm sitting in the chair, it's not even done, and I'm already thinking about the next. Twenty-one tatts later, and I'm still craving the next one." She waved her hand over her torso. "So much empty space."

Alex's head buzzed again. Not as bad as before, but the sensation was like the floor had moved.

"That's awful," Rachel said at Alex's pained state. "I can't even make out what they're saying, and it bothers you?"

Carrie shouted for them to shut their traps.

Alex was a little nauseous.

"Alex?" Eric was across the room, dangling his keys. "Care to get some air? I'm running to grab pizza."

"Go," Carrie and Rachel said together. Carrie added, "Really great meeting ya." As Alex turned to Eric, she heard Carrie gushing to Rachel, "I like her. More than I thought. She seems cool."

Rachel replied, "Nothing's gone to her head, not even a little."

Alex followed Eric. She didn't see Abby anywhere. Everyone waved her off.

Eric waited by the door, car keys jingling in his hand when Alex joined him. "I'm not one for this sort of party. You?"

"It's overwhelming," Alex replied, "I don't think I've ever met so many people at once."

"Ready to go?"

The random bursts of headache were becoming more frequent. "I should tell Heather I'm leaving with you."

"Let me." Eric leaned into the living room and shouted, "I'll be back with the pizza in twenty. Alexandrea is coming with me."

Everyone waved again. Colette just wiggled her gigantic blue fingernails.

Alex followed Eric into the driveway. He groaned. "Looks like we're taking the minivan." He pointed to the blocked-in white convertible and made a pouty face.

There was a white minivan parked on the street. Eric held open the passenger door. The interior was a mess, especially the backseat. Colored O-shaped cereal was scattered about, a few pieces stuck to the seatbacks. A collection of toys littered the seats and the floor. Bunches of tiny men dressed in military regalia rested beside a pile of stuffed animals with gigantic heads. Lions and zebras and warthogs smiling through their fangs and tusks.

Eric pulled onto the street. After a few turns, he began to tap the steering wheel, humming a tune Alex didn't recognize. He paused and said, "Heather told me what you did. William could have died if it weren't for you."

Alex didn't respond. She didn't know how to react. Saying anything felt like bragging.

Eric's tone darkened. "The irony isn't lost on me."

This confused Alex. "What do you mean?"

Eric hit the steering wheel hard enough to startle her. "I know it's not your fault, and you probably don't even know. No, you don't. Heather would never say something like that."

"Like what?"

"Did she ever tell you you're the reason we aren't together?"

"Me?" Alex decided she wanted to be back at the party.

"I believe in you, Alexandrea, really, I do. What your parents did." He blew out of pursed lips. "It goes beyond what any human should be expected to do for their kid, and I'd die for mine. I think Heather and Peter had everything planned out before he met Holly. I mean, by the time I joined the picture it was already the expectation."

"Really?" This was more information than she'd gotten all night. "What do you mean? What was expected?"

"When I met Heather, she told me." He took a breath. "I know I can't say it, but let's just cut the shorthand and say I thought I was on board. I really, really thought I was. I was all, *Yeah, change the world.* I called myself a feminist. I got those things. Then, after what happened to your dad, it kinda hit me. You know, changing the world requires sacrifice. Until then, I thought I understood sacrifice, and Heather was counting on me. I realized it was sacrifice in the biblical way, you know, chained up to the mountain, eagle eating your guts." He looked at Alex. "I just couldn't. No reasonable person would."

Isn't that Greek mythology? "Eric, I have no idea what you're talking about." As much as she wanted to understand what happened to her father, she was as confused as ever.

"Look, if I don't tell you these things now, you might not think much of me when you figure them out. I don't want to be on your bad side when you do."

"If you say so."

He stared at her a moment, taking his eyes off the road. "Is it true? I mean, you can't hear it when people talk about magic?"

"Magic?" *Is he making fun of me?*

He tapped the steering wheel. "Maybe Heather..." he didn't finish his thought. "So, when your mom was preggers, like, I don't know, maybe two or four weeks after they did the deed, that's when it happened." He paused. "You can hear all this?"

Alex nodded. She was finally hearing something real. If he was telling the truth, that is.

"Well, your father, Peter, he does this thing. Same thing, I think, that you're doing tonight. Only he comes home and, well, you know your dad. He didn't leave that way."

Alex realized she wasn't breathing. "My dad? That was because of me?" Her stomach somersaulted. *Is this why Heather can't tell me? I'm going to become a zombie tonight?*

"I mean, not because of you." He hesitated. "No, I guess it was because of you. Not you, you know, you, the general thing, but not you, as in the specific thing, the baby." He looked at her. "I'm trying here."

He was making her head hurt... figuratively. "Okay."

"Well, Heather wanted me to do the same thing. In the beginning, I was like, 'Sure, whatever.' Then all of a sudden, it's a year or whatever later, she's preggers with William and Rosemary. It's real. I mean really real, and she wants me to do the thing. I mean, crazy, right?"

Is that why I'm doing this tonight? Because he didn't? "Do what, exactly?"

"You really don't know? I mean all this time no one's bothered to tell you?"

Alex shook her head. She resented Heather. In ten minutes, Eric told her more than she ever had.

"You're hearing all this, right?"

"No headache." She speculated, "I wonder if it's because you're, you know, a guy."

"A guy." Eric nodded. "Could be. Never thought about it that way, but it makes sense. You know, the whole emotional thing. They explained that to you at least, the emotional thing?"

Alex shook her head.

"Unbelievable," Eric shouted. "Here's the story as I know it. Your mom is preggers and your dad does this thing where he—"

Her head felt like someone was forcing it into a grinder. She dug her fingers into her scalp and groaned through the pain. It ended quickly.

"Holy shit," Eric said to her. "You really can't hear it?"

Alex was still catching her breath. "I guess not."

"Wait, wait," Eric said, "so he goes and—"

Alex groaned at the intensity of the torment. "Please, stop," she whimpered, unable to breathe.

"Unbelievable."

"I'd ask what," Alex panted, "but I don't want to feel that again."

"Is it worse each time?"

"No, maybe it depends what you're saying."

"When I talk about your folks it's worse?"

She speculated, "I think."

Eric drummed a beat on the steering wheel. "You know, I'd be lying if I told you I don't want to do it, just to see how it works. You know, like at the doctor. Better or worse when I say—"

"Please don't," Alex gasped. She regretted leaving the party.

"I won't," he said. "But right after that, you were—"

Alex clutched her head, retching.

"Okay, okay," Eric said, holding up his hands. "Don't puke. I won't do it again, I promise." He laughed. "I just had to see; it was just a joke. No harm intended."

Alex thanked him, even though she no longer trusted him. *This was who Heather married? She best never lecture me about my judgment.*

After several silent minutes, he said, "I didn't do what Heather wanted. She was pissed. She even tried it herself. She hurt herself and worse, hurt William. I mean, he wasn't even born yet and, well, whatever. It's in the past, right? She and I, Heather, we weren't ever the same. But then it got bad. She started with her conspiracy theories. All these crazy ideas about who was actually controlling the world. She believed there was this cabal hiding the truth. I just couldn't sit there and let her spout her crazy theories. She'd tell anyone who listened. And that was the logic behind what she wanted me to do. I thought she hated me because I failed her. It took me years to realize that it was never her doing the hating. I don't think Heather's capable of the emotion. I had all the hate. Enough for both of us."

Alex didn't speak. Listening to her uncle bare his soul to her made her uncomfortable. Was he saying Heather was crazy? Was he telling her—without telling her—that she needed to escape before Heather made her a zombie? *Whatever's coming tonight, it's not about me hearing words.*

Eric whispered this time. "You have a huge burden, all these women counting on you. I mean, wow. I thought I had it rough. Anyway, I also want you to know, according to Heather, I didn't do the right thing all those years ago. I won't let that happen again—if the opportunity arises, I'll be there for you."

Alex was relieved they pulled in front of a strip mall pizzeria.

Eric parked and opened his door. "Coming?"

"I'll wait," Alex said. Eric left the minivan running and walked away.

Alex rejoiced in the silence.

What did I get myself into? She looked around the parking lot. Part of her was expecting to see Matthew, with his crooked neck, lurking, staring back at her. Her head was spinning. Twenty minutes with Eric and he'd already poisoned her to Heather. She convinced herself that's what this was, that Heather could never harm her.

She spoke aloud, "I should have stayed home Saturday. I could have just holed up in my room with a book." She took a deep breath. "If I didn't go, would all this have happened, anyway? Would Matthew have found me, anyway? He was in the house Sunday, waiting for me and Abby. If I stayed home Saturday, would I still be here today?"

She saw Eric leave the pizzeria. While he was still too far to hear, Alex said, "I do not like you."

Eric returned to the minivan, placing the five large white boxes on her lap. He stared long enough to make Alex feel uncomfortable. "You remind me a little of each of your parents, like, if I squint one eye and then the other, I can see a little of each of them. The whole ride I've been thinking you sound a little like your father, but you've got your mom's eyes."

"I sound like my father?" She wasn't sure that was a compliment.

Thankfully, the ride back was silent. Apparently, Eric had said everything he needed to. Alex worried he'd start trying to see what set her headaches off again. She felt so vulnerable; he could harm her with a word. He was the first person she'd met who weaponized her pain. Deep inside, that terrified her. In the silence, she only had to worry about the hot pizza boxes burning her thighs.

Pulling onto his street, Eric reached out and rested his hand on the top pizza box. "This was, you know, between us. Heather doesn't need to know what I said to you, okay?"

"Sure," was all she replied. She wanted to be out of the car and anywhere he wasn't. She wanted to be wherever Abby was; touching *base*.

His hand lingered on the box. He wasn't even touching her, but it felt lecherous. It wasn't until they parked that he slid it off.

Donna was standing in the driveway, wine glass in hand, talking with the woman with the piercings, who was smoking a cigarette. The sunlight caught her metal hoops and balls and her face sparkled.

Donna looked up as they parked.

Eric started to say, "Lemme help," but Alex let herself out of the car.

"We've been looking for you," Donna scolded. "You should tell someone when you leave."

Alex couldn't help but make a face. "Eric told all of you."

Eric interjected. "Heather asked me to get her out of the house. How else were you gonna talk without hurting her?"

Alex felt betrayed. *It was a plan? What would he have done if I didn't want to go? And Heather? Heather sent me with him. How did Heather not know who he was?* He disgusted Alex. Mystery be damned, all she wanted was to go back to Abby's and lock herself in the bedroom.

The pierced woman threw her cigarette down in the driveway and stepped on it. "I'm starving. Let me help you get this." She took half the boxes and waited for someone to open the door for her. Eric picked up her cigarette butt and deposited it in the trashcan beside the garage door.

Inside, Abby took the rest of the boxes. "You good?" Abby asked like she could tell something was bothering her.

"I think so," Alex felt better as soon as Abby was at her side. "I'll be better when we're done here. I've never felt so uncomfortable."

"Tell me about it." When Alex didn't answer, Abby joked, "I should have worn one of my good muscle tees." Abby winked and Alex laughed. "I hate these *gatherings*," she said, sarcastic emphasis on the last word. "Everyone has such high expectations. Lest everyone forget why they're really here."

"I'm glad you're here, Abby," Alex said.

Abby gently punched Alex in her arm. "Then so am I, kiddo."

Alex looked over the group. She studied Abby and wondered how she must feel, ostracized by a group Alex thought she belonged to. Alex was thoroughly confused and more than a little unhappy with Heather. She didn't believe Eric, but he'd sown enough doubt. All she wanted was for this day to be over. She told Abby as much, adding, "What's stopping us from just going home?"

Abby looked at her. "Do you want to?"

Alex thought. "I kinda do."

Abby's face twisted. "I get that, I do, but," she struggled with the words, "you need to stay. This is important."

Alex replied, "If you say so."

"I do." Abby's face relaxed. "As long as you agree."

Chapter Sixteen

here were a few slices of pizza left when Eric's second wife, Jennifer, came home with their two children, five-year-old Hunter and Caitlyn who was seven. Seeing Jennifer beside Heather, Alex wondered if Eric had a type. They looked like cousins, Jennifer from the city, Heather from the country.

"Hi, Heather," Jennifer's tone lilted from the weight of her sympathy, "I am *so glad* Bill is okay. Rosy too. When I heard, the first thing I thought was what *we could do* to help you."

Heather smiled. "Thanks, Jenn. I appreciate being able to stay for a few days."

"Of course. Your house was *burglarized*," Jennifer made the last word sound extra-special.

"I appreciate it. A lot."

Jennifer looked around. "There's a lot of estrogen in the house tonight," she said to Eric. "How are you not twitching?"

Eric laughed it off. "Pizza?" He opened a box revealing two wilted slices, the cheese dull and unappetizing.

"Um-no," she said.

"We're going soon. Thanks for letting us use the house for this. Oh," Heather addressed both Eric and Jennifer, "and for taking care of Rose and Billy tonight."

Jennifer looked around again. "When Eric told me there'd be a party, I thought Bill's friends." She glared at Eric, who pretended not to notice. "You know, *get well?*"

He's not a Bill. Why do they call him that?

"It's not really a party," Eric explained before Heather kissed his cheek and said, "See you later." He looked to Jennifer. "It's a meeting."

"Right, *meeting*," Jennifer said. "Which one of you is the *dungeon master?*" When no one except her laughed, Jennifer urged Hunter and Caitlyn upstairs. "Bye Heather, see you," she said before she left the room.

"I'll be back later tonight or tomorrow. I'll try to be quiet," Heather said. "Thanks for everything."

Eric said, "No problem. Not after your house got broken into. I mean, they're my kids too, and you're their mother. Something happens to you, it affects them."

"Well, I appreciate it. I hope Jenn understands."

"Ah, you know," he smirked. "She understands. She doesn't want to get involved between us."

"I'd understand if she did."

"She's good like that. She's not someone who pretends there isn't history."

Heather smiled and touched Eric's arm. "I'll say goodbye to the kids." Alex followed her out of the kitchen. She couldn't wait to get out of here.

The other women filed out to their cars. Heather hugged Billy. "Don't give your dad any trouble."

"Nope," he replied.

Alex was behind Heather, who said to Rose, "Take care of your brother tonight."

"I will. Wish I was going."

"You're not?" Alex was shocked.

"Mom says I can't."

"She needs to rest. It's been a trying few days."

"I'd like if Rose was there."

Heather made the face that meant *don't argue.*

"Yeah, but—" Alex started to say.

"No but," Heather interrupted.

"Mom, I feel fine," Rose whined.

"You," Heather pointed at Alex, "stop being wise and go to the car. And you," she poked Rose in the arm, "stop arguing with me. You're not going. Don't make me say it again."

"Fine," they said in unison.

Alex hugged Rose and Billy goodbye. She found Abby by the front door. "Ready to go?" Abby asked

The question felt weighted with extra gravity. "Ready to go," Alex repeated. "It's time." She took a long breath, wondering why she still worried Eric was warning her. "I'm not gonna lie, I feel a little queasy."

Abby rubbed her arm. "You'll do fine, kiddo. Just listen and do whatever you're told."

"Okay," Alex replied reluctantly. *Abby would warn me if I might end up like my dad, right?* "Are you ready?"

Abby echoed Alex's weighted breath, "As ready as I'll ever be."

What's that supposed to mean? She asked Abby in a hushed voice, "It'll be okay, right?"

"It's going to be fine." Abby put an arm around her. "I've got your back, kiddo."

"I'd rather you didn't call me that."

"Really? What's wrong with kiddo? Why not, kiddo? Huh, kiddo?"

"It makes me feel like a kid."

Abby raised an eyebrow. "Somehow you're not? Since when?"

Alex found it hard to argue against this without proving it right. "All this," she waved her hand around, "makes me feel like I need to be more mature. How can I act like a grown-up when no one treats me like one?"

"Makes sense. Okay, boss. Whatever you say, boss."

Abby was making a joke, but Alex's sense of humor had abandoned her. She felt called out again for being a child. Abby intended it as a term of endearment. She hoped that after tonight, after whatever occurred, things would feel right. She was tired of the anxiety, the uncertainty. Except for the charm, nothing in the past few days had made her happy.

Alex changed the subject. "We riding with Marta or Heather?"

Abby grinned as they stepped outside. She motioned to Marta's car. Marta stood by the passenger-side door with the pierced woman, gesticulating in anger. The pierced woman was bent in half with laughter. Etched in the dirt on the window were the words, "I'm a dirrrty car."

"That you?"

Abby grinned. "No idea what you mean."

"Marta's pissed."

"If Nancy keeps laughing, Marta will lighten up."

Nancy, Alex realized, that's who the pierced woman is. *I met her Saturday night at the hospital: the woman in yellow scrubs who took care of Billy.* She couldn't believe she hadn't connected it before. Abby was right. After a minute, Marta laughed. When she saw them, she gave Abby the finger.

Heather walked to her yellow car and waved them over.

Abby let Alex take the front seat. Heather pulled out of the driveway and joined the convoy.

"I'm glad that's over," Heather groaned. "I ha-ate that."

"Why do it?" Abby asked. "Why not just meet everyone at the site?"

"It was Donna's idea. She thought, you know, get everyone together, have a bite, and get lubricated. You know, break the tension and go over the plan one last time." Heather thought a moment. "Who brought the wine? I should thank them."

"I think it was Eric's."

"Oh dear," Heather giggled. "Jenn's going to be pissed. Did we leave any?"

"I wasn't drinking. I don't have the stomach for it tonight."

Heather looked into the rearview at Abby. "It's going to be okay."

"You asking or telling?"

Heather made a face. "I don't know."

Abby sighed. "It will be okay, whether it's okay or it's not."

Alex sat and listened.

Heather turned to Alex. "How are you? Where's your head?"

"I just want this to be over. I'm not having fun today."

Heather bit her lower lip. "Everyone was giddy to meet you. Were they too enthusiastic?" When Alex said nothing, she pushed, "Tell me, Alex. What happened?"

"Why did you send me with Eric?"

"So we could talk without hurting you. There's a lot at stake tonight, hun. I needed to go over things."

"But why him? Why not Abby? Why not make me wait outside?"

Heather and Abby spoke over one another. One said, "What happened?" The other, "What'd he do?"

She feared they'd disagree with her. "He's a creep. He started telling me things about you, Heather. Like, why you broke up."

"What did he say?" Heather's voice was cold.

"You hurt Billy. He said it was my fault."

Heather hit the steering wheel. "What else did the idiot say?"

Alex was slow to reply, "He realized he could hurt me by saying things. He said it was a joke, but he kept doing it."

Abby growled from the backseat, "When we get back, I'm going to—"

Heather interrupted, "You won't do anything, Abby. It's complicated."

"He's an asshole," Alex muttered.

"Don't say that again, Alex," Heather chided.

"Why'd you ever marry him?"

"Alex, I don't expect you to understand." She took a breath, recomposing herself. "He can be a jerk. He thinks he's being funny or charming. He wasn't trying to hurt you. He's just," she hesitated, "afraid of you."

"What does he have to be afraid of?"

Behind her, Abby cackled.

"It's not you, exactly," Heather explained. "It's Matthew." Heather patted Alex's thigh. "Sit tight, Alex. Tomorrow morning, you'll know everything. It will be a brand-new day."

Alex couldn't wait for that brand-new day to hurry up and get here.

Chapter Seventeen

lex felt her heart thumping rapidly in her stomach and down into her fingers and toes. So many somethings, so many unknowns, all culminating, all converging wherever Heather was taking her. *Maybe I should be happy. Maybe.* She wanted to feel brave, to find faith in her aunt, and in Abby, and in their Book Club, but Alex realized there was no base big enough right now. *Am I going to wind up like my dad?*

The setting sun strobed through the trees as the convoy turned onto the side roads nearing home. A few more turns and the cars ahead began to slow. One at a time, they turned onto a makeshift path through the dense woods. Her stomach reeled with the recognition. This was the route Abby had taken three nights ago, driving them away from the Old Witch's Shack.

Why come back here? Alex couldn't help but think about dragging Billy through the woods, her body in a state of complete and utter exhaustion, with Matthew giving chase.

The cars parked beside one another in a clearing.

"We're here," Heather unlocked the doors. Abby and Alex stood together as the others gathered.

Abby put an arm around Alex. She felt like Abby was sheltering her. She hoped Abby would say something but had to break the silence herself to fish reassurance from the woman, "You nervous?"

"A bit. Except it's so important. Remember, do whatever Heather says."

"Are you expecting something to happen?"

"I hope so. Your head should stop hurting."

Donna, the older woman, opened her trunk and pulled out a huge stainless-steel stockpot. It was larger than anything Heather owned. "Is this big enough?"

"When I said big, I meant like six quarts," Heather said.

Donna scowled. "Then say six quarts. You're not going to ruin it? I was hoping to return it."

Heather opened her trunk. "I hope not," she said under her breath. Bow-tied bundles of herbs and flowers lay on an old red and white geometric quilt. Heather grew the plants in her garden and tied them with bows to give as gifts. These herbs, however, were unfamiliar to Alex. They were not gift-worthy; they looked gnarled and brittle, dry and dusty. Even alive, they must have been ugly plants.

Linda-or-Lydia took the bundles and smiled at Alex. "I bet you're excited. I know I would be."

Alex smiled back. Linda-or-Lydia followed Donna, Nancy, and Marta as they walked, excitedly chatting, into the clearing where the old foundation rotted. Carrie, the tattooed chef, managed several reusable shopping bags, bursting with supplies.

Betty, her red hair looking bloody in the evening light, came to Heather and Alex. "You need me to carry anything?" After a pause, she asked, "Can I see the Book?"

Heather glared at her. Alex shrugged. Heather said, "Betty, stop talking about these things until she can hear them."

"I didn't think it was such a big deal," Betty said defensively.

"I'm sorry," Heather said to Alex. Then turning to Betty, "We just went over this. I don't have it yet." Betty backed away and followed the others.

Soon, only Abby, Heather, and Alex remained near the cars. The others gathered at the foot of the foundation.

Heather took Alex's hands. "This is probably... no, this *will* seem silly at first. Please," she said, her voice modeled sincerity, "please play along, no matter what you think."

"Um, okay."

"There will be some theater tonight. They need it to for the spirit of the event." Heather began petting Alex's hands. "No matter what happens, no matter what you see, please do what you're told. We won't get a second chance at this. Okay?"

Alex nodded. "Okay."

"And if, in the beginning, something we say makes your head hurt, I'm sorry. If I knew another way, or could guarantee this wouldn't hurt your head, I'd do it. Okay?"

Alex nodded.

Heather shared a serious look with Abby, each silently communicating their concern.

Abby took Alex's hand and forced a smile. Heather took the quilt into her arms, and the three walked to the clearing.

The ground was still rutted by Abby's truck. The churned-up grass made Alex's stomach wiggle. She could almost see Abby's truck pulling up to the foundation as it had that night. It wasn't long enough ago.

Six shopping bags sat in a line against the stony heap.

"Who could have done this?" Marta said to Heather, hands pinwheeling. "Tire tracks everywhere. Is nothing sacred?"

Under her breath, Abby repeated, "She doesn't know. She doesn't know."

Flames leapt into the air from atop the foundation. *Is it on fire?* Donna cursed. Her pot sat amidst the fire, resting in the circular pit Alex assumed was in the kitchen. *I knew it was the kitchen!*

The other women joined them, leaving the pot.

Heavy with anticipation, Alex found it hard to breathe.

"I can't believe we're doing this; we finally get to be—" Alex clutched her head for a moment.

"Jeez, Rachel," Carrie shouted, "you've got to be kidding me. How many times does Heather have to say it?"

"I'm sorry," Rachel apologized. "I'm just so fricking excited."

"It won't be long," Heather said to them, patting Alex's shoulder. "We've been planning and discussing tonight for years. It's time." She said, in her authoritative voice, "You all know what to do. Let's get started."

A random chorus fell short of a cheer.

"Okay," Colette said, "what's first?"

Heather rolled her eyes. "The first thing," she said in a near whisper, as though not wanting her voice to carry to the trees, "is to help Alexandrea to relax."

"Shouldn't we, you know," Abby whispered, "*theater?*"

Marta huffed, "Heather knows what she's doing."

Donna pulled her shirt, "Marta, we're not even dressed properly."

Heather held her palms out, "Donna's right. Alex is *vulnerable*. What was I thinking? Donna, please get the salt."

Donna rooted through one of the shopping bags. "What the hell is this?" She offered the jar for everyone to see. "Truffled sea salt? Will that work?"

Nancy blushed. "I food shopped for myself too. These bags are mine," she pointed at the first two. "Those others are for tonight."

"Sorry," Carrie apologized, "I grabbed everything in your trunk." She gestured to the jar in Donna's hand. "That's an excellent brand."

"Really? I bought the middle-priced one."

"Yeah," Carrie explained, "The truffle is really pronounced—"

"Ladies," Heather pleaded, "can we focus?"

Nancy pulled two red and white boxes from one bag. "There's eight more."

Donna discarded the fancy salt in a bag and grabbed two boxes. "Heather, is there any issue if the salt's Kosher?"

"It never came up. Peter only ever said salt. What difference could it make? Salt's salt, right?"

Peter? What's my father got to do with this?

"I think Kosher salt gets some prayer or something by a rabbi," Marta offered.

Donna's arms fell to her sides. "More male prayers ruining sacred things."

"I think it's more a style," Carrie explained. "It says *Kosher*, but I think it should say *koshering*, for making food *Kosher*. I use it all the time in the restaurant. It's less salty."

Marta looked surprised. "Salt that's less salty than salt? How is that even possible?"

Heather interrupted. "Focus people." Then she took Alex's hands and led her forward. Alex followed until they stood about ten feet from what Alex believed was the front of the foundation. Heather surveyed the spot as if to be certain it was correct, then she let go of Alex's hands. "Stand here. Don't move." She whispered. "Theater."

"'Kay." Alex made a face at Abby that said things were getting silly.

Abby mouthed, "Wait."

Heather addressed the group, pointing to spots on the ground. "We need to make three rings around Alex." Then quietly to herself,

"What did Peter say, six inches?" She continued, working it out aloud, "The first goes here, around Alex's feet. The other two, there and there. Pour a solid line. No gaps or breaks."

Marta took the first box and opened one end. She poured a thick line encircling Alex.

Donna pointed at the circle, "That's too thick."

"It's how fast it pours," Marta replied.

"We're going to run out if everyone pours like that."

Marta stopped pouring and held out the box. "You do it."

"Ladies!" Heather stood between them. "Is this how we're going about this?"

"Someone's always got to criticize," Marta complained.

"I wasn't criticizing," Donna defended. "I was pointing out a fact."

"Enough," Heather shouted. "You're worse than my twins. Pour the salt, no gaps, don't run out."

Donna started pouring the second circle and Carrie the third, following just behind her.

Colette pointed, "Um, there's a gap, she'll be in danger."

Donna sprinkled a little salt to fill the gap. "The ground's not even. Whoever drove here…"

Donna's box emptied halfway through her second circle. Betty, who was working in the opposite direction, completed it. June and Nancy finished the third.

They all seemed so serious, Alex wondered if Heather maybe lied to ease her nerves.

This must be the silly thing Heather mentioned.

"Good." Heather spoke once the salt rings were complete. "Where's our victim?"

"That'd be me," Abby cheerfully raised a hand.

Alex's heart dropped. "Victim?"

"It's an, um, expression," Heather chose her words carefully.

It didn't feel right to Alex. She worried she was spending her last conscious moments surrounded by salt. "Use better expressions."

Heather sighed. "I'm doing it how I was taught. Peter said that's how it works."

Is Heather gaslighting me?

Heather handed Abby the quilt. Abby rolled it up and placed it under her head as she lay down, between Alex and the foundation.

"Is this right, Abby?" Heather asked.

"Looks good. It's been a while."

Been a while? They've done this before?

Marta poured a ring of salt around Abby.

Nancy, pouring the salt about ten feet away from Alex, called to Heather, "We should have enough for the last ring. Is it a problem if we go a little thin?"

"I told you we were going too thick," Donna muttered.

Heather shrugged. "We use the truffle salt?" She looked around. "Just make sure it's not broken." Then she turned to Donna, "Could you add the liquid to the pot?"

Alex was glad Heather was sending Donna away. *She's getting on everyone's nerves.*

Donna rubbed her hands together. "Sure. Where is it?"

"The soda bottle," Nancy pointed at the last bag on the right.

Donna held up the two-liter bottle. She shook it, watching the dark liquid swooshing inside. "You sure it's not soda?"

"I don't drink soda," Nancy said. "I made it last night, exactly to Heather's instruction."

"Hold it up to the light," Heather explained. "If it's dark purple, it's not soda."

Donna held the bottle up to the setting sun, squinting into the bottle. It cast a purple shadow across her face.

"Donna," June said, "it's not soda."

Donna started for the fire, muttering. "I don't know why I'm doing the cooking. We have a chef."

Heather called after her. "The herbs should be ash first." She made a twisting motion with her hands, "Mash them up good. No chunks or bits. Everything has to dissolve." She turned to Alex. "How you holding up?"

Alex looked at the salt circles. "Wishing I didn't think this was so ridiculous."

"The salt provides protection," Heather explained. "Three circles just for you. One for Abby. Then one for all of us."

"Protection against what?" Alex asked. "Slugs?"

"Just put up with us a little longer." Heather looked around. "Where's Marta?"

"She left something in her car," Carrie replied.

Marta came running with a large, green duffle bag. "I borrowed it from the hospital."

"You took a responder bag?" Nancy asked.

"I wanted to be prepared."

"I don't think we'll need that." Abby looked to Heather, "You don't think we will, do you?"

Heather shrugged, "You tell me."

"What's that for?" Alex pointed. "Heather?" *What if Eric was telling the truth and Heather's crazy?*

Heather pointed at her own head. "Soon," she told Alex. Then she addressed Donna, "Is it boiling?"

"Just started forming bubbles," Donna shouted back from the fire.

Heather looked deep in thought. "That's good enough. It'll ruin if it burns. It's ready; bring it over. Carrie, help Donna with the fire. We shouldn't leave it burning."

Carrie hopped onto the foundation. Using potholders, Donna raised the pot off the flames. Carrie collapsed the fire with a large stick. The fire grew then died away. From where she stood, Alex could only see churning smoke. Donna returned, walking carefully with the pot.

Alex peeked into the top of the steaming vessel and saw a thick, purple fluid cooling from a boil.

Setting the pot on the ground, Donna wiped fruitlessly at the black scorches on the outside of her pot. She groaned, looking at the filthy potholder.

"It needs to cool," Heather told the others. "We're almost ready. We should get dressed."

"Oh," Lydia-or-Linda said, "I left them in the car. Be right back." She returned a minute later and handed each woman a black cloak.

Donna held hers up and grinned. Several others stared and marveled at them. Carrie and Rachel bumped their fists in excitement. They began slipping them on over their heads. Heather handed one to Alex. "Here's yours."

Alex looked at it. She couldn't understand the excitement. "Is this a graduation gown?"

Donna, who was taking her pants off under the long gown said, "It's easier than making our own. I got our first batch years ago when I was still teaching. These are new. Lydia ordered a few extra for graduation. Thankfully, the school colors are black and white."

"Yeah, this is so much better," Alex said under her breath. In her head, she repeated, *Lydia, Lydia, Lydia.*

Lydia was folding her sundress. "Yeah, tonight is important. We should have new ones."

Heather started undressing under her gown. "You should take off your clothes too," she said to Alex. "Leave nothing on under the robe."

Alex was about to argue, feeling a little weirded by the whole experience, but Heather interrupted her. "This is one of those things I said would seem silly."

Loud enough for Heather to hear, Alex said, "You think this seems silly? The salt seemed silly. This I don't have words for."

Heather gave her a look. The look.

"Okay, okay," Alex said. "Fine. I'll wear the graduation gown. Just tell me why I have to take off my clothes."

Donna stepped closer; Alex tried to not stare at the large tan panties resting on the pile of clothes in her arms. "It's tradition."

"Please, Alexandrea," Heather begged. "Just pretend we're nuts and play along."

"No pretending necessary, Heather. Why do I have to get undressed?"

Heather carefully stepped into the salt circles and whispered to Alex. "Because I'm asking you to. Because I can't tell you why. Because you need to. Because I won't ever ask you to do anything like this again."

Alex squinted at her.

"I swear," Heather replied. "Because if this doesn't work, I have nothing else."

Reluctantly, Alex undressed under her robe, throwing her clothes to the ground. The whole time, she cursed under her breath.

Once they were all wearing their robes, their clothes folded to the side, Heather scooped the thick purple liquid into a red Solo cup. It was dark and stringy.

Alex curled her lip. "I am not drinking that."

Abby sat up on one arm. "That's for me." She toasted Alex before tipped the cup back, gulping between thick slurps. She upended the cup as the stringy liquid slowly glopped out. "Hasn't improved any, Heather," she said, finishing it to the last. "You should work on the flavor."

"Who knows what it would do if I changed the recipe?" Heather replied. "Oh, that was a joke," she added. "I'll save the rest for you to use in a charm or something." It sounded like a question.

Abby put the cup down. "I wouldn't make this crap into a charm." She looked at Alex. "You still wearing yours?"

"Should I have taken that off too?"

"No," Heather blurted, as though dropping something. "You should always wear Abby's charm." She returned her attention to the group, signaling the women closer. "There are nine of you, so we need to make three groups of three surrounding Alexandrea."

"What about you?" June asked.

Heather thought. "I need my hands free. Besides, ten doesn't work."

The women spent the next minute or so organizing themselves into groups. It looked like an impromptu square dance, groups of twos and threes joining and parting in turn.

"What is taking so long?" Heather scowled. "A third of you are teachers!" She then directed the stragglers, giving them places to stand within the final salt ring until six women stood with their backs to Alex, the remaining three facing her and Heather, forming three triangles around them.

"Okay," Heather sighed. "Now what?"

Abby belched. "Ug," she groaned. "That might have tasted better coming up." She motioned with her hand, making circles in the air. All she said was, "Alex... relax."

"Why do you keep asking Abby?" Nancy called from where she stood. "Why would she know anything?"

"It's not like I have a manual," Heather replied. "I know we've been planning this for years, but it's a lot of pressure to get it right."

Alex pulled the hem of her robe tight around her ankles. "Cold," she said to Carrie, who gave her a quizzical look. "I'm getting a draft." Carrie pantomimed that she was cold too.

"Okay, remember we discussed how to do this?" Heather didn't wait for anyone to answer. "Any one of us is too weak to, um," she turned to Alex during her pause, "to do this. All of us working together should... be able to."

The other women nodded.

A second and third star glimmered in the darkening sky. It would be twilight for only a little longer. Alex tried to stay focused, but the dark revived disquieting memories.

"Like this?" June reached out to the two other women in her triangle. Each group of three clasped hands.

"Yes, exactly like that," Heather said. "You must keep Alexandrea foremost in your minds. Always think of her. Relaxing thoughts. Just like we practiced."

"How do we know we're getting it right?" Donna asked. "You said it was too dangerous to try until tonight."

"As soon as we start, we'll know. He'll know too," Heather warned.

They were all watching Heather. "Let's begin."

They began murmuring to themselves. At first, Alex couldn't discern any individual voice; they all overlapped, but she found she could focus on Donna's voice. As the eldest, her voice was raspier, a little lower in pitch, and louder.

Slowly, gradually, they fell into a cadence, their words becoming melodic and dancing with one another. As one would speak, another would drop off. Nancy, then Betty, then Carrie, then Rachel, Donna, June...

"...that feeling I get lying in bed, falling asleep when the bed falls away... lying in a warm bath, my head on a soft pillow, my body so warm... at the beach, floating in the ocean, feeling the waves carry me up and over the swells..."

Alex shook her head in exasperation. "This is bullshit."

"...when all the noise and disruption of the day ends, and my body unwinds... that first night after a trip, getting into my bed..."

Alex's fingers began to tingle. She shook them. Had she been standing still for too long? Her toes followed. Then her ears. It wasn't the pins and needles of a limb going numb, yet it was just like that. The sensation got stronger and then dissipated, washed away by a small wave of calm. Then another and another. Calm rolled through her body, each wave taking with it some tension, some stress. She could feel muscles in her back release, unclenching one at a time. She closed her eyes and took a deep breath. The waves took longer to wash over. *I was thinking something, wasn't I? Was it something about the woods?*

"...at the end of the night, the kitchen's all cleaned up, and the last customers leave... that sound my son makes when he's sleeping, his little snore..."

She opened her eyes and saw the nine robed women around her. Something wasn't right. She was seeing, hearing, but it felt alien; she didn't know what to make of it. Surrounding her, they held hands. There was Heather. There was Abby, holding her stomach, bent in half. *What is Abby doing? Should she be like that?*

Something seemed to distract the group; they all turned to look.

"That's supposed to happen," Heather said. "Keep going."

Heather's voice sounds so weird. So calm. When is Heather ever calm?

"Heather, I don't feel good." It was Abby. Her mouth opened and closed, gulping air, and her eyes widened and shut tight. "I don't remember it being this bad." She said other things too, but Alex had trouble registering them. Abby dug at the ground, touched her throat. *What is she trying to do?*

The women didn't stop, but their words were different now. "...that feeling when the kids are home and all the doors are locked tight... when I take out the trash at night and run back to the house, closing the door behind me... when I am in a warm bed, the covers up to my neck, and the house is quiet..."

What are they talking about?

Abby wheezed. Alex had a thought, a momentary flash, but it was gone before she could understand it. She couldn't discern what Abby's movements meant, what her expression meant, certainly not what to do about it.

Abby's skin and lips turned blue. *Why blue?* Abby made one violent thrash and was still. A small spot on her throat was the only part of her that still moved. It moved, was still; it moved, was still... Alex watched. Then it didn't move again.

Chapter Eighteen

bby looks so strange. Alex didn't know why she thought this should upset her, but she remained indifferent. Daylight vanished, and stars filled the black sky. There were so many. They were so beautiful, single sparkling dots and swirls that looked like smears across a dark, overturned bowl. So far out of reach. A giant silver disk Alex thought she recognized. "Moon," she said aloud, not knowing what the word meant; she just found it there, in her mouth. She felt like saying it and enjoyed the way it felt leaving her mouth. "Moooon," she said again.

All these shimmers gave the strangest, most unusual quality of illumination to the clearing. The light was so diffuse, so dim, muting the colors around her. *Moon stole the color?* "Give it back, moon," she said. "Mooooon."

When Abby scrambled to her feet, her face pale, Alex could hear the other women say a word. Several of them made a loud word with their mouths. A second moon glowed in Abby's chest. From that bright spot, a slender silver thread—a glowing, sparkling string—descended to the ground. Abby was there too! On the ground and standing above herself; two Abbys! Abby was not as nice a word to say, so although she looked at Abby and she called to her, what she said was, "Moon?"

The woods around them vanished. *Moon stole them too?* Fog rolled in but waited just outside the clearing. The moon wouldn't allow it to get any closer. "Moon," she said, nodding her head respectfully.

The moon in Upright-Abby's chest burned bright. Alex called to it; she sang to it.

Upright-Abby shuffled away from Lying-Down-Abby, the slender thread of light growing between them. It never stretched or became taught; it just hung upon the air. It appeared to be a composite of radiating waves, pulsing and interwoven. It sparkled and crackled, appearing almost as a moving afterimage, a temporary burning in the eye.

Alex saw the other women, their hands still clasped, each had a moon in their chest. *So many moons!* She looked at her own chest. *No moon.* She fingered the neck of her gown, hoping to discover her moon hidden beneath. Under her gown, she was naked. The air was cold. On the center of her chest, below Abby's charm, she saw a dark circle where everyone else had their moon. This void was so dark, so perfectly absent, she expected her poking finger would pass through, but she only felt her skin. She couldn't touch her dark moon, couldn't stick her finger in and discover what was there. She felt... disappointed.

Unconcerned by the women and their odd words, Alex watched them release hands and look to Heather, into whose palms Upright-Abby placed a book.

Where book come from?

Having delivered the relic, Upright-Abby shuffled back to her corpse and lay down, two becoming one. Only the moon with no thread remained.

The women spoke, their voices calm and unemotional, to Alex at least.

Donna spoke first, "What is that? That better not be what I think it is."

Alex looked at the book. It was thick, over an inch, and it was large; ungainly for Heather to hold open.

"Don't open that," Yellow Scrubs said. *Nancy.*

"This is my brother's Book," Heather explained. "He left it here for this."

"Left it here?" Donna said. "We do not use books."

Since when are books bad? Alex wondered. "Why you mad at book?" Her lips made no sound.

June backed away from the group. "You never told me we would use that... thing. That's not just some book, it's a life. It's the heart of a woman, a sister, and some man tore it out. All this time, all this talk about what's happened to women like us and you do this? I can't be part of it."

"This Book is the only way we save her."

"Then why not tell us?" Donna demanded. "In all these years, planning and preparing? You knew we wouldn't help you if we knew."

"June," Heather called, "don't step outside the circle. There's nothing to protect you if you do."

Alex watched. She understood their words. Each word was calm and metered. *Are they speaking like this or am I hearing them like this?* She decided she didn't care.

June paused at the edge of the last ring of salt. She considered the unbroken white line, then raised her head to shake it at Heather. "You tricked me. You tricked all of us. I expected more from you."

Nancy stared at Abby. "Not to interrupt; is she dead?"

"It's part of the ceremony," Heather said. "That's what Peter told me. She'll be fine, like before."

"What if Peter tricked you?" Colette's eyes filled with tears. "Then we killed her. Oh man, you ruined our lives. She's dead."

"Stop it. All of you," Heather said. *Is she shouting?* It sounded almost like Heather was shouting. "Each and every one of you knew this was dangerous. Abby too. She knew. The only one here who didn't know is right there." she pointed at Alex. "The moment Abby brought the Book to me, the moment we cast this spell, he knew too. He still can't find her." She pointed again. "He's not stupid. He knows why we have the Book. If we don't finish, he'll come; he'll find us. He'll find her. Who of you is strong enough to protect her? Or us? What do you think happens then?"

Donna slapped her sides. "Great. Great. What've you done? How do you know you can trust your brother? That was his," she pointed at the Book. "That was his."

Heather opened the Book and ignored Donna. She thumbed through large, thick pages, one at a time. Papers lay stuck to each page, as though to hide the contents from Heather as she flipped through.

Alex couldn't make out what little writing peeked through, but the lettering looked calligraphic and elegant, handsome swirls with illuminated boxes beginning each page. Even from the distance, Alex saw evidence of annotations from a second hand, modern scratch squeezed into the margins. Her eyes blurred, and her ears rang louder than before.

"You know what we came to do," Heather said to the group, "You know how important this is. When was the last time any of you cast even a small spell? None of us can. No woman can, because of Books like these. So what do we do? Do we walk away? Do we say that because a man made this Book, because he took the magic out of a woman, it's our moral imperative to say we can't use it?"

Heather pointed at Alex. "She needs our help. She needs us to finish what her parents started. None of us knows how. We're lost. We're weak. Right here, right now, this Book is our only guide."

Donna shook her head. "This isn't right, Heather. Reading those words aloud is sacrilege. We've talked about how dangerous these things are. All those meetings, all those times we came out here, most of us hoping it was true. We were pretending. We prayed there was something more to us, and Book Club gave us that hope. You taught us that using a man's words to make a woman's spell is the most evil, horrible thing we could imagine. It's not who we are."

"What would you have me do? We're not using their words." She looked at them all. "Peter translated the spells *back* to emotion; just like we calmed Alex with a spell; that's how we finish this. He even hid the pages from me, made sure I'd never have to read them." She offered them the open Book to see the redacted pages for themselves. "He didn't know if it could work without the Book."

"That Book may have been in Peter's hands," the tattooed chef interjected. *Carrie. She's cute.* "But what's in it belonged to a woman. If we use it, maybe we're taking back what's rightfully ours."

Donna shook her head. "You're siding with her?"

Alex was feeling something. Slowly it came to her, "This is boring."

All the women turned around.

"What's with her chest?" Minding the salt circles, Rachel stepped closer to Alex for a better look.

"I wasn't lying," Heather told the others. "Alexandrea has no soul."

Rachel stopped and clutched her chest, right where her coin shined. "I didn't think that was possible."

"Now you see for yourself," Heather asked, proffering the Book. "Which is more important? How else can we help her?"

Donna asked, "This is because of Peter? He did that to her?"

Heather nodded.

Carrie sobbed. "I know you told us, but until I saw it, I didn't comprehend. It's like she's alive and dead, but neither." She shook her head "If that Book is how we help her, then that sister didn't die in vain. Can't you all can see that?"

June put her hands on her hips. "I don't like it. Not even a little. But I didn't come out here, get undressed, and everything else to keep arguing. If this is the only way, let's help the girl."

Nancy and Lydia conceded too, then the others.

Donna was last. "I never thought I'd see a real Book before. A woman died to make a man more powerful." She turned to Carrie, "You're right. At least it's in women's hands now." She turned to Heather. "Maybe it's time a Book helps a woman."

The women reformed their triangles. "There's not a lot to this spell," Heather said. "Peter specified that it only works here, right here at the foundation."

"That's why we come here?" Donna looked around. "That's why this place has been sacred to us all these years? I thought you made up the witch stuff about this house."

"That means there's magic here?" Carrie asked. "Real magic?"

Alex was feeling less relaxed. Emotion returned to their words. Her ears rang, but the words now came through. "I don't think you need to do that, um, spell thing," she told them tentatively. "I can hear what you're saying, you know, about magic."

"Is that true?" Carrie kept looking between Alex and Heather. "We're done?"

"No," Heather said. "It's the spell we cast to relax her."

"I can hear," Alex said, "when you talk about magic. I mean, my ears ring, and my head hurts, but I can hear."

"You can hear it," Heather explained, "because we sent you into a fugue state. You're half awake, half asleep."

"Asleep?"

Marta interrupted, "Heather, does this mean she's coming around? Like she's waking from anesthesia? I mean, for a while there she sounded like a cow, mooing. Now she seems almost coherent."

Heather nodded.

"Then hurry," Donna urged, "before any of us loses our nerve or changes our mind."

Heather looked at the Book. Pieces of paper covered in notations stuck about the open page. Her finger drew a line from one to another, then went through the cursive notes written in the margins. "Oh Peter," she whispered, "I really hope you got this right." She looked up at the other women. "The spell has four parts. You need to dig deep, and always be thinking of Alexandrea." She cleared her throat. "Ready?"

The others made noise as they said some version of yes.

"The first emotion is dread."

"Dread?" Rachel had her right hand half raised. "Like, for ourselves, or over someone else?"

Heather looked panicked. "It just says dread. I thought like, you know, when you're alone and get that feeling? You know, *dread.*"

The women looked to one another for confirmation and once the majority seemed ready, they began. June started, followed by Colette. As before, they seemed to wait for a turn, each citing their own experience, and perhaps sharing those of the others.

"...being alone, hearing something outside... taking out the garbage at night, so far from the house... being followed... the lights going out in a storm..."

After several minutes, Heather spoke again. "Now it says here, death without sorrow. I think that means something that didn't affect you."

"...that raccoon, the sound the tires made... the mousetrap; the snap in the middle of the night... my dinner, that chicken, knowing it died for my plate..."

Carrie whispered, "Don't tell me you're thinking of going vegan."

Marta hissed, "Be serious."

"Next," Heather said once the women's remembrances had once again harmonized, "the third step, we need to add the sight of death."

Lydia asked, "What's that?"

Carrie asked, "Like roadkill? Or is chop-meat okay?"

"Seriously, Carrie? Don't screw this up," Marta chided.

Heather interrupted them. "I have no idea. Go with what feels right. Don't be silly."

"...the bloated belly of that deer... the flies and that smell... making me want to throw up, it was such a wet stench in my nose... the open casket at Grandpa's wake..."

"And last," Heather said after what felt like far longer, "losing someone close."

"Oh no." Colette looked around at the others, her eyes welling.

They began muttering. Donna was first, then one by one, the others had their turn.

"... that utter desolation in my heart... the emptiness, the endless sadness... every reminder sending me to tears... wondering how it happened... that voice message he left, *On my way, love ya, babe, see you later...*"

Betty gasped and said, "Colette, you never told me that."

"Don't stop, don't stop, don't stop," Heather chanted.

Colette started again, "Marcus was gone, and I was alone. I couldn't help wondering, did he suffer? For how long?" She sobbed. Carrie nearly broke the group to comfort her but Donna and Marta hissed. The others continued. "...every time I went into her bedroom to make her bed, finding it never unmade..."

Chapter Nineteen

lex shuddered. Her ears rang, and her body ached. She had never hurt so much before. Her stomach heaved, dry, repeatedly. She dropped to her knees. She clasped her ears, she was exploding in agony when, with one violent wave of extraordinary pain, it vanished. She froze. Was it over?

When she was certain the pain was gone, she stood.

Sounds swept back to her. Noises from the breeze, the trees, the leaves; birds, insects and small creatures rummaging through the underbrush as though they had all waited for her to be ready before beginning.

The sky was an expanse of rich blue, smudged with only a few white clouds. *Is it morning? When did that happen? Was I knocked out?*

Around her, the women were but specters, shadows frozen in sunlight.

The light, the air, the scent on the breeze, all felt new, unknown until this moment. The clearing was larger than she remembered. Tree stumps dotted the edge of the woods. "How long has that been here?" she said, noticing a squat house where the foundation had been.

The house was small and simple, sheathed in split shingles. Narrow wood stairs led up to the inviting front door, and small four-paned windows looked out from within. A stone chimney swirled gray smoke that dissipated into the gentle breeze.

The door creaked opened, and a bent and crooked old woman hobbled out. Her left foot pointed inward, and her brown right eye winced with each limping step. Her left socket was empty. Wiry, gray hair shaded her spotted scalp, and a crooked nose hooked over peeled-back lips. Three teeth poked through pink gums around a panting red tongue. Her jaw was thin and eroded. With twisted, crooked fingers, she clutched an equally gnarled branch for a walking stick.

"Have you brought it?" The old woman rasped. "Give it to me."

The hag stopped at the outer salt circle. One hand clutched the branch; the other fidgeted with her ankle-length dress. It was an ill-fitting mélange of patches in varied states of fade, from black to gray, all held together with ill-matched stitching. The woman's frail frame did little to fill the sagging, creased fabric. Large buttons marched from waist to neck, marred by empty spots where one or more had fallen off. Long ago the tattered collar may have been white. If Alex had tried to imagine a witch, this woman embodied the real-life cartoon she might have invented.

"Have you brought it?"

Jarred by the words, the accusatory tone, Alex wished one of the other women would respond or instruct.

"Heather?"

Heather didn't answer. She was like a vision perceived with one eye but not the other.

"Give it to me."

Alex stammered. "I, I didn't bring anything." Then she considered Abby's charm and reached for her throat.

"Keep your pretty baubles, girl with no soul." Her laughter concluded with an abrupt cough. She gestured at the shadows of the women. "They didn't bring us here with just a spell. They needed a sacrifice."

The words chilled Alex. *Sacrifice?* Abby was more visible than the others, laying in her own circle of salt. Alex couldn't recall seeing Abby until the moment she thought of her. The old woman's gaze followed. Alex remembered what happened to Abby, but hearing the word *sacrifice*, put the pieces together at once. *Could Heather be that cruel?*

"No, no, not Abby." Alex trembled. *There had to be another way, Heather. Not Abby.* She choked back her sobs. Abby was dead.

"That would be it, sweet one." The hag pointed to the glowing disk on Abby's chest. "Be a dear and get that for me. Give it, then let's go inside."

"I'm not giving you that."

The old woman motioned with a hooked finger. "If you don't, you'll waste her life." She grinned. Her remaining teeth, all rot and root, wiggled. "Come, dear. We go inside and the world opens to you. You'll get what you came for." She waited, her face growing long with frustration. "We could just wait here until he finds you. Which will it be? Out or inside?"

"Inside?"

"As soon as you give it." She pointed a gnarled finger at Abby. "That one knew the cost."

"I don't want to," Alex whimpered.

"You're here till you do. Or he comes. Maybe he'll take you last. Make you watch what he does so you know what's coming."

Alex tentatively left the inner-most salt ring. Her cheeks were wet with tears. She felt like she was being made to cut out her friend's heart.

"Careful dear. Don't break the salt. They worked so hard on them pretty designs."

Alex knelt beside Abby's body. Her skin was still warm. She would have felt alive not if not for her muscles. Abby was limp in places Alex never would have expected. Her arms flopped as though rubber replaced bone, skin hung from her face without life to keep it taught. Her eyes seemed locked on Alex, fixed in condemnation.

"Rest your hand right over the coin."

"Coin?" Alex knew what she meant, but the question slipped out. She placed her hand at the center of Abby's chest. All she could feel was Abby's breastbone and bra. Gradually, she felt a draw, a pull, almost a magnetic attraction. She could feel the faint impression of a disk against her palm.

"Clasp your fingers round it nice and slow."

Alex closed her fist. As she raised her hand, she could feel it radiating against her skin. It was heavy for something ethereal and typically unseen. She turned her hand over. Though not as bright as when it was a part of Abby, it was beautiful. Just as the spot in her own chest was darkness, she realized that what she'd perceived as a silver disk was *light*.

"Very good, child. Now give it here."

The old woman held out her hand, her fingers barely capable of opening.

Looking from Abby to the hag and back, Alex started to cry.

"Almost there, child. Hand it to me. Good girl. Sweet girl."

Alex recalled her dream, the cherubic child taking the disk from her mother. She placed it into the old woman's palm. Their hands touched. The old woman's flesh felt like burlap.

"Oh, Abby," Alex whimpered. "I'm so sorry." *Did I betray her?* What she gave away had to be special or the crone wouldn't want it. *Was I tricked?* There was no one to tell her what to do. If she were stronger, maybe she could have refused. Had she had a choice? Guilt and sorrow made it hard to concentrate. She wondered if the magical effects of emotional numbness had dissipated. She couldn't make sense of everything her mind was trying to tell her. "Abby's dead," she said to herself, "and I gave away her soul." She felt compelled to lie beside Abby and mourn.

"Little you know, girl. The way back is forward. Your friend remains dead as long as you remain here."

Alex stared at Abby, "Really?"

"Yes."

"Are you sure?"

The old woman cooed, withdrawing her hand. "Come into my home."

Around her, the house, the old witch, these were real; these were here. The women were but shadows. The women were nowhere.

The crone hobbled up the stairs to the house, her walking stick punctuating her shuffling and dragging steps.

"What about them?" Alex motioned to the phantom women.

"Take another step," the crone said.

Alex stepped over the last ring of salt, and as she did, the salt, the women and Abby vanished. Her heart raced. "Where'd they go?"

"Go? Ha," came the reply. "They stayed. You went."

Alex looked to where the circle of salt had been. She felt lost and untethered. "What did they do to me?" she muttered to herself. Whatever it was, she would have preferred the ignorance of her headaches.

She stepped back to where she had stood. Nothing happened. Nothing changed. Nothing was there.

"What do I do now?" Answered by expected silence, she mocked Heather, "*Just trust me Alex, do what I tell you.* You had no idea, did you? No idea at all." But Alex realized that there was only one thing to do, move forward. If not for her own sake, then for Abby's.

She paused at the base of the stairs, taking in the surroundings. She was not surprised that the circle of cars was gone, replaced by a militantly organized garden.

"Am I in the past?"

The old woman declined to respond.

Turning to find she was alone, she raced up the stairs. Each step creaked and bowed. Passing through the doorway, she took a deep, appreciative breath.

Inside, the house was dim. It took a moment for Alex's eyes to adjusted. First she saw motes of dust afloat on streamers of sunlight from the windows. Then she noticed the neatly tied bundles of all varieties of drying herbs hanging from almost every rafter, filling the space with a scent of home.

The structure looked like a completed puzzle of logs, boards and shingles, each shaved, cut or trimmed to interlock perfectly with one another. It was not assembled with nails and intent but honed and mitered with great purpose and care. Even Alex's untrained eye could appreciate the craftsmanship.

The kitchen, dining, and bedrooms were teased out of the single space using furniture as partitions, making three rooms out of one.

A wood-framed bed peeked out from behind one wall with a red and white quilt tucked around its mattress. A simple square table with four chairs sat in the dining room, and a large, ornate cabinet to her right contained dishes, jars, and other vessels. A washbasin sat atop one of several hip-high cabinets in the kitchen, and in one corner, beneath an immense wooden mantle, she saw a stacked-stone fireplace. A great metal hook hung from the mantle such that it could swing in and out of the flames, and from it dangled a blackened iron kettle, tended to by a young woman.

The woman ladled a bowl from the kettle before turning to Alex.

Alex held her breath. This woman was perfect and beautiful, her skin as soft as a peach's, her face round, her eyes large and brown with thick, dark lashes. Her hair was long, straight and thick, a dark chestnut close to black in the candlelight. Her figure, held snug by in the dress she wore, caused Alex to glance at her own shape, the graduation gown disappointing compared to this woman's luxuriant curves.

In a pleasant, smiling voice, the stranger said, "I'm Sara."

Alex extended her hand to shake, but the gesture wasn't returned. "I'm—"

"Alexandrea, I know," the woman finished with a gentle smile, looking up; Alex was taller.

"You must be hungry," the beautiful woman said in a soft voice, her lips a natural deep red. As she moved them around the words, her eyes brightened, smiling on their own.

"Um, no thanks," Alex replied. "I just had pizza, maybe two hours ago."

"Peet-za?"

Alex did her best to explain.

Sara shrugged politely. "I have soup if you like. You came all this while."

Alex knew that fairy tales with witches often started with tempting offerings, only to end someone thrown into an oven. Then she realized, however, that she was famished. "How am I this hungry?" Her hunger was greater than any fear of fairy stories.

The bowl clanked as Sara set it down. "It may seem just a few hours to you, but we are more than a few hours from when you last ate."

Alex sat. Sara presented her a spoon. She was famished; she couldn't think straight. She rested her elbows on the table then thought to take them off, unsure why she did.

Sara leaned on the edge of the table, her hair falling to one side as she hovered over Alex, "You're not obliged to keep good manners with me. Eat."

Alex looked at her doubtfully, accepting the returned nod. She put down the spoon, cupped the bowl in her hands, and lifted it to her lips to slurp hungrily at the hot broth. Chewing bits of meats and vegetable as they came, she only dripping a little out the corners of her mouth.

"More?" Sara asked when she'd finished. "It's not rude to eat, only to refuse if you're hungry. You've traveled a long time." It was like the woman had read Alex's mind.

"Okay. More, please. I didn't realize I was so hungry. It's delicious."

"I thought you'd like it. I made enough for you to have more, later." Sara skipped to the kitchen, looking back at Alex with a wink.

In a moment she was back. She presented Alex the bowl, and as Alex ate, she sat down beside her.

Lowering the near-empty bowl from her lips, Alex spoke. "There was an old woman..."

"Outside was a long time from now. In here, I am who I was."

Alex stared at her. As hard as she tried, she could not see in the perfect beauty before her, the deformed and decrepit creature who had greeted her only moments ago.

"Does that surprise you? Should I have lied and said I was her daughter?" The woman smiled. Then in a fluid flash, she rose from her seat. "When you're done," she said, wagging a beckoning finger as she glided into the bedroom, "there's someone I'd like you to meet."

Alex took a final mouthful of soup and then followed, her bare feet padding on the smooth wooden floor. Her stride felt ungainly, especially compared to the grace with which Sara skated across the floor.

The bedroom was small, a narrow bed, an ornate cradle, and a two-drawer dresser with a pitcher and basin beside a hand mirror and a brush. Sara caressed the two babies lying within the crib. Swaddled as they were, they reminded Alex of ice cream cones. One sleeping infant breathed rapidly, its face an expression of peace. The other fidgeted like a worm, whining, although not quite awake.

"This is Abagail," Sara breathed, rubbing the squat nose of the sleeping baby. "George here is not the sleeper his sister is."

"Twins?" Alex flinched at the stupidity of her question.

"Of course. Always twins." Sara rubbed George's belly. "I put them to nap just before you arrived. Jonathan is supposed to be hunting, but I know perfectly well he is finishing carving his name in the large rock at the divide. He is claiming the forest to the cliff."

Alex took a guess, "Jonathan William Frost, 1826?"

Sara smiled again, her eyes twinkling. "The same. Come back to the kitchen. We have much to discuss." They returned to the table. For a moment, the two women stared at one another. Alex could read little emotion on Sara's face, but she was sure she felt enough for the both of them: Confusion, guilt. More than anything she felt lonely. She recalled Abby, but the recollection took effort, as though her memory was fading. Standing, she walked to a front window. The view reminded her of all those Saturdays, atop the weather-worn foundation with Billy and Rose, wondering who once lived here, what happened to them, how it all looked. Now, here she was, granted the answers to questions that no longer mattered.

"How do I get back?" Alex asked.

"It will all be there," Sara said. "Just not now." She slapped her hands into her lap. "We have much work, you and I. Much to learn."

"I have so many questions, I don't know where to start." She faced Sara. "Why am I even here?"

Sara smiled, but this time Alex read sympathy in her expression. It unnerved her a little. "You and I, my dear, we are best of friends who never before met. A friendship arranged by men at different times of our lives."

Alex rubbed her head. "How is that even..." she realized where and when she was.

"You are here for a reason, Alexandrea Hawthorne." Sara pointed to a spot on the table. "You were meant to come here, now," she dragged her finger in a circle. "So that the loop may be closed."

"Loop?"

Sara nodded. "It is complicated. They took something from you. By coming here, you can retrieve it."

"You mean like magic?"

Sara forced a smile. "You have much to learn before you return. So you can. The loop awaits."

Alex eagerly returned to the table. "What do I do?"

Sara smiled, almost a grimace. "It is more complicated than that, Alexandrea. You are at the beginning, and while this may appear to be my beginning, I have already been to the end. It is a loop that keeps me waiting for you to come. And now, here you are." She reached into her pocket and pulled out Abby's vibrant glowing disk. She smiled genuinely at Alex. "I've met Abby before. Just as she sacrificed herself for you, she did the same for your father when he visited me."

Chapter Twenty

t surprises you that I met your father." Sara hadn't asked a question.

"I guess. I never knew him. There's a lot to be surprised about."

Sara fixed a lock of hair that had fallen in her eyes. "No, I suppose you would not know him. What if I told you he knew you would find yourself here?" She drummed a finger on the table, a tap accenting each word.

"He planned this?"

"He will. He knew you would follow in his footsteps." She laughed. "Follow. Exactly who followed whom is up for debate. Who came first? I guess it was you, but you couldn't come until after he was here. That is the trouble with loops. They become so confusing."

A gray tabby jumped to the floor and ambled towards the table. It avoided Alex as it snaked around the table and chairs, rubbing up against the wooden legs.

"Why am I here, Sara?" Alex said, breaking her attention away from the cat.

Sara held out the glowing disk in her palm. The cat let out a plaintive yowl and leapt onto the table. It shot out a paw, claws flexing, reaching for it. Sara pulled her hand away, and losing balance, the cat hopped back to the floor. "Brutus wants to help," she explained. "Once upon a time, cats knew about magic. Time has twisted that knowledge to instinct." She bent to stroke his flank as he sauntered off to the bedroom. "Always trying to protect. A little overzealous, though. They no longer understand not every word is harmful. Perhaps, rather than take the chance, they sit atop every sheet of paper they come across."

Alex remembered how Dolly always found whatever book, magazine, or newspaper anyone was reading to be the most comfortable place to sit.

"Protect?"

"Well, Alexandrea, some words are harmful."

Alex was unconvinced. "Now I have to worry about words?" She thought a moment. Heather had seemed so distant, so far away. "Heather had a Book."

Sara's face soured. "I know nothing about that." She faked another smile.

Alex glanced to the window. *This was a waste of time.* "I've been here a while. I don't want them to get annoyed because I'm taking too long."

Sara laughed politely. "They are not aware." She drew a circle on the table again, tapping at the top. "You left here this moment. There you'll return. Only the loop has time."

"How do you know so much about time?"

Sara looked sad. "The universe has ways of revealing truths to us. Never when the information would be useful."

"Is that why I'm here? To learn truths?"

"Learning is a part of your task."

"And what is that task, exactly?" Alex dared to say what was on her mind. "I feel like you don't want to tell me."

"Whether or not I want to tell you has no bearing on whether or not you'll find out."

"You said you've been through the loop."

"I have, but it's all so confusing."

"So how do I learn?"

"I can show you." Alex leaned forward as Sara rested one hand upon the table. The other held out the disk. The motion reminded Alex of the child from her dream. "Learning begins when you take this from my hand. I will not give it to you."

Is this a test? "What will happen to Abby? Without her soul?"

"Is that what they told you this is?"

Alex was speechless.

Sara took a preparatory breath. "Different people have different words for it. Some call it an anchor because it anchors your ethereal spirit to your corporeal body while you dream. I think of it as a coin." *Billy called it a coin before he attempted suicide. How did he know?* Sara's gaze guided Alex's to the shining disk. "Dreams and death are alike in many ways. You've seen the silver thread? The ethereal tether, binding Spirit to Body?" Alex nodded. "In dreams, the spirit wanders the world of the dead."

"I'm not sure I follow. I mean, it makes sense, I guess…" she trailed off.

Sara nodded to her hand. "There are things that can only be learned from experience. The longer this goes unclaimed, the longer you do not understand."

Alex almost reached out. "Will Abby get it back? Will she be okay?"

"Her fate is in your hands, or it will be."

"What happens when I take it? Do I do something with it?"

"Tell me, Alexandrea, why are you here?"

"I don't know. I need you to tell me."

"Try."

"It's a long story."

"Not as long as the one I have for you. So please, tell me."

Each time Alex shifted, her graduation gown tugged a little tighter at her throat. She fussed with it until it felt right.

"I started having this dream, every night. Always the same. Men come into the house, my father, who was kind of…" Alex did a quick impression of her father, making her face blank.

Sara nodded; her eyes sad. Alex hoped she'd find her impression amusing.

Alex continued. "Well, he—my father that is—tries to shoot me. I don't know; everything just happens so fast. My mother gets shot, sort of, then I think she explodes him. Then I escape. I go into this mist stuff. It's like the mist I saw Abby walk into, that was all around before I saw your house." She paused, trying to deny the connection she had just made. "That's when I wake up. Oh, and there's this child that turns into a monster thing, trying to collect the disks, but I don't have one."

"Very fantastic," Sara said plainly.

"Only none of it ever happened. My parents died in a car accident."

"Interesting. Not sure what a ca-raccident is, but no matter. They can't both be true." She paused. "Like when you found yourself here. You were there, you were here. Two different times, same place. Only one can be true, no?"

Alex shrugged. Nothing made sense and the more she listened, the less so.

"What happened after you started having this dream?"

"When I told Heather—she's my aunt, my father's sister—when I told her, she freaked out and that's when everything started. I couldn't hear some things people said. It's been happening my whole life, the headaches. I never realized why. Long story short, I'm here now because Heather told me this would stop them."

Sara smiled. "That was not a long story."

"I left out some things, like getting lost in the woods and my cousin trying to kill himself."

"That sounds dreadful."

"It was. Someone was watching us while we tried to save Billy. Then later, the same man attacked us. He almost killed Abby."

"You saw this man?"

"Yeah. He had a bent neck." Alex stretched her neck out, lowering her head to demonstrate.

"He didn't always. Do you know who he is?"

"His name is Matthew."

"You are important to him. You could not hear special things because of him."

Alex gasped, "What did he do to me?"

"Not him, exactly, but to protect you from him," Sara replied. "Don't you want to know what these things mean? What each piece of your puzzle has to do with all the others?"

"Of course."

"Shall we do something about your curse?" She held the disk closer to Alex.

"I can hear things I couldn't before. I think they broke it already."

"Not yet. Everything in dreams is possible."

"I'm dreaming?"

"Well," Sara drew out the word, "no. There are ways we may use dreams to go places." She pointed at Alex. "You, my dear, came here through a dream."

"I thought you said dreams happened in the *realm of the dead*." Alex delivered her words with a thick coat of sarcasm.

"I said that."

"So you're suggesting…?" Alex paused. "Are we dead? Or just you?"

Sara looked hurt. "You must understand, Alexandrea, you will travel this loop but once. This is *my* recurring dream. You are my salvation just as I am yours."

"Salvation?"

"The curse is to keep you from magic. To hide it from you and you from it."

"Magic? Like real magic? Hocus-pocus and all that?"

"Spellcraft, my dear, yes. You know, *Double, double, toil and trouble?*"

Alex's face wrinkled. "Macbeth?" Sara nodded. "You know Macbeth? I thought Shakespeare was, I don't know, taught in school."

Sara laughed. "That is where I learned it."

Sheepishly, Alex replied, "I'm sorry, I thought, you know, being a girl, in this era, that education... um, that you're only good for making babies or something."

"That fate befalls many women."

I can't believe I just insulted her. Alex wanted to change the subject. She thought back to the last thing Sara said before she put her foot in her mouth. "I preferred the Tempest."

Sara held up a finger. "Shakespeare was a brilliant man who understood magic better than most. Most men, that is. The Tempest is about a man who steals his spellcraft from a woman, kills her, and enslaves her child."

"But he releases Caliban and Ariel in the end. He breaks his wand."

"This is true. Does that make him a hero? Does he realize he was wrong or had magic served *his* purpose? Is he, perhaps, afraid someone will do to him what he did to Caliban's mother? Which is more important, the act or the outcome?"

Alex shrugged. "I guess the act. So Macbeth, huh?"

"The witches, the weird sisters. He was mostly right about them."

"Really? So I need to collect newt eyes and toad toes?"

Sara chuckled. "I forget how little you know. Spells are all emotional. That is, our emotions conceive and control them. A recipe like what the weird sisters recite only serves as an emotional map to more complex spellcraft. How each thing makes you feel: a dash of happiness, a touch of loss from a childhood pet. They are deeply personal conceits; we cannot share them among witches."

Alex remembered the four parts of the spell Heather used to summon Sara and how each woman spoke of different things. "I think I understand, a little. When you say it's emotional? How?"

Sara held out the glowing disk.

Alex studied the woman's face. She found her hand moving of its own accord, as though just thinking about the disk was enough to spur her arm to action. Finding her conviction, she took the disk.

In the distance, Alex heard men laughing.

Sara's tone changed. "Quickly, Alexandrea, put that someplace safe."

"What's happening?"

"No time to explain. You and I, we close the loop now."

"You're scaring me. Is this because I took the coin?"

"There are experiences we must share. Some will be difficult. Very. Horrible things will happen. Remember yourself. Do not lose yourself to me."

Alex pressed the disk against her chest with trembling hands. "Sara, I don't think I want to do—."

Sara interrupted. "There isn't time, Alexandrea. Peter created this loop for you. In doing so, he trapped me. You, me, together. This is the only way we each get what we want." She rose from her chair.

Upon hearing her father's name, Alex stood too.

They faced one another; Sara stepped forward. "Don't step away," she said. They were nose-to-nose. "You will have a moment of confusion. Don't lose yourself. You are not me. Do you hear me Alex? You are not me."

"I think I'm going to be sick," Alex said.

Sara took a sudden step forward. Alex tried to pull away, but she wasn't fast enough. She felt herself knocked to the ground, but her body never landed.

She was still standing.

Sara was gone. As was Abby's disk. Had she dropped it?

Alex scanned the room. The house. It wasn't there. No one was there, save for the sleeping babes in the bedroom.

She couldn't breathe, though she tried to inhale deeply. It was like she wore a mask, seeing out from recessed eyeholes. Her hands were not her hands; the skin was lighter, more calloused and worn;

she wore scars from small cuts and burns, which were not there moments before.

She walked towards the kitchen.

Alex tried to shout in surprise, but nothing came out. She hadn't set out to walk, and the movement startled her. Someone else was controlling her body. But... this wasn't her body.

Alex's body moved and spun without direction from her mind. Each motion, each step, each nod of her head disoriented her; it was like a carnival ride. She entered the kitchen and was about to wash her hands when, an instant before dipping her hands into the placid water, she saw her reflection. Sara's face returned her gaze.

She remembered the woman's warning, *Don't lose yourself. You are not me.*

There was a knock at the front door. Sara jumped. Alex could feel her heart beating faster, feel the tension rise in her shoulders. Her hands clenched.

"Yes?" Sara called out, her voice tense but melodic. Alex felt the word forced through her throat.

Someone pounded.

Sara took a deep breath and edged towards the door. "Who's there?"

Why are they banging so hard? Thinking, apparently, was all Alex could do. No reply came, no thoughts returned by Sara, no communication between them.

Alex felt her body—Sara's body—perspiring, a wetness in her armpits, down her back and between and under her breasts. Sara tiptoed to peer through the window nearest the door.

She saw four men. One pounded the door; the others waited impatiently at the bottom of the stairs. Their clothes were familiar, yet nothing like Alex had ever seen people wear in real life. The fit looked blousy. They might have been they were going to a costume party. She would have called it *old-timey.*

One of the three pointed to the window. The other two saw her, even as she ducked back in.

"She's in there," one of them shouted. "We know you're in there!"

The banging stopped.

Sara clutched her pounding chest. She edged back. She looked towards the bedroom.

She's worried about her babies.

The door crashed open. Splinters of wood spun across the room.

"When I said knock it down," one of them said with a hearty laugh, "I meant the door, not the whole house."

Sara took a step back as four men rushed in and started towards her. One carried a cudgel, another a hammer, another a nib pen. She tried to run, but hands were already on her. Alex tried to scream, tried to struggle, feeling their grasp bruising Sara's skin, rough hands pulling her to the ground, pinning her down. *If this is Sara's body, why does it hurt?*

Alex's head exploded. *Another headache?* It took a moment to realize someone had struck her. The second strike reverberated through her skull. The initial blinding white light became an all-consuming darkness.

Chapter Twenty-One

Distant male voices. Depth. Submersion. Blackness. Deadening darkness.

Rising. Slowly from the murk. Voices, closer. Darkness giving way.

A spark of consciousness. Mind aware of her body, aware of herself, aware she was Alex.

Alex didn't feel... well. *What happened?* The ache at the back of her head reminded her.

She was sore, uncomfortable in an unfamiliar way. She focused instead on her surroundings.

Then it happened. She took a breath, the deep, deliberate breath of someone desperately surfacing from a dreamless pool of unconsciousness. Sara was waking.

Something hindered the breath. Not her corset; this was a binding, biting, unforgiving rope, right below her breasts.

Alex was alert, Sara still groggy. Until the other woman opened her eyes, Alex remained in darkness. Until she breathed, Alex suffocated. Until she moved, even once she moved, Alex was restrained, trapped in a cage of someone else's body. She tried fruitlessly to pull in her limbs to ease her discomfort and curl into a ball. Alex felt her arms outstretched unnaturally. As they pulled back, something dug into her wrists. Her ankles were similarly bound. Her hands and feet were prickling numb and cold.

Sara's eyes fluttered open. Alex felt her panic, the fluttering heartbeat and nervous fear, the unwanted knowledge. She was—they were—bound to a chair with their arms outstretched and tied to a single iron nail driven into the center of the table before her.

Sara's mangled dress told a story in wrinkles and stains. *This is Sara's body; it isn't me,* she told herself. She wondered what Sara was thinking. She had no choice but to see what Sara looked at, spotting scattered buttons amidst broken table settings that littered the floor.

She felt waves of anger welling up inside Sara—muscles tensing, blood pressure rising—followed by much larger waves of terror. Tears pooled in her eyes. Her stomach twisted. It was all Sara.

This isn't me, this isn't me, Alex repeated hysterically. Sara's tears were the closest she had to her own. *It's not my body. This isn't me.*

Could Alex endure this? Could Sara? *She's from another time,* Alex asserted, intent on convincing herself. A whimper from her throat betrayed this hope.

"She's awake." The young man who spoke wore a black suit with a white shirt buttoned snugly to his throat. He rushed towards her. "Look, look, she's awake."

Alex watched through Sara's eyes, felt her withdraw, felt the bindings digging into her skin.

Two older men with leathery, pocked skin stared from the kitchen. One was balding, his hair fine and sparse, missing from all but the sides of his head. When a fourth man's hand clamped her shoulder, Alex knew who was in charge.

The fourth man was taller than the others, younger than all but the first. Alex refused to believe Sara's eyes as he came closer. His fingers squeezed her shoulder. His other hand was hidden from her view.

"It's good to see you're awake, my dear, Sara Frost."

Sara swallowed. Alex felt her fight to hold her composure against rising revulsion.

The leader continued, "Work must be done, and I apologize; you're necessary to complete it."

Alex tried to say, *I'm not Sara.* She wanted to scream it, to swear. *Can't they tell I'm in here?* What Sara said was more metered than Alex expected, "You have me confused for someone else, Matthew."

Matthew? The attack at Heathers wouldn't happen for more than a hundred years.

He sat across from her. Alex studied his face. "I think you've been expecting me."

He leaned closer, caressing her cheek with his knuckles. When they were nose to nose, Alex saw only his brown eyes, the deep, dark ridges in his iris, the yellow and green flecks. "I know," he hissed, his warm breath intruding in her mouth, "you are not alone."

"Babies," Sara gasped.

Matthew retreated to a less intimate distance.

I don't want to be here, Alex wanted to scream. Why does Sara want me to experience this? What did I do to deserve this?

"I did nothing wrong," Sara said with an air of defiance.

What are you doing? Alex tried to scream. *You're encouraging them!*

"We'll see about that, witch," one of the pock-faced men shouted. "If you're innocent, you'll celebrate in heaven tonight. But we know where you're headed."

Alex felt Sara's body react with anger. Alex wished what she felt and thought would at least be in tune with the body she inhabited. The discrepant emotions disconcerted her. *They just said they will kill you. That means me too.*

Matthew's scowl made his boisterous partner step back, shrinking in stature.

Alex felt Sara moving, like someone squirming right beneath her skin—or was it the other way around? She tried to relax, to let Sara flow rather than to fight her—to observe rather than participate. *This isn't me.* It was like watching an uncomfortable movie, unable to look away.

"You question my innocence after what you've done?"

One of the men laughed.

"Keep laughing," Sara protested. "You and your false holiness."

"False," one of them mocked.

Matthew looked away. "Keep quiet," he growled. He turned back to Sara. "These boys," he thumbed over his shoulder, "they like the sticky bits. They don't see the grand picture. They don't realize that of everyone in the room, you are the least expendable. If you could see the world from my perspective, you'd sympathize." He lowered his head to look directly at her, jutting his neck straight out from his shoulders.

"Huh," he said. "The boy was right. There is someone else."

Matthew. How? Alex tried to do the math; nothing made sense. The man in her house was not two hundred years old, but the resemblance...

"We both know how important this is. Things inside coming out, lessons to learn, magic to share." He sighed. "You won't agree, but a part of you deep inside, will one day understand; I am not a villain. Circumstances drive good men to do things to make the world a better place."

Matthew lunged. A loud snap shook the air. Sara stared at his once-hidden right hand. It held the hammer that struck the table. It startled any thoughts out of her.

The other men, also startled, laughed at her reaction. "The hammer!" the youngest among them shouted.

"Sara," Matthew said in a consoling voice, "I hope you someday understand; I take no joy in the things I do."

She answered. "Don't you?"

In Matthew's pregnant pause, one of the pock-marked men stepped forward. "You are a devil-fucking witch," he blurted. "Beat the devil out of her, Matthew. Beat it out of her!"

"Get away from her," a voice called from the door. Alex felt her head turn, and Sara's eyes fell on a man standing in the remains of the front door. She could feel the swelling in Sara's chest, love bursting from her to this man, blending with her fear. "No, no," she cried out to him. "Jonathan, no!"

The man with the cudgel attacked Jonathan without warning. Matthew screamed for him to stop. "What did I say?" It was swift and brutal. Jonathan's body crumpled. A second strike sounded, and a third, sounded wet. Jonathan convulsed briefly then lay still.

Sara screamed. Alex felt her throat going raw, the nausea, the pain in her chest. Sara strained against her bindings until they drew blood.

"What have you done? I said no killing. The boy was right."

Sara clenched her eyes as she thrashed and wailed. When she exhausted her breath, she collapsed against her restraints, sobbing.

The man answered, "What's the matter?"

A loud snap popped her ears. Sara looked up to find Matthew standing over the blackened and smoldering body of the man with the cudgel. Holding a Book. He snapped it shut, and it vanished.

Sara stared at the two bodies, her lungs paralyzed; her chest convulsed with sobs. The air stank, burned flesh, cooking fat, and a putrid scent, a dark, wet smell that made Alex sick. Sara's constitution was stronger, her grief greater, but her will was spent.

Matthew spun around, shouting at the remaining men. "You had instructions! Killing the husband was never one of them. You do nothing you aren't told."

The younger man defend. "He might'a been a danger to us so—"

Matthew interrupted, "I have worked too hard to suffer fools."

The bald man pulled the younger man back.

"Enough," Matthew thundered, turning back to Sara, striking the table with the hammer. "You, Sara, are a witch." The hammer punctuated *witch*, cracking again against the wood.

"Am I on trial?" Alex felt fear and rage in Sara's words.

Matthew leaned wearily on the table. "The last witch. The last one with any real power."

"I don't know what you're talking about," she whispered through her tears.

"If we *burn* you at the *stake*, it's supposed to cleanse your *soul*." His volume rose. The hammer cracked down on *burn*, *stake*, and *soul*.

Alex wanted to slink away, to slide through Sara and disappear. Sara's emotions, fear, hatred, grief, anger, made her feel sick. There was too much feeling. *Why did I take that disk? Sara tricked me. I was the sacrifice.* She was as afraid of the crash of the hammer as she was of the hammer itself.

Did Heather know? Heather gave her up to Sara; unwitting or complicit, she was here because of her aunt. "Trust me," she had said. She hated everyone. Venom welled inside like bubbling magma, ready to explode. Sara screamed her rage at them.

The two men retreated into the kitchen, but Matthew slammed his hammer again. He thundered, punctuating every few words with another strike. "Save your emotions, your magic won't work."

Sara wept.

Suddenly he was holding a Book. Different from the last, it was large, its leather cover shiny and new. He placed it on the table with a soft thump. He pointed to the bald man, who rushed over to open it. The pages were crisp and pristine-white. Matthew produced a dip-pen and handed it off. The bald man cleaned ink from the tip with his shirt and licked the nib. Then he waited, the pen trembling in anticipation over the book.

"*I* am a merciful *man*, Sara. Give up your *magic*." The hammer continued to hit the table, causing her to wince with every few words.

"Will you give your *magic* to me?"

Sara whimpered. "I don't want to die."

"Give me your *spells*." The hammer left half-moons on the table's surface.

"I'm not a witch."

"Don't *lie*. You're the *last* of your kind. Without *you*, I lose *everything*." Crack-crack-crack.

"I don't know, Matthew. I don't know any magic."

"After you, *Sara*, no one's left. Your *magic* must be kept *safe*." Crack-crack-crack.

"Please stop."

"If it's not *me*, it'll be *Jeremiah*." Crack-crack.

"Who?"

"You know who." Matthew sounded exhausted.

"No, I don't. None of it. I don't know what you're talking about. Please. Please!" Mucus and tears streamed down Sara's face. Alex felt the gaping hole in her heart. The chasm grew and threatened to swallow her. Sara collapsed on the table, straining against the rope around her chest. "I don't know. I don't know," she sobbed.

"It doesn't *have* to be like *this*." Crack-crack.

"I don't know. I don't know..." She sounded weak; exhausted.

Slowly, Sara looked up at Matthew, her hair falling forward and sticking to her wet face.

They stared at one another.

Alex could feel Sara's defiance, "You'll have to take it."

Matthew struck the table with the hammer, a jarring, sudden crack that startled Sara into a sweat.

"I haven't been *asking*, Sara." Crack.

"I don't... I can't..."

"Tell me *one*." Crack.

"I told you," Alex felt Sara's defiance, tears falling down her cheeks, her mouth sticky and ropy, "I won't give them to you. I can't." Her body strained against its binding, the coarse ropes becoming slippery with blood.

"Give me your magic now!" His voice thundered, full of rage. The hammer came down again and again.

On the crack accompanying his last word, Alex felt a sting in her left hand.

For a moment it only stung.

Then it flamed up the inside her arm, burning and charring the nerves until it exploded into her torso and into her skull. She wrenched, screaming. She looked at her left hand. One knuckle was crushed.

It's not mine, it's not mine, Alex chanted in her mind. She wanted to believe that because the pain was Sara's she shouldn't feel it. But she did. *It hurts it hurts it hurts!* Sara broke into a sweat. The pain eased for a brief moment before intensifying worse than ever.

"I'm sorry." He leaned in close. "Your magic?"

Sara sobbed and dry-heaved. She wanted to be away from here, anywhere, even dead. Alex tried to call to her. *Let me out! I don't want to learn this. I don't belong here. It's not me. It's not me.*

The hammer came down thrice more. Alex and Sara howled, writhing in agony, their left hand crushed from each blow. She twisted against her restraints, pulling, battering her body against the chair, wishing she could wrench her arm from her torso, willing the ropes to cut through flesh and bone if that would aid her escape.

A geyser of vomit rose inside her. She dry-heaved. She could feel it gushing up, an acidic tang at the back of her throat. Guttural noises retched out of her as vile dark fluids spilled from her mouth, splashing a cavalcade of strange shapes across the table. Twice more she spewed up, spitting disgusting vomitus noises. The bald man leaned forward, dipped his nib into the dark, swirling liquid and scribbled away in his book, his pen creating a series of meaningless shapes and designs as he frantically committed her fluids to the paper.

Sara gasped for air, spitting the taste from her mouth, adding shapes to the table. Her hand was a molten ball of fire, but the pain in her limb was secondary to the pain of magic being wrenched out of her. She felt like her insides had been torn out.

"You've done well," Matthew whispered.

Alex wanted Sara to catch her breath. She was hyperventilating.

"That was one. We have a long day ahead of us." Crack!

Chapter Twenty-Two

A lex awoke crumpled on the floor. She had never imagined it was possible to hurt so horribly. They made Sara give them everything before discarding her. Knuckles broken, left ankle wrenched and limp, nose cracked and bleeding, teeth knocked out or pulled. She lost consciousness for the last time when he took her left eye.

Alex waited for Sara, grains of the wood floor pressed into her face. She wanted to cry, to wail, to sob, but she had no control over this body. She could not vent her pain or fear or anger until Sara gained consciousness and did it for them both. Until then, she existed in darkness, breathed when Sara breathed, lying in a pool of all-consuming pain.

As the other woman regained consciousness, Alex could feel the utter desolation inside her. Eventually, Sara moved. She opened her eye and examined her hands. They were grotesque: twisted, bruised, and swollen. Her body felt like it smoldered following a raging fire.

Beside her were two corpses. Jonathan lay closer, his face turned away; just beyond, his murderer, the cudgel fallen from his black and charred fingertips.

Sara stared at Jonathan, his caved-in skull. She stared so long Alex wondered if she still saw him. She would sob, catch herself and then sob again. Her heart ached; it hurt differently than any part of her body; it was worse.

"Babies," Sara rasped through her split lips and dry, raw throat.

Alex couldn't bear to move, but Sara wouldn't wait. She yelped with each motion; a few times she screamed. Using the chair, her elbows, her battered body, Sara pulled herself to her feet. Step by shuffle by limp, clawing the walls, leaning, falling and crying out, Sara reached the bedroom. She collapsed at the sight of the empty crib.

"Abigail. George. Jonathan." She sobbed their names, repeatedly, until nothing remained inside.

How long can I endure? Sara lay still for a long while. Eventually, sleep brought her dreams of her pain.

When Alex opened her eyes, the day was bright. She felt no improvement. Her wounds burned hot; some were oozing. Skin, stretched taut with fluid and blood, was bruised red, purple, and black.

Why am I still here? Why is this happening to me?

Sara crawled to the front of the house. The two corpses looked like they were sweating. Thankfully, she looked away. She reached the splintered remains of the front door. She pushed through. She pulled herself upright and leaned against the house.

Wildflowers rolled on the breeze. Insects flitted in the bright, warm air. She watched bees and birds. She sat with the sun warming her face and the breeze giving her sweetened air to breathe. Alex was thankful for the view, for this one thing.

Sara closed her eye. The breeze whispered to her. The flower petals caressed her cheeks. Alex could feel it, the ever-so-subtle feeling of falling, like a cup that contained her had tipped, and everything was trickling out.

Sara took one lingering breath, taking in the forest.

Chapter Twenty-Three

*I*s *it over?*

Her body moved, and the carnival ride of vertigo as her consciousness was subjected to Sara's will began again. Sara looked down at her own mistreated body collapsed in the doorway. She looked at her hands; they were not mangled. *I'm dead. Sara's dead, and I'm still trapped inside her ghost.*

More than before, Alex felt Sara's presence, so close they occupied the same space. She felt the sadness and the relief, the bitterness as this other woman recognized her life had concluded. There was no sorrowful reunion, no loved one to hold her hand, no child she could gaze upon. She shared her last private moment of life with a man she feared. Her death came by his will. Somewhere, perhaps alive, perhaps not, her children were crying for their mother, and he would be the one to wipe their tears. Maybe he would feed them, clothe them, and teach them. Maybe they would call him papa. Sara hoped this was so. The alternative was too much to bear.

Why am I still here?

With the pain mercifully behind her, Alex looked on Sara's corpse. Sara's body was no more hers than Jonathan's was. So she told herself, at least; so she hoped. Sara was dead; Alex wasn't. Was she? She was still here.

Sara took the stairs, one at a time, walking towards an encroaching wall of mist that had emerged from the woods.

She saw the child. With small bare feet, it stepped from the dark cloud and trod on the green earth. Alex recognized it immediately, the many folds of fabrics wrapping its body. The child held out its other hand, fingers small and slender. It patiently awaited its payment. Sara clasped her chest. Alex expected her void, but this time, she felt it: Sara's disk.

"You want this?" Sara asked the child.

The child could have been either sex, perhaps neither. It looked on her tenderly, its cherubic face saddened, exuding silent comfort. Its hand was adamant.

Holding the disk, understanding the transaction that was taking place, Alex thought, *Of course it's a coin.*

Sara placed a fist on the child's palm. Its fingers warm and soft. The coin had such remarkable weight for its size, her hand lifted away as she let it go.

The child's fingers closed, hiding the glowing shape. Then the coin was gone.

It clasped Sara's hand, and walked with her, wordlessly leading her closer to the roiling edge of the mist. The forest was mute, save for their footsteps. Its hand was a comfort. It adjusted its grip more than once, making certain their hands were always together. It radiated love. She knew she was cared for. She knew at last, she wasn't alone.

The child paused and waved her forward. Alex feared where, or to whom, the path would lead.

Sara stepped from the world into the mist.

It may have been a moment or a hundred years later, Alex was uncertain of time, but she was back in Sara's house in the woods. The furniture was unbroken, the floor unsoiled. Everything was exactly as it was the moment Alex had arrived.

Sara pulled a chair out from the table and lowered herself gingerly into it. She placed her hands—gnarled and broken, but painless—in her lap and waited.

Alex sensed that time was not the same as it was for a living body. Sara did nothing but sit in her chair in her house. She felt her body changing, her skin thinning and shriveling, her hair growing long and wild; her vision yellowed and dimmed. Around her, the house decayed under growing layers of dust. The forest encroached upon then invaded it. The ceiling collapsed around her. The walls gave out. The floors sagged. Vines embraced the foundation, and everything rotted to dirt.

Sara said this was a loop, that she was trapped, and I would set her free. Did I? Did I free her and trap myself? Will I sit here forever or will the loop restart? Is this my fate now, enduring her death over and over?

She didn't notice when the sensation began, unaware until it reached a threshold. It was like a fishhook caught her gut, and whoever had the line was ferociously reeling her in. Everything felt different, strange. An unrelenting draw threatened to drag her if she resisted. A fallen branch in her crippled hands became her walking stick. She stepped to the edge of the foundation, the house like a shadow behind her.

At the foot of the steps, surrounded by a ring of salt, a woman lay dead. Sara took the stairs one at a time with both feet, careful and steady in her rising excitement. She felt alive again as she approached the outer layer of salt and the young man standing within it.

"Have you brought it?"

"I need it back." Alex heard it. It wasn't her voice, but the way her mouth shaped her words that reminded everyone of her father.

"Your name is Peter," she said to the young man. *Is Sara hearing my thoughts?*

"You know my name?"

"I know about you," she cackled. "Before anything else, I need something."

Peter, tall, thin, young, placed the Book he was holding upon the ground and stepped from the three circles of salt. He rolled the young woman over. Alex would have gasped if she could.

Peter placed his hands on Abby's chest.

Abby was only a few years older than Alex.

Peter held his hands out to Sara. She claimed the glowing coin.

It felt different. It felt warm, alive. It recalled Sara to the time when blood still flowed in her veins, and she was more than a specter in a dream. How long since they felt alive? The sensation was almost unfamiliar. Alex felt Sara's rising tide of jealousy.

"Come." She beckoned him, turning away. Alex could stare at him all day. Her father, whom she only knew as a living corpse, stood feet away, alive and vital. His dark hair, his tall, lanky form; she wanted to burn the image into her retinas, memorize every detail, every hair, before she lost him again. She wanted Sara to turn around one more time.

He wore dungarees and a plaid shirt, open at the collar. *Why does he get to wear his clothes and I had to be naked under a graduation gown?*

As she crossed the threshold into the house, her consciousness somersaulted, her entire existence shifting in a fit of momentary vertigo, as though the world slipped onto its side. Her appearance of decay, of brutality, of time, all vanished. She was young.

Peter stepped through the doorway. "You're beautiful," he exclaimed, startled.

Sara grinned. Alex, however, found the complements and intonation disturbing.

"Outside was a long time from now. In here, I am who I was."

"No offense, but out there, you were, um…"

"Hideous?" Alex could not believe her father was behaving this way.

"No, I mean, but compared to now, yeah, kind of." His cheeks reddened.

Alex slid to the kitchen, her feet gliding over the floor. "You must be hungry," she said.

"No, I just ate a few… You know what? I am hungry. If it's no trouble."

Sara looked back as she started spooning soup into a ceramic bowl. "Trouble would be you not eating."

She set the bowl in front of Peter, and he hungrily began to eat. He sat hunched over the table, using the bowl to catch his drippings as they ran down his cheeks. Sara took the seat beside him, her corseted frame accustomed to the restriction. The sensation was comforting. *Am I becoming Sara?*

"Tell me Peter Hawthorne, why did you summon me?"

Peter pushed his seat back. "I am the male twin of a witch."

"Is that an achievement?"

"I am wed to a witch."

"And?" Alex enjoyed Sara's snark and watching Peter squirm.

"She's pregnant."

"More twins." *Twins? Had she been capable, Alex would have gasped.*

"Yes, exactly."

Sara nodded, thoughtfully. "You still haven't told me about the woman you sacrificed to come to me. Is she your Familiar?"

"I came to you specifically. And no, Abby isn't my Familiar. She's my friend. I asked her to be my Familiar, but she refused. To me, that is. She said she'll swear herself to my unborn. To the girl."

Abby swore an oath to me? She's my Familiar?

He continued, "I'm learned, you know. I've studied. I've read hundreds of Books."

Is he bragging?

Sara's anger boiled over. "Do you expect me to think well of you?"

"No, anything but." Peter raised his hands defensively. "The Book I used to get here—to get outside—was yours."

"That Book was never mine, only what is in it." *Sara's book?* Alex could still see the vomited shapes spilling, the disgusting scribe dipping his pen and scratching symbols and designs into the paper, the pen driving his hand, the vomitus ink changing color on the page. If it weren't so horrific, it would have been miraculous.

Peter's Book. Alex recalled Heather's words. *She held Peter's Book, used Sara's own magic to send me back to her.*

"That—that's what I mean. The spells are yours. That's why I came to you. For your help. To ask you to save my baby girl."

"I'm listening."

"I need to un-twin her."

Alex felt the wind leave Sara's lungs. *Un-twin?*

"I have your spells. I need your help."

"Tell me why you want this?"

"I researched it all. A friend helped. I read all the notes, it's amazing how detailed they were back then, the bureaucratic forms they filled out to make sure no information was lost. I know they created *this* Book as they," his tone lost its excitement, "tortured you."

"Tortured me, did they?"

Peter nodded.

"That wasn't torture. All they wanted was my magic. That was murder, committed slowly."

Peter looked around the room.

"I would have confessed to any crime or sin to make it stop. But they wouldn't stop until they squeezed me of every last spell."

"They believed they were in the right. They think they're protecting the world."

"Hah. Rubbish they tell themselves to sleep at night. Their kind spilled enough innocent blood to overflow the oceans."

"They fear what would happen if your kind, if women, repossessed your magic."

Sara grinned. "They should."

"I agree. That's my point."

"Are you justifying their actions to me?"

"Not in the least. I want it to happen, the repossessing, to make everything as it was, as it was supposed to be before they knew they could take it. I want to see that world."

"I've read the myths and stories. They worshipped us. Women protected the world. Until men learned to steal it and wield it for power."

"Some of us want to end that. When my mentor, Matthew, came to me,"—Alex gasped—"he wanted to start it again. But I figured it out—me and my friend, William. Matthew thinks he's using me to do this for him, but he wants it all for himself. I know how to give it all back, and it starts with you."

Sara scowled, unaffected by Alex's gasp.

"Don't you understand what I'm saying? What you went through needn't be in vain."

"Let's not debate the past," she hissed, reaching out and touching Peter's cheek, feeling her father's stubble. *Is Sara flirting with my dad?*

"My mother taught me to respect the Moon. I want my daughter to be born a goddess. I want her to know she has the power to make right in the world." Alex listened in disbelief.

"You've practiced those words?"

He blushed. "Hundreds of times. They sound better in front of my mirror."

"Your mother taught you this morality?"

"My ancestors have always been a little heretical. My parents made sure I understood what I did to Heather; I diminished her because I exist. Witches weren't supposed to be twins. It happens to those with even a speck of magic left. It's the yin and yang, balancing where balance isn't necessary. I know it doesn't matter nowadays. There's no magic left. It's all in Books now."

"Un-twinning is possible," she mused, "but the risk is too great. It is not for a man to take upon himself."

"That's where you're wrong," Peter said with a little too much enthusiasm.

"Where I'm wrong?" Sara slid her chair back. "I think maybe we're done. *Wrong?* If you're so smart that you know when I'm wrong, you have no need of me."

Peter held out his hands in contrition. "All this, your suffering, it is because of men's meddling. Let a man's meddling fix it. Jeremiah can be stopped, but only with your help."

"You don't want your daughter to suffer that burden?"

"No."

"You will suffer for it."

"Whatever it takes."

"She will suffer for it." Alex waited to hear how her father would answer.

"I wish there were another way."

"You are certain?"

Peter stammered. "I, I am. I know it will work."

Alex listened, fearing what was to be revealed to her.

Sara leaned intimately close to him. *Is she going to kiss him?* "How far are you willing to take this?"

Peter lowered his hands to the table. His voice became somber. "As far as necessary."

"You will sacrifice everything?"

"I'm here aren't I?"

"You are asking for something whose cost you cannot comprehend."

"I'd die for my daughter."

Alex smiled inside.

"What if the cost is greater than death?"

Peter slammed his hand down on the table. "Dammit. I didn't come here to get jerked around. I came here to save my daughter. Can't you just help me?"

The sound of his hand slamming the table startled both Alex and Sara. It made them queasy. "Perhaps you'd better go."

Peter opened his mouth, but she interrupted him after a syllable. "Go. Now. Take yourself outside and return to the salt. Do not bother me again. Ever." His banging on the table had been too much like Matthew's hammer.

Don't go, Dad. All this time, all this waiting. This is what you wanted me to see.

Peter did not budge. He banged the table again. "Dammit, how do I prove myself?"

Sara jumped to her feet, knocking her chair over, her hand outstretched. "There's the door. Use it, or I will send you through it myself."

Peter's voice fell. "I'm sorry," he whimpered. "You're my only hope."

He stood; his head hung. He shuffled towards the door. "Sara," he began from the threshold, "the things I did to get here were not without consequence. Everything I do is in service of my daughter. They'll know I came. Matthew, my teacher, will know. He'll punish me, my wife, maybe even my unborn. Jeremiah, who knows what he'll do? I'll accept their wrath, but I mustn't fail my daughter."

Eric said the sacrifice was too great. Does Peter know that?

Sara said nothing. Her hand tightened around Abby's coin, feeling it radiating against her skin. *Does Sara mean to keep it? If she's sending him away, shouldn't she return it?*

Peter touched his chest then pulled his hand free, proffering his own glowing coin. "I'm prepared to hand this to you, right now, if it means you'll help me. I will do anything you ask, even give my soul to you."

Alex could feel Sara's growing desire for his coin. *Would this return her to life? What about these coins make her so covetous?* The upswell was short-lived, and she replied, "I am not the Ferrier of Souls. I do not accept this precious currency."

This time Peter did not answer. Alex's emotions were conflicted; this was her father, younger, in his prime, and yet he gave up all of that for her.

"Do you know why I test you, Peter?"

"Test?"

"Because you come here, asking me to help you complete an impossible task. You speak of your willingness to accept the consequences, yet you know not their impact on your daughter. How long before she understands?" *Is she saying this for him? Or is it for my benefit?*

He lowered his eyes. His voice broke. "I don't know if she ever will. I can only do what I believe is right and best for her and hope one day she can forgive me for it." He looked up as he finished, staring at Sara. "I hope she forgives me."

All her life, her father had been a shadow shambling through the house. Alex was about to see what made him like that. *Holly never told me because I wouldn't hear it. How many times did she try? How many times did my head ache too much for me to hear? All this time, I thought it was too painful for her, but she hid the truth because it was too painful for me.*

They stood, staring at one another. She clasped his extended hand. His palm relinquished the glowing coin, but Sara pushed it back. "You mustn't let go of this until the right moment."

"You'll help me?" She nodded. He breathed a sigh. "What do I do?"

Sara positioned his hands on his coin, both thumbs against the center. "Press down in the center. Will it to cleave. A coin doesn't just break because you try to break it." She touched his hands.

"What will breaking my soul in two do to me?"

"It is the most grievous self-harm. Break it with the desire to save your daughter. It is only by sacrifice that she survives the night."

Peter studied his coin. He closed his eyes in concentration. His fingers turned white as he squeezed and twisted at the coin. It snapped, and it was like the very earth they stood on was unmade. Waves of light nearly knocked them from their feet.

Grinning, Peter held two near-perfect half-moons of light. As he placed them in his right hand, his left hand darted to his pocket.

"What we do next, Peter, cannot be undone."

"I'm ready."

"I am a shade in the world of shadows, Peter. The journey to the place your wife dreams allows no living things. You must take a path neither a shade nor a dreamer can travel. This will require payment where none is expected."

How does she know these things?

"The universe whispers secrets that only the dead can hear," Sara replied. *Is she telling him... or me?*

Peter nodded. Alex felt Sara wish her home away. The walls dissolved, leaving them on the stone foundation, the only thing that was real about this place in Peter's time. Mist boiled up from the ground. When the child appeared, it regarded neither of them.

Sara could pass, but the child just stared at Peter. It made no request; it only prevented him from moving any further. Alex, for the first time, was unafraid of the child; it was beautiful.

"Give him a half," Sara told Peter.

Peter looked at the cleaved moons in his hand. "Does it matter which?" When Sara shook her head, he held out a half-moon. The child reluctantly accepted the gift. It turned it between its small digits. It closed its fingers and opened them again, its eyes widened as though shocked to see it still in its palm.

It silently motioned for Peter to pass. Peter studied the child. It repeatedly opened and closed its fist as though shocked the half-moon of a coin remained. Peter offered a gratuitous wave and smiled. The child—Charon—smiled back.

Peter followed Sara into the mist.

Chapter Twenty-Four

Peter caught up to Sara and stood at her side. He was tall, perhaps even taller than Alex, but she hadn't her own body to compare. Alex was unused to looking up at people. It felt unnatural, like she was standing in a hole. Peter was so young, so nervous. His anxiety was palpable. Alex could barely contain her excitement, knowing they were standing side by side, father and daughter. Sara reached up and placed a hand on his shoulder. *Did I make her do that?*

The words she said were unexpected. "Peter Hawthorne, welcome to the unimagined afterlife."

"There's nothing here."

"Hence the name."

Alex couldn't tell who was speaking. Thoughts were coming to her as Sara's mouth moved. *Is this the universe revealing itself, or am I losing myself to her?*

Peter looked about. "How long do we wait?"

"When have we been waiting?"

Peter motioned to the emptiness beneath his feet. "We're standing, waiting for something."

"A moment ago, you were at my house; a building that hasn't existed in one and three-quarter centuries. To cross a room, you believed you walked. How did you walk across something that is not there?"

"How else would I do it?"

She pointed down. "Like this."

"We're moving?" She nodded at his surprise. "Right now?" She nodded again. His face lit up, his eyes twinkling in a smile. "I was creeped out when I saw you glide across the floor before."

Alex felt Sara's amusement at his provincialism. "You and I are in a place with no walls, no floor. It's a place of nothing, yet to be thought into being. It is empty and as vast as, well, vaster than existence. Do you understand now that just because you stand doesn't mean we are waiting?"

"I guess," he mused. "It just doesn't feel like moving…"

"Emptiness doesn't feel like anything. Perhaps it's time we fill it. We need your sleeping wife. Think her here."

"Like imagine her?"

"She sleeps. When she dreams, she ventures into this world, tethered by a silver thread of light, leaving her body behind. We need to find her. We need her dreaming self to bring us to her sleeping self."

"I wish I understood what you mean, but I'll try." He closed his eyes in deep concentration. "I don't think this will work," he said, biting his lip. "This is ridiculous."

Ridiculous things can have very severe consequences.

"Keep trying."

"I am," he hissed, concentration twisting his features. "I don't know if I'm doing it right."

In the dark distance, a cavity of light appeared.

"You're doing it," Sara encouraged him.

In a moment, Alex's mother was standing beside them, the spot on her heart glowing bright, a silver thread trailing away into eternity.

Alex was unprepared for the intense feelings that exploded into existence at the sight of her mother, like her heart was recklessly over-inflated. Holly looked so young, so vibrant. It pained Alex to realize how the coming years would erode her attractive features. As desperately as she wanted to know her father better, it was her mother she wished to question.

"My Holly," Peter whispered.

"You're home already? It worked?" Holly asked. Around them, first the furniture, then the objects, and the walls of their living room, materialized from the darkness. Holly motioned at Sara, "Who's this? She's pretty." Then to Sara, she asked, "Who are you?" Holly leaned closer, as though using Sara's eyes as peepholes. "Who are you?"

Can she see me?

Holly stood before her, in a pink wide-ribbed turtleneck and jeans. Alex didn't think her mother looked pregnant, just young and beautiful.

"Holly, dear, you need to go back to sleep," Sara said.

"Sleep?"

"Yes."

"Aren't I? Isn't this a dream?"

"It is," Sara told her.

Holly caressed Peter's neck. "I like when you're in my dreams."

Peter grinned, but Sara stepped between them. She cradled Holly's arm, and they drifted along her glowing thread. Past the kitchen, the front door, up the narrow staircase. At the top of the stairs, into her parents' bedroom. Sara paused then stepped past and investigated the next door. Boxes stacked were stacked inside, two and three high from the door to the back wall. *Is Sara curious, or did she sense that I wanted to look?*

Peter noticed. "That's our storage room. We need to clear it out for the nursery."

Holly was no longer standing, but asleep in bed, a gauzy white cotton nightgown enwrapping her body. There was no silver thread, no coin. Peter sat beside her. Her body rocked towards him as his weight depressed the mattress. He touched her shoulder. His hand ran along her side from shoulder to hip to knee, following her curve. "I love her so much. She wants this too. But I can't hurt her. If this hurts her, we stop now."

Holly mumbled in her sleep. "Your professor came to check on you."

"Matthew? Matthew was here?"

"She's dreaming," Sara explained. "Whatever her experience, it will seem no more than a bad dream."

Peter scanned the room. "If Matthew's here," he began.

"If you're having second thoughts," Sara said.

"No," he replied. "There's no going back."

My mom knew Matthew, too? Well enough to have dreams about him?

"Please tell me what to do."

Sara sat on the other side of the bed, her corseted form upright. Alex understood; when Sara thought of herself, she wore a corset.

She reached across the bed and placed her hand on Holly's belly. Alex felt a tingle in her hand. *Am I in there? Little embryonic proto-me?* She shivered at the implication; she was inside and outside her mother.

"The babies are here," Sara said, patting Holly just above her pubic bone, "months from being born. They are not alive, not dead; they just are. They are in the process of being."

She touched Peter's left hand. "You left your time and journeyed to mine. You are a physical being in the world of shadows; your body lies amidst the circles of salt at the foot of the ruins of my home. And is also here. You exist in both places. However long you are here, no moment will pass for you, there. There is no in-between, just two ends of a loop. Do you understand?"

Peter nodded. *Really? Because I have no idea what she's talking about.*

Sara pulled his hand into contact with Holly's abdomen. "Holly is here, asleep on your bed, in your home, in your time. In her belly, swelling around two glowing coins are the things that will become your children. They're dividing, forming, transforming. Reach into her."

"Into?"

Sara nodded. "Press. You are not in the same world. You are here and she is there."

"I think I understand," Peter said.

Really?

"Do you?" Apparently, Sara shared Alex's doubts.

Peter held his hand to the bridge of his nose. "It's like you can see Holly with one eye and me with another. We appear to be in the same place, but there's a wall between us. Am I close?"

An uneasiness passed through Sara. "That is a very good example."

After a moment of pressing his hand against Holly, Peter said, "My hand isn't going into her."

"Visualize your hand slipping through. Pretend you can walk through a wall."

He pressed her belly. Holly stirred, groaning.

"You're not hurting her. Push, Peter, push!"

Peter pushed harder. Holly groaned. Just when he seemed about to push Holly onto her side, his hand slipped into her.

"Oh, that's disgusting," he said.

"Feel for her womb. Do you feel it? Inside, you will feel your children."

He was like a television surgeon conducting a complicated surgery, his hand fishing around in her insides. His complexion greened, his expression of disgust worsening.

"I feel them." His eyes alight, brimming with moisture. "I feel them. One, two. Both my children." He laughed with joy. "I'm touching our babies!"

Realization chilled his enthusiasm. He was more calculated than Alex expected, "How do I know which is which?"

"Take one in your hand."

"Okay, I'm holding one."

"With not too much pressure, squeeze."

As Peter said, "Okay," Alex's chest clenched.

"Not that one," Sara hissed. *Does Sara know only because I'm here? Is that why they needed me to be here?*

"Okay. I'm holding the other one."

Sara placed her hand on Holly's hip. Only Alex could hear her whisper, "Alex, I am so sorry. Please forgive us."

What is she apologizing to me for?

Sara looked up at Peter. "Listen carefully. In one swift motion, without releasing your grasp, you must pull your hand out. You mustn't stop no matter how the sensation compels you."

Peter's eyes went from Sara's face to Holly to her belly. "Will it hurt her?"

"For a moment, it will be excruciating. The faster, the shorter her suffering."

"I can't."

"You must, Peter. Now, or you lose both children."

"Wait."

"What are you waiting for, Peter?"

"It's not that simple. His coin... stays."

Holly's face was showing distress. "You will lose them if you take any longer," Sara urged.

"Shush. I'm losing my concentration."

Sara crossed her arms. "They're dying," she hissed.

"Just another second," he said.

"Now, Peter!"

Holly groaned.

Peter's back wrenched, his shoulder and arm withdrew in a single, fluid motion. Anguish washed across his face as the thing in his hand tore away from Holly's womb.

Holly cried out but didn't wake.

Peter opened his hand and looked at his palm. Panicked, he showed his empty hand to Sara.

"Unexpected," Sara said. Then she pointed. "Look closer."

Alex saw. She was chilled.

Peter brought his hand closer to his face. In the center of his palm, he observed a minuscule black pinprick. It was a void similar to her own, an absent soul.

"Now, blow it away. Let it go and never think on it again."

"Like wishing on an eyelash?"

Sara didn't answer.

Peter blew across his palm. The black spot seemed to flutter, its size and shape unchanging as it flitted into the air, a speck of oblivion carried on the draft of breath, lost to the darkness around them.

"It's done."

Peter shook his head. "But we're not." Sara's expression demanded further explanation. "They'll know I did this. I need to protect her until she's old enough—strong enough—to defend herself."

"Remember Peter, time is no longer on our side. You've brought a second soul here. What are you doing?"

Peter grinned mischievously. "Yours was not the only Book I brought." From his pocket, he pulled a tattered piece of paper, but Sara refused to look at it. "I'm sacrificing this woman to save my daughter."

Alex felt Sara's disgust.

Before she could stop him or say anything, Peter began the guttural translation, speaking the nonsense sounds from the book in his hands. He carefully tore the page leaving each symbol like a solitary glyph on its own scrap. He plunged his hand back into Holly's womb, emerging empty-handed.

"What have you done?"

"I cast the first part before I left Holly in the waking world and finished it here. To protected her. I did not waste her brother. He hides her. I hid magic from her. She will not know it, think it, hear it, or even see it."

Sara's curiosity overlapped with Alex's own, "You left her defenseless?"

"No," he said. "Hidden. They can't know where she is. She is invisible to them."

"She's powerless."

"Almost. She'll heal. Like most women, she won't know she's doing it."

"They will find her, Peter."

"My friend created a trigger. When she's in danger, she'll dream of her last real memory of me."

Her last real memory, the words echoed in Alex's head. All this time she'd assumed her headaches and ears ringing was evidence of malice. *My father did this to protect me?*

"There," Peter said. "Everything is set."

Sara touched his shoulder. "Peter, what have you done?"

Alex didn't know her father, but his expression said he wasn't telling the whole truth when he said, "The curse is complete."

"No, Peter. That's not true." Sara could see through him too.

"The curse needs to be undone at some point, no?"

Sara nodded.

"That's what we've done. I ensured it happens."

She metered her tone, expectant. "I need to hear you say it."

Alex did not like her father's expression. "You, Sara, will know my daughter."

He knew this whole time? Blood drained from Sara's face. "Peter, why would you do that to me? To her?"

Peter cast his gaze down. "I know you know now."

"You tricked me," Sara hissed.

"It's the outcome, not the path that matters."

"I wondered why I couldn't move on. *You* did that," she growled. "And to think I pitied you. You're about to get what you deserve."

"About to?" Peter turned to Holly and his demeanor changed. His shoulders fell, his face softened. He touched her shoulder. He traced her shape from hip to knee. "I've done what I came to do. Holly is sleeping, the baby is un-twinned. We need to leave before

Matthew or Jeremiah realize and find her. Tomorrow starts a new day for us."

"You mean, for Holly and the child. You knew the price was high."

"I did. Let's hope she is worth it."

This is how you talk about me? Dad, what did you do to me? Sara just said, "When will you know?"

He was silent. Sara fidgeted, allowing him to think. She wanted to be away. He whispered, "If I did everything right, she'll know. You'll know too." He made a face. "She has to be with you when they take your magic. That's the only way to make her receptive to it."

"You know my fate and yet send your daughter into my life? That's cruel."

"Magic won't come without sacrifice. Please, when you see her, don't tell her what's coming or that it's because of me."

"If it works," she mocked, "you just told her."

He didn't respond. "Let's be done."

She just told you I'm here and you have nothing to say to me? "I can't wait to be back with her."

Sara cupped Peter's head in her hand. "Oh my dear," she said, "once we leave this place, you'll never speak to your wife again."

Peter produced the remaining half-moon. He stared at the glowing form, the straight edge that wasn't straight. "This doesn't come when I leave." He wasn't asking.

"You paid to cross over; you must pay to cross back."

"That will kill me, won't it?"

"Yes. No."

"Which is it?"

"Both, Peter. Eternal twilight. Living death."

His eyes closed mournfully. "I hoped you'd know a way back without that happening. I knew you didn't, but I hoped." He looked at Holly. "We have time for this?"

"Be quick," Sara replied.

Alex seethed. *He did this to me? Even if Sara knew he could save himself, would she tell him now? He knew the risk and put it on Sara and on me. He cursed us all.*

He rubbed Holly's shoulder. Her eyes fluttered opened. Still mostly asleep, she mumbled, "You're back. Did it work?"

Peter nodded.

Holly's face darkened. "We had to, right? We did the right thing?"

Peter nodded. "We did." He smiled, but his eyes were sad. "I've got to go. I'll be back soon. Just, please know that no matter what, you are my life. I live to be your husband, your friend, your lover, your partner in crime."

"You sound like a greeting card." Holly stretched.

"We always knew there would be a price. Whenever you look at her, never doubt that it was worth it. Never wonder if I had doubts."

"What are you talking about, Peter? You're scaring me. What price? Doubts?"

Sara hissed, "You never told her?"

Peter turned to Sara. "I hoped to cheat my way back."

Sara shook her head. "No one cheats death, Peter."

Holly asked, "Who are you talking to?"

Peter didn't answer. "You'll raise her, teach her. Everything we talked about; I know you'll make her amazing. Heather knows too, how to break the curse."

"Peter," Sara said, clutching his shoulder. "You can feel them, can't you?" Outside Holly's bedroom window, in a sky that wasn't from the waking world, dark shadows gathered. "The living don't belong here, Peter."

Peter nodded. "I love you, Holly."

"Now, Peter," Sara hissed.

"Just a minute more."

"Peter, what they'll do to you..."

Peter kissed Holly's cheek.

"I love you, Holly."

"Now," Sara cried.

"Okay."

"I love you too... Where are you going? Peter? What price? Peter, don't leave me..." Holly's voice faded with the room. They were alone. Their surroundings faded into the darkness. The shadows, like floating paper jellyfish, disappeared into the black sky.

Peter sobbed, head in his hand. Sara touched his arm. "One day," she whispered, "she'll learn why you did this. She'll learn about your sacrifice. Things we do for our children aren't obvious at first. She may even feel guilty for doubting you."

"She shouldn't feel guilty," he replied. "This is my love for her."

"In time, she will understand. I am sure as I am of my own feelings."

Finally, Alex had answers, but also more questions. Her emotions were a Gordian Knot of confusion.

The mist broke before them. On the edge of the curtain of ethereal fog, Charon stood.

"Pay the balance," Sara's voice choked.

Peter approached the child, reluctance weighing on his steps. He produced his half-moon. He turned to Sara. "There's no other way? You're absolutely certain?"

Sara shook her head. "You can't remain here."

He nodded. Charon stared with curious expectancy.

Peter rolled the half-coin over in his fingers. "I know what you're going to say, but I don't think I can go through with it."

"I don't imagine you do, Peter."

"I have to, though, don't I?"

"The alternative…" Sara started to speak but didn't finish.

"I know, a living person can't stay in the world of the dead."

"Horrible things hunt the living. All this will be for nothing. The suffering you cause, it will be inexcusable."

"I guess my secret will be safe. They'll never learn the truth."

"Not from you. You guarantee her safety."

Peter approached Charon. He looked down, and it gazed back passively. He knelt. The child regarded him, its expression unchanged.

"You've probably seen it all," Peter said. "You bring everyone across, collecting your coins. I wonder, though, if you've seen the likes of me before." He proffered his half-coin. "Please accept this."

Charon looked to the offering and then back to Peter. Its hands gently relieved Peter of the coin. It inspected the glowing crescent with intense curiosity, turning it in its hands, running its fingers over the snapped edge.

"You have the two halves," Peter told the child. When its expression didn't change, he asked, "Do you understand?"

Charon produced the other half-coin. It held one in each hand and placed the broken edges together. A small divot was visible along the seam. The two halves came apart. It placed them together, again and again; they came apart each time. It showed Peter the two halves.

"Are you giving them back?" Peter reached his hand out.

"Don't, Peter," Sara shouted.

Charon pulled the halves away. With an unnerved expression, Peter pulled back his hands and held them at his sides. It showed him again that the two halves wouldn't stay together. *What are you trying to tell him?*

Peter moved closer to Sara.

Around them, the wooden walls and meager possessions of Sara's house materialized out of the mist.

"Nothing happened. Did I make it through?"

Sara produced Abby's glowing disk from her pocket. "This brought you home."

Peter looked at the glowing disk. "That Abby's." Although nothing about his tone insinuated he was asking, Sara nodded. Peter was silent.

"I know what you're thinking, Peter."

"Do you?" Peter asked.

"Is this how Abby's story should end?"

"It's not Abby's story. I'm only thinking about what's best for my daughter."

"You would make a lovely family."

You'd sacrifice Abby? For what? You're not who I thought you were.

"But this isn't how Abby's story should end," Peter answered.

"She's committed to your daughter."

Peter nodded. "She's in safer hands with Abby than me."

"You made difficult decisions today. Her Familiar will always protect her. Your desire to live may lead you to fail."

Peter said nothing. Alex wondered what he was thinking. Two options lay before him: sacrifice or self-preservation. One was best for him, the other for her.

"Peter," Sara said, "You know how my Book was created. You did this to her because there's no other way for her to be susceptible to my magic. You can't protect her from that. You'll want to. You'll try."

Peter didn't say a word. His lowered head spoke volumes. His eyes teared up. He pushed her hand and Abby's coin away. Sara allowed Alex to stare at him a moment longer. She took in every moment, studying his every motion. "I'm sorry," he sobbed. "I know what I should do. I just…" He took a breath but didn't finish.

"Don't want to die?"

Peter looked up at her and nodded. "I know there's no way back for me, Sara. I knew that at the start. I know I have to, but I don't want to."

Sara was silent.

"I know I'm being selfish. I chose this. I burdened her. It's up to that baby in Holly's belly to prove I made the right choice."

"We'll see, won't we."

"She'll be amazing," he told her. "You'll see."

Sara offered her hand. "It's time you returned this."

Peter's face was red and wet from crying. He was ashamed.

Sara took Peter's arm as he took the coin. They glided towards the front door. Alex understood the impact of his choices, the impact on their lives. To her, he was not even a person yesterday; today she saw the multifaceted, flawed, amazing man whose single act caused so many years of anguish and pain for so many people.

Alex's thoughts turned to her mother. She now understood why her mother cared so much, and for so long, for a man incapable of expressing any kind of emotion in return. It broke her heart to think of their love story, and how despite their shared adoration, her mother's love would forevermore be unrequited.

Sara's joints tightened. Her body sagged and shrank. Her hands, trembling as her fingers twisted, hooked the gnarled walking stick beside the doorframe. Air entering her lungs came with effort and required more frequent, shallow breaths.

They took the stairs slowly. Her knees protested, and she leaned heavily on her cane. Her body was so stiff and weak she could barely reach one step from the last. They approached Abby's body. Peter knelt beside her. Alex saw Abby, her youthful face, fleshy and child-like. It was gray and deathly. Peter placed Abby's glowing coin on her chest, his hand over it. With the same hand, he slid his book—

Sara's book—under her arms. Alex thought she saw him use his other hand to slip something into the pocket of her jeans.

Peter turned back to Sara. His mouth curled ever so subtly; his reaction disgusted Alex.

She was still the same woman inside, but he saw the decrepit crone. He had spent so much time with the young Sara, the beautiful Sara. His expression spoke to what he saw now.

"Thank you," he said. Sara softened. Perhaps she'd misread his expression?

Alex wanted to reach out and embrace her father. Her heart ached to feel his touch, to hear him say her name. It would be the first time.

Peter hesitantly touched Sara's shoulders. He embraced her. He placed a gentle kiss on her cheek. Had Alex the control to cry, Sara would have shed tears.

"There?" Peter pointed to the center of the circle.

Sara nodded.

Peter walked calmly to the center circle. He turned to her, eyes glistening, and sniffled. "Tell my daughter I love her, when you see her."

She smiled gently, "She knows."

Alex couldn't process what she was feeling in this moment. She missed her father so. She'd misunderstood him, seen him as defective. Now she understood. Was he brave? Conniving? Duplicitous? Whose sacrifice was greater, his or the one he gave to her? So much weight rested on a little girl he'd never know. He was flawed. He was just a man.

Peter reached the center and for one moment there were two of him; in the next, there was only one.

Abby coughed. Peter's sorrowful expression melted away.

Sara knelt by Abby's side and patted her arm.

Abby came around. Seeing Sara, she started.

"Let me help you," Sara helped Abby to her feet.

"Peter? Hey Peter?" Abby called to him. He replied with his vacant expression. "What happened to Peter? What did you do to him?"

"Nothing," Sara stepped back.

Abby pointed at the glowing coin in her chest. "Then where's his?" There was nothing, no glow, no dark void.

"He succeeded, Abby." Abby processed what Sara said. *Peter had to tell you something. You had to know what to expect, right? How else did he get you to agree to die for him?* "Everything rests with you now, until his daughter is ready."

"She's not even born yet. How will I know?"

"You'll know."

Abby looked from Peter to the old witch. "He told me to hide his Book." She examined the Book, the pages obscured with sheets of notes. She closed the cover, stepped over the circles of salt, and disappeared into the mist. Moments later she reappeared as though stepping into and out of a closet. "What now?"

"Take Peter home. There is nothing left of him, what you see is empty, guided only by the residue of what used to be inside."

"He's dead?"

"And alive."

"That sounds horrible."

Sara nodded. "I've heard about people like him, turned to slaves, unable to resist whoever possesses their coin."

"Who has Peter's?"

Sara motioned to the mist. "He paid with two halves for passage."

"Two halves?" Abby clarified, "Both?" She patted her pockets before looking relieved. *What did he give her?*

"Both," Sara said. "Half to enter and half to leave."

"What do I tell Holly?" Abby asked, a little out of breath.

Before she could explain who Holly was, Sara replied, "Holly will remember her dream. She knows, although she may not understand what Peter is now. Tell her he is both alive and dead. When his body ceases to live, nothing will be left but dust. He will never pass over again."

Abby thought a moment, and then she got to work. Sara allowed Alex to watch. Abby broke each circle of salt with her foot, then guided Peter down the trail to his car.

Alex watched them go. This was the man she knew. "Bye daddy," she whispered to the wind.

Chapter Twenty-Five

rossing the threshold to her house didn't restore Sara's youth. She collapsed into a chair, gasping at pain all the worse for momentarily experiencing her youth. She was complicit in Peter's self-destruction. The male twin was a curse on womankind for counteracting the female, diminishing her, creating balance where none should have been, weakening womankind's magical strength.

Assisting Peter had resulted in her own demise. Matthew killed her because of this. Peter trapped her in a circle created by her own meddling.

Sara's emotions did little to help Alex with her own. She felt like a little girl. As a child, she had learned right away to cry for mommy, because—in her perception—Daddy didn't care. How mistaken she had been. He cared too much. She had mistreated him a few times, and that was what she remembered now. She'd face Matthew's hammer again if she could take those times back, not for his sake, but for her own. Alex had come for answers, and now she questioned her own recollection. If the nightmare was real, did her mind create the car accident to protect her from her headaches?

There was a fear both women shared; was all this sacrifice and pain worth the cost? Would Alex live up to expectations that had driven her loved ones to make such extraordinary sacrifices? Could she?

Sara sobbed.

If she had been like a parasite when she entered Sara, now they were nearly symbiotic. Sara's body felt like her hers. She couldn't tell where she ended and Sara began. How long had it been since Peter left? It could have been years. Her body grew older and even more exhausted.

Alex didn't hear Sara's thoughts but felt them. Sara needed no words to express her darkening emotions. Her life was short, her death, eternal. Death wasn't an escape from life, but an extension, a sequel where all the rules change, a dream without end and Sara couldn't move past the death that was forced upon her. She envied

Peter. She hated him. He lost all consciousness forever. He was a flickered-out candle flame, smoldering, never to be relit. She was doomed in the extension of a life she wanted to forget but never could. *If this is death*, Alex could feel her wondering, *could there be another death from this?*

Alex felt something. This wasn't a novel sensation. The first time it snuck up on her, but now, understanding what it was, Sara and Alex understood the feeling in her gut. Alex felt Sara's expectation. It was frightening and thrilling. Sara's body protested the effort to stand, creaking in resistance, refusing to straighten. Shuffling to the window, what she saw outside made Alex want to cry.

Ten women bumbled about in the clearing, pouring salt circles and handing out graduation gowns. Alex saw herself. Sara's curious hands absently grasped the window frame. *Is that really me?* Alex had been inside Sara for—*how long*? Nearly two centuries? Seeing herself now made her long—and fear—to slip back into the skin of that body. Would it still fit her?

She recalled how being that person, that child, made her feel, and worse, how she felt about it. Looking at that woman, so young, Alex could not grasp how she never saw herself as beautiful. That girl was tall, trim and athletic, with muscular legs and shoulders. That girl always hated her slender hips and bust. That girl would look at beautiful Rose and wish she could be as pretty, as curvaceous, but now there was no one else Alex wanted to be. Sara cackled joyfully as that girl made faces at Book Club's apparent ridiculousness. That girl's face smiled at rest. Alex felt almost in love with that young girl she used to know.

Why did it take viewing myself as someone else to see the lies I told myself about her?

Alex knew she was smart; it was the one thing she was most proud of. She valued her intelligence more than looks because what were looks worth without the brains behind them? Standing at the window, looking through a hag's eyes, Sara's face reflected in the glass, she understood that a pretty face had nothing to do with the person inside.

Alex scanned for Abby. When she saw her friend, her heart warmed. She wondered if Abby would remember meeting Sara— what would it have been—nineteen years ago? Feeling an overwhelming pull, she grasped her walking stick and took to the stairs.

Outside, the child she had been was about to meet Sara. Only it was not truly Sara she would meet. *What am I supposed to do? How do I close the loop and get back? What happens if I fail?* She hesitated at the bottom step. *If I turned away, would I spare her the pain?*

She saw the bewildered face of her younger self.

*   *   *   *

The exertion of the stairs caused Alex to gasp for air, "Have you brought it?" *Was that Sara, or history, or time, repeating?*

Alex shuffled her crooked feet to the edge of the rings of salt, her hand extended.

Young Alex did not know what was being asked of her. The expressions that crossed her face—the animation and life behind her eyes—as she mentally ran through a checklist before settling on the charm Abby made for her, amused Alex.

Alex grinned, exposing her few remaining teeth. She hadn't remembered it until now, the clarity of the glass, the depth of the swirls, the perfect darkness of the small center. *How long ago did Abby give me that?*

As Young Alex's hand wrapped around the charm, Alex felt the breath leave her lungs. *I'm supposed to take Abby's coin; that's what Sara did. Don't I still have it?* She reached into Sara's pocket and stroked Abby's coin. *How can this be here,* she regarded Abby, *and there?*

I'm supposed to tell her I don't want the charm. Alex could barely breathe. She couldn't find the words. *The first time I have control and I wish Sara were here to tell me what to do.* She searched her mind for a hint of Sara but found none.

She watched her other self finger the fine silver string for the clasp. *Stop, girl. Heather said that must never come off.* Alex as Sara lunged, grasping at the charm. Her foot crossed the circle of salt. She felt the smooth charm of burned herbs encircling each other in her palm. She fell into Young Alex's defensive arms. She anticipated the collision of bodies, of ground, of bones breaking. The world spun, her stomach uprooted itself and convulsed. She could not tell up from darkness, down from cold. She was a creature of divine proportions, multiple arms, legs, heads, entwined and devouring one another.

A moment later, Alex gained her bearings. Her head swam as the world twisted into place.

The sky was dark. She stood in a salt circle beside the rotting foundation. Her youthful hands ran over her graduation gown, feeling the form beneath. *Is this really me?*

She held the charm. *Is this why I needed to keep it on, to bring me back?* Had the charm saved her from Peter's fate? She possessed no coin of her own. She had nothing Charon wanted. Did this mean she was free to pass unhindered to the realm of the dead and return? In her dream, Charon allowed her passage without payment. *Does that mean I'm not really alive?*

Alex could not find Abby's coin; she no longer had pockets. *Did I lose it?* She tried to think. *Technically, Sara hasn't asked me to take it yet.* It was hard to fathom that something she remembered hadn't happened and perhaps never would. *Sara was right, loops are confusing.*

Abby woke when Peter returned her coin. Alex stepped from the circle and fell at Abby's side. She looked dead. She gently slapped her face. "Abby? Abby, wake up!"

Around her, the women were suddenly alert, panicked, and confused.

"Alex, why did you leave the circle?" Heather admonished. "The spell won't work if you don't do as you're told."

Alex shook Abby's limp form. Her skin and muscles were relaxed and rubbery.

"Is something wrong?" Carrie looked around at the others. "Did something go wrong?"

"Help me," Alex pleaded. "She's not breathing. She's supposed to wake up."

Donna pointed a finger at Heather. "Isn't it supposed to work this way? That's what you said? Abby will seem dead and then be fine?"

"Maybe it didn't work." Marta's inflection left the ambiguous potential for a question.

Heather lowered the book in her arms and shook her head. "I did everything exactly as Peter wrote. Everything."

"Marta, please," Alex cried, "she's not breathing; I don't feel a heartbeat."

Marta pushed Alex away and examined Abby. She checked her pulse, stretched open an eye. "Oh no."

Nancy fell to her knees across from them. "She shouldn't die for real, should she?" She directed the question to Heather. "I mean, not permanently?" Heather looked confused. "Heather," she screamed, "what did you make me do?"

Heather froze. Marta instructed the other women as she started chest compressions. She sent Carrie for the green responder bag. Using shears pulled from an outside pocket on the bag, Nancy cut open Abby's shirt and bra, exposing her chest.

Alex couldn't take her eyes off the drama. *After all of this, Abby is going to die.*

Heather was frozen, still holding the Book, pages turning in the wind.

"Give that to me," Alex demanded.

Alex could tell Heather was panicking. Abby was dead and Heather was responsible. When the police arrested them all, they would label them a cult, making a human sacrifice. Their Book Club would be revealed as a witch's coven. Their children, their spouses, parents and neighbors, would all wonder when the quiet woman next door had become a satanic killer. "She seemed nice," they'd say. Heather might never see her children again, except through a glass prison partition.

Why isn't she doing anything? Alex tried to wrench the book from her aunt's unwilling grip. "There's got to be something in here to help Abby." To Heather, it must have seemed like the girl who called their ceremony silly was fighting to take her Book, but for Alex, nearly two hundred years separated those moments. She was a much-changed woman.

"If there's something in this Book that can help her, you won't find it standing there."

Heather released the Book like she no longer wanted it. Alex cradled the heavy tome in her arms and thumbed wildly through the pages. Peter's notes covered every page, and she discarded these markers as she went. Moonlight glowed off the beautifully illuminated pages. Different colors of ink, swirling boxes, and shapes were displayed on every page, accentuating what appeared to be words and sentences, though not a single shape formed anything she would call a letter. It was a beautiful maelstrom of gibberish. *Nothing makes any sense!*

Alex recalled Matthew's scribe dipping his nib in her—in Sara's—vomit. She'd experienced the creation of page after page. Boxes outlined the text, curved lines separated one spell from another. *I can't read this. It's just random shapes and designs.* It looked foreign and alien. Her eyes gave up their search and, in their desolation, just stared. Something in the ink of the shapes caught her eye. Looking closer, she saw that each shape contained more. *Are these shapes magical letters? Words? Spells unto themselves?* She squinted, going deeper and deeper. Each individual form was made of hundreds more, and in each of these hundreds more still. She felt like she was falling in, spiraling deeper, level after level, each form containing thousands of words, and then thousands more; spells within spells within spells within spells.

How deep did they go? Was there a depth where she'd find crusting ink staining a page and nothing more?

She couldn't stop, she had to reach the bottom, to see the last, to discover the true spell. She wasn't just standing in the clearing, holding a Book, she was soaring through the universe, a galaxy of magic surrounding her. It was then, as she was gasping in marvel at the splendor, that a thought crept into her mind. *These are not just spells, not just magic.* Alex was reveling in the essence of Sara. All around her, she was not seeing creation; she was seeing the parts of the woman Matthew stole. He took all this, everything that made her. *Sara is magnificent.*

And then Alex saw forms, shapes and designs writ on the page, and there were no layers to them. They were gibberish to her eye, but in her mind, she recognized the vomitus she and Sara had spewed. That act may have been perpetrated upon Sara, but Alex was coupled to her pain. This was her anguish on the page, her blood in the ink. She could hear the hammer splintering her bones. In each spell, she felt the horror that had become stains upon the page.

Pain consumed her, like rusty nails and old razor blades flaying her skin, licking at her insides. She screamed, certain she was spewing a vapor of blood. She was back in the clearing, staring at the Book. She grasped the open page before her and clenched. She could hear the paper crinkle, see it give, the old, fragile sheet cracking instead of bending, breaking in a spray of dust. Her hand tightened, and she could feel the sheet tear away from the threads in its binding. These pages were pain. The pain felt like the hammer shattering her.

Alex screamed again, trying to ride the pain. It only intensified. Shapes, forms, and the designs followed her hand across the page as though swept into a dustbin. Her wipe scattered them from the page, sending them flitting to the earth. She shook the Book, turning its cover to the sky and watched as the words of pain, Sara's pain—her pain—fell to the ground where they crumbled and vanished.

Alex looked at the cover, the name *Sara Frost* inscribed in the binding. She ran her finger over the letters.

Earlier this evening, that name would have been a mystery. Now, feeling the embossing under her fingers, Alex knew what each letter meant with an intimacy she could not even assign to herself; she had been Sara longer. *How much of Sara is inside me? Is Sara in the Book the way I was with her?*

The paper fibers still remembered what was writ upon them. Alex thought of the hammer and the man wielding it. This Book was his legacy. She felt the rage and heat building up inside, and at once the Book burst into flames.

Flames enveloped her, creeping from the cover to her flesh where, with a roar, they consumed her. The screams around her mixed with her own.

Heat held the Book, flames consuming the pages. The pages browned and dried, darkened and cracked. They did not burn away; they were consumed. The Book transformed to ash in her hands. It was unbearable, yet there she stood, the center of the flames, fanning them with her rage.

Heather's face reflected the fire, its violent dance sparkling in her eyes. The heat made her body ripple and sway.

The Book crumbled away.

Alex felt lighter. The flames vanished. She expected to see her hands blackened and sooty, but nothing of the Book remained. *How is the graduation gown intact?* Heather embraced her, chest heaving with sobs.

"Are you okay? What happened? Are you hurt?" Heather patted her down, looking at Alex through tear-filled eyes.

The women gaped at Alex. Then, as though forgetting what they just saw, they returned their attention to Abby. Marta resumed her chest compressions. *Why isn't Abby waking up, like she did with Peter?* Alex's mind swirled. *What's different this time?* Alex thought through the details of her encounter with Sara, step by step, comparing the first time she met Sara with the time she *was* Sara, meeting her younger self. *The coin.* It was like a voice whispering behind her ear. Abby had revived when Sara returned her coin. But Abby's coin hadn't yet been removed.

"Let me through." Alex pushed through the circle of women and knelt beside her friend. Watching Marta force herself against Abby's chest was stomach-churning. Abby's chest collapsed and rebounded, her breasts falling in and out during each compression. Alex placed a hand on Abby's chest, closer to her throat than where Marta was working. She looked at Marta. Sweat drenched the other woman's face. Her eyes were wide with panic.

"Do you want to take over?" Marta was breathless, sucking air. At a nod from Alex, she withdrew.

Alex placed her hands in the center of Abby's chest. She pressed her hands down as Sara had once instructed. She could see the glowing coin rising to meet her palm. She was too deep in concentration to hear Marta or other women's cries. She pulled the coin from Abby's chest.

"What are you thinking?" Marta screamed. "She's dying and you're taking her soul?"

Alex opened her palms to reveal the glowing coin before lowering it back to Abby's chest.

Marta prepared to restart compressions, but Alex stopped her. "Wait." Before Marta could argue, Alex said, "It's got to work. Her coin has to be removed and returned before she comes back."

As Marta was asking, "What's a coin?" Abby coughed. She opened her eyes. Her hands grasped her bare breasts. "Why am I naked?"

"You were dead," Marta replied, confused by her own words. She eyed Alex in stunned relief.

Abby groaned as she tried sitting up. "Feels like you took turns jumping on my chest."

Marta cradled her. "Basically. You sure you're ready to sit up?"

Abby winced. "This isn't my first rodeo." She looked at her shirt and ruined bra. "Damn," she said, "I liked that one."

Carrie handed Abby her graduation gown as she finished changing. The other woman changed, asking one another if they understood what they just witnessed. Abby immediately rolled the sleeves to her shoulders.

Marta said to Alex, "What happened tonight?"

Nancy added, "Aren't you even a little wigged out?"

"Should I be?" Alex was grateful to be back. She'd seen enough. This was nothing. Abby was fine.

"Abby almost died. Death freaks people out the first time they see it."

Alex considered, then said, "Let's get Abby to the car." She turned to Nancy, "Can you get the others to help clean up?"

"Okay." Nancy shook her head and started delegating cleanup to the stunned women around her.

Alex and Marta helped Abby to her feet. Abby groaned, complaining about her chest. Alex embraced her and whispered in her ear. "I met my father tonight. I know what you did for him. Thank you, Abby. Without you, I wouldn't ever have learned the truth."

Abby tightened her embrace. "I didn't do anything for him."

Alex smiled. "Thanks, Abby. This is too much to ask anyone."

"You can ask me anything, Kiddo."

As they plodded to the cars, Abby asked, "You can hear now? No headaches when we tell you your parents didn't have a car accident?"

Alex nodded. "We broke the curse." A tickle in her ear, like an intimate whisper, distracted her.

Marta shouted, first in excitement, then to the others, "Hallelujah! We did it! Our spell worked!"

Marta grinned at them both, traded hugs, then went to the other women to share her excitement.

Once alone, Abby said, "Your father asked me to help him. I agreed. Then he asked me to be his Familiar. I refused. He believed in protecting the women around him. If I became his Familiar, he couldn't protect me. I promised I'd be your Familiar, and I'd protect you. He didn't think twice."

Alex hugged her. Like waves of heat from the mid-day sun, she felt herself radiating affection for this woman. Just as Abby sacrificed for her, Alex knew she'd do the same. When they released, Abby took an intentionally deep breath without wincing. She looked with surprise at Alex. "You've gotten a lot better at that. My chest doesn't hurt at all." Alex recalled the times she'd healed Abby without realizing. She had never felt it like this time. She had felt her love radiating, only it wasn't just love; it was magic.

Once Abby was resting in Heather's car, Alex approached Heather, who hadn't left the burned patch of grass where Alex had consumed the Book.

Heather looked up, hands on her hips. "It worked?"

Alex nodded.

"It happened so quickly, I thought we goofed. At least we didn't leave you feeling confused and ridiculous for long."

"If you had any idea, you would never have let me go."

Heather's face fell a little. "But it was over so fast."

"For you."

Heather digested these words. "Was it bad?"

Alex considered lying. "It was... difficult."

Heather embraced her. "I'm sorry it hurt you."

"I know you'd never intentionally put me in danger. There were times I felt so alone. I don't know which was worse."

"Times? How many times could there be in three minutes?"

"Three for you, Heather. I've been away a very long time."

Heather stared. "You seem different. Not just the fire thing with the Book, whatever *that* was, but you seem, I don't know." She waved her hand in the air. "It's probably just the magic," she said with excitement.

"Probably," Alex grinned. *Heather is adorable.*

"I'm so proud of you. Your mom and dad would be too."

Alex couldn't help but smile.

"So what's next?"

"I'm so tired. I feel like I haven't slept in years. I just want to get to bed." She motioned to the foundation, "I'm tempted to sleep right here."

Heather looked to the night sky. "I don't think anyone here would turn down a little sleep right now. Crazy night."

"How soon can we go home?"

"Home-home? Not until we're sure it's safe. Matthew knows where we live."

"I have to think it's okay now."

Heather looked surprised. "What makes you so sure? Did something happen during the ceremony?" Colette appeared holding their clothes.

"I have a sense that for me, anyway, it's as safe as anywhere."

"We'll see." Heather started putting her clothes on under her gown.

Alex dropped her gown to the floor and finished dressing unencumbered.

"Did you learn what the Book said?" Heather asked after she dressed. "I would have given anything to read it."

"It was here for me. That Book was only one part of what was important."

"But those spells, all that magic, they're lost. You burned them up. They're destroyed."

"I don't think they're gone. I was there when they made that Book and took her magic. I went through that so I could take it back. That's what Sara suggested broke the curse."

Heather looked confused. "Are you saying you have them; the spells, I mean?"

"I think so." It may have been the joy at her ordeal being over, but Alex felt different. Was that the magic? She looked at the starry sky. "Can we leave soon? I need to sleep."

"So that's it?"

"We'll see, won't we? My father wanted me to have this gift. I don't know what cost it carries."

"You seem so mature." Heather gazed a moment longer, then shouted to the others. "Let's make sure we take everything we brought. Break the circles of salt."

They walked back to their cars. Marta approached Abby, who was waiting in Heather's car.

"Hey," Marta said.

"Hey," Abby replied.

"You gave us a good scare back there. You sure you're okay?"

"I'm good."

Marta turned to Alex. "You too? You're good?"

"I think so," Alex replied.

"So no hospital?" Alex shook her head. Marta's attention returned to Abby. "Before, when you said this wasn't your first rodeo, what did you mean?"

"I've done this whole thing before. Didn't end so happily last time."

"No?"

Abby shook her head.

Marta said, "At least it's over and you're okay. Both of you. But, Abby, I bet you're glad you never have to do that again."

"I took the oath to serve Alex. If she asks, I'll do it again."

"You're insane. She'd never do that." Marta turned to Alex, "You won't make her do that again, right?"

"No," Alex said.

"You never know what the future brings," Abby replied.

Marta shook her head again. "I just can't believe... I mean, I saw you die. I can't imagine ever agreeing to that, especially knowing. You've died twice? I don't know if that makes you the bravest or dumbest person I know."

Heather climbed into the car. "Abby, you're welcome to stay the night at Eric's."

"Thanks," Abby replied. "If it's okay with Alex, I'd like to be home."

Alex nodded. "Sure, Abby. Whatever you need."

Abby said to Marta, "Would it be too much to ask you to drive me?"

"Of course not," Marta replied.

"We can drive you, Abby," Heather said.

"Alex needs to get to sleep," Abby explained, sliding out of Heather's car. "Come here," she said, extending her arms to Alex.

"I'm so glad you're okay."

Abby rubbed Alex's back. "How about you? You okay?"

Alex's reflex was to say *Sure*. "I don't know." she sighed. "I really don't."

"So it worked?" Marta asked Heather. "Like he said it would?. We cast those spells? We did witch things tonight?"

Heather answered slowly. "Only Alex knows if we succeeded."

Marta walked around the car towards them. "You're a brave kid," she said to Alex. For once, Alex didn't mind being called a kid. "Ready to go home?" she asked Abby.

"Absolutely. See ya, kiddo. Talk to you tomorrow, okay?"

"What would you say about grabbing a bite tomorrow?" Marta asked Abby as they walked away.

"Sure. If you're up for it, we could stop on the way. There's a diner off the interstate. I'm starving. If anyone asks, we can say we're celebrating my graduation."

Chapter Twenty-Six

Alex watched the outside blurring past the car. *Could it have been an illusion? Did I experience those things or just think I did?* In the moment it seemed real. It seemed horrible. It seemed to last for years and years. *How could that be real?* Alex wanted to feel magical. Do I feel different because I'm expected to?

She felt the vibrations where her head rested. She realized she might never know whether it was a delusion or a real experience. Even a bad dream, however absurd, could leave a person shattered. All she knew for certain was her exhaustion.

Closer to Eric's house, the streetlights and landscape lighting painted the streets in a perpetual twilight, denying the silent peace of darkness.

Heather turned into the driveway. Neither spoke during the ride. The car rolled to a stop and Heather turned the motor off. The silence was like a sigh, shrugging off tension. Alex could have slept right there.

They sat in the car for a long minute. Finally, Heather turned to her. "We should go inside."

Alex nodded. They climbed out of the car.

Heather put her arm around her. "Come on, let's be done."

"I'd like that."

"Did we do the right thing tonight?"

"Why are you asking me?"

"I know you pretty well, Alex. I see the change. I see the pain in your face." She rubbed Alex's shoulder. "Not to mention you burst into flames. That's not exactly normal. I almost shit myself." Alex was too tired to laugh. "You said tonight took longer for you. Did something hurt you?"

Alex thought about what to say, how to say it, where even to begin. She held Heather, wishing Heather could take her pain away.

"Did we do the right thing?" Heather asked again.

Alex looked at her hands. She remembered them broken. What mattered, memory or reality? Intention or outcome? Her mouth opened. "I think so."

The front door opened. Rose ran out in pajamas: sweatpants and a t-shirt. "I've been waiting behind the door since you pulled up. You gonna stand out here all night?"

"We were just coming in," Heather said. She turned to Alex. "Ready?" Alex nodded.

Rose skipped a circle around them. "You're home so soon. I guess I missed all the fun. Tell me everything!"

Alex embraced her cousin in a desperate hug.

Together they walked for the door. Eric opened it at their approach. "Was it everything you expected?"

Heather regarded Alex. "And then some."

Eric nodded. "Abby okay?"

"She's fine." Heather gave Eric a polite embrace. "Thanks for letting us stay."

"No problem," Eric said, looking Alex over. "Jennifer and the kids are asleep. Billy should be." He glared at Rose.

"I'm up," Rose volunteered.

Eric stepped closer to Heather. "She okay?"

"I'm fine," Alex told him.

"No more screaming headaches?"

Alex sneered. "They're gone."

"It really worked." His voice carried the weight of disappointment.

Heather touched Eric's forearm. "It's been a trying night, especially for Alex. We have a lot to talk about, but that's for tomorrow. Okay?"

Eric pointed at Alex. "You sleep with Rose."

Rose clarified. "I share my room with Billy here too, so you and I'll share my bed." Her hands shook with excitement.

"I need to shower," Alex said.

Eric didn't seem to know how to respond to the statement. "Um, I guess. Sure, yeah. That's fine." He nodded for emphasis. "Rose will show you the bathroom. Towels in the linen closet."

Rose looked at Alex's empty hands. "Where's your overnight bag?"

"Huh?"

"You didn't bring a change of clothes?"

"I didn't realize…"

Rose fluttered her eyelashes, "Daddy, Alex has nothing to sleep in or wear. Could you find something for her to wear, pretty please?"

Eric eyed Alex head to toe. "Nothing's gonna fit, but I'll leave something with Rose."

Heather said, "Thanks, Eric. For everything."

"No problem. You're welcome to stay until your house is safe."

Heather repeated, "And thanks for making it okay with Jennifer."

He held his hands up. "Look, she's not thrilled my ex-wife is over, but she gets it. If the tables were turned, she knows you'd have us."

"You think so?" Heather winked.

"Thanks, Eric," Alex felt the need to thank him herself.

"No sweat," he replied.

Heather took Alex's arms. "Sweetie, you sure you're okay?"

Alex didn't want to nod; she had to.

"Okay, that settles it," Heather said, "I'm going to bed." Heather hugged Rose and left towards the kitchen for the fourth bedroom in the back hall.

Eric looked at the girls, "I'll dig out something of Jennifer's for you, Alex." Then he climbed the stairs.

Rose led Alex upstairs. Outside their bedroom door, Rose whispered, "I'll wait up for you. You'll tell me everything I missed?"

Alex smiled politely. "Sure." This time she didn't check her reflex reply.

She closed the bathroom door and turned on the hot water. Undressing, she unceremoniously tossed her clothes in a pile. She didn't look in the mirror. She stepped into the shower and cried.

The water felt a degree from scalding. She hoped it would wash away everything she was feeling. *What happened to Sara.* "Not my body," she whispered. She felt bones break as Matthew tortured her, but her body—Alex's body—suffered not a scratch. She lived for decades and was no older than when she left. Was it ridiculous that she felt assaulted? It was Sara who'd suffered, Sara who died, Sara whose children Matthew stole. Alex feared she was co-opting Sara's pain. The shower wasn't helping. It wasn't easing her pain, wasn't easing her guilt, wasn't easing her confusion.

A timeline of events swirled and reconfigured in her head. Things she thought she knew clouded. Things she didn't understand cleared. She understood why her mother remained so devoted to her father when he had nothing to give her in return. Alex missed them.

She scrubbed until her skin was tender. The car accident that took her parent's lives was fading, faulting, fracturing. In its place, a nightmare became memory. She remembered standing at Heather's door, Heather opening it and staring at her. In the kitchen, she saw Billy and Rose. Heather looked at her kids and back at Alex before letting her in. They spoke no words.

Alex dried off and changed into the pajamas Rose had left for her. Exhaustion became so overwhelming her thoughts no longer mattered.

She skulked into the bedroom. Rose slept peacefully, her reading light left on. Alex climbed into bed, shut the light and, holding her cousin, barely had a moment before she fell asleep.

Chapter Twenty-Seven

lex's sleep was restless and fractured by dreams. She wandered Sara's house, abandoned and fallen into disrepair. Detritus covered the floor. Leaf litter mercifully hid the broken table settings, human remains, and other evidence of suffering. Three chairs remained tucked to the table; the fourth sat askew. A single bent and rusted nail punctured the center of the stained table like a crooked exclamation mark. Alex wandered the space; disturbed dust and cobwebs dancing in her wake.

The hearth in the kitchen was long cold. Black soot ran in tears of rainwater leaking through the unpatched roof. The pot that once held soup brimmed with a fetid mix of rainwater and rotting leaves; Alex wasn't used to smells in her dreams.

Barefoot, her steps shuffled through leaves and dirt to the bedroom. The red and white rotting quilt was shoved aside. The threadbare sheet was tanned with water and time.

Dead leaves filled the crib. Under matted, wet layers, she felt a form, cold and still. She feared it was Abigail or George, returned to their crib, no more alive than the rest of the house. She uncovered it. In her own fingers, she held the hammer. Alex could almost feel the countless other hands the cold object had impacted, none of them hers. She didn't remember putting it down, only realizing she no longer held it.

Where is Sara? She paced the house, finding neither the old woman nor the young. She longed for either, wishing Sara were there to answer a question or twenty. Perhaps Sara was finally at rest.

Alex awoke alone.

It was morning.

A narrow galley separated the two twin beds. Nightstands and dressers stood at the heads and feet. Off-white walls, a few frames with generic childish imagery, boring sheets. This was where Billy and Rose stayed when they visited their father; it wasn't their room.

Alex slid out of bed. On a chair beside the closet door, Rose had left clothes for her. Alex did not feel comfortable enough to ever imagine wearing Jennifer's underwear.

The sweatpants were too large and too short. The pink t-shirt with its glued-on gemstones spelling out "Believe" was too big, especially at the bust, ill-fitting Alex's tall and slender frame. She looked in the mirror, wondering if her ridiculous appearance in them would embarrass Jennifer too. She tried to cute them up, rolling the waistband or tying the t-shirt, but nothing helped.

As Alex stepped into the kitchen, Rose cackled.

From the table, Heather, Billy, and Eric followed Rose's cackling gaze. Heather smiled tactfully, but both Billy and Eric were unsure what Rose found funny.

Eric slid his bowl of cereal closer to Rose. "Let me get you a chair."

Alex assumed two extra chairs in the corner were for when Billy and Rose were in residence. It seemed that Jennifer took the kids out to allow Eric time with his *other* family.

Eric produced a bowl and utensils for Alex. She took her seat between Eric and Billy, poured some cereal, filling the bowl almost to brimming with milk.

"Have some cereal with your milk," Eric said.

"Is there a sudden milk shortage, Dad?"

Surprised, Eric refrained from responding to Rose.

"Coffee?" Heather offered. She filled an empty mug at Alex's nod.

Rose was bursting with curiosity. "Come on, don't keep us waiting. What happened last night?"

Alex's eyes pleaded for Heather to intervene.

Heather's words came out slowly. "I truly am not sure."

Alex nearly leapt to the ceiling when Rose hit her hands on the table. "Come on, Mom!" Alex felt the blood slowly returning to her face.

Heather said, "It was over as soon as it began."

"For you," Alex said to her cereal.

Concerned, Billy stared at Alex. "What's that mean?" Rose asked.

Heather could read Alex's discomfort. "Alex can hear magic now."

"Really?" The twins asked together.

"I guess so." Alex said.

Eric left the sink and walked closer to the table. "What of that Book? Where is it?"

"The Book is gone," Heather said.

"How could you let that happen? Don't we need it?" Eric's eyes accused Heather and Alex equally. "When you say *gone*, what do you mean?"

"It's gone, Eric," Heather replied with exasperation. "It's no more. It—"

Alex interrupted, "It's destroyed."

Before Eric could say anything, Heather said, "Destroyed is maybe the wrong word."

Eric made a face. "Did you keep the spells?"

Silence pressured Alex to respond. "I think so."

"You think so? Is that an answer?"

"Eric," Heather started.

"Don't *Eric* me," he interrupted. "We could've used that Book. It's important to know where the spells went or if they're gone."

"We? Since when do you care about witchcraft?" Heather spoke to Eric while looking at Alex.

Alex didn't look up. "It's not gone."

Eric edged closer. "You know the spells?"

Alex spooned her cereal-sweetened milk and looked at Rose and Billy's expectant faces. "I wouldn't say *know*," she said. "It's different. It's like knowing you know but can't quite remember."

"Does she always talk like this?" Eric asked Heather.

"Cut her some slack," Heather demanded. "She had a rough time."

"What?" Eric's pitch was near-falsetto. "If you came back any sooner, you would've bumped into yourself as you left."

"Please Eric," Heather pleaded.

"Give it a rest, Dad!" Rose hit the table, startling Alex again. Milk splashed to the table as her hands trembled.

A red-faced Eric turned to Rose, but he spoke to Heather. "Are you going to do something about that?"

Heather tried to diffuse Eric's frustration. "We're all a little tense."

Eric blamed the failure of their relationship on magic, but Alex saw what their dynamic must have been. Before Heather said anything contrite, Alex interjected. "You think they're just words because that's what you think you know. Spells are emotional. They're," she held her hands out, her fingers still trembling, turning her palms forward and back, "inside. They're like a whisper in my head, always talking. I don't know what it's saying or how to make it work. Maybe if I get angry, sad, happy? Maybe it needs to be really, really intense. Maybe that's how I'll cast a spell."

Heather looked at Alex with an expression Alex wasn't used to. Pride?

"Maybe?" Eric stepped closer to the table. "Maybe's the best we get?"

Heather hissed, "Eric, what is wrong with you?"

"Wrong with me? What about her? You put all your faith in her for *maybe*? Maybe what? Maybe it worked and maybe it didn't?"

"Dad, stop it!" Rose hit the table again.

Billy joined in. "Leave Alex alone!"

"Has everyone here lost their minds? Look at her." Eric motioned to Alex. "People died for her. Peter sacrificed for *maybe*?"

Under her breath, Heather hissed, "What do you know about sacrifice?"

Eric raged. "That's where you sink?" He telegraphed striking the table. Alex flinched, her eyes tearing.

Rose shouted, "Stop it Dad! Stop fighting!"

"Not until we know." He pointed at Alex. "Do something. Cast a spell."

"It doesn't work like that," Alex pleaded. "Please stop."

"Then how does it work? You said emotion, Alex. Cast a spell." He turned to Heather. "There's no *maybe*. All your hope was for nothing. She's not special. She's just—"

"Normal, like me?" Rose struck the table. "Just say it, Dad."

"You can't understand, Rose," Eric growled. "You're just a child."

Rose ran from the room. "You're an asshole," she screamed from the stairs, stomping each step for added drama.

"See what you've done?" Eric leaned into Alex's face. "You've hurt a lot of people. You keep saying, *That's not how it works*," he mocked, "because you have nothing. You pretend because your Dad killed himself and you want to believe it was for something. You pretend because these women believe in you. You're just a stupid girl, pretending."

"Why are you doing this?" Alex glowered through her tears.

"Cast a spell, Alex."

"I can't. I don't know how," she cried.

"Cast a spell," he shouted.

"Leave her alone," Billy screamed.

"Stay out of this," he shouted. "Go to your room."

Billy shook his head.

"Cast a fucking spell!"

Alex screamed, "I can't!" Her chest was heaving, her hands trembled. If there was magic inside her, she would have obliterated him. She wasn't sure whether that relieved or disappointed her.

Eric's voice lost its affectation of anger. "See, Heather? If she had magic, if it were emotional, she would have cast a spell. It was all a fantasy. Pretend conspiracies. Now do you see how pathetic this game you've been playing is?"

Heather's eyes welled. "This was an act? You're proving a point?"

"I am not your trick pony," Alex scowled at Eric, her voice rising in volume. "I don't perform for you. You don't tell me what to do."

Eric huffed. "Calm down. You're all being irrational." He looked at each of them as he spoke, "You thought something, and it wasn't true. Don't tell me you're not disappointed, Heather."

Alex turned to Heather. "I can't stay here, Heather."

Heather was about to reason with Alex when her demeanor changed. "You can stay with Abby. Would you like that?"

Alex nodded.

Eric sighed contritely. "Come on guys. I didn't mean it; I was testing her. We had to see."

"Please help Billy upstairs," Heather said to Alex. "I'll call Abby. I'll tell you when she's here, okay?"

"Thanks," Alex stood. Billy joined her.

"Guys, come on," Eric pleaded. "It's okay."

"No, Eric," Heather snapped, "it's not okay. You don't know what happened. You didn't stop to ask. If you knew what that girl's been through—"

"Tell me, Heather."

Alex helped Billy up the stairs. Rose was waiting in their bedroom.

Chapter Twenty-Eight

orry my dad's such an asshole," Rose said as Alex entered the room. The two embraced. "I don't want you to go."

"I know."

"So you'll stay?"

Alex shook her head.

"Please don't go," Billy pleaded.

"It's for a few days," Alex said. "Eventually, Heather will realize home is safe."

Rose brightened. "I can't wait."

Alex tugged at her pink *Believe* shirt. "Jennifer probably wants her clothes back."

Rose cackled. "I *believe* she does!"

All three laughed.

"You never told me what happened," Rose said.

"You were sound asleep. I didn't want to wake you."

"You snore."

Billy fell on his bed laughing.

"What are you laughing at?"

Alex looked at the clock. "Abby should be here in under an hour."

Alex sat beside Rose. "Abby grew up with your mom and my dad. She promised my dad she'd always be there for me."

Billy said, "That's good."

"At least you'll be with someone who loves you as much as us," Rose said thoughtfully.

Alex felt her cheeks redden. "Stop it."

"I love you, Alex," Billy giggled in falsetto, with kiss-noises.

Rose's face went cold. "Shut up, Billy."

"Yeah," Alex said, crossing the room, "shut up, Billy." She wrapped Billy in a bear-hug.

"My leg, my leg," He called out, giggling.

Alex kissed his cheek. "I love you too, Billy." Playing with her cousins was the first fun she could remember. Was it only yesterday she knew nothing of witches or spellcraft?

From downstairs, Heather interrupted, "Alex, Abby's on her way."

"'Kay," she shouted. Then she said to Rose, "In a few days, we'll all be back in our own house like nothing happened."

"That'd be nice," Rose replied. "Everything normal."

"I look forward to normal."

Billy mumbled, "Nothing's ever normal."

Alex cast Billy a glance, but whatever he was thinking passed. She sat beside Rose. "I'm sorry I'm leaving. I wish I had time to tell you everything."

Rose jokingly pushed her away. "You did this on purpose so you can't."

Rose's playfulness always made Alex feel better. "I can tell you a little," she said, feeling no judgment from her cousins as she had from Eric. Though she would avoid the darker memories for now.

"It was so weird. You met the Book Club, all those women. They seemed normal, right?"

"Yeah," Rose answered. "Mostly."

Billy rubbed his arms. "Except the one with the tattoos. She's a badass." Rose grinned at him.

"I thought they were all out of their minds. They took me to the stone foundation, you know, the Old Witch's Shack. They put on these black graduation gowns, I guess like witch's robes."

"Witches robes?" Rose shook her head.

"They made circles of salt. Then they cast a spell. All at once, there was a house there. I was there—as in a long time ago. Then she came out." Alex lowered her voice dramatically. "The witch."

Billy's mouth was agape. Rose's eyes went wide until they squinted with a smile. "You're lying."

Alex shook her head.

"What did she look like?"

Billy perked up. "Was she old and all ugly?"

"When I first saw her, I thought she was horrible." Her eyes welled with tears. "I saw her when she was younger, and she was so beautiful. Her name was Sara Frost, and she was the most beautiful woman I've ever seen. And these men came to punish her."

Rose was quiet. Tears clung to Billy's eyes. "I don't want to hear about what the men do."

"It happened a long time ago," Rose reassured him. "Right Alex?"

Billy shook his head.

"If he doesn't want to hear it," Alex intervened, "I'll just tell you another part."

"No," Billy pleaded.

"What's the matter with you?"

Crying, he looked at his sister. "I know what she did. Mommy wanted to do it to us too. It's all my fault."

"What do you mean?" Rose stared at him. "What did Mommy do?"

"She wanted to make you like Alex," he sobbed.

That's what Eric meant; he couldn't go through with it once he knew the risk. Heather tried? Why was it so important to her she'd risk becoming a zombie?

Alex envied Rose and Billy's relationship, a friendship born at birth, maybe before. The possibility that Heather nearly did the same to Billy made Alex consider how her parents changed her life. *I almost had a brother.*

Rose looked at Alex, her face worried. "What did they do to you?"

Alex watched Billy as she told Rose, "I should be a twin like you. My father undid that."

Rose's shoulders collapsed. Billy was sobbing. "I'm so sorry, Billy. I didn't know."

He wiped his nose and whispered, "Mom tried. She wanted it to happen. Maybe it would be better if she did. What if it's all wrong? What if I'm not supposed to be here?"

Rose leapt between beds to embrace her brother. "You're supposed to be here."

Alex followed. "She's right, Billy. Rose is right. We both love you. Heather loves you. Eric... I guess Eric loves you."

Rose laughed at Alex's sarcasm.

Alex wrapped her arms around Rose, whose arms were around Billy. She loved her cousins so much. All the adults around her thought they knew what to do, yet it was these two she most wanted at her side. It didn't matter to them if she had powers, they loved her no matter what, and she loved them.

"Okay, enough with the hugging." He wiped his face. Any sign of self-pity vanished in his smile.

Rose returned to her own bed. "What are you grinning about now?"

"Nothing."

"You're all smiles," she said accusingly. "You touched a boob."

He shook his head but laughed.

Alex said, "Okay guys, that's just creepy."

"Not mine," Rose defended. "Gross. He's my brother."

"Not mine, either."

Billy blushed. He held up his hands. "You two are sick." He walked towards the door. "I'm going to find someplace to not be around women for a while."

Rose made an obscene gesture with her hand.

"Gross," Billy said. "No."

Once he was out of earshot, Rose turned to Alex. "What came over him? He didn't cop a feel?"

"You're gross," Alex said through a smile. "No, he didn't."

"I wouldn't put it past him. He's always staring at you."

"We're cousins, Rose." She tried to change the subject, "Did you feel anything when I hugged you?"

"See? I knew it."

"That's not what I mean. Did you *feel* anything? Not with your hands. You know, emotionally."

"You about to confess your unrequited love?"

"Be serious."

"Like what?"

"Think. I healed Abby last night when I embraced her. Maybe I made Billy feel better too."

"That's not how it works."

"You know how magic works now?"

"I know it's about actual pain and injuries."

"But what if it isn't? You know, when it's," she couldn't believe she was saying this, "stronger."

Rose mulled over the possibility. "I'm probably remembering it this way because you asked—I don't know how to explain it—I felt like I was part of a complete whole. Like, we were one. It was, maybe, really comforting."

"I think I made him feel part of us just as he was feeling unwanted."

Rose changed the subject. "What else happened last night?"

"They broke the curse."

"Curse?"

"I couldn't know magic. I couldn't hear it. Now I do." She looked past Rose. "I did these things even though they already happened. I wasn't just remembering them, I was," it was hard for her to say it, "inside Sara, the old witch, as she was doing them. Someone took her magic and made a Book."

"That's horrible. Those things are dangerous." Rose paused. "I wish I could have seen it."

"I destroyed it, but I think I took the spells."

Her cousin's eyes widened. "Say what?"

"I think I took them from the Book."

"That's what Dad was carrying on about? You have magic? Do something cool! Like make me have me wings!"

"It's not like that. I don't know what spells I have."

"What good is that?"

"Maybe I'll know when the time is right."

Something caught Rose's eye. Reaching out, she asked, "What's this?" She touched Alex's charm.

Alex smiled. She had fondled the charm a few dozen times just today. Touching it made her feel better. "Abby made it for me. It's glass and some herbs from Heather's garden."

"Alex," Heather shouted from downstairs, "don't keep Abby waiting!"

Before she could react, Rose lunged across the bed and hugged her tight.

"I'll miss you, Rose."

"I love you, Alex. I wish you didn't have to go."

"Alex, did you hear me? Abby's here."

Alex shouted back. "Be down in a minute."

Rose grinned. "Get out of my room. You smell."

"You snore," Alex retorted.

"You talk in your sleep."

"You fart a lot."

"I'll see you."

"Smell you, you mean."

Alex grabbed her small pile of clothes and headed downstairs.

On her way to the front door, she hugged Heather goodbye. Heather's embrace was fleeting. "I'll call tomorrow and check up on you," Heather said. "I'm really sorry, sweety. This isn't what I want."

Alex moistened her lips. "I'd rather be with Rose and Billy. I'll be fine with Abby."

"We'll get there to spend time with you or have you here for dinner."

"I'd prefer not to come back here."

"He's sorry for what he did."

"He should say that himself, Heather."

"He should. Come here, sweetie," she embraced Alex again, for real.

Alex held her, feeling love for her aunt.

"Sorry Alex," Eric said from behind her.

Alex turned around.

"I may have pushed things too far. Sorry." He held out his arms like he expected an embrace.

Alex would not hug him. If she could give someone good or ill feelings with an embrace, she didn't want him to know.

"Um, I'll get the clothes back to you next time I see Heather."

Eric grinned. "That shirt's best off lost."

Alex forced a smile.

"I'll leave you two. Jenn should be home soon." Eric walked away.

"Aunt Heather," Alex began tentatively when he was gone, "can I ask you a very personal question?"

"Depends what that is."

"Remember when I said Eric told me about what you tried to do for Rose?"

Heather interrupted her. "Abby's waiting. That's a conversation I don't want to have."

Alex was used to parents avoiding the truth. She started towards the door.

"Alexandrea," Heather said after her, "Don't leave on that note. I love you, Alex. See you soon."

Chapter Twenty-Nine

lex stepped out of Eric's house into the bright June day. Abby waited beside her truck, bare arms folded, grinning. Alex felt free. She climbed into the passenger seat.

"That's some getup," Abby smirked.

"Don't get me started." Alex tugged on the loose shirt. "I can't wait to change."

"Even with the sleeves torn off, I wouldn't touch that." Abby winked.

"Thanks for coming to get me," she said as Abby backed out of the driveway.

"No problem." Abby's tone was more enthusiastic than her words. "It's great to have you back."

After several minutes of silence, Alex caught Abby glancing in her direction. They weren't far from the farmhouse. "Did you have breakfast yet?"

"Yup," was Alex's monosyllabic reply.

"You maybe want to pull some glass? I started the kiln before I left. It'll be searing hot when we get back."

"That sounds like fun," Alex said. "Is it safe to leave it unattended?"

Abby's mouth pinched. "About that," she said at last. "Marta's over."

"Really?" Alex couldn't help but grin. "You two?"

"No," Abby laughed. "So not my type. We ate breakfast and got to talking. When Heather called, she asked to stay. She wants to get to know you."

Alex slumped in her seat. "I'm not a fan. Marta's a bitch."

"I know," Abby replied. "She does too." The truck slowed and Abby turned onto the rutted driveway and past the cornfield and farmhouse to the barn and the trailer.

They pulled up alongside Marta's car, now caked with dust, Abby's handiwork no longer legible.

As Alex hopped out of the truck, Marta came from the barn, waving.

"Hey Alex," she said. "It's good to see you again." She hesitated. "You okay?"

Alex tried to smile. "Hi, Marta."

Before she could figure out how to evade the question, Abby asked, "Lunch, drinks, or glass?"

"Maybe a little glass," Alex replied.

Marta agreed. "I'm curious to see you do your thing."

"Glass it is." Turning to Alex, Abby said, "As soon as you change."

Marta guffawed. "I didn't want to say anything, but that's some outfit."

As Alex walked to the trailer, she replied, "Trust me, I know."

* * * *

It was well after four when they closed the barn door, a handful of charms and a single vase left in the annealer. Abby fired the grill. She and Marta opened a plastic folding table and chairs and set out some dishes. Abby shooed Alex every time she tried to help.

They sat to eat, and Marta opened a bottle of red wine and poured for Abby and herself.

Abby coughed, pointing with her eyes at Alex's glass.

"She's only, what, eighteen?"

"Really, Marta?"

Marta shrugged and poured Alex half a glass.

"Last night," Marta began, "what happened?" The other two looked at her quizzically. "I saw the flames and Alex and the Book. It freaked me out. I mean, I'm giving you chest compressions," she gestured at Abby, "and there she goes. Whoosh! What fucking happened?"

"I died," Abby snorted.

Marta put her fork on the plate. "Heather made it sound like you'd only seem dead. What the hell?"

"It's part of the process."

"That's some effed-up process," Marta exclaimed. "Was it worth all that... drama?"

Abby looked at Alex. Marta's gaze followed.

"What?"

Abby placed a hand on Alex's. "You don't have to talk about it. We're just curious."

"What do *you* think happened?"

Marta shrugged. "Heather had us try to cast that spell. I expected something special or miraculous, but it was over so fast."

Alex looked at Abby, not sure how to say she wasn't ready to talk. *I will not cry.* She took a gulp of red wine, then another. She preferred it to beer but didn't know why people claimed to enjoy it so much.

Alex watched Marta shrink in disappointment. "Sorry I brought it up," she said. "I don't want to upset you."

"I don't even know what to think about it," Alex explained.

"You know," Marta said in a hushed, serious tone, "at the hospital, when something really tough happens, they get us in a room to talk about it. It's okay to be vulnerable. Sometimes things happen that really fuck with our heads. You can't just move past; you need to work through. We're here, but only if and when you're ready."

Alex looked from Marta to Abby and back. "After you cast the spell, a house appeared, and an old woman walked out."

"You're screwing with me." Marta looked at Abby. "She's screwing with us, isn't she?"

Alex finished her glass. Abby refilled it, emptying the bottle. "She's serious," she said, disappearing into the trailer.

"I had to give her Abby's coin."

"Coin?" Marta touched her chest. "Oh, you mean the silver token?"

Alex stifled a laugh. "Everyone has a different name for it. Why token?"

"Token, as in pay with your token for passage," Marta explained.

"I get that," Abby said, returning with another bottle. "Coin, token, aren't they basically the same?"

"No," Marta replied. "I can use a coin for all kinds of payment. A token on the other hand has only one use, like years ago in the city on the sub—"

Abby glared Marta to silence.

"She took Abby's *token*," Alex sarcastically emphasized Marta's word. "Then we went into her house."

"You followed her into a house that wasn't there? That's too freaky."

Alex closed her eyes, clenching her jaw. Tears fell as she spoke. "I don't know how to make you understand. What was an instant for you was years of hell to me."

Marta's hands went to her mouth. "I'm so sorry Alex."

Abby touched Alex's arm. "You want to stop?"

Alex could tell her face was a ruddy mess. "No. It's probably good that I talk." Abby nodded. Marta leaned in closer. "The woman—Sara—needed to show me something. I became a part of her. I was stuck *in* her. I saw through her eyes. It was like a body-shaped prison." She told them about the loop, and struggled when she got to Matthew; all she could manage was, "They took her magic to make Heather's book."

Marta rested her trembling hand on Alex's, hesitating twice before taking hold. "I am so sorry, Alex."

"They even took her babies."

"Who could do something so horrific?" Marta asked.

"Sara called him Matthew." She looked at Marta, "That night we came to the hospital with Billy, someone had been following us in the woods. It looked like the same person, but how could that be?"

Marta shrugged. "If you went back there, why couldn't he?"

"I don't know," Alex sighed. "Matthew killed her. She paid her coin, and we waited."

"You were in a ghost that died? That's some circular logic."

Alex heard Abby kick Marta under the table. Marta winced.

Alex sipped her wine. She felt relaxed. *This is why people like wine.* "Then Sara was summoned. I thought we would see us," she made circles with her hands to show her inclusion of Abby and Marta, "but there was Abby and my father."

"That just gave me chills, full-on heebie-jeebies." Marta showed the hairs standing upright on her arm.

"My dad asked Sara to un-twin me. He had the Book Heather used. Sara made him break his coin in two, and when it was over, he had to give up both halves. But he tricked her, making it so I would be there. He knew I was inside Sara and never once said anything to me."

Marta's face turned ashen. "How are you sane after this?"

"Then you summoned her. Sara had sort of gone. I'm standing face to face with myself, but it's been so long I almost forgot who I was. Then I was just me again. I had been away for something like two hundred years, but no time had passed."

Marta poured herself another big glass, emptying the second bottle. "Alex, I am so sorry. What you went through—if I had any idea, I mean—do you blame us for what happened?"

Alex shook her head.

Abby lowered her face. "I'm sorry I wasn't there for you."

"You couldn't have known," Alex said. "My father knew. He believed it was important to put me through that."

Marta nodded. "That's a real mind-fuck. Your own dad? Wow."

Abby looked teary-eyed. "I caused that to happen to you?"

"I don't know what to think about it," Alex said. "I mean, when will I know it was worth it?"

They watched her but said nothing.

"So," Alex broke the silence, "that's my story."

Marta waited a minute and said, "I saw the fire, the Book, and you. Did the Book do that to you or you to the Book?"

"I'm pretty sure that was me, but maybe it was me *and* the Book. I felt like I was the fire."

Marta nodded. "Did you take her spells or are they gone?"

"I think I took them."

"Can you do one? I mean, you really have them?"

"Everyone keeps asking that. I don't know. I think so. I feel like they're in here." Alex pointed to her heart. "When it's quiet, I can hear a whisper that wasn't there before."

"Who else asked you?" Abby asked.

"Eric."

"Heather said something went down with him. What happened?"

"He tested me. He tried to get me all emotional, but nothing happened. He's such a dick."

Abby grumbled, "Why didn't Heather stop him?"

"Heather was so certain the spell would work," Marta remarked. "I mean, she knew it would. But then it's over and she didn't seem sure of herself. At Book Club meetings, we were just a bunch of middle-aged women in the woods pretending to be witches.

She made them believe. When nothing happened—or seemed to have happened—she looked lost, like for the first time, she doubted herself. Maybe that's why she didn't stop him. She used to be so certain and now maybe she isn't sure, either."

"I thought you knew you were a witch," Alex said.

Marta straightened up. "I didn't have a twin brother. Heather once told me that a long time ago, all women had some power. Some more than others. Those women are born twins now. Some curse from eons ago."

"That's why she hated me," Abby cut in.

"I didn't hate you. I misunderstood you."

"Felt like hate." Alex muttered.

Marta lowered her head. "I didn't understand. You were the only one who didn't pretend or hope they had something special. You were the only one confident in anything, and it was that you were normal."

"I never thought I was normal. I just knew I wasn't a witch. I'm Alex's Familiar."

Marta continued. "Heather was so certain. I couldn't help but believe her. Because of her her, I knew. The more time that passed, though, the easier it became to give in to doubt. While we're all battling our uncertainty, you were like, *Nope, I got nothing.* I resented you for your honesty. It was threatening. It made me doubt everything I believed."

Abby laughed. "Sounds like you've seen a shrink about it."

"If you know one who handles insecure witches, let me know."

Abby almost fell out of her seat. "I think I'm drunk."

Marta tried to stifle her laughter. "Me too. Witch shrinks; who would have thought? How am I going to get home like this?"

"Can you get a ticket for broomsticking while intoxicated?"

Marta erupted in laughter. Alex laughed too. She was feeling woozy. Worse than with her single beer the other day. "I might be drunk too."

Marta pointed a finger at her. "You can't be drunk. Someone's got to drive us home."

Alex giggled, "I don't drive."

"And I am home," Abby replied. "You're the only one with a problem."

"What am I going to do?"

"You either share a bed with me, Alex, sleep in your car, or the barn. Or we all sit here until we sober up." Alex started collecting the dishes. Abby clasped her arm. "Stop. You're my guest. I've got this." She turned to Marta, "You can help."

Marta looked at Alex. "I will never understand her."

Later, Alex collapsed in her bed, groaning when the room seemed to keep moving. "People like this feeling? I'm never drinking again." Both Abby and Marta cackled. "What's so funny?"

Abby took the couch. Marta followed Alex to the bedroom. Standing in the doorway, she said, "I promise not to take up much space."

Alex opened one eye.

It seemed like minutes later that Dolly woke her, curling up beside her head. She petted the purring ball of fur and dozed off again, her head feeling unwell.

Chapter Thirty

Nearby music. Loud. Tinny.

Alex groaned. Her head throbbed. The noise was too intrusive to ignore. It sounded like a tango, played in the style of thrash metal. It went quiet then started up again.

Marta groaned. "Alex, shut off your phone."

Alex struggled to open her eyes and saw a glow on the nightstand. "I don't have a phone," she protested. "That's Abby's ringtone."

Marta pulled the pillow over her head.

Alex picked up Abby's phone. The screen read, "Heather". Above that it read, "3:58 AM."

"Hello?" Alex tried to whisper into the phone. A little louder, "Hello, Heather?"

"Alexandrea?"

"Yes?"

"Why are you answering Abby's phone? Where is she? Are you okay?"

"Yeah. Abby's sleeping." Alex took a breath. "Heather, are you okay?"

"No. Not really, sweetheart."

"What happened?"

"I need you and Abby." Heather sounded like she was crying.

"What's happened? Heather, please, you're scaring me."

"There's been a fire. I can't find Rosemary or William."

"We're coming."

"Please hurry."

Alex woke Marta and then Abby, repeating to each of them what Heather had said. After a large glass of water and several aspirins, they were in Abby's truck, racing to Eric's house.

From the end of Eric's street, they saw the road littered with fluorescent orange cones crisscrossed with thick-textured hoses, the wet road reflecting flashing light, turning everything red and white and red and white.

They parked on an adjoining street. Dirty faces moved from truck to truck to house—or what remained of the house—carrying tools, talking on radios, or exchanging the depleted air bottles on their ringing packs.

The roof was open, the windows like glowing mascara-streaked eyes. As the firefighters doused the house with geysers of water, steam and smoke boiled into the air.

They found Heather sitting on the curb in a bathrobe over mismatched clothes, phone in hand, soot-smudged cheeks lined with tears. As soon as she saw them, she jumped up and hugged Alex and Abby.

Marta spoke first. "Holy fuck, Heather, what happened here?"

"The smoke detector woke me," Heather sobbed. "I—my room was downstairs, away from the twins"—I tried to get to them. It was so hot; I couldn't see." Her voice cracked. Abby rubbed her arm. "I couldn't get through. I couldn't save them. I, I..." Marta gasped. "Eric and Jennifer were there when I got out, with their kids. I, I asked, but Eric didn't know." She stared at Alex, as though waiting for permission to fall apart.

"Where's Eric?"

Marta looked at Alex. "You're calm." Alex shook her head, tears in her eyes. She recognized what she was feeling. It was the same as when Sara discovered her children were gone.

"Over there," Heather pointed. She crumpled into Abby's arms, sobbing, "My babies are dead."

Alex embraced Heather. "You don't know that," she whispered. "I'm sure they're okay." She needed this to be true. "Let's talk to Eric. We'll talk to the firefighters. Okay? Someone here has to know."

"You're right. It's probably fine." Heather wiped her eyes. "They're probably..." She trailed off. Confused, Heather wrenched free from Alex's embrace. "What did you... How dare you?"

"What?"

"My babies are dead and you're trying to take my pain away? Don't you dare!"

Alex stepped back, aghast. "I wasn't trying to do anything. I wouldn't do that to you," Alex couldn't find her defense. She wanted

Heather to feel better, and couldn't deny she felt something while holding her. She just didn't know it was her doing.

"Alex? That you?"

Alex turned and saw Eric holding Caitlyn. Jennifer gripped Hunter in her arms beside him.

"I'm so sorry, Eric," Alex reached out to touch him.

He nodded curtly. "We need to talk. Not here."

"Why not here?"

Eric shifted his feet. "The fire people are saying it looks like an electrical fire."

Alex looked back to Marta and Abby, who were consoling Heather. She turned to Eric. "You don't agree?" There was silence. "What's going on, Eric?"

"I have a message for you." Alex felt the blood leave her face. "He told me he needs to meet with you. He said something like he needs to see if it worked. He's waiting at Heather's house."

She knew who he meant. Still, she asked. "Who?"

"He didn't exactly give his name." Eric crossed his arms.

Alex crooked her neck.

"Yeah, that's him."

"I can't go until I know Rose and Billy are safe."

"That's just it. He has them."

Heather looked up, enraged. "Matthew took my children? When were you going to tell me?"

"My instructions were to tell Alex and no one else." Eric defended. "He threatened to hurt my family."

Alex bristled. Heather screamed, "Rose and Billy are your family!"

"You know what I mean," Eric said, repositioning Caitlyn to his other side.

Alex sneered. "You promised me you wouldn't fail again. You'd be there when the time came. Doesn't that include saving your kids? Or did you mean just to watch?"

Jennifer interrupted her, jabbing the air with an accusing finger. "Listen, little girl. They threatened us. They took everything from us. Eric wasn't about to let his children lose their father too. This isn't even about us, it's about you."

Abby pushed past Marta and Heather. "You don't talk to her like that."

Jennifer made a face. "Or what? My husband's ex-wife needed a place to stay. Sure. Her kids, of course. This girl. We've got room for everyone. Now because someone is after your niece or whatever she is, my house is gone?" She looked past Abby at Alex. "I lost everything because of you."

Alex stared at Eric. "You let Matthew take your kids?" In her head, Sara cried over an empty crib.

"He didn't let anyone do anything." Jennifer gestured at the house. "They destroyed our lives."

Abby put a restraining arm around Alex. "It's time we go. We need to think this through."

"I think the coward isn't telling us something," Alex said.

Jennifer handed Hunter to Eric. "My husband was heroic tonight. Don't speak to him like that."

Abby stood between them. "Calm down. We need to know everything to find Billy and Rose."

Jennifer screamed at Abby. "Who do you think you are, telling me to calm down? How does this even concern you?"

For a second time, Alex was grateful her emotions couldn't cast spells.

Abby nearly threw a punch, pulling it at the last. Jennifer flinched. Abby threatened her with her closeness. "You deserve this." She pointed at the remains of the house. "The kids don't, but you two do. These people win because it's safer not to fight them." Alex was about to pull her back, when Abby said, "Let's go."

Alex followed. Marta too. Heather took a minute. Her emotions turned all to rage. She frothed at Eric and Jennifer. She stammered and made fists, but finally marched away.

The four women piled into Abby's truck.

"What do we do now?"

Everyone looked at Alex.

Alex wished she could shrink away. She was furious, but she wanted someone else to decide what came next. *What am I walking into?* She pictured the night ending with her tied to a chair, her hands under Matthew's hammer. "Why are you looking all at me?"

"You're the only one who can save my children," Heather said, sounding to Alex like she did when they were misbehaving, and she unsuccessfully tried to control her anger.

"Who else has a bad feeling about this? Why didn't he just come for me?"

"Maybe he still can't find you," Marta offered. She looked to Heather. "That's what you said, right, that Matthew can't find her? Once we started the spell, he'd know. I don't know, maybe that's why she can't do magic too. Maybe we only fixed part of her."

"You think he came assuming I'd be with Heather?" Alex took a deep breath.

"That means he won't see you coming, either," Heather postulated.

"I don't have magic, Aunt Heather. How do I defend myself or protect you?"

Abby groaned, "I don't like it."

"He has my kids," Heather pleaded. "We have to try—"

Alex interrupted. "We're walking in there unprepared."

Marta spoke up, "It sounds like we have to."

"I've got your back, Alex," Abby said. "We all do."

"It's decided." Heather wiped her face. "I'm not sleeping until I see my kids again. I don't care how long it takes or if it kills me."

"Hopefully it won't come to that," Marta said.

Abby nodded. "I'm with you on that. You sure about this, Alex?"

"Nope, but I have to." Alex turned to Marta. "You don't need to be a part of this."

Marta looked hurt. "If you don't want me there, just say so. This is kind of personal, so—"

"That's not it," Alex interrupted. "I mean, if you want to, you know, not be involved, we're okay."

Marta looked outraged. "I've been with Heather since the beginning. I'm a nurse in an emergency room. My job is to save lives. There's no way I'm walking away from this."

Chapter Thirty-One

hey climbed out of the truck. Birds were calling on the sun to rise. Alex started towards the dark house.

"Wait for us," Abby hissed.

Alex waited.

On the porch, Alex took the key from Heather and opened the front door.

Heather gasped as they stepped inside. "What the hell?"

Abby replied, "I'll help clean up."

"Not what I expected," a raspy male voice spoke.

No one had noticed Matthew seated on the couch. His neck stuck out from between his shoulders at nearly ninety degrees. At his knees, opened on the broken coffee table, lay a wide, elaborately illuminated book. The thick pages were yellow, nearly to brown, but with embellished writing and gold leafing sharp and crisp as wet ink.

"You've met my boy," he said to Alex, motioning to the young man approaching them.

Alex couldn't take her eyes off Matthew. He was the man who shattered her hands and took her eye. *That wasn't me; that was Sara.*

"I'm glad you came, Alexandrea. Please follow George, and I'll return the children."

Alex's gut knotted. "Your name is George?" She tried unseeing everything that reminded her of Sara.

He nodded.

It's got to be a coincidence. It can't be them. She told herself she was seeing the resemblance because she wanted to. That was two hundred years ago. She felt sick. How do you defeat immortals?

"He doesn't like hearing how much he looks like his mother," Matthew said. "Sara Frost was a beautiful woman, but you know that, don't you, Alexandrea?"

"You stole Sara's babies." Alex pointed to George.

"Stole? No," Matthew said. "Sara couldn't care for her children. I brought him up as my own. Showed you the world, right George?"

George nodded. "Taught me everything I know."

"You believe him?" Alex asked.

"Matthew told me. He extracted her magic," George said matter-of-factly.

"That was two hundred years ago." Behind her, the other women tried making sense of what was happening.

"Come with me, Alexandrea." George stretched out his hand.

Abby clasped Alex's shoulders. "Don't."

Alex hissed, "I wasn't gonna."

"You're special, Alexandrea." Matthew leaned back to raise his sightline. "I don't know why I can't find you. It's like you don't exist. Except," he rubbed his crooked neck, "for that one time several years ago."

Alex glared. "Where are my cousins?"

"That's not the question you should be asking."

"What is?"

"Where is George taking you?" Matthew explained, "To a place no woman has ever gone; where the lucky ones go. Call it a test."

Alex crossed her arms. "A test for what? Why should I?"

George started, "Because if you—"

Matthew interrupted, "Two good questions. Either you take my test, or I'll milk these women for their magic."

"Abby doesn't have magic," Marta interjected.

Matthew made a face. "*She's* the Familiar?" He grinned at George.

Alex's anger welled up, bubbling past her fear. "Don't threaten us."

"Don't you want to know why you don't have magic?"

"Shows what you know," Alex bluffed.

"Alexandrea, please. If you had magic, I *would* know."

Heather said something to Abby too quietly for Alex to hear.

"Go with George and everyone goes home tonight. I won't have to milk these other three."

"Don't do it," Abby warned.

Alex refused to be intimidated, "That's what you call it now?"

"Too coarse? Am I triggering you?"

"You're disgusting," Alex sneered. "It's murder. You call it *milking* to make yourself feel better."

"When will women learn? Magic wielded by emotion is dangerously unstable. It's not murder, Alexandrea. Once safely written into Books, magic can be controlled, harnessed for good, used to protect. Emotions are fickle and unpredictable."

Heather growled ferociously. "What have you done with my children?"

"Your children are fine," Matthew looked away. He looked uncomfortable. "Your son is an intriguing boy. There's something familiar about him. He's like a child I might raise on my own. Your daughter is ripe for extraction." He turned his attention back to Alex. "Better? Is it less demeaning than *milking*? Call it what you like; that's what we'll do unless you go with George."

Alex wanted to explode with rage. "Bastard, give Heather her kids back!"

"Maybe I'm not making myself clear. Maybe you're not good at being told what to do. Some women can't help questioning what's best. One way or another, you're leaving with George. How else can I know you're the one I need?" Matthew leaned forward to look down at his book. His mouth opened, and his words sounded like a hundred foreign languages poured from a blender. His coin appeared below his bent neck.

How much more emotional do I need to get?

Matthew finished, his coin glowing. Everyone's was shining now, except for Alex's. A black hole hung in the center of her chest.

A dreary haze materialized behind Matthew, growing darker and thickener by the second. Its roiling edges twisted and turned, smoking angrily, but inside it had grown so featureless-black it appeared flat. A pitch of nothingness. It made her eyes ache. She couldn't focus, couldn't tell how far or near it was. Alex took a step back. She could barely breathe. It was the same as the hole in her chest.

"As I was saying," Matthew said, "to the universe, you don't exist. That shouldn't be. But here you are. I need to know. You *will* take my test."

"Come with me." George's hand was still outstretched.

"Oblivion," Matthew said. "Isn't it remarkable? You're seeing pure nothingness, an absolute, perfect void. The eternity of an entire universe, absent everything."

The blackness grew larger. Alex guessed it was probably coming closer.

"She's not going anywhere with anyone but us." Abby stepped in front of Alex.

Marta whispered to Alex, "What are you waiting for? Cast a spell. Do anything!"

Heather shook her head, "Is that thing getting closer? It hurts my eyes."

"Get back, Alex," Abby demanded.

Alex held up her trembling hands. "Nothing's there. There's no magic."

Magic or not, Alex knew it was up to her. The responsibility hung on her shoulders like heavy timbers. Everyone was counting on her. She saw two options. She quickly weighed them, judging distances and positions. *Is it worth the risk?* "When I move," she whispered, "get to the car."

"What about you?"

"Just run."

"I'm not leaving you," Abby hissed.

"You say something, dear?" Matthew mocked.

In two quick steps, Alex lunged at Matthew and his Book.

Her hands snatched at the open cover. the Book spun from her grasp. Matthew's hand snapped like a striking snake, his fingers snagging the spine in one perfect snap. "No, you don't!"

She tugged at the cover, but in his death-grip, her tug only pulled them together.

Abby wrenched the door open. Heather started through. Oblivion poured through the air toward Abby, who had nowhere to go. Marta stepped between them and with a yelp, vanished into the dark cloud.

George clasped Alex's arms, trying to separate her from the text.

The Book slipped from Alex's grasp, and the room vanished.

Chapter Thirty-Two

lex stood at the intersection of two unending aisles. The dark granite floor was so perfectly reflective, it mirrored everything above. Immense rows of fantastically ornamented bookshelves came together in unending repetition. Thick shelf fronts boasted stories with menageries of carved creatures from reality, myth, fantasy, and ones wholly unrecognizable. The bookcases towered as high as she could see in the inconceivably vast space. The ceiling and floor seemingly vanished in the distance before any walls stood between them. Books beyond count, books of all sizes, crammed shelves and lay piled on tables at each corner. Several men, made minuscule by distance, mulled through the stacks, oblivious to her presence.

Where's George?

Two dozen books formed a skewed tower on the table beside Alex. The top book's leather cover was crisp, oiled, and new. Inside, the paper was pure white. It smelled of new paper and ink. On the pages, ornate but obscure shapes impersonated letters and words. *A witch's Book.* Alex trembled. The discovery sickened her. The vastness of the Library came into perspective as each Book announced its kinship with the one in her hands. She was in an ossuary of women's magic.

Music drubbed in her ears, a fast, accentuated beat. Her heart pounded. Her chest heaved. She was running.

The ruddy gray of dusk overhead, the rumbling traffic and city sounds, were not distant enough. She was alone on the footpath, exhilarated, the cooling air a salve for burning lungs. One foot in front of the other, her breaths partitioned by her footfalls; in-in-in-out, in-in-in-out. Then the music stopped. An interrupting voice said she had run four miles in twenty-nine minutes, eight seconds.

Alex felt—the woman she was felt—strong; she increased her tempo. One mile to set a new personal record. Push a little faster, exhaustion be damned.

Ahead on the trail, a man monitored her approach, his eyes but slits on his squinting face. She increased her rhythm to sprint past. *I'll never make time; too fast too soon.* She hated these guys, salivating on the exercise paths, lurking, as though their wolf-whistle was encouragement. *Sleazebag.* She wasn't running for their entertainment. Her feet caught the edge of the path furthest from him, lungs aflame, speed increasing, eyes cast downward so he'd know she refused his regard. She just wanted to run. Relief smothered tension as she passed him. Only when she was thrown to the ground did she realize there was another guy.

Alex dropped the Book, her hands prickling with heat. This was no ancient witch from some savage, uncivilized time. This woman went out for a run maybe last month or last week.

She felt crushed, drowning in the vastness of the surrounding Books. Her chest heaved with panic. Her head swam with a nearly audible warning. Spinning, she found herself face to face with George. For a moment, she nearly clung to him, but not for her safety, for his.

"Matthew wanted you to have this," he held out a slender volume. Alex warily accepted the Book. "Open it."

Alex wouldn't look at it. She didn't want to look at the embossed name on the spine, certain it read, "Rosemary Hawthorne."

"Open it, Alexandrea."

She would not willingly experience her cousin's fate.

"Open the damn Book," George shouted.

Several distant figures craned their heads, taking notice. All men, all with Books. A few began towards them, towards her.

George acknowledged the distant figures. "If they catch you, you'll never get your cousins back."

Reluctantly, Alex opened the Book, staring at the yellowed pages. She placed her hand over the symbols and designs. She thought she would feel angry, as when she held Sara's Book. The sound in her head grew loud as though all the Books whispered to her. On the illuminated pages, the shapes and designs called to her. She felt herself flowing into them, past them, beyond them.

A woman was screaming, begging. Alex felt her breath in her throat, the words formed by her tongue, begging her brother to stop, "Please, George, please, not again."

The gush of vomitus forced itself through her jaws.

Alex lowered the Book, its symbols still swimming in her head.

Sara had thought her babies were dead. George now served the man who caused her untold pain. Abigail wasn't raised by Matthew. Imprisoned until she was old enough to be milked, or extracted, or whatever Matthew called it. Her own brother, her executioner. This Book was his creation. Alex had seen, felt enough. She sobbed, crushed, broken. *What hope is there if this is okay?* She cried for Sara.

The tears on her face belied the anger of her words, "How could you do those things to your own sister?"

George replied, "She did them to herself."

"Is that what you tell yourself to sleep?"

"You don't realize how dangerous you are with even a little power."

"Tell me, George, how dangerous am I?"

"Here, in all these Books, safe in this Library, are all the spells of every witch who ever cursed an innocent man or killed an unbaptized babe."

"All these Books, George? Really? You know that's not true. Most of these women were innocent."

"It doesn't matter."

"Yes, it matters."

"Until women can control their emotions, they have no right to this power. It is because Jeremiah took the first spell that we can live in a better world."

Alex could see Sara reaching into her crib, stroking her babies. When she discovered them missing, whatever dark possibility most haunted her, the truth was worse.

The men were getting closer. The closest was two, maybe three aisles away. One called out to her. "Women aren't allowed here!"

George ignored them. "When you opened it," he said, "I saw something in your eyes. You felt something."

"Abigail's pain."

George looked taken aback. "You felt her pain?"

She looked up at the stacks. "I feel all their pain. I know the suffering that made each Book."

George almost looked like he believed her. "I'm so gullible. Manipulative witch." He lowered his voice. "Everyone knows women secretly enjoy having their burden removed."

The first man reached their aisle. He waited for others. George eyed them nervously. "George Frost? Why did you bring a woman here?"

"It's fine. I have permission." At his words, the other seemed to relax. Most remained close, however, watching with curiosity or concern.

Alex ran her hand along the Book's spine, over the gold embossed letters of Abigail Frost's name. *Is it wrong I'm relieved it wasn't Rose?* Thinking about Rosemary experiencing what made these pages coiled a rope about her stomach. All these Books smothered her. Amidst the rising din in her head, Alex made out a whisper, three barely audible words, "Read my daughter."

George hissed, "This is Matthew's test. Tell me, what is your reaction to this amazing place?" At her drawn silence, he dropped his guise of sincerity. "Magic is all but out of the world. If not for these Books, every time a woman burned a dinner, she could obliterate her family with her emotional rage."

Without taking her eyes off George, Alex snapped open Abigail's Book.

"What's your game?" George sneered. "Everyone knows women can't read Books!"

Perhaps seeing her open the Book, several men rushed forward. They shouted at George, accusing him of defiling their Library with this woman.

Alex stared into the page, losing herself again.

Hands grabbed her, pulling as they wrestled her to the ground. She felt hot breath wet on her face as voices shouted at her. Alex only heard Abigail's screams.

One man tried to wrench the Book from her hands. Another grabbed her wrists. Another pried at her fingers. They fought to take Abigail from her. What they didn't know, couldn't know, is that Abigail had suffered enough at hands like theirs. Alex would not let anyone hurt her anymore.

Her fingers bunched and tore the pages from threaded binding. One man screamed in horror or anger or hatred at the damage. He stared wrathfully at Alex. He shoved her, trying to take

Abigail. Alex stumbled; the Book jarred. The men cried out when they saw the written symbols and shapes thrown from the page and scatter into the air.

"She is mine!" Alex's fist crumpled the pages. The men gaped at the disordered Book, watching their precious spells falling away. One hissed and backed away. Then another.

Alex felt heat rising.

The Book burst into flames in her hands. The blaze wrapped up around her arms, snapping into her hair and at her face. Searing heat forced the men to retreat as brittle pages crumpled. Alex was the flames. She consumed the Book. As ash drifted down to soil the floor, she rediscovered the table and reached for the precarious pile. No hand slapped the stack, only flame. Her heat was so intense the Books erupted in a whoosh of fire, covers thrown open, pages blackening, curling. Ink bubbled and sizzled, evaporating into dirty smoke.

She cried in hunger; these Books were not enough. She pressed her body, her limbs of flame, against the bookcase, a single tower among thousands. Book after Book, shelf upon shelf screamed. They begged her for her release, willingly overcome by her inferno. Ecstatic agony tore her apart.

Each text, each page cried its story to her. A thousand hammers, a thousand rocks, a thousand hands all lost their grip on women who slipped from the imprisonment of their pages and sought sanctuary in her fire.

She heard other cries, not of pain but of outrage, of anger and hatred. She need not turn her head; her fiery visage was all-seeing, all reaching. As her thousand hands scoured more Books, she watched men racing towards her.

They screamed at George, demanding he make her stop, lamenting her destruction. They approached, and she welcomed them, watching them withdraw from her heat. They cursed her, spit in disgust at her wanton desecration of their sacred place. They pulled unburned Books from endangered shelves, saving as many as they could, passing small piles, like a fire brigade; hiding fuel from her flames.

Others thumbed hastily through their own texts. One man began reading, then another, and another and another and another, their nonsensical words no more than overlapping noise.

"We hold you accountable, George Frost. You brought her here!"

"Make her stop!"

"Get her out of here!"

"What were you thinking, George? This is why women are forbidden!"

"She'll destroy it all!"

Sparks shot from hands like electric bolts. They passed through her flames and splintered off charred hunks of bookcase. Others tried to scorch her with flames of their own. Their lesser fires vanished, swallowed by her greater.

"What can I do?" George's crying voice whined as the mob encircled him.

An entire bookshelf lay in her embrace, swallowed within her body.

Through folds of hot air and dark, sooty smoke, Alex saw a short, old man in a three-piece tweed suit standing at the end of the aisle. While everyone else rushed towards or away from her, this white-haired, mustachioed little man stood akimbo, observing. A tall, thin man approached him. Tattoos covered his arms, neck, face and much of his scalp, a dirty greenish-blue, painting him nearly solid. The old man gestured for the tattooed man to watch with him.

A voice in Alex's head whispered, "Jeremiah."

Alex looked from this bookcase to the next and the next. Could her flames reach?

She felt something. Soft. Alive. Touching her. Entering her, parting her flame.

George wailed as the men force-fed him into her.

Alex's flames saw for her, felt for her, feasted for her. *Am I anymore? Am I only fire?*

Inside her fiery body, George cried out, pushing deeper, reaching for some mote of her in the inferno. She consumed him, her sharp tongues flicking his blackening skin. She caressed his hair, watching it sizzle, curl, and become part of her. His clothes withered from his body; his skin bubbled and spit, leaked and charred. She felt him within her expansive body, the ecstasy of his tiny death; he embraced her flames like a body, urging them to burn him, to consume him. And with one final willing touch, he sent her away.

Chapter Thirty-Three

aylight streamed behind Heather and Abby; transfixed by Oblivion, their retreat through the front door halted.

Alex found herself beside the coffee table, exactly where she stood when George grabbed her. He hadn't returned.

Between Alex, Heather and Abby, Matthew leered into the blackness. A small glow emerged at the edge of Oblivion. The brightness grew like a fistula sprouting from an impenetrable fluid. The contrast hurt Alex's eyes.

Matthew plucked a glowing coin from the shining edge He placed it on his tongue like a communion wafer and swallowed. He quivered. Shock consumed his expression like a sudden downpour. "It was him all along." He looked at Heather, his words so cold they frosted the air. "You knew?"

He started, seeing Alex suddenly beside the coffee table. He yelped like someone stepped on his tail. "Where's the boy?"

Was that real? The truth hollowed Alex out. Whatever George deserved, he hadn't deserved that. She told Matthew. "I burned him."

Matthew froze, perhaps trying to control his reaction. His face reflected a parade of divergent thoughts.

Marta was gone and the dark void roiled closer to Heather and Abby. Alex had to act. Without magic, she had but one move. She leapt at Matthew, reaching for the book in his hands. She didn't care if she burned the house down if that's what it took to protect Heather and Abby.

Matthew tried to wrench the Book from Alex's grasp.

"Help me," he screamed, stumbling to the ground. Alex pulled and twisted, but Matthew held the Book fast.

"Look out!" Heather and Abby shouted together. Alex saw only darkness.

*   *   *   *

"No, no, no," Heather cried when Alex disappeared into Oblivion.

Abby could barely breathe. "Where'd she go?"

Matthew threw his Book to the ground and pulled himself to his feet.

Heather buried her face in Abby's shoulder. Abby's hands trembled, she felt eviscerated, her insides emptied out. "Not Alex." Her face contorted. "Not Alex." Tears rolled down her cheeks. "Not her."

Matthew rubbed his crooked neck before kicking his Book across the floor. It flipped inside out. He screamed and upturned the coffee table, "That wasn't supposed to happen. I need her. I needed her." He turned to Abby. "What do I do now? He'll know. Jeremiah will destroy me." He turned to Heather. "This wasn't supposed to happen. Not like this. It's over. What am I supposed to do now?"

"Go fuck yourself," Abby screamed through her tears.

He shook his head. "She meant a lot to each of us. More to me than you know." He collected his Book.

As he found a page, Abby asked, "Haven't you done enough?" Heather wiped her face, holding onto her.

Matthew's jaw locked in position as he read, speaking in tongues.

Abby and Heather winced, but he and the blackness vanished. "I'm alive?"

Heather couldn't answer. "I, I think," Abby stammered. "You're okay, Alex?"

*   *   *   *

Sitting on the floor where the black void had been, collecting her knees against her torso, Alex sobbed.

Abby touched her with a poke. "That really you?"

Alex brushed her hand away. "Of course it is."

Abby fell to her knees and embraced her. "I thought Matthew killed you with that thing."

Heather scrambled over, tears streaming down her face. "I was sure you were gone. He killed Marta. She's gone, and we thought you too." She touched Alex, making sure she was real. Then she froze as if struck by a thought. "Matthew thinks you're dead," she said.

"What was that thing?" Abby asked.

"I don't know," Alex replied as they released her. "Everything went dark, like pitch, total blackness. I was floating. Cold; alone. Like it wasn't me that vanished but everything else. And then, I was here." She stood and scanned the room. "He's gone?"

Heather answered. "He said some man's going to kill him."

"He needs you for something," Abby added. "He said you're important."

"He has an odd way of showing it." Alex started towards the door. "Let's get out of here."

Stepping outside into the morning light felt surreal. This was Alex's home, yet all she wanted was to get away from it.

"I don't know if I can ever come back here." Heather stared at the house. Her breath trembled. "Last week, this was my home. Now I don't know if I'll ever see my babies again. And Marta died here."

They approached Abby's truck. Abby walked in silence. Alex put her arm around Heather. "We'll figure this out," she said.

Tears streamed down Heather's face. "Hug me, Alex. Take this away. Make me forget. It hurts too much. Make me forget Billy and Rose and Marta. I don't want to wake up tomorrow without them." Alex embraced her, but she was conscientious not to think too much. She would only give Heather strength. If only she had strength to give. She lost them too. Her arms around Heather, her aunt's body sobbing, Alex held her close, tight, and loving.

Heather touched Alex's face. "Oh, baby," she sobbed, "I've made a mess of everything, haven't I?"

Alex didn't know what to say. *He wanted me. People around me are collateral damage.*

"Come on, guys," Abby opened the truck. The doors squealed, like lamenting wraiths.

They climbed in. Sitting in silence, Abby wasn't starting the engine. *They're both waiting for me to talk, to say their names. Why me? I'm the child. Not only don't I have magic, I destroy everything that does. I'm not special, I'm useless. Worse than useless.*

The silence gave Alex opportunity to hear the din ringing in her head. It was like a thousand whispers, a constant rolling white noise. The longer the truck remained silent, the louder the hiss became. The silence was deafening.

Sara showed me why they aren't doing anything; adults don't have the answers; they don't know any better. They're just older.

Alex mustered the courage to be the first to speak.

"What would Marta want us to do?"

Abby nodded. "I think she'd want us to bring Rose and Billy home."

As though finally receiving permission, Heather sobbed freely.

Abby offered Alex a weak smile. "She'd want us to get through this before we grieve." She paused. "She stepped in front of me. I don't know if she realized, but she saved my life. Her sacrifice shouldn't be in vain."

Heather sniffled. "What was that thing?"

Alex touched her chest. "It was *nothing*. When I fell in, it was like, I mean, I understood what nothing means." Alex tried to explain as best she could. "It's unending darkness. A whole, vast universe, only completely empty. Marta died thinking she was alone in all existence."

"How do you know that?"

"That's how I felt."

Abby whispered, "It spat out her coin, and he put it in his mouth."

Why would he do that? What does he gain by eating her coin? "Why eat her coin?"

Heather's face was red and washed with tears. "He ate her coin?"

Alex nodded.

Abby said, "Alex, how'd you get out."

Heather choked back more tears. "Did you find your magic?"

She doesn't believe anything is possible without magic, does she? "I passed through it," she said, trying to make sense out of it. *Why did it let me go?* "I was there and then I wasn't."

"Why you and not Marta?" Abby asked. "I mean, could she have done something?"

"I don't know." Alex touched her chest. "Maybe because I don't have a coin?"

Heather sobbed. "Is that what happened to my babies? He ate them too?"

Alex shook her head. "I don't think so. He used them. To get to me. You said he was upset I was dead. Maybe now he'll let them go."

"What happened to you, Alex?" Abby whispered, pausing before speaking at normal volume. "Before, when you and that George disappeared? You came back alone."

Alex described the Library. Its innumerable Books, all made from stolen witch's magic. "They really believe they're keeping the world safe." She explained Abigail's Book and how, as she had with Sara's, she had turned to fire. "But I didn't stop with one. I burned a thousand or more."

Heather cheered. "Bastards deserve that."

Abby fretted, "Will they want retribution? Did you keep the magic?"

Alex rubbed her ears. "I think I hear it. It's like all those Books are whispering. Like a thousand whispers all overlapping. I can't tell what they're saying."

"Is that why the magic doesn't work?" Heather asked.

Alex bit her lip and blinked back her tears. Every time Heather asked, she heard it as an accusation. *She doesn't mean it that way, but what if she's right? What if I'm defective? What if there's something wrong with me?* "No," she answered.

Abby touched Alex's shoulder. "We'll figure it out, Alex."

Alex saw in Abby's eyes, her Familiar could tell she was upset. Abby asked, "Mind if we start driving?"

Heather didn't wait for Alex to reply. "The further away the better."

"Rosemary," Heather whispered, "William, please be okay. Please be safe. Mommy loves you." Then she added, "Please don't be dead."

Abby drove back to her trailer, Heather sat sideways in the front seat, keeping an eye on Alex in the back.

"Tell me about the Library. Peter mentioned it but never said much about it."

"What did he say?"

Heather replied, "He said it was a place for study. A repository of knowledge. When he said they kept all the Books there, I assumed books, you know, normal books."

Alex didn't want to talk about it, but she had to. She described the Books she discovered. She told them about the jogger.

Heather shivered. "They're still doing it? What magic are they getting? I held a Book just two days ago and I could feel the pain in those pages. To think about hundreds more like it is overwhelming."

"Millions," Alex corrected her. "Books everywhere I looked." *Each like another Sara.* Her heart broke.

A few silent minutes passed. It was too much to bear. Alex only saw Sara's daughter Abigail twice, once as a sleeping babe and when she held her Book. *That poor girl; they kidnapped her when she was an infant and killed her to add to their collection. How many women also lived and died like that?*

Alex explained, "The Book you used, that was Sara's. The *old witch's shack* was where she lived. George is her son. I know," she prevented Heather from interrupting her, "it doesn't make sense. He doesn't look old but is. I don't know how. Matthew kidnapped him and Abigail as infants. He raised George, convinced him Sara got what she deserved. In the Library, George handed me Abigail's Book. He told me he made it. He murdered her to take her magic."

Abby looked at Alex in the rearview. "His own sister?"

"That's horrible." Heather's voice choked with rage and sadness.

"When I open a Book, I feel the woman. I feel what happened. Them taking her spells; killing her." Alex's voice started to break. "It hurts. It hurts like it's my hands they're breaking, me they're burning. I know it's not, but it feels real. It's so hard. All that pain and hatred. They die without pity, surrounded by people who hate them so much they're celebrating. How can they believe hurting people like that is a good thing? I feel like I'm holding all these lost stories in my heart."

The other two were silent, looking at Alex in sorrow-filled awe.

Heather whispered, "Is that why you, you know, do the fire thing?"

Alex didn't know and said so.

"There's got to be an easier way," Abby said. "You shouldn't hurt so much."

"I don't know any other way," Alex replied. "I didn't want to open one Book and then I was this gigantic ball of fire, burning hundreds—"

"You were in the fire?"

"I *was* the fire. Each Book is its own torture."

"That's not fair," Heather said softly. "I'm so sorry, Alex. I had no idea. Your father convinced me he'd done all the hard bits. I bet he thought so. To think I tried to burden Rosemary with this. I'm grateful I failed. She could never be as strong as you."

"This is what we're up against," Alex continued. "Matthew convinced George, who did it to his own sister."

"Is it possible," Abby said, pausing in thought, "if *we* sent *you* back to Sara—that Matthew went back too?"

"He didn't seem aware of the future. Maybe he did his research so he'd fit in back then."

Abby nodded. "Maybe I'm grasping at straws to make them less scary."

Heather leaned forward. "How does knowing he can time travel make someone who commands a black hole less scary?"

"They have all their spells," Alex said. "I mean, the Library has all the magic. Matthew ate Marta's coin. Like, he ate her soul. Is it that far-fetched that he might have figured out how to live a really, really long time?"

Heather hadn't stopped shaking her head. "How do we defeat immortals?"

Abby banged on the steering wheel. "This is all terrible. It wasn't supposed to be like this for you. What was Peter thinking?" She hit the steering wheel again. "There's no way to keep you safe. How do I protect you when Matthew can send you places like the Library? If you had magic and could protect yourself that would be one thing, but this? When Matthew made you disappear, I thought you might be gone, you know,"—she choked up a little—"forever. How did you get back from the Library without magic?"

Alex hadn't had time to understand the event's emotional gravity. Thinking about it made her want to cry. The answer was she did nothing. It was George; he'd burned his flesh to touch her, and part of her still ached for his pain. "Like I told you, I am the fire. I punished them. I touched all the Books I could reach. I burned them all. It hurt so…" Alex couldn't find words to describe the immensity of her pain.

Heather gasped. "I can't imagine how horrifying that was, but it must have looked amazing. I would have loved to see you destroying their collection."

"Ironic, no?" Abby interjected. "Burning Books?"

"It's not ironic," Heather said, "and those aren't Books, they're tortured witches. They have no right to them. They don't belong to them."

Alex continued, her tone a little softer. "Men from all over the Library threatened me, and George for bringing me. George found me deep in the fire." She recalled how he felt, how she tasted his pain as he moved inside her. "He touched me. That's all it took to send me back. I think I killed him."

"Serves him right," Heather muttered.

"I burned his skin away. *I killed him.* Sure, I wanted to hurt him for what he did to Abigail, but not like that." She paused, trying to push the memory away, but it was like a sticky nettle she couldn't release from her fingers.

Heather laughed, "I bet Matthew regrets sending you there."

"I don't understand. What purpose did that serve?" Abby added.

Alex shook her head. "I don't know. I think he wanted to see what I would do. I wonder if he knew, and that's why he had George do it."

"I don't understand." Heather's words may not have been meant for any ears but her own. "He takes my babies to show Alex his Library. How else is he using my kids? I thought it was you, Alex, but what if it's something else?"

Alex almost whined, "I don't know anything. He said it was a test, but I don't know what that means."

Chapter Thirty-Four

hey came to a stop and Abby shut the engine. The three women sat silently as the late morning light and daytime heat rose outside.

Abby was first to step out. Her door creaked. She unlocked her trailer and cranked open the windows.

Alex wanted to go with her, but Heather showed no inclination to exit the truck. She didn't know what to say to her aunt. She couldn't understand what Heather was feeling. They were her cousins, but they were Heather's children. They were missing, and possibly dead. Alex had nothing but hope; Heather, reality. It reminded Alex of the physics thought experiment where a cat is both dead and alive in a box. For Heather, both realities existed with equal uncertainty. Only once they were found would one become true. Marta's death, however, offered a third possibility. Heather might open that box and find it empty.

Until this moment, Heather and her diverse Book Club got together to *play* witch. One death had made it real. Heather was drowning with little hope of reaching the surface. Whatever she'd started, finishing now seemed impossible. As long as she sat in the truck, Alex would keep her company.

The luxury of time introduced new doubts to Alex. Facts seen from new distorting angles introducing possibilities she had never considered. What if her father wasn't the hero of her story but a villain alongside Matthew? What if his plan all along was not about saving witches but damning them? Give them a powerless messiah to wither their hopes. Was it all just an ingenious plan to wipe them out, the last few who believed, and Alex was the key? If they believed in her, she endangered them. Or, more troubling, what if Matthew wasn't lying, and they were on the same side? What would it mean if she had to align with someone so cruel?

Alex spiraled through sadness and depression until Heather interrupted her thoughts. "Are you ever getting out?"

"I was waiting for you."

Heather smiled weakly. "Oh dear, I was waiting for you. I thought you needed some time to process."

"That's what I thought, but about you."

"I've processed enough," Heather answered. "I'm ready to figure out what we do next."

Alex jumped to the ground, and Heather wrapped her in her arms. "My sweet Alexandrea. It's not fair, you're too young for so much responsibility. If I could do it in your place, I would." She touched Alex's hair. "I wish I knew what to say to make it easier. I know I'm just your aunt and will never replace your parents, but you're my family."

Alex hugged Heather. "Thanks," she replied. "I love you too."

Heather stepped back. "We'll find a way. We'll save your cousins. Together. You're not alone. We're all here for you." She glanced at the trailer.

Abby was setting up chairs in the shade. She handed each of them a tall glass of ice water. "Sit," she told them, "we need to rest. It's been a long night."

They sat. Alex drained her glass then chewed on the ice. Setting the cup down, she closed her eyes and listened to the peaceful noises from the farm, the rustle of the cornstalks, the shifting breeze, the calls of birds. *A little more of this, and I might fall asleep.*

She climbed out of the lawn chair and wiped drool off her face.

"You were in a coma," Heather said. "You slept for hours."

"I was?" Alex asked. "Sorry."

"Don't be silly," Heather dismissed. "Abby just put chicken on the grill."

Abby came out, arms laden with plates. Alex stepped over to help but Abby refused her. "Sit," Abby ordered. "Food'll be ready soon. I was waiting for you to wake up." She disappeared again, but only for a second, returning with a trio of slushy, green drinks in one hand and a full pitcher in the other. "I made margaritas."

Alex took a quick sip, not expecting to like a beverage that required salt on the glass. She tasted the alcohol, but it was sweet and pleasantly tart. Like candy in a glass. *This is why adults like these drinks.* When Heather saw her drinking, she blurted out, "What are you doing?"

Alex didn't have an answer; Abby let her drink. She looked from Heather to Abby, hoping Abby would take the blame. She offered, "Abby lets me."

"I don't care." Heather raised her glass. "You're supposed to toast before you drink. Were you raised by wolves?"

Alex cracked up.

Abby raised her glass. "To Marta."

Heather's smile dimmed, but she nodded solemnly. "To Marta."

"To Billy and Rose," Alex added, "and getting them back safely." The others repeated with enthusiasm. The three glasses clinked.

"I was thinking," Heather said when they were winding down, "maybe we should get the Book Club together."

Alex didn't think this was a good idea and said so. "I worry that makes it more convenient for Matthew."

Heather opened her mouth to argue the point but stopped. "Okay, I won't. I trust you."

"I'm not so sure that's a good idea, either."

"What? Trusting you? Don't be silly."

"Heather," Alex made her tone less whiny. "I can't do any magic. Why put your faith in me when I'm, what? Broken?"

"Alex, your father gave his life for this. He wasn't stupid, he knew what he was doing. We'll figure out why things aren't working right. It's going to happen. You'll be amazing."

"I wish I could have your faith in me. Maybe there's a reason it doesn't work. Maybe I'm not really a witch. Maybe I'm like Abby."

Alex worried she'd insulted Abby, but her Familiar wasn't bothered, "You're not like me. Trust me."

Alex didn't see further reason to argue her point. "I'm just concerned your faith in me is misplaced. I know magic is real, I've seen what men do with it. Maybe that's the only real magic. When was the last time you saw a woman cast a spell? Not a group, but one? I can't. Maybe that's how it should be. I only have," she tugged her earlobe, "noise." She groaned. "I traded one type of ringing for another."

"I understand how you can doubt yourself, but look at what happens when you touch their Books."

"What if you're wrong?"

Heather put her arm around Alex. With a nod, they started towards the trailer. "If I had to bet on you, I'd be all in." She rubbed her eyes. "My kids are missing, but I know—*I know*—that because of you, I will get them back."

"I hope you're right, Aunt Heather."

Heather mused a moment then theorized. "Maybe you need supporters around you for the magic to work."

"Are you all going to clap like I'm a fairy?" Alex joked.

Heather made a face. Abby looked amused.

Alex shrugged. "I don't know. Do you think it'll be any different with an audience?"

Now Heather shrugged. "I've practiced healing my whole life. I feel like I intuitively know what herbs to use. It's not real magic. The summoning spell was the first I've ever cast in all my life."

Alex pondered that a moment. "How were you so sure you could?"

Heather looked at Abby, who had just plated the chicken and was returning to hand them their plates. "I knew it would work."

"How could you be so sure?" Alex wished for Heather's certainty.

"Because I have faith in the things I was told. Like I would cast that spell and you would be amazing. I just believe. Being born a twin is—I guess it's like two magnets—one cancels the other out." She shrugged. "That's why I think more women would help, sort of amplifying the signal." She held up her drink and looked at it. "Or it could be the alcohol talking."

Alex and Abby laughed politely.

They began to eat. Alex realized she had been starving. "I wish I knew it would work," she replied with her mouth full. Abby watched her closely, and Alex wondered what she was thinking. "I think having them all around would make me feel pressured. Even if I could do a spell, I don't know if I could with all of them watching. Does that make sense?"

Abby laughed, "Classic performance anxiety. Kills the mood every time."

Heather snorted, trying not to spit out her margarita. Alex wasn't sure she got the joke but assumed it was about sex. She didn't understand how some adult jokes were so unfunny to kids and vice versa. She guessed it was more about the emotional release than the actual joke; the more stress, the better it felt to laugh.

"It can't hurt to try." Heather pressed. "I knew I couldn't do it alone; I needed others. I just didn't know if I needed five people or fifty."

"I think you could have done it alone," Abby remarked. "Your brother did it by himself."

"It's different," Heather protested. "Peter explained it to me. Once they put emotion to paper, the spell is pure and unadulterated by emotion. That makes them more powerful. Each spell is perfect."

"Then spells aren't as good when witches cast them?" Alex asked.

"It's different. Peter said it's like cooking. The Book tells the reader how to perfectly make a generic cake. Emotion adds all the flavor and filling and frosting. It might not be as pure and strong, but it's better suited for the moment."

Abby shrugged. "I never thought about it that way. What do I know?"

"I couldn't have done it without you, Abby. You were the key to this whole thing."

"What did we accomplish exactly?" Alex wiggled her fingers. "No magic." She looked into the distance. "I don't know what's supposed to happen, and the whole experience has been horrible. All I want is to wake up and find it's all a bad dream or have someone tell me all I have to do is twitch my nose or say a chant or pinch my left boob."

Abby laughed. "Have you tried any of those?"

"No." Alex's reply sounded like a question. "Should I have?"

Abby refilled her glass. "I'm just saying, before you get frustrated, try everything that comes to mind. Something is bound to work. Right?"

Alex thought for a minute. "You're probably right." She looked to Heather. "Sure, call the Club. I'll try with them all watching."

Heather stood and grabbed the table. "Wow, I didn't realize how that hit me until I tried to get up."

Alex felt a little woozy. She remembered the way she felt the last time she had too much to drink—*was that yesterday*—and thought better of it this time, nursing her single glass.

Heather went inside to her purse and cellphone. She started making calls, and Alex could hear her negotiating with each woman. *All serious requests come with short notice; that's what makes them serious; can't you change your plans? Why do you even come to our meetings if you can't help?* And on and on. Eventually, she came out and announced, "Tomorrow night, after dinner. Six of them can come."

She came back to the table and started cleaning up.

"Did you tell them about Marta?"

Heather's face became a knot of emotion. "My kids are missing, Marta's dead because of the man who took them. At what point am I scaring people away?" She looked to Abby then back to Alex. "I thought, better we tell them tomorrow in person. Before they figure it out for themselves. She's gone. There's no crime scene. As far as anyone is concerned, she's about to go missing."

Abby added, "Everyone saw me leave with her."

Alex pointed her finger at Marta's car, parked to the side, covered in dust.

"Well," Abby said, "there's that. I should probably take care of it."

"You can't leave it there," Heather said. "If people come looking for her, you don't want her car here." Heather looked at the barn and the fields. "They'll think you're a serial killer the second they see it."

Abby nodded.

"It has to be gone before we tell them what happened to her," Heather said looking at Alex.

"We? Or do you mean when I tell them?"

Heather took a preparatory breath but let it go. Taking a moment to gather her thoughts, she finally said, "I didn't tell them because I couldn't. I'd have to tell Donna then tell Nancy, then tell Linda, then tell Carrie. Saying it once is hard enough."

Alex shrunk in her seat. She'd be the one tasked with telling them. It, like everything else, weighed heavily on her.

Abby joined Heather clearing the table. They made a single trip, leaving Alex alone outside.

Alex looked up at the darkening sky, struck by the deepening, almost cobalt blue. The sun was at the horizon. A gathering of clouds bloomed at the edge of the fields. The whispering in her head was nearly as loud as the breeze. When she concentrated, she heard what sounded like words, but there were too many to make out. Venus, the evening star, sparkled overhead. Untethered, perhaps from the alcohol, her mind ran freely. Venus was a planet, another world she could see from where she sat, the first sparkle in the sky. In mythology, Venus was the goddess of love. The day was ruled by the sun, Helios, a male, but Selene, the moon, was female. She felt like it should mean something significant, but that meaning was just out of reach. She found herself thinking how the bright star reminded her of a coin, like the goddess's coin sparkling in the sky. She wished she could unravel the riddle her mind had uncovered. No additional revelations came. She only felt exhausted.

As Alex headed into the trailer, Abby and Heather were coming out.

"Where you going?" Abby asked.

"I'm tired," Alex said. "Mind if I go to bed?"

"Everything okay?" Heather looked at her phone to see the time. "It's not even nine. You slept most of the day."

"Yeah," Alex sighed. "I'm just wiped." She rubbed her face. "I'm just so tired I can't think straight." She pulled on her ears. "The noise isn't helping."

Heather nodded. "The booze didn't help, either," she said matter-of-factly. "Drinking makes me sleepy too."

Abby motioned back to the trailer. "The cats are all waiting for you on the bed. They're reluctantly getting along."

Alex smiled. She looked forward to cuddling something small and warm. To Heather, she said, "We're sharing the bed tonight, I think. Don't worry about waking me when you come to bed."

Heather gave Alex a hug. "I can't sleep," She said. "I don't think I'll be able to relax until I know Rosemary and William are safe." She walked Alex to the trailer. "If I get tired, I'll come in, but I think Abby and I'll be up a while."

Alex hesitated, holding the door open. She looked first to Abby and then to Heather. "Thanks," she said.

"For what?" Heather and Abby replied almost in unison.

Alex's eyes watered. "I'm feeling like I'm letting everyone down. Especially Billy and Rose. I feel like everyone expected me to be magical." She took a slow breath. "You, um, you two make me feel like it's okay, like we're in this together."

"Oh, sweetie...," Heather touched Alex on the shoulder.

"We are in this together," Abby jumped in. "You, me, Heather, the Book Club, we're all in this together. Your father and mother may have started it, and they're gone now, but you were never alone. We will never leave your side."

Alex nodded tearfully.

"It's true, Alex, a lot of people are counting on you," Heather said. "No one expects you to do it alone. Even if you had magic, we'd all be at your side." She took a breath and rubbed Alex's shoulder. "Get a good sleep. We'll figure things out in the morning. Okay?"

Alex nodded. "Goodnight."

Alex used the bathroom and washed her face before changing. She slipped under the covers, briefly petting the cats, and lay there quietly, her eyes closed.

The cats purred at her touch. Dolly stood and stretched, walked over and threw herself against Alex's hip. Alex rested her hand on Dolly's flank and flexed her fingers to knead Dolly's fur. She heard murmurs from Heather and Abby outside but could only discern every few words and so couldn't reconstruct their conversation. It wasn't that different from the cacophony in her head. She wondered how Heather was holding herself together.

She was sick with worry about her cousins. Thoughts of them mixed with horrors replaying in her head. *Maybe that's why Heather doesn't want quiet time with her thoughts.* Alex couldn't blame her. She tried focusing on other things. Outside, the night-breeze picked up, fluttering leaves and corn stalks tapped against one another. The gentle rustling helped soothe her mind and drown out the constant whispering.

Eyes closed, Alex felt like she drifted in and out of sleep, never falling deep enough. She couldn't tell if she fell asleep or only drowsed. The minutes passed in groups. Maybe she was sleeping five or ten minutes at a time. She found her thoughts drifting to Rose and Billy.

Are they sleeping now? Are they safe? Do they know I'm thinking about them? Her heart felt banded in iron, hard, cold, and rusting. It ached. *I wish I could tell them I'm thinking of them, worried for them. Then they could know they aren't alone.* She imagined her thoughts finding them as she drifted into a deeper sleep, creating a dream they all shared or bringing them to a place where they could dream together. This all started with a dream. She replayed the nightmare in her head, and with that, her mother's voice came to answer her.

Chapter Thirty-Five

lex lay in bed, a pillow to three cats, not quite awake and not quite asleep, drifting between the two realms. The room's acoustics altered as though the trailer slowly submerged into water. She heard her mother's words from the dream. *Bring the mist, Alex. There's nothing more for you here. Alex, please focus. Now go.*

And she found herself staring into a gray mist. *Did I do this?* Looking back to the bed, she expected to find herself asleep. Save for the cats; the bed was empty. She wasn't dreaming. Her black spot was awake. The mist was here.

"I'm coming, Rose. Soon, Billy," she whispered. Her heart pounded in her throbbing head. *I should tell Heather, but what if I can't bring the mist back?* Nerves boiled her stomach into a froth. Finally, she was doing something no one else told her to do. She wasn't about to ask permission. Alex crossed the threshold into the afterlife.

She surveyed unimagined dream-space, as Sara had called it. No silver thread tethered her. To cross over in corporeal form, Peter had sacrificed his coin. She just came here. *Maybe I don't pay because I don't have a coin?* Her cousins could be anywhere. Alex believed there was one place to start looking.

There was no sense of travel, of distance, but Alex moved. She kept her focus singular until arriving at her destination.

Stepping through the mist, she stood at the crest of a mountain, sloping into the dark valley below. Beside her sat a giant stone: Picnic Rock. The night sky was a wondrous explosion of stars and constellations. *Billy was right.* She scanned the firmament. *You can see every star that ever was.*

No one knew she was here. No one would come looking for her. The night air chilled her nervous perspiration; she shivered. She was actually here, at Picnic Rock, and yet the leaded weights of dread that permeated her nightmares clung to her like anchor chains.

She wandered past the rock, looking for a path she knew wasn't there. Grass and twigs crunched under her feet. She discovered the winding trail and followed it. It snaked and switched, leading eventually to a white door. She watched as the entire house around it came into view, perhaps into being, as she noticed the door.

Her hand paused at the knob, apprehension slicking her skin. This house was Rose's dream. The ornate white door creaked open before her hand. She entered into a warren of rooms, decorated with boldly patterned wallpapers and elaborate window treatments. She was in Rosemary's safe place.

Alex noted how the décor evolved room by room, as though first designed by a child, then growing in excitement and sophistication. One room was an assault of primary colors and stuffed animals. Another vibrated in sunny lemon yellow. Photos of kittens and ponies dressed rainbow-colored furniture that had sparkling clothes draped out of the bubble-shaped drawers. Toile wallpapers, red on white, patterns of women in dresses with horses and carts of produce. Silk and satin pillows piled on beds, lace in the windows. Furnishings entirely made of stuffed animals that dispensed gumballs; a chair made of candy with odd corners bitten off or licked smooth. It wasn't just a house, Alex realized, but a collection of Rose's wants and desires from given moments in her life. One room reflected a childish desire and the next, choking on tulle and lace and round tufted chairs and fainting couches, a cliché of femininity.

She proceeded deeper, turning randomly but never returning to a room she'd already been. It was a maze, each room fenestrated on all walls, each window viewing different outsides. Colors and patterns took on a grotesquery of exaggeration, painful to look at for too long. Scents of baking cookies and potpourri and popcorn tightened her throat. Walls twisted, losing their shape, their structure, their purpose.

Alex's heart thundered with anxiety. The feminine comforts were no longer comforting but threatening and violating. Nowhere could she avert her eyes from the deteriorating creation. The house felt unending, trapping, consuming.

Alex called for her cousins. Floorboards creaked the only reply. The rooms became dusty, disused, then worn, then dilapidated. *When did it get like this?* Moth-chewed, stained curtains hung, torn, on broken valances. Dust covered the floors, like a gray morning snow. Discarded furniture lay disused and broken, like rotting corpses, the fantastic facades degrading into wet papier mâché and cardboard. She rubbed her neck; the hairs stood on end. Each subsequent room suffered greater deterioration. *What happened to Rose?* Fancy yellowed wallpaper curled from the walls. Plaster cracked. Filthy windows stared out without their panes. Exposed lathing peeked through holes in the walls.

Alex entered one final room. There were no further exits. She felt trapped in Rose's torment. The room seemed to teeter as she moved. Floorboards opened to darkness, water dripped from pregnant stains in the ceiling and bled down the walls.

In one corner, a set of stairs led through a rupture in the floor. Frightened, Alex continued towards it.

Cobwebs dressed her face and body, encumbering her trembling descent. The staircase groaned beneath her. Finally reaching the bottom, she stepped onto hard-packed dirt in the center of a vast, unfinished basement. Wood slats haphazardly nailed to studs separated inside from out. The smells of must and decay infiltrated her sinuses. Alex pulled cobwebs from her hair and face, worrying about what tormenting creatures crawled in these recesses of Rose's mind.

The underside of the floor was distantly visible through a haze of cobwebs above her. Sweat chilled Alex's skin. She was a vulnerable interloper inside Rose's dream house. This was the place Rose escaped to in her sleep, her unconscious safe place. How horrible was Rose's dread to influence the design, or was something more insidious responsible for the house's dilapidation? She dreaded what she would find when she came upon her cousins.

Through the slats, she spied Picnic Rock. Four torches glowed in the darkness. *Did those get lit while I was in here?* She shimmied through a crevice between slats and cautiously followed the winding path back to Picnic Rock. Climbing the makeshift stairs, the first thing she saw—besides the four torches wedged into the cleft in the giant, flat stone—was a solitary hitching post amidst bundles of twigs and brush.

"Sacrifice Stone," Alex whispered Billy's words. *This is too crazy to be a coincidence. What does Billy know?*

Near where they had sat when Billy leapt from the front of the stone, she found her cousins. Their hands and feet were bound, and they appeared to be unconscious. The vastness of the night sky glistened like a swallowing maw. She spun, scanning for a sign of

Matthew. The thought of him creeping towards her was an unwanted hand caressing the flesh beneath her skin.

Without losing focus of her surroundings, Alex approached and began untying her cousins.

"She's here," Billy hissed, and Alex realized they had only been pretending to sleep. "Alex came for us." Once free, he worked on Rose's bindings.

Where's Matthew?

Alex didn't help Billy untie Rose; everything felt dreadfully wrong. *What is Matthew waiting for?*

Once Rose was freed, Billy helped her to her feet.

The twins looked haggard and filthy.

The fact that they needed her to hiss, "Come on," to consider escape—and even then they didn't move—troubled Alex.

Rose's voice sounded poorly rehearsed. "I can't believe you found us."

Billy and Rose crumpled to the ground like marionettes who had discovered their strings were severed. Dread paralyzed Alex.

"You're alive," Matthew's voice was thoughtful, both stating and asking. "No one survives Oblivion." He rubbed his crooked neck. "I can't figure you out. It was supposed to be simple. Then Peter double-crosses me. Now I can't find you, Alexandrea. How did they hide you?" He motioned to the twins. "I hate resorting to petty tricks like kidnapping, but I'm a desperate man."

Matthew stood opposite her, the crease dividing them like a line neither yet dared to cross. "What did you do to them?" She motioned to her cousins.

Matthew's head wobbled as he struggled to look up at her. "They're in no pain. Just darkness. They'll revive little worse for wear." He took a small step.

"Why me?" Alex had nowhere to retreat; the edge hung behind her. She wouldn't abandon her cousins.

His smile looked forced. "Your demonstration at the Library was a proof of concept." He stepped closer, judged Alex's body language, and stopped. "I didn't know what to expect. You performed beyond my wildest expectations." He touched his glowing chest. "I can track most any soul, but never yours. That deception has considerable value to me."

"I've always been like this."

"Peter never inquired about anything like that," Matthew mused. "If not him, could Holly figure it out?"

Alex knew he asked rhetorically, but shrugged. "Is that what you want?"

"It's *part* of what I want-*ted*," he replied precisely. "The Library proved your value. He was right. Again. This will work." He crept forward.

"This? Who?"

"I thought your invisible soul was a flaw. It protects you. You've destroyed irreplaceable Books. Jeremiah knows you exist now. He'll want you destroyed. But if he can't *find* you…"

"Destroyed?"

"You burned his house, Alexandrea. You disfigured my son." He was nearly halfway to her, the seam at his feet.

"George is alive?" Her concern surprised her. Like heartburn, but not as unpleasant.

"I should have retained Marta's soul for him. When I was young, a dear friend named Laurent Robaleaux explained that once upon a time, witches could conjure real magic. Sara Frost—I know you know who she is—was the last of her kind. Now *witches* pretend with crystals and nature communes. Nearly all their magic is safe in Books." He eyed her, adding, "Nearly all."

Alex responded sarcastically. "So I'm interesting… and Books." She shifted her weight. "When do you get to the evil plan?"

Matthew laughed, genuinely. "There's no easy way to explain it, Alexandrea. I need you."

"Need me?"

"If you could go back to the Library, what would you do?" Another step.

Alex didn't have to think. "Destroy it."

"Exactly what I want! It doesn't belong to them." For the first time, he left her speechless. "Your fire doesn't destroy Books, Alexandrea. They become a part of you." Another step. Alex bristled. Matthew smirked as he crossed the crease in the stone.

"You want me to take all the Books? Why? What then?"

"Take their Books, take their strength. The Library belongs to Jeremiah. It is the source of his power. It was a brilliantly simple plan. But you were invisible. You can take the Books but have no magic. But you escaped Oblivion. I've tried provoking you. But every test, you surprise me by finding an answer no one knew before."

"Testing? Provoking? For what?"

"The Library contains all the magic that ever was. Look what happens when you touch it. If you were able to express your magic, you'd become a weapon I could wield. I can control their magic and use it against them."

"I am not your weapon."

"No," he grinned, stepping forward. "You're my thief. If you can't make magic, can I extract it?"

Her words came angry, her breath acidic from her churning stomach. "I guess you'll have to break my fingers to find out."

"I have to know it would work before I hurt you. I won't just beat a woman. Until I know they won't be lost, you burn Books but nothing more."

Alex's anger rolled her stomach acid into a froth. She half expected her words to burn. "You kidnap my cousins; you murder Sara Frost; you hurt everyone I love. Why not just ask me, 'Hey, Alex, those Books you burn, did you keep 'em? Can I have 'em?' Instead, you tell me you'll terrorize me until you're sure it's okay to beat me to death?"

"Magic can only be taken by force."

"You're disgusting. That Library is disgusting. If I could, I would burn it all."

Matthew roared. "We agree on something, Alexandrea! Once again, we are on the same side."

"That's what this is, Matthew?" she asked as snottily as she could. "A heist? A robbery?"

"Imagine the Book you'd make. A single tome of all magic." His grin sickened her. "My Book."

The Book I'd make? The notion eviscerated her. She felt opened before him, as though his hammer were already smashing her to a twitching pulp, but her nerves hadn't told her yet. She wanted to escape. She wanted to save her cousins. She wanted to understand the parts her family had played in this. *I can't leave them.* He had forced her into a decision. She would never again lie to herself that it wasn't her body. She didn't know what to do. Rage answered for her.

Alex charged at Matthew, hands balled into fists.

Matthew's face told her everything. This was not the solution he'd anticipated. A Book appeared in his hands and he hastily read from it.

She punched and clawed at him. Underneath his clothes, he was bone thin but sinewy and solid like stone. Their faces close, she inhaled and felt in her mouth the patterns of words on his breath. She had vomited similar words from Sara's lips.

Two sets of hands pulled at her shirt and clawed the skin underneath, wrenching her from Matthew, kicking and screaming. Seeing her assaulters, she fell into broken stillness.

"Thank you, children," Matthew said to Billy and Rose, who dragged Alex away; their faces torturously acknowledged his voice. "Put her to the stake."

"Rose, Billy!" Alex cried to them. "What are you doing? It's me." She hoped they might acknowledge her. *Why are they helping him?*

Alex could not wrench free. Their fingernails cut half-moons in her flesh. She thrashed; her foot snapped Billy's head back. Alex's eyes welled at the expression of betrayal on his face. "I'm sorry," she heard herself whimper. Billy looked at her with the forgiveness of a priest at an execution. Her apologies foundered, broken by tears from the realization that she lost them.

They forced her against the rough wooden post. Splinters and knots stuck into her back. Rose now possessed enough strength to keep Alex pinned as Billy collected the ropes that had bound them. He walked around Alex, lashing her to the post. The ropes bit into her.

"Billy, Rose, please," Alex begged, "you're hurting me. He's going to kill me." She'd been fearful before but never so certain that harm was coming. Her insides churned like water slopping from an upturned bowl. Raw loathing glowered from Rose's eyes; her cousin was a ravenous animal whose only emotion was contempt. It crushed Alex. If not for them, why was she here?

"What are you doing to them?"

Knots secured, Billy and Rose pushed the bundles of timber and brush, to surround Alex. They ambled to the edge of the stone, staring into darkness.

"Cast your magic." Matthew said, "I'm not sure which I believe more, that you can't or won't. I keep wondering, *what is she waiting for?*" He nodded his outstretched head. "I need to know you can express the magic in the Books inside you. I don't want to do this, Alexandrea, but if lighting these flames—if causing you immense pain—frees you from whatever is suppressing your magic, then I have no choice." He looked the greenish of seasick, as though unsettled by his own words. "I only hope it doesn't kill you in the process."

Alex struggled against the biting ropes. Blood swelled into clefts in her flesh gouged by her cousin's feral nails. She remembered being immobilized inside Sara. She possessed dozens more experiences—now memories—of other women tied up moments before death. She had lived this fate a hundred times over. How would this be different?

"I can't do magic." She watched Matthew's surprise. "They all hoped I'd be special. I don't know what they were thinking."

Matthew stepped uncomfortably close. He whispered, "You are special." He pointed at her eyes. "I saw you, all those years ago, hiding inside Sara Frost."

Having another confirm the incident made it suddenly real. Had any fight remained in her limbs, she would have thrashed uselessly against the ropes. She understood the coming pain. This time it would be her body.

"I've waited a dozen lifetimes to meet you, Alexandrea Hawthorne. We've been plotting to overthrow Jeremiah for a hundred generations. I sacrificed my life for that cause. When he told me, when I saw you in there, I knew I could wait a century to find you again." He petted her shoulder. "I found Peter and made him my student. I let your father find clues, let him think he was sneaking, answered his questions, feigning ignorance. He thought I didn't know. He never realized he only did what I wanted him to. I gave him Sara's Book so he would find her. It was simple, tracking what would be. Tracing the lines that led to you.

"You were inside Sara when I took her magic. Only she, and now you, could take it back. That's why your father did this. To give you magic, to give it to me."

She whimpered, "He didn't do those things for you. He'd never help you."

Matthew touched her head like he soothed a kicked puppy. "Willingly or not, your father served me." His words left Alex chilled.

Matthew directed Rose and Billy to a spot near the front edge of the stone. A Book appeared in his hands and he turned to Alex, "Perhaps the pain you need isn't just physical." He mused. "It's ironic; I used the same Book for thirty years. It disappeared the first time we met, and I worried I'd never find its equal. But this one has a unique spell. It rattles the minds. When I command them, any conflict brews their worst fears to reality into their minds. Watch."

"What's happening Alex?" Rose sobbed, holding her head. "What's happening? Is mommy dead? Is she dead?"

Billy collapsed; his face swelling from Alex's kick.

"Rose," Alex called, "Heather is fine."

Rose's body convulsed. Alex knew her words offered no comfort.

Matthew drew a deep breath. "One final test," he offered gravely. "You have magic, Alexandrea. I sincerely hope you find it soon."

He navigated to a page. His mouth moved, whispering a guttural language, repeated like a chant. The Book disappeared. Branches and twigs swelled around Alex as buds emerged and matured before her eyes. They opened, and what should have been bright blooms emerged as flame, flickering and dancing, spreading across the pile.

"Show me, Alexandrea. Please. Don't make me hurt you. Show me you hold those Books inside."

Hot air surrounded her like a suffocating blanket as the flames crept from twig to branch, growing larger, closer.

"Show me," Matthew repeated, scrutiny and disappointment written on his face. He would watch her burn alive but wouldn't enjoy a moment of it. With her death he would watch his grand scheme literally burn up in smoke.

Sweat burned her eyes; flames tickled her ankles with poison stingers. "Matthew," she begged, "please. I don't have magic. Not like this. Not like this. Please, Matthew."

Matthew's face dripped with pity. "It has to be you, Alexandrea."

"No, please..." her cries were lost to the choking claws of smoke.

Matthew produced his Book again. Holding it out, he hissed to Billy, "Come here son, hold this."

Billy dragged his feet, his body slumped. His tortured expression evidenced the agonies in his mind. He stared at Alex as though watching her burn would offer a reprieve from whatever visions he suffered. His arms awaited Matthew, who perched his open Book in them.

Matthew flipped to a page and produced a pen.

The flames combusted larger branches and logs. Alex's stomach burned like a mirror fire consumed her within. Not even her adopted experiences had prepared her for the singeing pain as flames lashed her skin, or the throbbing, billowing heat inflating blisters the size of cherries on her ankles and fingers. She panted with fear, incapable of screaming. Terror menaced her like a monstrous figure cloaked in smoke.

"Put the fire out, Alex," Matthew begged. He studied the page before him. "If you can't, try to force it out. Vomit it. Give me your magic." He glanced at Rose. "Perhaps I should have burned her and made you watch. Would that have done it?"

Alex couldn't believe the heat could get any worse, and the flames weren't yet at her. Her throat snared closed with each choking breath and her eyes burned like they'd been clawed from their sockets.

"Now, Alex," Matthew ordered, "put out the flames!"

Alex chanted, "Not like this." She recalled the horrors she'd experienced trapped within Sara, believing she would survive because it wasn't her. The heat played lasciviously with her hair, which stuck to her sweaty face. This time it was her, her body, her life that was ending.

Magic whispered in her head, the voices growing louder than the roaring flames. *It never says anything. It's useless.* As the flames roared, the whispers grew louder and frenzied. Whispers became shouts and screams.

When she'd held Sara's Book—Abigail's—they had transformed her. She had become the flame. She burned George just as she was now burning. A shock of panic rose in her like a hurricane wave crashing on rocks. A shift in the wind fed her a sip of cold air. She thought to scream but knew this last breath shouldn't be wasted.

"Matthew," she croaked, "turn them away. Don't make them watch. Turn them away."

She thrashed desperately and felt the pole budge. *Can I lift it free?* Sweat poured off her body, saturating her clothes. She felt the urge to pee. *Now?* Tears stung her eyes, running down her sweaty, sooty face. Mucus burst from her nose as she convulsed with sobs.

The flames reached her, its brightness still no match for the dark hole in her chest. Fire teased her skin like a puppy with razor blade teeth. With the last breath in her lungs, Alex cried. The flames began taking her flesh.

Chapter Thirty-Six

ndrea? Andrea, wake up."

The voice sounded distant.

Sweat spilled down the center of her back. Her skin felt scraped raw.

"Sweetheart." A woman's voice, soothing, concerned. "Andrea, I need you to wake up. It's important. Right now. Be here, not there."

Angry flames sticking her with knives made of light.

Alex gasped. The air was clean. Familiar, though long forgotten.

The choking smoke churned powerfully against her. The hurt was extraordinary; she cried out in anguish. Twisted and straining, her body thrashed against restraints.

"Andrea, I'm not kidding. Wake up right this second." The familiar voice was stern and right outside the dark place containing her.

The roaring flames tried to mute the words, pleading for her to come back.

A hand touched her cheek.

Alex jerked awake.

"There isn't much time, Andrea."

Alex knew the voice. Her chest banged like a door holding back a mob. Her eyes opened. Instead of her expected disappointment, she was captured by Holly's loving gaze.

Alex was stiff, sore. *Was that a dream? A bad dream?* "My head hurts, Mom," she groaned and rubbed her temples. It ached worse than ever. Made her sick. Flashes haunted her: her body consumed by flame.

"I know, dear. It's going to hurt a bit longer. Stay alert. Don't fall back to sleep. Can you do that for me, Andrea?"

Sleep begged for her return, promising freedom from her throbbing migraine. Alex looked at her mother. *Something's not right.* She sat up. "Why do you keep calling me Andrea?"

"It's your name," Holly replied.

Alex squinted through her pulsating misery. *She's my mother. Something seems off.* "It's not Andrea, Mom. Remember? *Alexandrea.*" Only that wasn't true, not anymore. "Since I started living with Aunt Heather, after you... ever since I... Everyone calls me Alex."

Her mother smiled. "That's a sweet way of honoring your brother's memory."

"My... brother?"

"I'm sure I told you this story. Didn't I? I'm sure I did, you know, before." She shook her head at Alex's uncertainty. "Maybe it made your head hurt? The story of when I found out your dad and I were pregnant. I knew right away it was twins. It's always twins in my family and Dad's. Dad and Heather, and me and your Uncle Steven."

"I don't remember. You had a brother?"

"Have. You still haven't met your Uncle Steven? You'll like him. He has a farm and knows all sorts of interesting facts about everything. His daughter is your age. Not a twin, though. That was a first." Holly shook her head. "I digress. It's been a long day and, I missed my afternoon nap." She touched Alex's arm with a smile. "Anyway, Dad and I were so excited." Holly's smile darkened. "It was probably premature. You were nothing but a soup of cells, barely even a sea monkey, but we named you. Andrea," she poked Alex on the nose, "and Alex."

Holly's eyes narrowed. "It wasn't meant to be, though, we lost the boy only days later, but you know about that by now." She stroked Alex's face. "I wish you could understand how I feel, looking at you. You're so grown up, so amazing." Her eyes looked away. "Anyway, I had spent so much time talking to you both, narrating my day-to-day, it felt wrong to stop saying his name, like I abandoned him." She paused. "After what we did, it was like erasing him. Part of me wanted to always remember." Holly wiped her eyes. "I told your dad. He agreed. We would name you Alexandrea. Alex and Andrea, all in one."

"Dad agreed?" Alex had trouble thinking. Her headache was a rock, smashing her skull. She had witnessed what happened when he un-twinned her.

"You know how he is. I told him. It wasn't like he said, *Great idea, Holly*. It was the way his eyes sparkled that he told me." Darker emotions roiled behind her smiling eyes.

The headache grew, threatening to rupture Alex's skull. She winced but smelled smoke. She looked at her hands. They appeared fine, but wet blisters stung under her skin. It jarred Alex to her feet. She fully opened her eyes. She was downstairs in her childhood house. Out the window, she saw a lovely late spring day. Her mom was a beautiful woman, but today she looked tired.

Her father staggered over to Alex from the kitchen, his eyes sweeping past her vacantly. As he tottered by, he seemed to lose his balance, bumping her, shoulder to shoulder.

Alex looked at him incredulously. "What was that for?"

Holly beamed. "He loves you so much. That's his way of telling you."

Alex almost choked on the notion. *Would he understand if I told him back?* As he wandered away, Alex asked Holly, "Why is he going upstairs?"

Holly's eyes grew misty. "Alexandrea, we all know what day today is. Your father's friend William told me to expect you, warned me they're coming. A car will pull into our driveway. Your father seems to sense that." She paused, "He's going upstairs for one last look at you, how you were before."

"I'm upstairs?"

"You and Charissa. I wish I'd known sooner. I'd never have allowed her over." Holly closed her eyes. "It's unfair."

"Today?" Alex's heart thumped like a parade band. Her dream, the trigger her father placed in her head. *That's today?* She remembered giving her father an unrequited hug, only to have him bump into her as he left the room. *He was telling me he loved me back?* She ached to see her father, to see herself, "Can I look?"

Holly's eyes popped wide. "See yourself?" She pointed up and then at Alex to differentiate her two *selves*. "You think your head hurts now? You're here *and* you're at that stone. You're in the final throws of the final loop to bring you to the beginning. You remember, right? You remember what *has* *to* happen, what *happened?*"

"What? The beginning?" That meant watching her mother die, watching her father turned to dust. All the goodness she felt seeing her mother again melted away, like she stood at a desolate beach waiting for Matthew to return with his tsunami. "I can't do this, Mom. I can't go through that again." She recalled the sting of the fire. "I'm on that Picnic Rock, aren't I? With Matthew. He's killing me because I have no magic."

Holly looked exasperated. "We protected you. Sacrificing everything. We unmade your twin, made you unable to even hear someone mention magic, and then we hid you from the world."

"Why?"

"You're so special, Alexandrea. If Matthew found you before you were strong enough, he'd use you and kill you." She stared at Alex. "Sweetheart, we *had* to let him think we were going along with his plans. This is so serious. No one could know. Your father's best friend warned us, no one could know what triggers the loop. We had to prevent anyone from giving you magic."

"Aunt Heather put all her faith in me because Peter promised her. I've done nothing but disappoint her. Because of me, Heather's friend Marta is dead."

Holly closed her eyes. "I knew that was possible. We never meant for others to die, but," she struggled for the words, "sometimes that's what it takes. I couldn't tell Heather. She'd try to fix it. She's prone to think every moment of peril is the right time. Heather is impetuous; I think that's why she tried to do what your father did. It nearly killed her and ruined her marriage." She touched Alex again. "She's a good woman, a good mother. She never knew the sacrifice we were asking of you."

"You knew?" Alex pulled from her mother's touch.

"I'm sorry, Alex." Holly's hand hovered tentatively in the air between them. "I don't expect you to understand."

"Everything I've been though. How could I?"

Holly wiped her eyes. "For what it's worth, I'm sorry. It's always life and death, Alexandrea. You're alive because other people die. Your father, Sara, me." She sighed, "You."

"Me?"

"You feel it. The beginning and the end. A moment of time outside of time. A trap sprung by death."

Abby died to send me to Sara. "I'm dying? In the fire."

Holly nodded. "Let's close this last loop. It was the only way to protect you once we were dead."

Peter stumbled down the stairs, his face slack and expressionless, one very busy zombie, getting in his last steps.

Alex looked from him to Holly. "I wish I saw the big picture as clearly as you."

Holly didn't wipe her falling tears. "Alexandrea, I watched you go upstairs an hour ago. All of fourteen. Here you are, an hour later, all grown up. All those years lost in one hour. All the years after this hour. I know what happens today. I know you're the only one leaving this house. Believe me, I don't see the big picture, only the tiny part I play."

"What part do you play?"

"All that matters is what we do now."

Holly opened her empty hand as though offering Alex something. "I can tell you about it or I can show you?"

Sara. Alex gasped. Smoke burned her eyes. She hesitated, "I'm ready." *Could this be worse than burning alive?*

Holly raised an eyebrow. "You don't want to hug your parents goodbye?"

Closing the loop means losing them again, watching it— again. After so many years she hadn't given it a second thought. The realization that this moment was temporary crashed upon her. Tears welled in her eyes. She sobbed. Fire crackled in her ears, choked her throat, bubbled her skin away. She clasped her mother like she feared falling from her. Her arms wanted to hold her close enough that her own body might absorb her. "I love you, Mommy."

"Alexandrea. My sweet, sweet girl." When they released, Holly wiped tears from Alex's cheeks. "I love you, Alexandrea. More than you can comprehend. I'm so proud of you. You've grown up so beautifully and strong. You are a better version of the best woman I could ever want you to be."

Comprehending that each second was one fewer they had together made her recognize this loop was a tease, a torture, but also the greatest gift anyone could bestow upon her. "I never thought I'd see you again. I should ask you about everything I don't know about you."

"Some questions go unanswered, sweetheart. Most people don't realize how little time they have. There's only so much." Holly smiled warmly. "Say goodbye to your father."

Peter stood, face slack, eyes unfocused somewhere in her general direction. Only his breathing indicated life inside. Alex pulled his form against her. She smelled his skin, his day-old whiskers scratching her face lovingly. He stood unresponsive, his arms limp at his sides. She whispered to him. "Goodbye, Daddy, I love you." His mouth moved against her cheek. *Is he telling me something?* She withdrew to see what he might be trying to say; he was swallowing.

He stumbled past, bumping her shoulder. He lost direction like a drunkard, bumping her again before resuming and striking her shoulder a third time.

Alex turned back to her mother, tears rolling down her cheeks. "I'm not ready to lose you. Not again."

"Find me, Alexandrea, in your dreams. It's time we set everything right."

What if this doesn't work, either? "Okay," Alex whispered.

Holly touched her shoulders. "Whatever happens, what matters is that you never give up.

"Do you know how to pull dreams into wakefulness?"

"I don't." She watched Holly's face for a sign of disappointment.

"It's okay, we only want the glow."

"I don't—"

Holly stilled Alex's mouth with her fingers. "Now," she breathed, "let's fix you."

Holly's coin glowed brightly. Alex looked at the hole in her chest, the darkest black, an absence where there should have been light. "That's all I have," she whispered. "Just a hole."

"Shh."

Holly's fingers encircle the dark spot and took hold of it. She looked lovingly in Alex's the eyes. "When you were conceived, you had a coin. It was bright and beautiful. But it wasn't alone." Holly's fingers held the disk of darkness by its edge. Her face wrinkled in concentration until a faint line of light circumscribed the coin. "Twins. His coin to hide yours." The sliver of light grew as Holly peeled one coin from another. "Male and female. Like magnets." The further she separated them the more the dark face diminished. Brought closer, the darkness returned. She flipped their dark faces towards one another, holding them, just apart. "And now we close the loop."

As Holly's hands drew closer, the two coins snapped together, leaving a bright, glowing disk in the center of Alex's chest.

Her ears popped.

"There," Holly said, a bittersweet smile on her face. "Everything is right again."

Alex couldn't help but stare at the glowing circle below her charm. She looked at her mother. Both their eyes were wet with tears. She knew it wasn't a soul, but the bright glow made her finally feel complete.

The comfort was short-lived. Like a cold hand squeezing her heart, a familiar anxiety returned, clutching covetously. Outside, the faint rumble of a car engine approached the house.

"That was fast." Alex recognized the sound immediately, bitter that Matthew darkened her moment of wonder.

"They're coming," Holly explained. "As soon as we flipped the coin, Matthew saw you."

Alex's eyes widened as she realized what this meant, both now and four years ago. "That's why he came upstairs for me. He thought I," she pointed up and touched her glowing chest, "was me."

"He can't know you-you are here."

"Where do I hide?"

A car pulled up the gravel driveway. Remembering her younger self's fear, Alex's face drained. She knew what would happen. What if she failed to escape this time? She started explaining to her mother, "When Matthew takes over Dad—"

Holly interrupted her, "Don't tell me what happens. If I prevent something from happening, it'll screw the whole thing up. You're here. That means it works. There is no then, all is now. You're here. You're there," she pointed upstairs.

The circular logic hurt Alex's head. "What if it worked the first time because I told you everything?"

Holly grinned devilishly. "Smart girl. Do it my way."

Alex could hear the car stopping on the gravel. 7756672 County Road B—drive right up to the house.

Car doors opened. Feet on gravel. *That's Matthew.* The thought brought her mind to Sara. Now Matthew was coming for her.

"Hide in the basement."

"I can't Mom." Holly tried to argue, but Alex talked over her. "I've done this before. It was horrible."

Jocular conversation drifting from outside. *You sure this time?*

"Fine. We'll do it your way. What's your plan?"

"Matthew needs to think that young me," Alex pointed upstairs, "is why he senses my coin, coins, whatever. I should be near her."

"You can't be in the same room, Alexandrea." The sound of car doors slamming startled her.

"Okay," Alex conceded. Seeing herself could be awkward. She heard familiar patterns of conversation as the four men approached the house. Footsteps on the porch stairs. Fear settled in Alex's gut like a punch, winding her. "Your bedroom. Right next to mine."

Holly agreed. The footsteps were nearly at the door. "You remember where the creaks are? Be silent."

"I love you Mom."

They were on the porch. About to knock on the door. She felt like Sara. Were Charissa and her younger self upstairs, like George and Abigail?

"I love you. Please, go."

Alex ran up the stairs, carefully avoiding the steps that creaked. It amazed her she could remember; had someone asked her yesterday, she mightn't have recalled that they creaked at all, but being here she knew how to avoid making a sound. Her heart pounded like a caged beast against her ribs. The next time she saw either of her parents, they'd be dead.

Chapter Thirty-Seven

There was a polite rap on the screen door.

Alex reached the top of the stairs. She hesitated, torn between fleeing what was about to unravel downstairs and peeking into her old bedroom.

As silently as possible, she crept to the doorway, her lungs frozen with expectation. Downstairs, her mother moved towards the door.

Inside her room, Charissa, a cute, young girl chatted away, playing with her phone. Next to her, Alex saw her younger self. Tall and slender, still going by Alexandrea. Alex could barely believe this was *her*; this girl, this child, not entirely oblivious of what the next few minutes would bring. Alexandrea was ill at ease, holding her breath. Charissa turned to her, "What?"

Alexandrea looked to the door, locking eyes with Alex. Alex froze in Alexandrea's sightline; Alexandrea cringed and cradled her head.

At the second knock at the front door, Alex ducked away, grateful. *I saw heat rising in the doorway. I couldn't see myself, so I saw blurry air. That means...* Alex looked at her hands. *That means I have magic!*

Alex slipped into her parent's bedroom.

"It's time, Peter." Holly said downstairs. The front door creaked open; the storm door screeched. Four sets of footfalls entered.

"Hello, Holly," a male voice said. "It's been some time."

"Not long enough," Holly replied. "Lose something?"

"Something," the man echoed.

"Are you listening to me?" Alex looked up. Charissa's voice was closer and louder than the ones downstairs. Alex kept missing what they were saying.

"I know she's here," said the man.

"She's my daughter. Where else would she be, Matthew?"

Did he just laugh? "You stole her from me. You went with the plan until it stopped suiting you."

"She was never going to be yours," Holly snapped.

"That wasn't your choice," Mathew said. "Peter was willing to die for our cause."

"Peter knew what he was sacrificing. He did that willingly, not for *you*."

"And where did that get you? Look at him."

Charissa again accused Alexandrea of not paying attention.

"Don't you dare," Holly spat.

"Was it worth it? Fifteen years, wiping his ass? Maybe Peter knew what he was sacrificing, but did you? Tell me, Holly, is your life everything you expected?"

Holly's tone changed. *She wasn't expecting him to say that.* "You'll never understand. It was always me and him; there was never room for you."

"Why are we talking to her?" A second demanded, brash and impatient. "What are you waiting for?"

"Isn't that so adorable?"

Alex turned towards her bedroom. Charissa was as loud and oblivious as she remembered. *How does she not sense what's coming?*

"What?" Alexandrea asked, the annoyance obvious in her voice. "Oh. Whatever."

Alex almost shushed Charissa when she spoke again. "Oh, here's another; it's even more adorable." She groaned. *Won't Charissa ever shut up?* She couldn't make out any of the escalating tones downstairs; this vapid girl spoke over them.

"Come on, Matthew, what are we waiting for?"

Alex jumped. *That wasn't a gunshot.* It was sharp crackling, like electricity.

The girls in the next room fell silent.

Downstairs, there was a rush of people. Fear snatched Alex's breath and curdled her innards with cold hands. *What's happening down there?* She knew her parents would come upstairs. *What if this time it's different? Could one action change everything?* If she raced down to protect her mother, would she compromise everything else? She couldn't save her mother and sacrifice herself. They could all die. Matthew could capture Alexandrea. She knew she had no choice but to hide like a coward as her parents gave their lives for her.

I'm trying to remember what happens, so I know what to do. Whatever I do now will make what I remember happen. The thought was freeing. Her memories from four years ago were being made now. Nothing can change what happened. She recalled Sara drawing the loop. Then—now—the same moment. Thinking about it hurt her head, and her head hurt enough just being here; being there.

"She's right up those stairs. I'm claiming what was never yours to keep."

"She has a name," Holly screamed. "She's a child, my child. Why her? Why now? There's got to be some other way. Some other child. Just let her alone!"

"You knew. Or why hide her?" Alex could hear Matthew's patience. *Is he explaining himself to Holly? I don't remember it like this.* Maybe Holly was getting him to explain things for Alex's benefit. She choked up; her mother was eliciting information for her daughter from her murderer.

Matthew continued. "Jeremiah doesn't know, but he's no fool. He'll figure us out, and when he does, he'll destroy us all."

"Everyone knows his name, but no one's seen your bogeyman. Maybe you made Jeremiah up to scare children. As though you'd need help." Holly sounded like she was trying to convince herself.

"Holly," Matthew said, "Jeremiah is very real. He won't talk. He won't negotiate. Not when he figures out we've betrayed him. You understand that, don't you? If we don't go through with this, we're all dead. She's the key, the only chance we have. There's no other way."

"Why her? Shouldn't she get a say? Shouldn't she hear what you plan for her?"

"Holly, we all agreed to this. You lied; you stole her; you hid her. You had to know I'd come looking. You had to know I'd find her."

"I knew you'd try."

Alex listened, expectation writhing in her insides. *How close was Matthew all these years?* She imagined Holly worrying every day that he'd discover their whereabouts. What pressures had she endured with a husband incapable of comforting her?

As though hearing Alex's thoughts, Matthew asked, pityingly, "All those years, you've lived dreading today would come, didn't you?"

Perhaps Holly was secretly relieved. The worrying was over.

"How sad, always looking over your shoulder, waiting, knowing I was behind you. You're both such idealistic fools. Did you really think you could betray me? You made promises, swore oaths and broke them. Where did it get you?"

"Stop it, Matthew," Holly demanded.

"Look at Peter. There's nothing left. He gave up everything! He made that sacrifice for the greater good. Not for you, or even her."

"You can't know him and say that. Peter protected her." Holly sobbed. "Don't do this to my little girl."

"Enough stalling," another male voice growled. "Why are we talking to her if the girl is here?"

"If you think I'm just going to hand her over, you're crazy." Then Holly's tone rose sharply in horror. "Peter? How? Matthew, stop it! You're hurting him. What are you doing to him? What have you done?"

"Yes, hi, hello?" Alex cringed at Charissa's voice, calling the police, leaving no space between the words as she spoke.

"We don't want to hurt you or Alex. Don't make this more difficult. Don't cause someone to get hurt." Alex listened to this third calming voice. There was something familiar about it, not just the sound but the cadence and the shape of the words, but for her life, she couldn't place it.

Holly cleared her throat. "You will *not* take my daughter. Not today. Not ever. I won't let you have her."

"Holly, please. You're giving him no choice," the familiar voice begged.

From her childhood bedroom, Charissa recited the address, practically shouting into her phone, "Seventy-seven, fifty-six, sixty-seven, two…"

Downstairs, there was a sudden flurry of activity, bodies crashing, the sounds of people colliding with walls and furniture. Holly cried out. "Alex, don't let them take you!"

She hadn't understood before, but now she knew her mother was calling to *her*, not younger Alexandrea. Any thoughts of action evaporated when Holly screamed. A crackling pop, like an electrical circuit sparking washed Alex's skin with cold sweat.

A body crashed to the floor. *Was that my mother dying?* Following a struggle, a single set of footfalls stomped up the stairs.

"You better be in your bedroom." Alex knew her father was climbing the stairs with a gun. But when Peter stopped just short of her open doorway, it was a Book open in his hands. The sight of the text made Alex sick. *I couldn't see magic. Instead of a Book, did my mind show me a gun?*

Her father, or his body, looked upon the Book, and his mouth moved, whispers too soft to hear. The door exploded into splinters.

Charissa screamed and Alex lost sight of Peter.

"I've waited a very, very long time," her father growled.

Everything seemed to happen at once. Someone took to the stairs. Charissa was begging anyone to, "Do something; do something; do something..."

Alex wanted to scream. All around her, people she loved were in pain, were dying.

Holly paused in the doorway, her blouse char stained. She supported her weight, clutching the doorframe in agony. She looked up and cried, "Get out, Alex!"

What am I supposed to do? Alex's hands trembled; she knew what was about to happen in the next room and couldn't sit idly by as Matthew murdered her mother. She raced into the hallway. She watched Holly push past Peter. Holly turned and Peter continued muttering nonsense from the Book; Holly stared right at her and shouted, "Go!"

Sparks flew from Peter's fingertips. It was the first time Alex saw real magic, saw the bright bolts of electricity sparking from her father's outstretched fingertips, striking her mother's chest, burning her shirt, her flesh, making her writhe with each successive strike.

It happened too fast to act, too fast to think, the cracking lightning, like Matthew's hammer coming down again and again.

Alex felt the scream in her mouth but clamped her hands over her face to keep it in.

Her mother was dying. Holly told her to leave. Although she looked at Holly, she saw Sara, tied to a chair and table, her fingers hammered to splinters. Holly's cries gave voice to Sara's pain. *Matthew can't get away with this, not anymore.*

Matthew was hurting her family, killing her mother—again—and Alex could not let that happen twice in one lifetime.

This was not her father. A rising wave of heat blossomed inside her. Her father's coin glowed. *That's Matthew's.* She grabbed hold of her father.

Alexandrea and Holly screamed. Alex's rage was sucked from her like a tablecloth in a magic trick. Lightning, crisp and blue from Peter's fingertips struck Holly and the resulting explosion threw Matthew, as Peter's form vanished in a roiling swirl of dust.

The concussive shockwave popped Alex's ears. Matthew crashed across the hallway, twisting his head and neck into an impossible angle.

If not for her purchase on the doorjamb, the discharge would have thrown Alex into the wall, just like Matthew. She hoped the confusion, dust and terror, would conceal her. *I shouldn't be here, what if I see myself? What happens?* She hoped her younger self was too distracted and confused.

All around her was destruction. Alexandrea was too preoccupied with Holly to notice her. Alex watched her younger self help her mother to stand as three additional footsteps raced up the stairs. Once again, Alexandrea stared right through her.

"Why are you still here?" Holly clutched Alexandrea's shoulders. "You have to go. Now." She pointed to the wall beside the bed. "Take Matthew's Book." Her face softened. "It's okay, Alex. You know it turns out okay." She looked at Alexandrea. "Now, call the mist and go."

Both Alex and her younger self looked to Charissa, unconscious at the foot of the bed.

"Leave her. Bring the mist, Alex. There's nothing more for you here."

Just past her father's shoes, layered in a thick coating of dust lay Matthew's Book. As two men stood over Matthew, a third approached the Book. It was out of her reach but within his.

Alex couldn't jeopardize Holly getting Alexandrea to safety. She wanted to hold her dying mother but could only walk past her battered body.

"Momma," Alex said. *Did I ever call her* Momma *before?* She didn't think so. "I can't leave you."

A confused and terrified Alexandrea asked her mother for clarification.

Alex had summoned the mist before. She could do it again. She concentrated. A glowing coin appeared on her mother's chest. Alexandrea had nothing but the black absence. Alex looked down on her own chest, and there it was just below Abby's charm, her glowing coin.

"Momma," Alex whimpered, "I'm afraid." Her father had to hand Charon his coin halves to cross over. But she wasn't crossing, she was stepping through. Would that be different?

As he entered the bedroom, stepping over Matthew, Alex recognized George right away. *George.* He looked the same; this was years before she would burn him up. He glanced in Alexandrea's direction, did he know their fates would intertwine? She studied his panic. *He doesn't have a clue.* She watched him with enlightened eyes. *Why did George step over Matthew and not help him?*

The man kneeling beside Matthew called to George. "Matthew's neck is broken, George. Did you hear me?"

"Yeah, Gary," George replied. "I heard. Is he dead?"

"You're not here," Holly whispered to her. "You're not here, you're there, Alex."

"Gary, I asked you a question," George shouted. *What answer is he hoping to hear?*

Gary touched Matthew's neck. "He's alive, for now." He motioned to the dust-covered shoes Peter had left behind. "Peter's obliterated. George, it wasn't supposed to happen like this. No one gets hurt, remember?" He stared towards Holly and Alexandrea. "She wasn't supposed to be this strong yet."

George shook his head. "I don't know. She did this?"

Mist slowly washed over the wall.

"You're not here. You're there, Alex," Holly repeated like a breath, "burning."

The man standing over Matthew's Book was older, perhaps in his thirties, his face a complexion of soft wrinkles and unshaven stubble. *He's so familiar.* He pointed at her, not Alexandrea. "It was her." His voice was familiar.

George panicked. "Be careful, William." He looked at Alexandrea.

William nodded. "I am."

How does William see me? Do the others?

As George and Gary debated what to do next, Holly weakly implored, "Alex, please focus. Go back through the mist. Take Matthew's Book. I love you. Now GO!"

Alex looked at her mother. Grief weighed on her like heavy chains. "Don't make me leave you again," she said. "How many times do I have to watch you die?"

Holly turned away to face Alexandrea. William caught her eye. *How do I know him?* His foot pushed Matthew's discarded Book closer to her. *What is he doing?* His eyes smiled as he mouthed the word, "Hurry."

Alex reluctantly stretched for the Book. William saw her hesitation. He moved. *It's a trick.* But instead of an attack, he retreated half a step. Alex grabbed the Book.

She turned between him and her mother, her heart machine-gunning in her chest. "Momma," she whispered, "I love you." Holly didn't respond, didn't acknowledge her. Holly refused her, and in her refusal, told her it was time to leave. She could already feel the pain contained in the Book like needles sticking her hands.

"William?" Alex repeated the name in the hope it would jar a memory loose. She took a step, her fingertips entering the mist and passing beyond the bedroom wall. She looked at him one last time as she crossed through. *He's so familiar. I don't know anyone like him; not old. It made no sense. Matthew didn't age, but what if he did?*

As the mist clouded her sight, she spoke the name that came to her. "Billy?"

Chapter Thirty-Eight

lex was in darkness. Pain leeched through the cover of Matthew's book into her hands. She heard the cries of women, their pains scorching her insides, making her gasp and wretch. Matthew's Book felt especially toxic in her clutch.

She stepped from the mist. The sudden onset of agony was like being struck by a freight train made of shattered glass.

The fire roared; her hair danced in the rising heat as flame blackened her skin. Towards the front of the stone, Matthew stood with Billy, who unwillingly held his book. Rose stood a few feet to the side, her body wracked with sobs, watching her cousin burn.

Matthew pointed to the flames, to the glowing coin in Alex's chest.

Alex screamed in pain. In anger. In rage.

Rosemary broke from Matthew. Buffeted by heat, she fought to rescue Alex.

"Alex, I can't." Rose pulled at branches, trying to move them away. The pile collapsed in an explosion of sparks. Flames roared as loud as Alex's cries.

Rose nursed her smoke-stung eyes. She kept reaching forward and pulling back heat-slapped hands.

Alex couldn't concentrate. Heat addled her mind, confusing her. Had she returned to her house or was that a fever dream? She had no fight left. She wanted to look on her cousin one last time, but when she saw Rose shaking, saw her despair, her guilt, her blistering fingers reaching repeatedly into the flames, her head cleared.

As though chastened by Alex's hatred, the stinging, licking tongues of light instantly flickered out. Fire shriveled into the charred wood, leaving glowing embers. With the intense heat suddenly absent, chilled air brought painful goosebumps to Alex's flame-ravaged flesh.

Rose kicked the still-hot char away. She struggled to untie the ropes binding Alex to the pole. She cried at the sight of Alex's arms and face. The ropes added blisters Rose's hands.

Matthew whooped in celebration, cackling joyously. "I was right! You did it!" Tears swelled in his eyes. "I knew it! I had to coax magic out of you!"

Without the ropes' support, Alex dropped to her knees. Angry blisters covered her blackened fingers. Her clothes had burned to skin that was red, black, and oozing. She shivered uncontrollably. Rose crept closer and knelt beside her. With tentative tenderness, she attempted to hold Alex.

Alex pulled Matthew's Book closer, scraping it through the ash.

The white-noise whispers grew louder, becoming shrieks. All urging her towards the Book.

"Rose," she croaked, her dry throat cracked, "please, move away."

Rose held her tighter. Contact was healing agony.

"Please, Rose." Alex remembered how it felt to burn George when he got too close, consume him. She didn't want to do that to Rose.

"Rose, please."

Rose backed reluctantly away. She looked betrayed, taking Alex's request personally.

Alex picked up the Book and struggled to her feet.

"When did you get that?"

Ignoring Matthew, she opened the Book. Heat and smoke blurred her vision, but she knew what was on these pages. She could see the ornate designs and shapes as though they cut through her heat-blindness. Clawing the page, watching the symbols shift and fall away, tearing the fibers away from the spine, she screamed as both transmuted to flame.

A pillar of fire swirled into the star-filled sky. Alex screamed in unison with the voices she heard crying out. This Book wasn't a single woman, but a very personal collection compiled by Matthew over the decades since Sara.

The fire roared with countless voices, embracing her as though in a frenetic dance, healing her, enraging her.

Looking out through the flames, she saw Rose, a tiny child, alone and devastated, looking in horror as her cousin disappeared in the conflagration. As though with her thought, the flames evaporated. Before she could even comfort Rose, her cousin's face blossomed a look of relief.

"They must have loved that trick at the Library." Matthew seemed mystified at Alex's fiery display.

Alex touched the glow on her chest, recalling Holly flipping her coin, recalling the love she shared with her parents just moments—and four years—ago.

"The day I broke my neck." Matthew's voice dropped to a whisper, "That was... you." A smile came over his face. "That's why I can feel you now." He nodded his crooked head. "Clever Holly. I thought I saw you, but it wasn't you *then*. It was you, *now*." He laughed. "That's why you couldn't do magic." He stared at her with a dumb grin. "You have it," he said, beaming. He laughed in triumph, jumping a little, "You have it. You finally have a soul."

"It's not a soul," Alex screamed, as though someone else compelled her. "It's a coin, for paying passage."

Billy lowered the Book he still held, "You give Charon your coin, just like the stories say, to pass when you die." The strangest expression slapped across Matthew's face, as Billy continued. "You throw a coin in the fountain for luck. Silver dollars are the luckiest, but most people throw pennies. They never get luck, though. But you're not buying luck; you're tossing coins to confuse Charon. I think that's where the tradition comes from."

Matthew's face filled with wonder, mesmerized as Billy continued. There was something more, the excitement of recognition, as though something Billy said helped him make a connection that had long eluded him.

"Toss a fake coin," her cousin continued, "so Charon goes looking for it and won't come for the real one. They're not the same kind of coin." He pointed to Alex and her glowing coin. "I keep you safe. I walk with you to your dream. My coin is tarnished because Mom didn't keep it safe for me. She ruined it. She meant to but didn't mean to. I protect you, but I can't do everything that I should do to keep you safe, but I will when I have to."

Billy's words mesmerized Matthew. His face was bright with surprise, as though he heard an echo through time, questions pairing with disparate answers, a single truth becoming known. A solitary word left his lips like a whisper, "William?"

Without warning, Billy crashed into Matthew. All three of them, Billy, Matthew, the Book, disappeared from the rock and into darkness.

Alex couldn't catch her breath. The sudden absence of Matthew and Billy was as though they'd not only fallen from the rock but vanished into oblivion.

As though fearing falling herself, Rose raced to Alex. Her grasp shredded Alex's tattered and burned clothes. She buried her head against Alex's tender shoulder, and wailed, lamenting her brother.

Shock from watching the darkness swallow Billy, from witnessing him leap again from Picnic Rock, crept over Alex like a wet, frigid breeze. Her fists clenched, and she screamed, throwing her rage into the black valley. Her parents were dead; Billy was gone, Rose hurt, and... Alex was at the center of their pain because Matthew had played all his pawns to this failed checkmate.

The rock beneath them heaved, lurching upwards. A sharp crack, like a thunder-strike, reverberated all around her. Rose grabbed at Alex just as the rock beneath them cleaved at the seam. The far half rose upward as it rolled away, disappearing with a thunderous rumble into the darkness of the valley.

Chapter Thirty-Nine

Alex's legs gave out. Before Rose could help, she was already fighting back to her feet. She clawed to the new edge, looking out over the darkness. Her head was a thousand whispers, but nothing could silence Alex's feeling of dread. She embraced her cousin, "You saved me."

Alex felt Rose's heart fluttering in her chest. The girl looked up at Alex and then over into the dark valley where the other half of Picnic Rock had vanished. "Billy's okay, right?" Giving voice to Alex's grief, she was practically panting.

"It's so damn dark." The torches had fallen when the rock split. Only one remained lit.

"What was he going on about?" Rose studied the darkness. "He said those things last time… didn't he?"

Many things repeated tonight. Alex couldn't remember ever missing her parents this much.

Rose turned back to the dark valley. "He's got to be okay, right?"

Alex held her, struggling for comforting words. "He saved us both." *The boulder rolled right over where he would have landed. The boulder I… I can't* feel *him.* It wasn't as if the sensation in her heart that represented Billy knew he was dead; it was like the moment he leapt from the rock, Billy ceased to exist.

Besides the stars, the single torch was their only illumination. "How badly hurt are you, Alex? Can you find him?"

Alex's blistered skin was raw, peeling, and throbbing. It gave off heat. "I think I'm over-done." *The Book healed me.*

Rose half-sobbed and tightened her grip around her. "You were on fire. And then you *were* fire. You burned so much tonight."

Alex thought about the flames. The Book, a source of so much pain, had taken hers away. Was it like a trade, taking their pain for her own? Her body was still disfigured; one Book hadn't been enough. "It was. I was…" She couldn't finish.

"Am I hurting you?"

"You're healing me. It's itchy."

Rose giggled but quickly lost her joy. Her hands slipped from Alex and she turned to the darkness. "I shouldn't need to ask," she pointed to the cleaved edge of the stone. "Was this you?"

Alex wanted to deny it; she had only her feeling when it happened. Admitting it might also mean admitting she killed Billy. "I think so."

"I want to go home," Rose whimpered. "Is the man gone?"

"Matthew?"

"Yes, him."

"He's probably wherever Billy is." Alex stepped to the edge. The stone was cleaved straight through; its rough-hewn edge disappeared in darkness. She claimed and then lowered the torch. It cast a weak circle of bouncing light, swallowed in milky darkness. The flame flickered and danced, its shadows shifting wildly.

Rose sounded defeated, "I can't see anything; you?"

Alex closed her eyes. She'd broken the stone. She put out the fire. She had magic. She felt the torchlight's warmth, heard it flickering, sputtering. *How do I do this? How does magic work? Sara said it was emotional.* She desired to find Billy, hoping the torchlight would locate him safe. Her heart swelled with hope and she focused on the belief she'd spot him clinging to some roots. She blocked any creeping doubt from her mind, repeating to herself, *he's alive. I know Billy's alive.*

"Wow," Rose gasped.

The torch roared with a towering flame, bright enough to light the ruinous cliff-side below. A wide crevasse marked the slide of the other half of Picnic Rock. Grasses and boulders were shorn from the ground in the grinding rush and pushed aside. The rock lay at the furthest limits of torchlight, a giant slab at the end of a long, naked runway.

Rose shaded her eyes, "You're doing magic."

Alex knew it wasn't a question; she heard the wonder and pride in Rose's voice. She didn't reply. Part of her knew nothing would be the same, and that frightened her. She finally had what Matthew wanted. She was no longer hidden from the world, from Matthew, from Jeremiah. But, only finding Billy alive mattered. She scanned the cliff-side. No one was there.

The landslide had erased the place Billy landed from his first leap. The torchlight fizzled with her dwindling hope, returning them to starlit darkness. Her insides felt something stir inside them. The grim thought that Billy lay crushed beneath the boulder was forming in her mind, building the strength it would need to escape her mouth.

What if he's on the far side?

"We have to look for him." Alex walked to the back edge of the half-stone, and the stairs.

Rose followed. "What if Matthew's down there?"

Rose seemed so much younger than Alex remembered. Perhaps because Alex felt so much older. "Does it matter?"

She led the way, her eyes adjusting to starlight. Every excruciating movement felt like fresh cuts to each crease, blister, and joint. Curls of turf and uprooted trees gave them footing on the steep decline as they descended to the giant ruinous boulder. They crept around it. Stones, tree trunks, and all manner of detritus piled against the front-facing side; Picnic Rock appeared to have burrowed into the ground. *No one will ever know that Jonathan William Frost 1826 existed.* His name and many others now marked the rock's new bottom. Her heart weighed with a tinge of sadness to think she'd erased these last traces of Sara.

Coming around the far side, they saw no signs of anyone. Alex pulled Rose to the new front, the rough edge of the rock that for millennia had been its center. It smelled of dust and stone. Touching it, Alex almost understood history, feeling the great expanses of time this face of stone would now measure; the age of the center had begun.

"There's no one here," she said.

Rose peered into the darkness. "Where else could he be?"

Alex didn't answer.

"He's here, somewhere?" She motioned to the darkness. "He's not... under... you didn't... you wouldn't..." Rose's tears tore at Alex like barbed accusations.

"I don't see anyone," Alex tried to modulate her voice. Nor did she *feel* anyone.

"You broke the stone and sent it all this way. You wouldn't have done that to Billy, right? You knew he wasn't there when you did it, right?"

In the smallest voice, Alex replied, "I don't know."

"He's not dead. He can't be. I'd know. Wouldn't I, Alex? He's my twin. If he were dead, wouldn't I feel it? Feel something?"

"I don't know, Rose," she repeated louder, more defensively than intended.

Rose looked at her, her wet eyes glinting in the starlight. "Tell me, Alex. Pretend you know and tell me he's okay."

Alex couldn't tell Rose that Billy might have been crushed because that would mean she'd killed him, and that was a pain she was unprepared to bear. "Maybe," Alex sniffled and wiped her face, wincing at the burns on each, "Matthew realized."

"What would he do?"

Alex searched desperately for an explanation like it was the antidote to her poison. George sent her from the Library with a touch, a half-completed spell. *Maybe he planned for things to go wrong here too.* "Matthew could have disappeared them. Him and Billy."

Rose wiped her running nose. "That means he still has my brother, right?"

Alex nodded.

Rose said hopefully, "That means he's alive. Somewhere."

Alex looked up the cliff-side. "We should go home."

"What do you think he'll do with Billy?"

Before she could answer, her thoughts shifted to William. The idea that he was an older Billy seemed as unlikely as Matthew being the same man who murdered Sara. The more she considered it, the surer she became. The man that night *was* Billy; it had to be. But even as a spark of hope rose within her, her stomach twisted, like a towel being wrung out. *Does that mean he's with Matthew now? Which fate is worse?*

Alex crafted the lie carefully, choosing words she desperately wanted to believe. "He doesn't want Billy, he wants me. They'll turn up again." *William. That was four years ago.* She tried forcing herself to doubt they were the same. Alex didn't want to tell Rose, didn't want to tell anyone, but maybe there was more to Billy. She pictured him leaping off the stone tonight and last week, clutching air or Matthew and disappearing. *The same action, separated by time. Nothing makes sense.* She could hear Sara say, 'Loops are confusing.'

They climbed up the cliff, shorn curls of turf became steps. "Do you think he'll do something to Billy?"

Alex clutched at tufts of grass. "He might try brainwashing him."

"Isn't that just in movies?" Rose breathed heavily.

"Matthew and the others like him believe," Alex explained. "He'll try to get Billy to believe the same thing." *William gave me the Book. He was helping me, wasn't he?* Alex's stomach felt like an empty pit. *We can't lose Billy to Matthew.*

"Billy won't believe that," Rose sounded smug.

"I hope not," Alex replied, reaching the top. *What about George? Matthew had convinced George to do those things to his own sister. What chance does Billy stand?* She shuddered at the idea that George and Abigail were analogous to Billy and Rose. *The next time we see him, he might not be the same Billy.* She voiced her confusion aloud. "Sometimes, I think people try so hard to believe, it makes them crazy."

They left the remains of Picnic Rock. Looking back, it was a hulking silhouette against the night sky. *What was it Billy called it? Sacrifice Stone? Could he have known? Had Matthew already gotten to him?*

Chapter Forty

Walking along the dark, wooded path, neither had much to say. They had taken this route, also in darkness, seven days ago—if it was after midnight. They walked faster without the burden of dragging Billy on his stretcher, a reality of which Alex was sure they were both guiltily aware.

The black forest had once seemed frightening. The shadows and silvery reflections of waning moonlight peeked and hid as the cooling breeze passed, but nothing dared approach. They walked without fear; Matthew would not haunt them tonight.

For most of the way, Alex and Rose walked side-by-side, hands gently clasped between them. Occasionally, Alex found Rose looking back as though searching for Billy.

Alex's wounded skin made walking painful, especially where her tattered and abrasive clothes rubbed. Though she found herself near the limits of her endurance, there was something about the pain that felt like flagellation, atonement for failing to save Billy, failing to defeat Matthew; failing to save her parents; failing to realize the answer to where magic hid was with her the whole time; failing to do anything of real grandeur once it was revealed to her. She had magic; how had she not saved them all?

When they reached the clearing by Sara's house, what they once called *the Old Witch's Shack*, Alex's exhaustion, guilt, and pain overwhelmed her. She hadn't slept tonight and had slept poorly for the last few. The safety of *base* called to her.

They wandered to the front of the foundation. Alex wasn't sure if Rose stopped for the same reasons as her or if they were so in sync that their decisions came simultaneously.

Tire tracks, remnants of salt, and a circle of scorched ground reminded Alex of how this all started. *Was that only four nights ago?* "Could we stop here?" she asked, wearily. "Is that okay? I'm just, I mean, I can't…"

Rose dropped her shoulders with a sigh. "I'm exhausted. I've been giving everything to keep up with you."

"You should have said something," Alex offered her concern.

"Look at you," Rose motioned to Alex's burns. "If you can soldier on like that, I can walk tired."

Alex found the way Rose spoke too funny not to laugh.

"What? What's so funny?"

Alex told her.

"No, I mean it, Alex." Rose's words were less amusing, more concerned. "You look like shit. That maniac burned you alive."

Alex cringed when she realized how close she came to death tonight. "I never want to go back there."

"I hope I never see that stupid rock again."

The two stood in awkward silence for a long minute. Each one wanting to say something but holding off. Alex worried over Billy; she feared for him, but being sick with worry still felt better than being sick with guilt. She needed to stop: worrying, walking, thinking. It would be better perhaps if they just slept.

Is there an easier way? A better way home? She had seen the mist roll up on this place before. This place was powerful; that was how Heather had explained it. She traveled to Picnic Rock by walking through the mist. Could she go back the same way? Could Rose? If bringing the mist summoned Charon, Alex feared what would happen when they denied it their coins. She knew what Charon could do.

Alex took Rose's hand, and they climbed the old foundation. She led her cousin to a wide, flat spot. "Here." Wincing, she knelt slowly to her knees. "We'll sleep here. This was Sara's bedroom. Right here was her bed."

Alex didn't bother wiping the stone, she just lay down on it, looking up at the night sky, hoping to lose herself in the sparkling firmament.

Rose joined her, inching as close as she could for extra warmth against the chilled night air. Alex's skin itched at Rose's contact. They lay side-by-side. As tired as they each were, neither closed their eyes. They stared into the sky, neither ready to let go of the day, neither ready to talk about it.

Alex took Rose's hand. "I love you, Rose."

Rose faced Alex, tears spilling from her eyes. "I didn't want to do those things," she whispered. "I didn't want to hurt you." She turned back to the sky, "I've been sick thinking you'll hate me."

With her other hand, Alex wrapped Rose in an embrace. "Matthew controlled you. I know you didn't do those things."

Rose burrowed her head into Alex's shoulder. "That's just it, Alex. He wasn't."

The words chilled Alex. "What do you mean?"

"He didn't make me do anything. He made me want to." She sniffled. "It was the only thought in my head: to hurt you, to tie you up, to protect him. If I didn't, if I tried not to…" She sobbed. "It was awful. It was so real. They weren't thoughts. I could see him killing Mom every time I thought of helping you."

Alex tightened her embrace. "That's the same as making you, Rose."

"No," Rose wiped her face. "Because hurting you also felt good."

That's was why Rose hasn't talked the whole way. It wasn't Billy, or anything I assumed. It was her guilt. What Matthew did to her, to them, was inexcusable. Hating him hurt. Alex had so much hate for him; it made the whispers in her head grow so agitated and loud she was surprised Rose couldn't hear them.

"I love you, Rose," she repeated. "There's nothing to forgive. He used you and made you do those things."

Rose pressed her face to Alex's chest and sobbed. Alex rubbed her hair, touched her cheek, and let her cry. *My burns will heal. Everyone will see my scars. No one will know Rose's are there.* She held her cousin, trying to give her strength to never suffer like this again. She loved her cousin deeply and listened as her sobs subsided.

Rose wiped her face with two hands. "I must look great. I have snot everywhere."

Alex giggled. "You're pretty gross."

"Thank you." Rose's answer wasn't sarcastic. She meant it.

"For what?"

Rose smiled. "I felt what you did. It was like your love pushing into me, pushing everything else out."

"It was okay?" She thought of Heather's reaction, before Alex even knew she could do it, when Rose and Billy first went missing. Heather had not appreciated her taking away the pain.

"Because it came from you."

Did I heal her or just make her feel different?

Rose whispered, "Let's talk about something else, okay? Something happy." Alex wasn't sure how to feel happy right now. "This was where Sara slept?"

"Yes."

"So we're in the same place? Just a different time?"

"Yes," Alex repeated. "Except she slept on the bed. Technically, we'd be under it."

"So it's like we're sleeping in a ghost bed?" Rose mumbled sleepily. "That makes it so much more comfortable."

Alex giggled at Rose's sarcasm. There had to be more comfortable places to sleep, but Alex was drawn to Sara's home. The rock was hard and cold, coarse and uncomfortable. Touching it made her skin throb. It opened her blisters. It made her hurt all over. Perhaps this was a place that could only cause her pain, and yet it was the only place she wanted to be if she couldn't be in her own bed—be that at Heather's or Abby's.

"I love you, cousin," Rose said.

"I love you too, cousin," Alex replied.

Just as Alex felt herself dozing, Rose whispered. "Back there, Picnic Rock, that was really you?"

"You asked me that already."

"I mean, I think it would take a lot of really powerful magic to break a stone like that. It's been in that same spot, like, always. And then it wasn't. It would have been there forever, but you moved it. I don't think *he* could have done that."

What else have I changed that would have been forever? "I hope not. I worry that—"

Rose shushed her. "I prefer how it feels when you think good thoughts. Go to sleep."

This amused Alex. "You asked."

"And you answered. Now go to sleep."

"Goodnight."

"Goodnight."

Alex listened to Rose's breathing as she drifted off to sleep.

Alex was exhausted. She knew she wasn't alone, but that didn't help her feel any less lonely. She kept her eyes closed and tried to keep her mind empty. The constant white noise of her whispers blended with the breeze as it gently pushed and pulled the trees, singing to the night sky.

Alex again found herself walking around Sara's house.

Rose slept soundly in Sara's bed. Alex covered her with the red and white quilt and watched her smile at the newfound warmth. She approached the front door. No one was there. It was difficult to discern whether this was now or then, but it didn't matter. No one was here, no one was coming.

She leaned on the doorframe and breathed in the night air. Here was finally peace.

In the kitchen, a small fire licked the bottom of a simmering pot. Alex left the door and stirred it gently with a wooden spoon from the mantel. She lifted the spoon to her lips. The broth was warm and delicious.

She remembered Sara telling her, 'I made enough for you to have more, later.' Was this what she had meant?

"I wish we could talk," Alex said to the pot. "I wish I could tell you what happened." Tears pooled in her eyes. "It's probably best I can't, it would hurt you so much to hear about your children. I just wish I had you here. I know you'd understand. You're the only person who would." The whispers within her replied. She could almost hear individual words, individual voices, but they spoke over one another.

Alex left the stew. There were no place settings on the table, but two tucked away in the hutch. She took a bowl and a spoon and was about to put them on the table when something caught her attention. Setting the bowl aside, Alex wrenched the nail from the tabletop. She stared at this little piece of rusty, bent iron. *Is it even a nail anymore?* She wondered if she should feel something about it. Did this object share in the responsibility for what happened, or had it been like Rose, compelled by Matthew to take part in an act of cruelty? She put it down. It too deserved to rest.

Sitting, she blew on the stew to cool it and slowly ate until her bowl was empty. She rinsed the bowl in the basin in the kitchen, dried it, and replaced it in the hutch. Then she doused the kitchen fire and closed the windows, setting their locking pins. She returned to the front door. The not-yet risen sun reddened the dark sky, dimming the stars and claiming the day for itself. She shut the door on the coming day and engaged the lock. The house would be empty again. She walked into the bedroom and sat on the bed, where she caressed Rose's head.

"I wish you could have been here with me Rose," she whispered. This was Sara's home, and in a way that made it hers.

Opening her eyes, Alex stared into the pale-blush sky. She was still in Rose's arms. Returning to wakefulness, she felt the onset of chilly morning air. Her healing had progressed through the night. No one would have mistaken her injuries for anything but mild burns now. They appeared less angry now.

Rose whimpered in her sleep, as though feeling the chill.

Rose rubbed her eyes. "I had the most peculiar dream." Her voice was nearly drowned out by the chorus of birds celebrating the dawn. "You must have suggested something to me because I dreamt I slept in a bed last night." She looked around as though confirming she was indeed not on a bed. "It was way better than sleeping on stone. I had a quilt. It was so warm." She shivered for dramatic effect.

Alex felt disgusting. Her tattered clothes smelled of soot and sweat. She started to her feet. "Heather's probably worried sick. We should get going."

"I'm starving," Rose replied. "I don't think I've eaten in days."

Alex sheepishly grinned. "If I'd known, I would have fed you last night, but I didn't want to wake you."

Rose sat up. "Wait... are you saying? That was real? The bed was real? I really smelled food last night?"

Alex half-nodded, half-shook her head. "It was a dream of a place I'd been before. I was hoping to find Sara."

"You didn't?"

"She's gone. I guess she's finally at peace."

"I'm sorry you didn't find her." Rose stood and brushed herself off. She ran her fingers through her hair, catching and pulling on knots. She picked out a leaf. "I'd like to have met Sara."

"In a way, I'm glad I didn't find her. She's suffered enough. Sara deserves to rest after all these years."

Chapter Forty-One

The foundation seemed different, like a house hadn't existed here in a century. Alex noticed vines growing around and over it and weeds sprouting through the cracks and between piles of stones. She wondered if the forest was reclaiming it, hiding it from future adventurers now that it had finally served its purpose.

Tire tracks and salt still bothered the ground around it, but that too would disappear.

Rose pointed at the burned grass, "This is where it happened?"

Alex told Rose about the salt circles. She recounted the whole story, everything she'd left out that morning at Eric's. It felt good to hear Rose laugh when she again told her about how ridiculous it all seemed at first. She showed her the place where Abby had lain when she died. She directed her to the foundation. "When I looked up, the house was here." Alex motioned with her hands to express the dimensions of the house. "And there she was." She pointed to where, in her minds-eye, she could almost see Sara descending the stairs.

Rose gasped as though she could see it too. She turned to Alex and motioned to the clearing. "It all happened here. You, Mom, your father, Abby, Sara. All of you, here, at different times and yet, all together at once." She stared at Alex in wonder.

Alex looked at the tired grass. Rose was right. And now she and Rose were here too. Perhaps this was an important place, as Peter told Heather and Heather told her. Perhaps this place was special in ways she had yet to grasp.

They set upon the trail. Their mood lifted slightly with the daylight. They held hands, their silence no longer weighted with guilt but buoyed with expectation. Soon they'd be home.

They stepped from the woods to the field that led to the road that led to their home. *This field feels special too.* Maybe it was because leaving the oppression of the trees for the open sky let Alex's spirit soar.

Crossing the field, Rose talked about all the foods she wanted to eat. "Waffles and French toast with maple syrup, fried eggs, and toast to sop up the runny yolks. Oh, and I want a grilled cheese sandwich and an egg crème for lunch with so much chocolate syrup that I can scrape it off the inside of the glass."

"You'll eat all that?"

Rose put her filthy hands on her hips. "Might I remind you there are no calories when you fantasize about food."

"Fantasy food?"

"Well, it's not ghost stew, like you eat, but it's something to keep my mind off how hungry I am. And worrying about my brother." Her silence was filled with many things left unspoken.

They meandered along the winding path, crossing the fallow field to the road. "Ghost stew, huh?" Alex said.

"You ate it; you didn't just dream you were eating, right?"

"I'm not hungry now."

"So tell me," Rose pressed, "how does it work? Is it a special diet stew? I mean, how many calories are in a serving? You ate it, but it wasn't really there, right?" Rose went on and on. Finally, she asked, "Could you make more?"

"Why?"

"Why?" Rose stared. "You have no imagination. Imagine the money we could make selling ghost stew. Eat as much as you want and still lose weight. As fast and effective as starving yourself but full of flavor."

"I hadn't really thought about it like that." Alex shook her head.

Rose stopped and turned back to the distant woods across the field. "It all really happened," she said to no one in particular. "Those things I remember all happened."

Alex wasn't sure if Rose expected confirmation or was declaiming. "They did."

Rose turned to her. "Good."

"Good?"

Rose nodded. "Because otherwise, I'm crazy. I mean, everything seemed real, yet who would believe."

"I get what you mean. It seems too much."

They reached the road. The reassuring sound of sneakers on gravel and then on blacktop confirmed that it was real; they had finally returned. Away from the valley, away from the woods. They were nearly home.

The road didn't change every time the wind blew; it didn't change with the seasons; it was just a dark gray street. It was easy to remember all the times the three of them walked this way in the past. Alex half-hoped that if she looked up at the right moment, caught the sunlight in just the right way, squinted long enough, she'd see Billy walking beside them. Maybe not Billy from right now, but Billy from another time, maybe older, calling himself William. Alex missed him so much and worried even more. *What is he thinking right now? Is he scared? Hurt?* She thought about Rose, about the guilt Matthew had caused her. Billy would have to live with that guilt until he saw her again, until she could tell him it was all right. She wished she could send her love over the miles.

They arrived at their home, at Heather's house. Alex stood outside, reluctant to enter. She contemplated the last two times she was here. Marta was gone, and part of Alex felt it was disrespectful to re-enter the house the day after she had lost her life. *I can't let him take these places away from me. I can't keep losing people and places because he wants to cut my circle tighter and tighter until I have nowhere left but to be with him.*

Rose opened the door. Seeing the destruction, she refused to enter. Alex summoned the courage to push past.

"What happened?"

Alex told Rose what had happened, everything except the Library. She wanted the story to be about Marta. She pushed a broken end-table and discovered the phone in a sparkling puddle of broken glass. Delicately, she retrieved the handset and checked for a dial-tone. She dialed Heather's cell and listened to it ring.

Just when she expected it to go to voicemail, a voice that wasn't Heather abruptly answered. "Hello? Who's this? What the fuck do you want?"

The voice made Alex smile. "Abby, it's me, Alexandrea."

Abby gasped, then sighed with relief. "Oh, jeez, Alex." She spoke slightly away from the phone "It's Alex. She's calling from your house." Then she returned to the phone. "Are you okay? He isn't there, is he? If he's there and you can't tell me, say something strange so I know, like you love beer."

Alex laughed, spilling tears of relief. They had probably panicked when they discovered her missing and then got this call. What came up on Heather's phone? Was the number labeled "Home" or "Rose and Billy"? Alex pictured Heather handing Abby her ringing phone, sick that Matthew was taunting her.

"Abby, can you please pick us up?"

In the background, she could hear Heather asking, "Alex? It's Alex? She's home?"

Abby replied, "Of course, but hold on; Heather wants to talk to you." Abby handed Heather the phone and Heather whispered that she didn't mean to take it away from her.

"Alex, sweetie," Heather said. "I came to bed, and you were gone. We were sick. You can't just sneak away, Alex. You can't do that to us."

Alex thought better of getting defensive. "I'm at your house. Rosemary's with me."

"Rosemary? Really?" Heather squealed joyfully, making Alex hold the phone away from her ear.

"Hi, Mom," Rose shouted.

In the background, Alex could hear them climbing into Abby's truck.

"We're on our way," Heather said. "Is she okay? Is she hurt? How is she?"

"She's okay." Alex looked at Rose. "A little banged up, but in one piece. She can't wait to see you."

"You? Are you okay?"

"Mmm-hmmm," was all Alex could bring herself to say, waiting for the inevitable.

Heather's voice became tentative. "William?" Alex was unprepared to answer. "Is he... with you?" Heather's voice softened.

Alex's inability to answer wasn't caused by guilt, but by the tone of Heather's question. Her words lacked the weight of desperation. They sounded nearly rehearsed, as though Heather had anticipated this outcome. *Or that's what I want to think.*

Alex swallowed. "He's not here, I mean, at the house."

"He's missing?" It was there in her tone again, as though Heather's question was leading her to the answer.

"He saved us, Heather. He was amazing and brave and helped us escape. I don't know, I mean, I think he's probably okay; maybe not safe, but okay. We couldn't find him."

"I know you did your best, sweetheart. I know my son will be fine."

Heather is doing her best to avoid casting blame. She's trying to protect me.

Guilt compelled her. "I'm sorry, Heather." She had to say it, even if that made it real. "He's with Matthew."

Heather was silent. As was her way, which in this case Alex did not expect, Heather looked for the good things. As she spoke, her tone rose. "With Matthew?" Her voice trembled with anger. "But you found Rosemary?" Her questions were leading again; it was as though Heather found comfort in asking them. "William was brave? That boy. We should look for him, don't you think?"

Alex nodded. She found Heather's tone forced enough to exhume something Eric had said: *She even tried it herself. She hurt herself and worse, hurt William.* Billy had known: *My coin is tarnished. Mom didn't keep it safe for me. She ruined it.* Alex couldn't believe she was actually thinking that Heather might be relieved her son was missing, perhaps finally free of her guilt.

After a minute of silence, Heather said, "Thank you for finding my daughter, Alex. I can't thank you enough." She seemed happy to have her one child returned. "Can I speak to her?"

"See you in a minute, Heather."

Alex passed Rose the phone.

"Yes, Mom, I'm okay. Yes, I saw Billy. He saved us both. He was so brave, Mom. Yes, Alex did, she found me. I wouldn't be okay if it weren't for her. I love you too, Mom. I can't wait to see you either. Oh wait, Mom? Are you still there? You're not going to believe this: Alex has magic."

Chapter Forty-Two

s soon as Rose hung up the phone, she went to the kitchen and opened the fridge. She made cereal for breakfast. She asked if Alex was hungry, but—and Alex had a hard time explaining it—ghost stew still satisfied her.

While Rose ate, Alex sat at the table watching her, mind racing. A week ago, she had thought her life was normal, and that it would continue that way. Now, she was unsure about tomorrow, and every tomorrow after it. There were too many unknowns, too many uncharted territories, too many unexplored shadows. Uncertainty was discomforting; it was exciting; it was dangerous. Tomorrow had never been so obscure.

It soured Alex's stomach to understand the greater scope of the world now opened to her. The only person qualified to explain it had tried to burn her alive. Perhaps this was why she felt such a strong bond with Abby, a woman willingly in a situation she couldn't comprehend. A woman who believed in magic but had none. Maybe that was why she made Alex feel safe.

She felt connected to the many women whose pain was inked in the pages of the horrible Books she'd burned. Their pain was now inside her. If she let the maelstrom of her own thoughts quiet, an impenetrable wall of impenetrable whispers formed in her mind. She'd originally thought that was the magic but now knew better. Innumerable women whispered to her, trying to tell her something so important they never quieted. *What was so important it became the voice they left behind?* There was no comfort in them, a sea of faceless shadows, unaware she was in their midst. She missed Sara. Of all the whispers, she most wanted to hear from her. She had spent so long with Sara, she was no longer certain what memories were hers and which belonged to the long-gone witch.

A vehicle pulled into the driveway and Rose slurped the rest of her cereal before racing to the window. "They're here," she wiped her mouth with her wrist. "Shouldn't we go out?"

"Let them come in. Heather needs to decide to come home."

Rose looked at Alex inquisitively. "Look at you, deciding for my mom. Way to go!"

Alex laughed. It was strange, but it felt right.

The front door opened. Rose raced into her mother's arms.

Abby slipped around them and over to Alex. When she saw Alex, her hands covered her mouth. "What the hell happened?"

"I'm healing fast."

"I know you'll heal. Does it hurt? What can I do? What happened? Are you okay?"

"I don't know." It was like answering all the questions and none.

Heather finished hugging her daughter, rocking her back and forth, and inspecting her from hair to toes. She saw Alex, her face drawn in surprise and horror.

"I'm okay," Alex said.

"You don't look okay." Heather's eyes teared over. She looked at Rose and back to Alex. "This happened to you saving my baby?"

Alex nodded. "It's okay, Aunt Heather." She took Heather in her arms, feeling her aunt's straining as she held on as tight as she could.

"I don't know how to thank you," Heather whispered into her ear.

Alex held her aunt, recognizing for the first time how fragile and birdlike her frame felt. *Has worry withered her away?* For so long she had been a rock in Alex's life. Now she felt brittle, breakable.

"Tell me what happened," Heather asked when they separated.

"The usual thing that happens to witches, apparently," Alex looked at her hands.

"He burned you?" Abby asked.

Alex nodded.

Heather bit her lip and stared a moment longer at Alex's burns. She seemed to recognize that Alex wasn't ready for that discussion. "I don't know how I'll ever feel comfortable enough to come back here," she said, turning her attention to the living room, eyes pausing on the broken furniture and shattered dishware.

"We can fit in the trailer," Abby replied. "That's no problem."

Heather put her fingers to her lower lip. "I appreciate the offer, I really do, but four people and three cats is asking too much from you."

"Not at all," Abby said, looking at Alex as though expecting her approval. "We'll make do."

"No," Heather thought a moment. "I really appreciate it, but this mess is my home. I need to reclaim what he took. We cannot let him take things from us so easily."

Alex was exhausted and hurting. She wanted to hide and heal and discover who she was now. Who was the girl who survived Sara's life, who survived being burned alive, who survived her parents' death twice? Who was this girl, this woman, who had magic?

"Okay," Abby conceded, "what do you need from me?"

Heather looked around. "I'll need my car, eventually."

"I'll drive you back to Eric's."

"Eric," Heather sighed, "lost everything because of Matthew."

Rose was confused; she didn't know. "Is Daddy okay?"

"He's fine," Abby explained. "Matthew burned his house down when he kidnapped you."

"What?" Rose looked accusingly at Alex. "Why didn't you tell me?"

"He'll be happy to know you're okay," Heather said, looking at both Alex and Rose. *Do you really believe that, Heather?* "I don't want to inconvenience you, Abby, but the sooner I can clean up this mess, the better I'll feel; if you don't mind, that is."

"It's no problem. We can get right on our way."

"About that," Alex interjected, "I need to change and pack. And," she sniffed her armpit, "I stink. Give me a few minutes so we can all go together."

"Oh, I'm sorry," Heather apologized like she had poked Alex in a burn. "I wasn't thinking. You probably don't want to be alone after all this."

"That's not it. I'm going back to Abby's."

Heather looked wounded. "You mean you'd rather stay with Abby than us?"

Alex heard the hurt in Heather's voice, and her heart nearly acquiesced to please her aunt. She reflected on the realities of staying. "Matthew can find me now. If he comes back—when—I need to know you're safe. I think it's best if I stay with Abby to think things through."

Heather turned to Abby. "You'll take care of her?"

"You know I will."

"I just feel like I can't take care of my babies if they're not under my wing." Heather sighed. "You're probably ready to take care of yourself."

"You have no idea," Rose said with an exaggerated laugh. "You should see what she did."

Heather and Abby both looked curiously to Alex.

"I'm going upstairs. Rose can tell the story."

As Alex walked away, she heard Rose's tone rise and fall through excitement and terror-filled descriptions. Either time had already distanced Rose from the menace or Alex had made her feel safe again. The girl was in awe of what she'd seen Alex do. She spoke of her brother in the most heroic terms. The one part of the story she didn't know and couldn't share was Holly's courageous last act to give her daughter back her soul.

Listening, Alex couldn't help but doubt some of the things she had done. She knew in her heart she had, but her mind made every effort to prove otherwise.

Matthew needs me. Was I in real danger or was it a performance? She couldn't say the burns weren't real; she was alive. When so much of her life seemed to be part of Matthew's plan, how could she assume this wasn't as well? *Why am I doubting myself?* She climbed into her bedroom. *Because I don't want to be responsible for everyone now.*

The artifacts of her last exodus remained scattered in her bedroom. She looked at the corner where George had appeared out of the shadows. *Is he really alive? In some hospital somewhere covered in disfiguring burns, or did Matthew lie? Did I burn him up like another Book? I did to him what Matthew tried to do to me.* She could still hear his screams. Thinking about him made her heart ache like she'd learned she lost something precious. She didn't want to think of George ever again.

She laid her clothes out on the bed and attempted to place them in her large satchel, so they'd be unwrinkled and drawer-ready when she unpacked, but there was too much to fit. She crammed it all into the bag, the last few items bulging out.

"I'll be down in ten," she shouted as she undressed. How she had already healed. Her body was a motley of scars and raw flesh. She took a quick shower. Everything hurt, and the water made her burned skin slough and peel. She gently washed the dirt and stench away. She patted herself with a towel and put her clothes on, still damp. Everything hurt.

When she came downstairs, the line of inquiry had shifted.

"I didn't want to do the things. He didn't tell me to do them, not really. Like when I tied Alex to the post. I'd never do that." Rose looked up as Alex came down the stairs, her eyes swelling with tears. "You know that, right? I'd never do that."

Alex tried to assuage her. "I know."

Heather stared at her daughter, a hand over her open mouth.

"I just felt so empty. All I could think is that if I didn't get Alex tied to that post the entire world would end, my family murdered, everything good and happy turned to ruins. I could see it happening." She looked at Heather. "It was like I could either tie her up or watch him murder you."

"Fucking bastard," Heather cursed. This was not the first time she had something to say about Matthew during Rose's explanation.

Rose continued. "I couldn't think of anything else. It was so real, I thought he was really killing you, Mom." She had discussed this with Alex last night, but it was important Heather know what they were up against. "She was burning and screaming and then her coin just turned on." She motioned to her chest with her hand opening from a fist. "As soon as Matthew saw the glow, the spell stopped, and I was free. It's like it made him... happy. He practically danced."

Alex interrupted them. "We should get going." Although Heather and Abby wanted to hear more, they agreed.

Following Abby, they walked out to the truck and piled in. Heather locked up the house.

The drive to Eric's home was quiet. As they neared, Alex said, "It might be good for Dolly to be back home too."

"I miss Dolly so much." Rose motioned with her hands like she was half scratching an invisible cat's head and half crushing it.

"You can follow us back to Abby's, to get Dolly." Alex hoped they'd stay for lunch. She wanted some time that didn't feel like they were in a trauma recovery group, but it wasn't her place to ask them to stay. She needed them to want to. As though hearing her thoughts, Abby asked, "You should stay for lunch."

Did she just read my mind? When Abby noticed Alex's intense stare, she mouthed, "What?"

Heather looked at Rose, Rose at Alex. Rose nodded and whined to Heather. "Please?"

Eric's house was a charred ruin. The smell of burned wood and plastics hung thick in the air, a rank and filthy smell, keeping the neighbors inside. Heather and Rose got out and walked to Heather's car. When Abby slowly rolled away, Alex looked back to make sure Heather was following.

Pulling past the corn into the narrow rut of a driveway, bouncing all the way to the barn and trailer, Alex felt oddly comforted. This wasn't home, but it felt like a safe place.

When the vehicles stopped, Alex pointed to where Marta's car had been. Abby grinned. "When Heather saw that you disappeared, we freaked. I figured if anyone came by, we needed to put the car someplace that wouldn't draw suspicion."

"Where?"

Abby wasn't telling.

When they arrived, Alex grabbed her satchel and dragged Rose into the trailer. As Alex unpacked in the bedroom, Rose rolled on the bed with Dolly. Quest tentatively observed them from atop the pillows jealous of the attention Dolly was getting. Marty was having none of it and skittered from the room.

Rose's question came as though released from a gate where it had built up momentum. "Why did he have to burn you?"

Alex knew. *Holly needed someone to die to trigger the loop open. Like my Abby for father and Heather.* She didn't want to talk about it in detail. She knew as soon as she started describing what happened, her emotions would swell over her and she'd drown in them.

"Do you think he had to? Like it was the only way to make your magic take hold?"

My parents un-twinned me for a reason. Matthew was part of that. Maybe this was all part of their plan. Burning her alive felt no crueler than trapping her inside Sara. "Maybe," was all Alex could manage. She couldn't help but feeling betrayed.

Alex and Rose headed out, passing Abby in the kitchen. The small refrigerator was packed with food. "We were up all night," Abby explained. "We worried Matthew got you and tried to figure out what we could do. I promised myself that if you came back, I'd have everything you wanted so I went to the store and got a little of everything."

"I'm sorry I made you worry, Abby."

Abby rubbed Alex's shoulder. "Goes with the territory. I guess sometimes you can't tell us what's going on."

Alex nodded.

"You'll try?"

"When I can, I will. Promise."

Heather sat at the table outside, lonely in her contemplation.

Alex sat across from her but said nothing. She was sure Heather was thinking about her son.

Heather shook her thoughts away and just started talking. "I'm so relieved that you and Rosemary are safe. Every now and then I realize I haven't worried about him enough. Maybe there's something wrong with me because I'm not constantly overwhelmed with grief. Then I start wondering what he's going through. I want to tear out my hair and cry. Am I a horrible mother? He's the one missing; he's the one going through whatever he's going through, and I'm making it all about me."

Rose hugged her mother. Alex was thankful that Rose took point on this; she remembered the last time Heather worried about her children, and how she'd lectured Alex for changing her mood. She looked at her hands. The burns went away a little more every time one of them embraced her. There was something about the burns, maybe sympathy for George, maybe knowing she got them at the same time she got magic, that made her want to keep them around a little longer.

"Mom, if you worried about him nonstop, it would exhaust you, and when he needed you, you won't have the strength to be there for him."

Heather forced a smile. She hugged her daughter back. "How'd you get so smart, Rose?"

Rose laughed. "I'm guessing not from dad." Heather laughed too.

Abby started the grill. "What's next?"

Heather turned to Alex. "The Book Club should know about Marta and Billy. They should know you have magic."

It felt like Heather was asking her for permission. "You'll tell them?"

Heather nodded.

Alex was reluctant to bring more people into danger. *What am I going to do with them? They'll look to me for guidance. Can they help, or will they be risking themselves for nothing?* The Book Club existed to make her a witch. What would happen to it now that she was?

Abby looked up from the grill, watching Alex and Heather's exchange.

Heather straightened in her seat. "Okay, well, I can call tomorrow, right?"

Alex nodded.

Abby broke into the conversation. "Let's have lunch."

Abby didn't allow Alex to help as they brought food to the table.

"So what's the plan?" Heather asked as they finished eating.

Alex thought for a few minutes. *What kind of plan does she expect me to come up with? Just because I have magic doesn't mean I can just summon Billy back. The plan is get Billy, but this is Matthew; this won't be easy or simple.* Finally, she said, "We should make our plan as a group. You know, focus on the coven's strengths."

Heather nodded. "Good point. That's probably best. Good idea." Alex wasn't sure she heard Heather's voice perk up.

Abby started taking up the plates. Heather gave her a hand. Alex and Rose retreated inside to find Dolly and get her into the carrier to go home.

In the bedroom, Rose sat on the bed petting Dolly. "It was amazing to watch you," she breathed. "You were so angry, so impassioned. You just did those things that we all dream we can do."

Alex stood with her back to the door. "It's not so great. Now everyone thinks I can fix everything. I don't know any better than I did when I didn't know there was magic."

"You'll figure it out," Rose replied cheerfully. "Only, when things get tough, you have an easier way through them."

This supposition riled Alex. It was with difficulty that she didn't raise her voice. "Nothing about what I've been through this past week was easy. I'd give anything for my ignorance back."

"You don't mean that. You can't. I'd give anything to have magic, and not be weak when men like Matthew come for us." She wiggled her fingers in the air, grinning.

"Rose," Alex protested as lovingly as she could muster, "they have magic too. They have more of it and they're much better at it. There are more of them, and they kill people like me. They think they're keeping the world safe." She sat on the bed. "I'm terrified. I have..." She didn't know what she had. "These spells or whatever they are, but I don't know what they can do, or even how to make them work. I didn't intend to destroy that rock; that just happened. What if they're right? What if I accidentally kill everyone I care about because—I don't know—I ruin dinner?"

"Since when do you cook?"

"Be serious, Rose. Maybe there's a good reason women don't have magic. Maybe me having magic is more trouble than we understand. Maybe we shouldn't."

Rose was silent. She made a whining sound in her throat, stifling the desire to say something as Alex's reality sunk in. "You don't mean that."

"I'm scared. I've had horrible things done to me and felt even worse things done to other people. I don't know if I want this. I don't know why anyone would."

Rose stared at Alex. "This really changed you. You're different."

"I'm still Alex."

"What I mean is, you never let anything scare you before."

Alex looked away. "I couldn't see the scary things before. Everything's different now. It's real."

Rose gave Alex a hug. "I'm sorry," she whispered.

"All I know is that Billy's missing because of me."

"You didn't cause that."

"Matthew took you and Billy to get to me. He won't give him back until I give him what he wants. To kill me."

"Why does he want to kill you?"

"I've burned thousands of their Books, and each one's inside me now. He wants me to do it to *all* the Books. Then, he kills me and makes one Book with all the magic. Imagine that, someone— someone like Matthew—with that kind of power."

"Maybe you should," her cousin whispered.

"What? Let him kill me?"

"No," Rose said, "Take all the magic. Take it for yourself. What could he do to you when you're that powerful?"

"What if I can't control it? Haven't you been listening?" The thought formed a pit in Alex's stomach. "He doesn't have to do anything to me. Not as long as he has Billy."

"Then you have to do it. To save Billy and yourself. Take everything."

Rose doesn't understand what she's suggesting. What's the point of arguing?

Alex tried resetting the tone of the conversation. "I have magic. I'm the only one, and that makes it my responsibility to get Billy back. That's all that matters, and that's what I'm going to do." She tried to feel the confidence the words possessed. *I can do it. I have to.*

Rose hugged her. Alex could feel her cousin's tears against her face. Alex hugged her back. She wanted this conversation to be over.

Rose smiled sadly at her. "I guess I should go. Mom wants the house cleaned up before dinner."

"I know. To take her mind off things," she added, "Wait till she sees the bowl you left in the sink." Rose laughed. "Never mind the whole house is trashed," Alex joked, "you left a dish in the sink."

"I love you, Alex."

"I love you too, Rose."

Rose stood and took the cat carrier. She offered a wave and left the room.

Chapter Forty-Three

lex and Abby watched Heather and Rose climb into Heather's car and drive off, tracking the rising cloud of dirt as they disappeared through the field and eventually found the road.

They stood wordlessly for another few minutes, when Abby finally asked, "Do you want to pull some glass later? I'll fire up the kiln."

Alex mulled it over for just a moment. "Sure." *Anything to feel normal.*

Abby didn't move.

Why is she stalling?

"Care to share your plan?"

Can she read my mind?

Alex touched her chest, below Abby's charm. "The way I see it, Matthew knows where I am. I have two choices. I can wait for him to come..."

"Or?"

"I have no idea where Matthew is or where he's keeping Billy. Either he'll come when he's ready, or I make some noise, and make him come."

Abby gently patted Alex on the back. "I like the second one too."

"I thought you might, Abby." Alex said.

Acknowledgements

Writing a book is a solitary experience, but the creation of it never is. There are many people who helped the process along. Beta readers helped by sharing their opinions about what worked or didn't. Others helped with their encouragement or enthusiasm.

Laura, my alpha reader. You had to contend with chapters not yet ready for general consumption. You participated in the conception of innumerable ideas that became this book. Your support, your willingness to lose me to hundreds of hours of writing over the years is why this book exists. Had you known when you told me to find something easy to write that this would be the result, you might have chosen to be more specific.

Mom, my other alpha reader. I cannot stress how important your enthusiasm and excitement were every time I emailed you the next chapter.

Peter Aperlo. I am grateful you were willing to beta-read. Meeting you at that hotel table for the Devil's Gate premier at Tribeca was a wonderful and fortuitous experience. Your notes and suggestions didn't just make this a better book, they made me a better writer. Thank you for the generosity of your time and wisdom.

My editor, Adam Wing. When a book is completed by its author, it can still have rough edges. A good editor grinds them smooth. It was amazing to see how much better my writing can be with a little polish.

My family. This is an expansive group that includes not just my wife, my parents and sister, but my in-laws, cousins, and those close friends who are too important to be considered anything but family. Your support, enthusiasm, and love made this journey possible. I would like to single out my father, who showed me the value of storytelling when, as a child, he'd wake me to re-tell the entirety of the movie he'd just seen. Years later, when I was old enough to watch those movies—The Shining, Apocalypse Now, Caligula—you cannot imagine my disappointment when they failed to live up to your rendition.

My teachers. Belinsky, Gerhardt, Eberhardt among them. You all helped show me the love of language and storytelling and encouraged me to find my voice.

The Book Club. My beta readers. You took the time to not only read this book before it was ready but also answer my endless questions. It can be difficult to take criticism, but you made it painless and even a little wonderful. In no particular order:

Michael Rubino, Jackie Gallo, Richard Gallo, Jennifer Maertz, Jason Grisafi, Melanie Yancey, Darrin Yancey, Susan Thonger, Marie Grisafi, Joseph Morris, Christopher DeFilippis.

The Wading River Fire Department. Becoming a firefighter taught me a lot about myself. I faced and overcame my greatest fears. That allowed me to redefine how I saw myself. Leaving allowed me the time to write these books.

The Corning Museum of Glass for answering all my questions. I can't wait to visit again.

And finally you, Kind Reader. Writing these books has been a thrilling experience. Knowing that one day I would share the world I've created with others made it more so. If you've come this far, here's where I get to thank you. Writing a book is a strange experience. When you read this book, it was your imagination that gave the story life. You completed what I began. I hope you enjoyed our time together at least half as much as I enjoyed creating it. Thank you for accompanying me on this journey.

About the Author

JH Nadler

This is Jason's first novel.

A former volunteer firefighter, when he's not writing, he works as a project manager.

He founded North-Forks, a blog of wineries and breweries of the North Fork of Long Island, where he lives with his wife and two insanely co-dependent cats.

You can find him at jhnadler.com and across social media @jhnadler.

Alexandrea Hawthorne's story continues:

The Books of Alexandrea
Book 2: The Between

Coming in 2022.

Made in the USA
Middletown, DE
23 October 2021